ECHO
OF
LIONS

OTHER BOOKS BY
BARBARA CHASE-RIBOUD

NOVELS
Sally Hemings
Valide

POEMS
From Memphis & Peking
Portrait of a Nude Woman as Cleopatra

ECHO
OF
LIONS

Barbara
Chase-Riboud

WILLIAM MORROW AND COMPANY, INC.
New York

Copyright © 1989 by Barbara Chase-Riboud

Silhouettes after engravings from *A History of the Amistad Captives,*
by John W. Barber, 1840

LIBRARY OF CONGRESS CATALOGING-IN-PUBLICATION DATA
Chase-Riboud, Barbara.
  Echo of lions : a novel / Barbara Chase-Riboud.
    p. cm.
  ISBN 0-688-06407-8
  1. Amistad (Schooner)—Fiction. 2. Slavery—United States—
Insurrections, etc.—Fiction. I. Title.
PS3553.H336E24 1989   88-13538
813'.54—dc19   CIP

Printed in the United States of America

First Edition

1 2 3 4 5 6 7 8 9 10

BOOK DESIGN BY KATHRYN PARISE

This book is dedicated
to the memory of my father,
who believed irrevocably in the
Constitution of the United States
of America

ECHO
❧ OF ❧
LIONS

BOOK I

"You are saved," cried Captain Delano, more and more astonished and pained; "you are saved: what has cast such a shadow upon you?"

"The negro."

—*Herman Melville*

ᥫᩭ Mendeland ᥫᩭ
January 1839

The echo of lions rumbled across the cold, humpback mountains, and the black winter sky was luminous with constellations reflecting undiluted in the quick, nervous river that ran by the compound. The brightest star was Konunqui, which shimmered to the east, and the steadfast Ndeloi and the blazing Sokolequli shone like fiery altars straight ahead over the curve of the world.

Today is the day of the trial. The drums had tattooed the words into his consciousness, awakening him. Sengbe Pieh lifted himself from the warmth of Bayeh Bia. It was the first time he had taken his wife since the birth of his son. Bayeh Bia had returned from her parents' home, where she had lived for almost two years while she nursed their only son. During this time, a wife was not allowed to consort with her husband. Copulation with a nursing woman was a strict taboo. The health, character, even the life of the child, was at stake. But his wife had finally returned with Gewo, who now slept in his hammock suspended above their bed; a fat walnut-colored doll of such beauty, Sengbe Pieh spent hours simply watching him. Gewo had been named four days after he had been born. He had taken him out in the early morning just as the sun rose and, facing east, had spit in the child's face, saying, "Resemble Him in all His ways and deeds because you are named after Him." Then the young father had exploded in laughter. He had named him Gewo, *God.* What a good name for a man! Now the second wife he had taken when Bayeh Bia had left, and who slept in a separate house, was expecting a child and would soon leave for her family's house. Tau already wore the tiny bell attached to her lappa to ward off evil white spirits. She carried a knife with her at all times since, in her state of pregnancy, she was considered a warrior and, if she succumbed in childbirth, that she had died in battle.

Sengbe Pieh slipped quietly from the beautiful, elaborately curved marriage bed he had lovingly sculpted out of the trunk of a single ash tree. Polished and oiled, its incisions and gouges, arabesques and geometric shapes glowed in the half light. His fingers still ached with the trace of every line, circle and curve. It was to him both raft and root, the glowing wood as anchored to the packed earth of his house as he was to his rice fields beyond. Sengbe Pieh pulled off his sleeping shirt. Bayeh Bia's hands, blackened from the cloth-dying that was the prerogative of her aristocratic class, were folded around her torso. She had fallen back asleep. Sengbe Pieh stooped to cover his wife, then rose to stand just outside the doorway of his house. The fading moonlight filtered through the shade tree, outlining a silhouette that was long, compact and powerful, with wide shoulders, narrow waist and high hips. For a long moment he stood there, immobile, the moonlight dappling him like rivets of caraway seeds, draping the perfection of his body in pellets of silver. He looked up into the driftless stars and whispered the name of his son. He felt supremely happy and safe. Just beyond, the river swept by on its way to the Gallinas, which hundreds of miles away emptied into the sea. One felt rather than heard it—a troublesome long sigh, a lament dancing on the stones. Sengbe Pieh had never followed the river to its great tributary. He had never had any desire to do so. He had met river people only once. He was a strong, generous, intelligent man, a hard worker, son of a village clansman who had married well. He and his brother-in-law possessed a large rice plantation. To be a rice planter had not been his first desire, but now all that was behind him and he worked hard at it. He was stubborn and vain of his superior mind, passive yet capable of severe exertion under great privation. He could hunt, walk, or fight until he dropped. He had no notion of compromise nor of defeat. His life was as static and unmoving as the great flat-topped acacia overhead. It took centuries for a man like him to move five hundred yards to the left or to the right.

Of course, his uncle had been right, thought Sengbe Pieh, and now his sculpture tools were neatly wrapped in bark in the bottom of his clothes basket.

"Warriors use their hands either to kill or to eat," he had

said. "No one in our family has ever worked with his hands. We have slaves to make sculpture. Everyone in this village can make sculpture. Carving a beautiful bed for yourself is one thing; magic is something else. Has any astrologer told you that you were a sculptor? Were you born under the right sign for a sculptor? Has any Mori-man spoken to you of sculpture? Has God spoken to you of sculpture? It is true that you carve well, but from now on I forbid you to do so." No, thought Sengbe Pieh, no astrologer, Mori-man, or god had ever told him he was a sculptor. . . . The matter was closed. In terms of family, to disobey one's uncle was an even greater offense than disobedience to one's father. Sengbe Pieh's village was part of the *Kuwui* of the neighboring town some ten miles away where the trial would take place. There were 104 members of his village. Of these, thirty were Sengbe Pieh's paternal kin, ten his mother's kin, and thirty-two were connected to him through marriage. They were Sengbe Pieh's own father and his wives, including his own mother, his six brothers and half brothers with their respective wives and children, his two sisters living without their husbands, his five sisters and half sisters with their respective husbands and children; the father of the husband of one of Sengbe Pieh's sisters and his wives; the nephew, his wife and children; the husband of one of Sengbe Pieh's half brothers and her husband; a paternal aunt and nine strangers with their wives and children.

As far as the trial was concerned, his obligations were clear.

"Who do you stand for in this contest?" the viceroy had asked.

"*Nge gbembi*, my line of blood relatives."

It was a matter of *ndewe*, a cousin. And it was a matter of honor.

Bayeh Bia came to stand beside him. She was dressed in a cotton lappa draped and pulled over her right shoulder. She had brought his lappa to him, which he threw forward over his left shoulder, bringing the other end around his body, under his right arm and backwards over the same shoulder. His right shoulder and arm were uncovered. Bayeh Bia had done the same but in reverse, so that her left arm and shoulder were free. This was the only difference in their dress. The intricate network of delicate scarrings on her shoulder and back glistened. Not long ago they had been under his eager, loving fingers, the feel of them sending swirls of excitement from the tips of his fingers to the core of his being. Even now, the memory of the touch of that marvelously exquisite relief remained with him.

"I'll be glad when it's over," said Bayeh Bia.

"The trial you mean?"

"Yes."

"In three days the whole dispute will be settled. And in four I'll be back home."

"The appeal to the Paramount Chief has made this thing all too famous. Too many people are talking about it. My lineage people have always been discreet. We don't like notoriety," complained Bayeh Bia. She was still angry with Sengbe Pieh over the quarrel he had had with his uncle, as well as Sengbe Pieh's stubborn insistence on taking sides in the suit of his cousin, which, after all, was *her* family's affair. In Bayeh Bia's neat, orderly world, her husband lacked discretion, tact, even a certain worldliness. His stubbornness was unseemly, even vulgar. His incessant arguments, his questioning of her parents' authority over their household, his strange name for their only child, all roused in her tranquil nature a sense of unease. Why was it he felt personally responsible for everything and everybody in the whole world? This trial, for example, wasn't even their family's business. She sighed. Sengbe Pieh was different from the men she had known, and she didn't like it. Yet it had been this very difference that she had fallen in love with.

Sengbe Pieh could smell the rain coming. Behind him, he heard Tau's little bell. She was bringing hot water for Bayeh Bia's bath and that of the child. Bayeh Bia was standing slightly behind him, and now her jet black hands came around him, stark against the white drapery.

"Forgive me," she murmured, "for speaking out. If you like, I'll go with you. My uncles will be there and we can pay our respects to Mama and the family, our *ndehun-bla.*"

"No, I'd rather you stay here with Gewo." Sengbe Pieh glanced at the beautiful triangular-shaped face, its classical features and up-slanted eyes.

"I'll travel with Kabba Sei. The roads aren't safe."

Sengbe Pieh and his brother-in-law set out at daylight. They had to arrive before the sun was high. The trial had dragged on for moons, for it had been appealed twice and was now before a Council of Paramount Chiefs. The matter, not a small one, had started out simply enough. The plaintiff, a noiseful, obstinate headman with old-fashioned ideas, had made his complaint to the viceroy and had given him a *famalui*—the bail to open proceedings. The defendant, his cousin, had been summoned to trial, and the sub-chief had informed him of the charge.

"Mba bdoe lu hwei lo?" Will you cross the summons? His cousin had, of course, not pleaded guilty, and had crossed the summons with a *famalui* of equal amount. The trial had opened and both men had stated their cases, then Lumaka, his cousin, had defined the points on which he took his stand and had planted a stick in front of him to show that he would not diverge from these points. At this point the trial had gone into its second day and from opposite ends of a bridge constructed for that purpose, the suitors themselves cross-examined each other. Standing directly opposite each other, they had questioned one another, each trying to get the other to cede a certain point. It had been a stormy session with howls and shouts of "Order." The long-winded emotional accusations and utter chaos in the end had been barely controllable. Then the witnesses had been called and sworn in, each on each other's medicines. It had been the first time Sengbe Pieh had ever sworn an oath on medicine, a serious undertaking since perjury along with treason were the worst crimes. The viceroy had then questioned witnesses, defendant and plaintiff in the presence of the elders, and the trial had gone into closed session with the Paramount Chief questioning the witnesses separately one by one. After this, the witnesses themselves had been asked to withdraw and hang heads on it, but despite Sengbe Pieh's eloquence and determination, they had been unable to come to a unanimous decision and the whole case had been appealed from the viceroy to the town clansman and from the town clansman to the Paramount Chief. The Paramount Chief had formed a Council of nine Paramount Chiefs who would now retry the case. The costs, thought Sengbe Pieh, were going to be staggering, since new fees had to be paid in each court.

When Sengbe Pieh and Kabba Sei arrived in town, the palm wine had already been sent to the Council as a Summons to

Court, and the Paramount Chief had already asked how much damages were being asked. The amount had already been deposited in a nearby house. It was impressive: fifty-five fine cloths, sixteen goats and two domestics. "A-wa-o, A-wa-o. All come, all come. This court now sits." His cousin and the plaintiff had already staked out their case, planting their staffs at either end of the bridge. They began arguing their points before the Paramount Chiefs, who sat on a wide-shaded veranda. The whole town had turned out, and Sengbe Pieh and Kabba Sei found their *ndehun-bla* and Sengbe Pieh's grandmother, where they would stay the night. But Sengbe Pieh was not called as a witness until the next afternoon. He would be the last. He was sworn in on the plaintiff's medicine and then gave his version. The Paramount Chiefs then questioned him and the other witnesses in closed session. Sengbe Pieh had argued vehemently and eloquently, but he could read nothing in the dark faces of the Chiefs. Again, all the witnesses were questioned. Again, his cousin and the plaintiff cross-examined each other on the bridge. Again, the witnesses tried to get one another to cede. Again, for the last time, the case was summed up by the two parties. The Paramount Chiefs retired and the town settled down to wait. After almost half a day of deliberation, the Council brought in its verdict. It was proclaimed by the Speaker.

"Sore losers," said Kabba Sei.

"I'm glad that's over." Sengbe Pieh sighed. "If my cousin had lost, Bayeh Bia would never have forgiven me . . . nor my uncle. And, if he had lost the caution he posted as damages, which he put himself in debt for, who would have had to pay the money-lender? Me? You? The *Nge gbembi*?"

"Well, everything went surprisingly well, considering the Speaker," said Kabba Sei. They had enough time to make it back home by nightfall. Gewo would be asleep, thought Sengbe Pieh, but he would wake him up—just for a little while. They were both loaded down with gifts from the *Nge gbembi* and his grandmother's messages, to be delivered to the clan. The old lady had kept them for hours with her list of message commands, admonitions and gossip. The venerable white head had wagged from side to side as his grandmother's wickedly malicious tongue lovingly recounted every indiscretion, insult, birth, marriage, and political intrigue of the past six months. The young men started back the way they came. To the left, about a mile out of town, there was a small footpath which Sengbe Pieh knew led down to the river they could follow home. As they approached it, he saw a large scrub tree creak and fall with a crash across the road, blocking their way.

"What?" he cried out as Kabba Sei slumped at his side, a head wound spattering him with blood. Sengbe Pieh pivoted his powerful frame just in time to grapple with, it seemed, two or three converging bodies. He fought desperately, sensed a fourth presence, felt the blade of his knife sink into flesh, heard a howl of pain. His nostrils took in a strange, foul odor he had never smelled before. He retched as a boot caught him in the chest. He lost his weapon. A club landed on his left eye. He went down.

"Bayeh Bia," he cried out. *"O Gewo! Ngi namubo, ga gula kotima be hongē! O ma gewo ge jondu gilima, hongē!"* If I slip, that I do not fall on the stone here, O God! O God I swear not by heaven!

Just before falling into unconsciousness, Sengbe Pieh had a terrible vision, that of childish nightmares: a toothless monster, white as the devil, with holes instead of eyes through which the sky shone, and bloodred snakes and snails growing out of his head and the bottom part of his face. A rancid odor, which he could not recognize as that of an unwashed European body, made him gag. The wound on his forehead oozed blood over his eyes, blinding him. With his last strength he gathered his saliva and spat into the beast's face.

"Sonofabitchblackbastard," it jabbered.

He fainted. When he awoke, he was lying on the ground and it was morning. He tried to move but found he was pinned to the ground by chains. An iron collar had been placed around his neck, to which were attached chains that held his two wrists and two ankles. He had been dragged for a distance, for his back was raw, the back of his head burned, his throat was dry, and his eyes were almost swollen shut. He was chained to another man. They lay on their sides, attached by the neck, unable to turn on their backs or sit up.

"Mende?" whispered Sengbe Pieh to the stranger's back.

"Mende, by the grace of God," came the answer.

For Sengbe Pieh this meant the man was Moslem and Poro.
Safe. The smooth, powerful black back and the nape of a small
curly round head was all he could see of the man.

"I am 'Have-Mercy-on-Me'—Grabeau."

"I am 'Drummer,' Sengbe Pieh. Are we dead?"

"No," said Have-Mercy-on-Me. "If only in Allah's mercy we
were. We are . . . stolen on the War Road."

"Then . . . then the creatures with the arrowless bows are
white men?"

"Yes."

"How do you know for sure?" asked Sengbe Pieh suspi-
ciously.

"You ever see anything look like that before?"

"No."

"Well, that's what they look like, and they are not beasts.
They are humans."

"No!"

"I assure you, Drummer. They do not have tails. They walk
upright on two legs. That which grows from them and on their
head is hair much like fine cotton threads. They speak a kind
of gibberish between themselves of which I understand a few
words. They smell like that because they do not wash. There
is no magic to it."

"How do you know all this?" asked Sengbe Pieh suspi-
ciously.

"It is not the first time I've been captured. I escaped the last
time . . . and I'll do it again."

"What will happen now?" asked Sengbe Pieh. His greatest
fear had always been to be taken captive on the War Road or
in battle or held hostage for ransom in another village. But his
town was at war with no one. He had not seen the Poro war
sign—a burned palm leaf. . . . When he explained this to Have-
Mercy-on-Me, his back shook, Sengbe Pieh assumed, with
laughter. But this was no laughing matter.

"You think they will hold you for ransom? And your father
will come and get you, little boy? You think white men respect
your rank, negotiate with your village and your *Nge gbembi*?
Exchange slaves for you? They will take them too! These men
will kill you, or eat you, or sell you to other white men who
own giant houses topped with many roofs of cloth which swim

across the waters. . . . Do you have an enemy? Your own color?"

"The waters!" cried Drummer, not really hearing the rest of what Have-Mercy-on-Me had said. "You mean where the spirits live? Are we on our way to Hell, then? And the white men are ghosts sent to conduct us?"

Grabeau sighed. "More or less." He tried to touch the other man, but even with his enormous strength he could not pull the chains high enough. . . . The man beside him was young, thought Grabeau, and well-born. He would have to frighten him to death if they were to escape. First, before he did anything, he had to exorcise the young man's fear of white skin and blue eyes. Maybe his luck had run out, he thought. Perhaps this time there would be no escape. He had never been chained before. There would be no quick sprint into the bush, no strong hands would close around white throats that stopped breathing just like black ones did, if one could endure the stench long enough.

"No," repeated Have-Mercy-on-Me. "They are not supernatural. They have bones that crack and teeth that can be knocked out, flesh that burns, blood as red as ours, which flows as easily. They have lungs which hold air, stomachs which spill intestines, and the same thing between their legs as we do, and for the same reasons. And they even have women—who resemble them. You must cease to be afraid of them. Be afraid only of their awful cruelty and lack of morals. In this, yes, they are beasts. The first time I was captured I didn't escape until I had reached the waters. I have seen the sea. It stretches to the end of the world. I have seen white men almost as dark as you. Their eyes are not sightless, but pale colors like sky and water, but some have eyes as dark as ours. They seem to want us even more than ivory or gold or cloth or *anything*. And they possess a terrible power; their weapons which open horrible wounds. And their cruelty knows no measure, neither to us nor to each other. And they are ignorant, yet our nations trade with them, make war for captives for them. We could have swept them off the coast once, but now they are too powerful. For generations they have been too powerful. Some, farther down the cost, even have fortresses; giant stone houses as big as their giant canoes. *Why* they need us, I do not know."

Sengbe Pieh listened carefully without interrupting with a thousand questions. He realized his life had become more complicated than he had ever dreamed. He began to reason.

"If we don't escape," repeated Grabeau, "you will never see your village, your mother, or your wife, if you have one, again."

"Two," said Sengbe Pieh with sudden coldness. "I have two wives and a son, Gewo." He had said it swiftly, but he felt the sob deep in his chest. He was afraid. They would be taken onto the depthless waters over the Spiritland, where they would die. He relieved himself on the ground. Shamefully, his own urine stung his nostrils. He apologized.

"It's all right," said Have-Mercy-on-Me.

"My brother-in-law was with me."

"Then perhaps he is still here, although some men were taken away when they brought you."

"How did they capture you?"

Grabeau hesitated a moment and then said only, "I was captured on the road going to Taurang in the Bandi Country to buy clothes. My uncle had bought two slaves in Bandi and had given them in payment for a debt; one of them ran away, and I was taken for him. I do not know what has become of my wife. I thank God I have no children," he repeated softly. "Oh, God, I'm glad I have no children."

During the night other coffles of chained men arrived. At the second dawn the chains connecting the collars together were released, allowing the men to turn around. Sengbe Pieh and Grabeau could finally face one another. Their eyes locked for one second, each sizing up the other, then their chained hands made the secret sign of the Poro. Ignoring their pain, they looked around. There were a hundred or so chained men— Kissi, Mandinka and Sherbro, as well as Mende. Sengbe Pieh counted the white men. He could see three patrols of seven men each. Twenty-one armed men, he thought, against a hundred chained and unarmed warriors. He saw no women at all. The light had swelled in one second to bright sunlight, and the arrowless bows were held cocked by the white men and gleamed in the light. Sengbe Pieh now had a dozen white men to contemplate. He concentrated on overcoming his fright and his repugnance. Have-Mercy-on-Me hadn't convinced him they were human, although now he saw that they had human form. But how to account for their color? God had made all men. He hadn't said anything about making them different colors. And why white? The color of the Devil? And why with tails growing out of their necks? And why that smell (although he didn't smell too good himself)? Sengbe Pieh fought his rising panic. It was the white that frightened him so—if only they were another color. . . . Obviously if they were to escape he would have to touch one of these men. Could he do it? Could he actually touch something so repulsive? He remembered the first time he had been forced to touch a snake. . . .

"Were you serious about the waters and the houses that swim?"

"Yes."

"And the arrowless bows, for example . . . can you use one?"

"No."

"Well, watch carefully. Watch how they hold them and where they put their fingers. . . . Watch how they put the iron pebbles inside. . . ."

Grabeau looked surprised and then said, "All right."

Sengbe Pieh forced himself to look at his white captors, although most of the men looked at the ground. Deliberately he slowed down his racing heart and then stared at one or the other of them until they appeared less frightening. He found a young man he guessed was his own age. He had brown eyes and brown hair and no beard, so it was easier. His mouth was full of beautiful teeth and he spoke and laughed a great deal when he was not coughing. Laughter and coughing were the first human sounds he recognized.

Besides their arrowless bows, they carried whips and long cutlasses that astonished Sengbe Pieh. They dressed in white skirts sewn up the center and wore black skins in the shape of a foot and lower leg. On their torsos they wore belts of shiny pellets and white tunics. Some wore a kind of armor of blue cotton with gold balls sewn down the front. The young man began to be able to differentiate one from the other, although they looked all alike to him. They had ears—all of them—and out of the slit they had for a mouth came an exceedingly strange gibberish resembling the rough growls of a baboon. He had already seen how much pain they could inflict. One white had beaten a man—a Mandinka—to the ground and to death, lashing and lashing on the bare flesh with his whip for no reason Sengbe Pieh could discern. He prepared himself to endure a great deal of pain. He squeezed his eyes shut, hoping all this was a nightmare. When he opened them, there was a white man standing indecently close to him. He recoiled.

"*Hereeatthis,*" he said, and forced a bowl under Sengbe Pieh's nose. It had corn mush inside.

"*Eatthis,*" the man repeated to the uncomprehending Sengbe-Pieh. The man's hand came up and smashed against the side of his head. If he had not opened his mouth, the iron bowl would have broken his front teeth. He swallowed again and again until the man was satisfied. Then another came with a bowl of water. He understood he was to drink.

"*Swallowthis.*" Sengbe Pieh had not had either food nor drink since he had been captured.

The next day the captured men were rechained together and the caravan moved out, marching, according to Grabeau, to the sea. More and more slave coffles had joined the original caravan, so that it stretched beyond the sight of Sengbe Pieh. He noticed that several white men had six legs.

"Hah," he laughed. "I told you they weren't human. Nobody has six legs!"

"They have two legs sitting upon four. Surely you've seen a *man* on a goat! There are only bigger, swifter and stronger. Surely you've seen four-legged animals . . . surely you've *heard* of elephants and *ca-ball-iyos,*" said Grabeau.

"Yes, of course," lied Sengbe Pieh.

"*Ca-ball-iyos* are of great use. They never attack men, and transport men long distances. White men tame and ride them instead of walking. They trample slaves. They can catch any running man."

Sengbe Pieh had once heard of a man riding a tiger. On the other hand, he found the *ca-ball-iyos* very beautiful. Another weapon, he thought.

"The women and children are in a different coffle," said Have-Mercy-on-Me.

"Women and children," cried Sengbe Pieh.

"Of course, you think they capture only men? You think," he asked brutally, "they have no use for our women?"

"For work?" asked Sengbe Pieh.

"For work, of course, but also for intercourse," said Grabeau.

"They copulate with their own slaves?" asked Sengbe Pieh. Both he and Grabeau knew this was *simongama*, incest.

Other slaves joined the caravan as it marched slowly towards the sea, until the ranks of chained black men had swollen to almost six hundred. Moans and cries escaped the men at night. Names of women or pitiful cries of "Mother" studded the night. From time to time a scream of terror rang out, bringing the guards rushing. The early morning hours, just before light, was the time the sick slipped quietly from sleep to death, or convulsed in agony, thrashing with dysentery or shivering with typhoid, malaria, or yellow fever; their delirium, their cries and shouts and screams, suddenly silenced. The guards would find them stiff and already cold in the sudden morning light, and cursing, would remove their valuable chains. The body would be dumped into the bush or, if a river were nearby, into the river, otherwise it was left where it lay when the coffles moved, for the vultures that followed the column from the interior.

Sengbe Pieh always recited the prayer of the dead for those who had died during the night, if they were Mende or not. Grabeau would also repeat his prayers for the dead, not knowing what religion the dead man had lived and died. Sengbe Pieh began to feel responsible for every death.

Sengbe Pieh began to memorize the position of the sun, calculating the direction in which they travelled; he began to fix landmarks with the distances between them, the length of the marches, the stops, how many days and nights, the changing vegetation and lowering temperature, where rivers and streams crossed their path. He had to get back to the Vai country and home. The chains had given all the captured men wounds and running, infected sores. The guards began to pour palm oil between the skin and the iron collars and anklets, and then sprinkled a white powder onto the oil which made a kind of paste. Often the infection spread and the man would die horribly of lockjaw. To his surprise, the tallest, strongest, most fit men seemed to succumb first, Sengbe Pieh noticed within the week of the march, while the smaller, wiry, stocky fellows doggedly rose every morning, weakened, sick, but still alive.

Grabeau, too, noticed that valuable fighting men were being lost by the dozens. One man managed to commit suicide by grabbing the bowie knife strapped to the leg of one of the guards and plunging it into his throat. It took him six hours to die on his feet, while marching, chained to two others, the razor-sharp, triple-honed, four-pound knife still protruding from his neck. Sengbe Pieh, too, began to think of killing himself.

The white men screamed and slashed with their whips but they could not make the slave coffle move any faster. It was a fifteen-day march to the sea. With the Africans hobbled with chains, it took twice that. At the end of the thirtieth day, when the sea was in their nostrils and the shore just over the horizon, there were four hundred slaves left of the original 550. Of the women and children who followed, there were only sixty. The body of the caravan consisted of some six hundred people, three thousand hides, nineteen tusks of ivory, sacks of gold powder, six hundred pounds of ivory, nine hundred pounds of beeswax and fifteen tons of rice. The only merchandise that carried itself, the slaves, preceded the bullocks, sheep and goats. As the head of the caravan moved beyond the horizon, the Atlantic Ocean came into view. For most of the men, including Sengbe Pieh, who had never seen the sea, they had reached the end of the earth. Beyond stretched the kingdom of spirits, the underworld, and petrifying eternity. A moan of fright and protest rose from the exhausted Africans while a shout of joy filled the lungs of the guards. Now they spurred the slow line with whips and sticks. The sooner the caravan arrived at Pedro Blanco's barracoons, the sooner they were free of terror of insurrection, exhaustion and fever.

"We have our full contingent of slaves!" Sengbe Pieh heard the cry to the lookouts perched like birds of prey on platforms scores of feet in the air.

"Tellpedroblancotogetondownheresowecangetoutofhere!"
"Thesoonerthebettertogetridoftheseniggers."
"Thetecoraisfittedoutandreadytosailinafortnight."
"Hurrahhurrahhurrah."

Sengbe Pieh knew now he would never see home again. They had not escaped. He felt his chest tighten as the clean sea breezes cooled his sweating body, and for the first time he tasted brine carried on the wind. But he did not know if the salt was in the air or in his tears.

* * *

Along the labyrinth of swampy marshland islands that reached out into the estuary of Gallinas, surrounded by sinister-looking mangrove forests, lookout seats were planted on poles some hundred feet above the ground. From this vantage point the horizon was swept constantly by the powerful telescopes. The lookouts could then announce the approach of either British cruisers or slavers. The barracoons themselves were made of rough logs driven five feet into the ground and clamped together by double rows of iron bars. The roofs were constructed of wood and overlaid with long, wiry grass. At each end were watchtowers manned by black sentinels with loaded muskets. Each barracoon held five hundred slaves and was tended by a group of Spanish or Portuguese guards who lived or died according to which disease—malaria, leprosy, dropsy, or yellow fever—chose them or passed them by. Some of them had never laid eyes on the man they worked for, Don Pedro Blanco.

Don Pedro Blanco's slave factories were famous throughout the New World. Known as the "Rothschild of slavery," whose bills on banks in England, France, or the United States were as good as gold, he had lived for nearly a lifetime amid the pestilential swamp and murderous climate, trafficking in human flesh, provoking wars, and bribing and corrupting native chiefs. Don Pedro was thought to be (and was in fact) an ex-naval officer from Malaga who had come to Africa in command of a slaver, the *Conquistador*. Failing to complete his cargo, he had sent his vessel back to its owners, remained on the coast with his share of the cargo and begun to trade with the natives and the slaver captains. That had been a quarter of a century ago. His debt to the owners of the *Conquistador* had long been paid, and he had flourished on his own. In all that time he had never passed the bar of the river, living on one of his islands with a sister no one ever saw, and on another, maintaining a harem of favorites, some of whom were white. Cavernous and swarthy, exceptionally tall for the times and always dressed in immaculate white in the manner of a Cuban colonial, he wore the arms of a grandee on the thumb of his left hand. No one knew what Don Pedro Blanco's real name was, though no one believed it was Pedro Blanco. Famous for his remarkable memory and unlimited cruelty, he had once killed a man for asking permission to light a cigar from his, but his face had the sublime purity of a saint, free of both fear and greed. When he visited the barracoons, as he did this day, it was usually in the uniform of a Portuguese navy officer. This was how he greeted the slave caravan that approached the slave factory of Man Rock, just south of the parent corral which already housed a full cargo waiting to be loaded on the slaver *Tecora*, at anchor in the estuary. With a slight movement of the fingers of his left hand, he greeted the patrol and watched impassively as the columns moved into the barracoon. He might have been greeting an acquaintance in a café in Barcelona, or acknowledging an homage in the opera house of Madrid. When the last of the black men had filed in, he gave the signal to close the stout doors of the barracoon and unfetter the slaves. Then, without speaking to anyone, he returned home, a specter in white, the lord of man-merchants.

The slave factory was the largest and most solid edifice Sengbe Pieh had ever seen. It loomed stories above him, the heavy log fortresses seeming as impregnable and impossible to unlatch as the bolt-lock carbines of the caravan's guards. There was no way around these walls, he thought, nor under them, and Grabeau was strangely silent that night as they sat closest to the fortress doors and ate the cooked rice served by the black guards. Perhaps Grabeau had a plan, but it would have to include his wife's brother, Sengbe Pieh decided. He would never leave him behind—if he were still alive.

"Find him," said Grabeau, "tomorrow." Then he took a small gold nugget out of the hollow of his ear. "This will open the doors of the barracoon. The rest is up to Allah."

"But why didn't you bribe one of the guards to let you escape on the road instead of waiting until now?" exclaimed Sengbe Pieh.

"And how was I to do that? In what language? There was no one who spoke Mende. Bargain with a white man who would take my gold and then shoot me dead or simply recapture me? Besides, how could I escape loaded with chains? Now at least we are unfettered, free to run, hide, and if necessary, fight. . . ."

Sengbe Pieh looked at the weak, wretched men around him. He turned to Grabeau more for comfort than anything else. But Have-Mercy-on-Me was saying his prayers.

* * *

Sengbe Pieh found Kabba Sei alive. Grabeau's gold was sufficient to get the three men beyond the doors of the fortress and into the swamps. Naked, they plunged into the tall reeds and murky waters and sandbanks, surprised that they had lost so much strength during the forced march, struggling against the shifting sand and the dangerous, briny undertow. The disappearance of three men was not noticed and the alarm given until the next feeding. A patrol set out and the lookouts trained their telescopes on land rather than sea. Unknown to the two men, Man Rock was not the only slave factory. Five others studded the islands, and by midday all the satellite factories and their guards were on the tracks of the three fugitives. Sengbe Pieh tried to lead them north, back towards the dense forests behind the desolate islands, but one of the slave barracoons stood directly in their path. It was the Spanish guards from the Mount Dinghy barracoon, very near Don Pedro Blanco's own harem, who finally captured the three men. For some reason Pedro Blanco decided that only Kabba Sei would be punished with thirty lashes.

Sengbe Pieh was stiff from the chains and the blows and cried out in protest as the guards jerked him to his feet, pulling Have-Mercy-on-Me with him. Before the barracoon was fully awake, the two were marched towards the sea. Seeing it this close, inflicted the most powerful sensation of terror Sengbe Pieh had ever experienced. He squeezed his eyes shut. He would never cross it. It was all over for him and Have-Mercy-on-Me. He thought of Bayeh Bia of the thousand braids, with her firm breasts, her open arms, her lavish flanks and exquisite back. The memory of their last night together made him swallow hard and squeeze his eyes even tighter. Bayeh Bia's breath, her soft voice, kept whispering to him *ndoma nyahanga, ndoma nyahanga.* I love you. I love you. "Father Siaffa, let it reach you." He whispered the Poro prayer. "Let it be laid down to Gewo." He repeated: "I love you, Bayeh Bia." He was twenty-four and he didn't want to die. Beyond was the great house on water that swam with its trees in the shape of crosses. They were going to drown him! They were going to send him down into the spirit world at the bottom of the sea. He would rather burn, he thought.

The two men were put into a long boat of the *Tecora* and rowed out to the ship. They were taken aboard. They looked up and saw a forest of sticks higher than century-old palm trees, higher even than the lookouts that seemed to pierce the sky, all draped with white cloth lashed tight. The first thing Sengbe Pieh and Grabeau saw as they were led onto the deck, was an enormous gun, turning on a swivel on deck. Then they noticed rows of these cannons—ten,—to each side. With a sickening lurch of his stomach Sengbe Pieh saw three immense cauldrons for cooking, and piled on deck, neck collars of iron, handcuffs and shackles as he had seen in the barracoons, and chains attached to black balls of iron.

The two captives were handed over to two sailors who took them down to the empty slave deck where, in the dim half light, they could make out row after row of wooden planks double stacked, no wider than the span of a man's two hands stretching, it seemed, to infinity, like some giant honeycomb reeking of a strange smell. The vaulted oak beams above were too low for a man to stand upright, barely four spans. They were the first two men to be chained to the ledges, on their sides in a half-crouching position. Their guards placed them in the first two slots of seven hundred, one above the other, next to the trapdoor and the first porthole. This proximity to light and air would save their lives, but they could not know this. Sengbe Pieh was sure Kabba Sei had died under torture and been eaten by the whites. Shamefully, he could do nothing to stop the hot tears of rage and despair streaming down his face. His chains rattled in the cavernous space like a spectral, rhythmic chant.

❧ The *Tecora* ❧
March 1839

On January 27, 1839, a three-hundred-ton Spanish ship, mounting eighteen guns on her deck and carrying the license of the House of Martinez—her crew of sixty assembled from Havana's jails and crimping houses, the captain having signed on a surgeon and three mates—had lifted anchor and set course for the windward Guinea coast. Captain Joshua McClapp of Rio de Janeiro held a receipt for the 2400 dollars he had given the House of Martinez as security against the slaving merchandise he was transporting.

Joshua McClapp had served indifferently under the Dutch, English, Portuguese and Brazilians, though he was, in fact, an American who had commanded several American ships and would spend his late years in the United States. He was wily, suave, ambitious, poetic, ruthless and vengeful. He had no religion, many vices, few weaknesses and no redeeming virtues except exceptional physical courage. His feelings, mostly repressed, broke forth occasionally in terrible rages. He was a lonely man, the last of six children, and had been kept in school to study geography, mathematics and languages until he was fourteen. He was then, for the time and the profession, well educated, and shortly after his birthday had embarked as an apprentice on the American slaver *Galaten* of Boston. He had seen the sea and his first Negro almost at the same time. And he had stuck to slaving for twenty years, giving it his youth and health. Despite his robust good looks, he was infected with syphilis. And, if he could still say he was in the prime of life— a life he risked every day—he lived only for the riches that black flesh brought.

McClapp's vessel was a relatively small brig, yet she would carry a cargo of 747 Negroes if Pedro Blanco could provide them. And the captain counted on a mortality rate of twenty-five percent, not an unusual number. The captain neither hated nor feared the dark human beings he carried as cargo. Nevertheless he did nothing to alleviate their suffering or to reform his own coldbloodedness. He knew, as every white man on the Windward Coast did, that once humanity seeped into one's heart, one's constitution, or one's calculations, one was not only a poor man, but a dead one. McClapp would just as soon have commanded one of the British cruisers that suppressed the trade and hanged pirates like himself, but the ten dollars a head in bounty offered was hardly equal money.

In the hold were Manchester cottons, Birmingham muskets, Sheffield cutlery, Rouen cottons, Marseilles brandy, Nantes taffetas and Hamburg looking glasses. In addition there were eight hundred leg shackles, five hundred iron collars, handcuffs, balls and chains, and four hundred wooden spoons. There were forty Winchester rifles, seventy sacks of horse beans, Peruvian bark, chainshot, gunpowder and rum. There were 126 water casks with a capacity of 150 gallons each, 120 pounds of farinha for slave food, and a slave deck ready for laying.

His ship was not only an illegal slaver with false papers, false insignia and several flags proclaiming false nationalities, she had sailed under many aliases: she had been the Spanish ship *Madrid*, then the *Alerta*, the *de Souza*, and now, in her decrepitude, garish lettering declared her to be the *Tecora*. She was a broad-decked ship with a towering mainmast, a brig rigged for speed. But her great finesse was the formidable gun behind her foremast, which turned a complete 180 degrees, mounted on a wide, revolving platform of iron which enabled her to double as a pirate ship if her slaving expedition failed. The *Tecora* could outrun almost anything on the sea, and if escape were impossible, she was equipped with a method of dumping the chained slave cargos, which served as evidence, into the sea. For the captain knew that if he were caught on the high seas by a British cruiser, the penalty was hanging for piracy. Even with all the slaving equipment on board, no vessel could be confiscated unless Negroes were actually found on the ship. This had suggested an admirably simple method of avoiding capture, and many had adopted it, but none more grandiosely than Captain Homans of the *Brillante*. Trapped, late in the afternoon, by four cruisers approaching from different quar-

ters, and with no chance of escape, Captain Homans, hidden
by darkness and as the light breeze died away, had prevented
the first of the British vessels from coming within gunshot and
set his largest anchor ready for dropping. He had then brought
on deck his six hundred slaves, bound by their ankles to one
long chain, which he attached to the anchor. When he heard
the long boats of the four cruisers approaching, Homans cast
loose the anchor. A confused wail of iron links and human cries
had risen, as the chain with its load of living bodies sank to
the bottom of the sea. When the British boarded the boat, the
smell of cooking still clung to the vessel, the kettles for cooking had stood full, but there was not one slave left on board as
evidence. Homans had gone free.

This system had been refined, mused Captain McClapp, until now there was not even the need to bring the slaves out of
the hold. The slave deck was built on a slant with a trap door
at the stern. The slaves were all shackled to the same chain,
which ran the length of the deck on both sides, and to which
was attached a heavy iron ball. The trapdoor could be opened,
and the iron weight falling into the sea would drag with it every
human attached to the chain.

The crossing had been without incident. After fifty-nine days
under sail, the ship had passed into the white line of surf, the
yellow line of beach and the green line of jungle that marked
the Guinean coast. Soon the jade-green hump of the Sierra
Leone mountains had come into view and they reached the
Windward coast, and that tangle of lagoons where their cargo
awaited. The *Tecora* anchored at the mouth of the Gallinas
River, where they found fifteen other vessels, English, French,
American, all with false papers and false insignias, waiting for
Pedro Blanco's sixty manned war canoes to come slipping down
across the foamy surf with their cargos. The crew stared wide-
eyed at the marine cemetery on a sandy spit, studded with
white crosses commemorating sailors who had died of scurvy,
dysentery, white flu, ague, yellow fever, typhoid and cholera.
The air was almost solid with mosquitos, and around the spongy
Banana Islands, crocodiles and sea cows swam and the bodies
of slaves washed backwards and forwards with the tide. Joshua
McClapp had often remarked that the women always floated
face downwards and the men always floated on their backs,
staring into the sky.

*   *   *

"The coast is clear." The message came down the length of
beach from one sentinel to the other, although several British
cruisers including the notorious *Buzzard* had been sighted pa-
trolling the coast. McClapp rushed to the beach. The twin masts
of his clipper scraped the edge of the horizon. Four hours short
of daylight to load seven hundred humans in a moody surf.
The captain began with the females, the most difficult cargo
for embarkation. Seventy reached the brig safely. Then came
the men, but by this time a sea breeze had set in from the
southwest like an incipient gale, and the swells upset almost
every other war canoe sent out. Negro after Negro was rescued
from the surf. The sun was rapidly sinking, and only two thirds
of the slaves were safely aboard. As night approached, the wind
increased. The *Tecora*, with topsails back, signaled impa-
tiently for despatch. The captain bribed the canoemen with
coral branches for each slave embarked, and the mothers, sisters and wives of the boatmen took charge of the embarkation,
coaxing, commanding and threatening. Before the sun's rim
dipped below the horizon, a few strands of false coral had sent
one hundred more Africans into Spanish slavery. Even so, seven
slaves fell unrescued into the shark-infested waters as the *Tecora* took flight under darkness without the remaining 120 to
fill her hold. Her final count was 670 men, women and children. McClapp had just lost 3,500 dollars in the surf.

A slave leaped overboard. Another broke his own neck with
his chains during the night. Two suicides in twenty-four hours
caused Joshua McClapp a great deal of uneasiness. This was a
potentially mutinous slave cargo. Mutinies occurred, he knew,
at the onset of a trip or at the end. Very soon the sea, the best
guardian of man, imposed distance, solitude and such fear on
the slave cargo that it subdued them—better than the whip,
torture or deprivation did. He had his own methods—he always had a sailor who knew the tribes well enough to separate
men from the same nations. And Africa, with its Babel of languages and dialects, made this quite easy. The real danger was
the lechery of the sailors. It incited the black men to revolt,
and led to lack of discipline on ship. But he had his methods
for that as well. He always brought a parcel of young females,
whom he kept apart from the rest of the cargo for the use of

the crew. And if they arrived pregnant, so much the better.

Sengbe Pieh and Grabeau watched the endless line of men, many of whom they recognized: Kimbo, Burnah, Shuma, Bau, Ba, Shule, Fooni, Berri, and Bartu,—all passed by the two men. Sengbe Pieh lurched out, almost choking himself with his chains. His brother-in-law had just filed by.

Almost at once, a squall broke from an almost cloudless sky and the boatswain's whistle piped all hands on deck. Amidst the confusion of the rising gale, a group of slaves, including all those whom Sengbe Pieh knew—plus two other Mendes called Belewa, "Great Whiskers," and Kosokilisia, "War Sparrow"—knocked down the sentry and poured out on deck. The sentry seized the cook's axe, and sweeping it around him like a scythe, kept the men who sought to escape from below at bay. Meanwhile, the women slaves had risen in a body and the helmsman was forced to stab several with his bowie before he could drive them below again. By this time forty slaves were on deck, armed with the staves of broken water casks or billets of wood ripped from the sides of the hold. The captain raced to open the arms chest on the quarter deck. Forwards of the main mast four of the crew were downed by clubs while the rest defended themselves and the wounded as best they could with hand spikes or whatever was at hand. The cook had been trained to throw scalding water on the rebels, but dinner had been over for so long that the slush poured down on the men was only lukewarm. Finally McClapp gave the order: "Aim low and fire at will!" The muskets, loaded with buckshot, brought down several of the slaves. Still, the remaining men neither fled nor laid down their weapons. The crew retreated towards the bowsprit as the slaves surged forwards despite the buckshot. Finally a dozen more rounds forced the remaining men, amongst them Grabeau, Sengbe Pieh and Kimbo, below deck. Just in time, for the sails, tacks and sheets were flapping, whipping and rolling about the masts and decks, and a British cruiser was near the coast. The captain forced the women from their quarters onto the deck and had the crew remove the boards separating the cabin from the hold. When this was done, a dozen sailors entered on their hands and knees and began to push the mutineers forwards to the forecastle with whips. The men defended themselves with their staves. By this time the cook had his water boiling. All who were not in rebellion were forced to come singly on deck. As only about six remained below, the captain ordered holes bored in the deck and buckets of boiling water rained down on them.

Kimbo, Sengbe Pieh and Shaka held out against the water as well as the gunfire. The captain strove to save their lives, but Shaka's resistance was so prolonged that he finally shot him to death. The two others he wounded. Three of the crew were injured. Twenty-eight balls and buckshot were extracted from wounded slaves. One woman and three men had been killed, and of the ringleaders, only Sengbe Pieh was alive. He was taken on deck, lashed to the mast so that his feet did not touch the planks and given twenty lashes. Sengbe Pieh had vowed no sound would escape him, but even the first blow, with its inexpressible pain, brought a scream, and a stream of urine ran warm between his legs. As blow followed blow and made delicate, crisscross scars, the shrieks became whimpers, then silence, then darkness. Gunpowder was rubbed into the expert pattern of wounds, and Sengbe Pieh would remain on deck until he began to heal. The revolt, so quickly sprung up, had as quickly been smashed. But from now on the crew of the *Tecora* lived with a pent-up volcano under their feet and the specter of the *Buzzard*, stalking them.

Sengbe Pieh awoke with a shout. At least he thought he had shouted. But the cry had come from the recesses of some deep nightmare, not from his parched throat. He could not turn his body to the left nor to the right, nor could he sit up. He could not move his legs because of the wounds, and for a moment thought he had lost the use of them, just as he had lost count of the suns that had passed. The rectangle of light above his head seemed to cast gloom over the multitudes that lay around, under and against him. He imagined, as he did every day, the fathomless deep under the creaking planks of the ship, and the spirit world drifting and churning below, horrible and eternal. "Bayeh Bia," he cried out as he did every day, but his cry was lost in the collective sob of a hundred men pleading for their mothers, their wives, their fathers. Men who, despite all their efforts, found themselves choked on their own vomit, or fainted again and again from lack of air and from the stench that rose from their bodies packed so tightly, there was not the space of

the width of a palm. He shifted his eyes to the left. He could
see grotesque crouched figures, carrying lanterns which cast
long shadows, moving amongst the men. The oil lamps fretted
and flickered, hardly able to burn in the airless hold, and
threatening at any moment to pitch the sailors into blackness.

Sengbe Pieh felt a sudden congestion in his chest as if his
heart had failed, but what broke forth was a long, helpless,
racking sob that sucked in the putrid air. *"Gewo! Why? Why?
Why me?"* He was now only a disembodied soul that would
soon join the spirit world beneath the waters. Why, then, did
he still have his body that knew pain, bled, stank? He tried to
sit up but the length of chain was too short unless the stranger
to the left of him, to whom he was chained, sat up as well.
With all his strength he yanked the man beside him to a half-
sitting position.

The man screamed with pain as the chains cut into his neck
and ankles. "Mercy," he moaned. "Who are you?" he whispered.

"A Mende like you," said Sengbe Pieh, "who wants to live,
and since we are chained together, you must live as well."

One of the sailors, hearing the noise, arrived with a lantern.
A man who smelled bad leaned over. The other man held the
light. The second sprinkled white powder all over him. Surely
this was the sign of death, thought Sengbe Pieh. *"Elonga Koe
hui! Elonga Koe hui!"* he shouted. "We are dying! We are
dying!"

This was the fifth voyage on a slaver for Dr. Raphael Jesus,
the ship's surgeon, and he had now refined his ministrations
to the deck beneath him. The rules for successful medical
maintenance of a slaver were purges and vinegar for slaves
and crew alike, force-feeding, disinfection, quarantine and immediate jettison of corpses. His medicaments were few: tinc-
ture of iodine, Peruvian bark, opium, morphine, laudanum, lime
mercury, camphor, lead, tobacco, arsenic, camomile, vanilla,
amputation for gangrene and infection, bleeding, cupping,
cauterization, quinine, turpentine and rum.

The slave deck of the *Tecora* had been constructed in the
classic manner of nineteenth-century slave ships, perfected by
the British two centuries before. A row of narrow boards were
set between two decks laid in wood, cutting the space into less

than four feet between the bodies on the bottom slave deck
and the planks. Each man had five feet five inches in length
and sixteen inches in width in which to lie or sit up. No slave
would see daylight for sixteen or seventeen hours out of twenty-
four. In good weather the cargo would be unchained and herded
onto the main deck, handcuffed two by two. Dr. Jesus was very
strict in his insistence on the maximum of fresh air. Each man
was fed once a day: a bowl of cooked cornmeal with palm oil
and yams or Spanish black beans called negro beans. The men,
by this time in a stuporous state, moved docilely, chewed slowly,
let the sea breeze blow on raw wounds or the hot sun beat
down on skulls that no longer functioned in thought. They endured the lashes from the crew's whip, which fell seemingly
without reason on this one or that one until finally the blows
fell without their even flinching.

Sengbe Pieh knew he must rid himself of the inexpressible
terror of *Pumui*, white skin. He knew from Grabeau that white
men grew old, fell ill, died in the same manner as black men,
but he wondered if the color of their blood was the same. Was
it a lighter or darker red? Or some other color? Blue? Green?
Did the profusion of hair on their bodies mean they were closer
to beasts who, after all, had blood as red as human beings?
Were they human beings? This day, when they had been let
upon deck for air, a commotion had broken out behind him,
and before he could act, two men, chained hand and foot, had
suddenly leaped over the side of the ship. Couple after couple
commenced jumping overboard. The sailors attempted to fish
them out with pikes, but they made no effort to save themselves. The crew fired several rounds over the heads of the
agitated men. Sengbe Pieh and Grabeau exchanged glances.
What if they had by chance been chained together? Would they
have chosen the undulating shadowy depths of the sea? Dr.
Jesus adjusted the mortality rate accordingly. He always had
to count on several, or even mass, suicides.

Raphael Jesus surveyed the slave gang from the quarter deck,
sized up the possible leaders of the cargo now that Shaka was
dead. Jesus' eyes lingered on Sengbe Pieh. His officers had
often urged the captain to follow the example of many slaving
captains and cut off the arms and legs of the most willful of

the slaves to terrify the rest, but he refused even to consider the thought, much less put into practice such cruelty to poor creatures who, excepting their want of Christianity and the true religion (their misfortune more than fault), were as much the works of God, he thought, and no doubt as dear to Him as themselves; nor could he truly imagine, looking down upon the pitiful huddled mass, why they should be despised for their color, it being something they could not help and the effect of the climate it had pleased God to appoint them. He personally did not think there was any intrinsic value in one color more than another, nor that white was better than black. We are just as prone to judge favorably in our own case, he thought, as the blacks judge *our* color, the color of the Devil. And here we are, he thought, doing the Devil's work and proving them right!

Days after the revolt, the *Tecora* passed the slaver *Si*. They saluted one another and loud-spoke congratulations on having avoided the British cruisers. Too soon, not a half day later, a midshipman entered the cabin of Captain McClapp to say there was a sail visible to the northwest. The captain rushed on deck, and the slaves were hurried below under whip handles and prodding lashes. McClapp set his glass and saw the large three-masted ship stalking them.

She tacked, as if not liking their appearance, and stood before the wind. The breeze freshened and her hull became distinctly visible. It was the famous British cruiser the *Buzzard*. The *Tecora* doubled in all directions, changing course and zigzagging to avoid her pursuers. Five guns were successively fired and the *Tecora* hoisted the American flag, but without effect. McClapp kept a sharp lookout, leaning over the netting and silently handing the telescope to one or the other of his mates. The slaves were kept below deck. At dawn, the captain saw the *Buzzard* was still a speck on the horizon, standing due north. The breeze increased as the British brig of war began to gain on the *Tecora*. The slaver dressed more sail to escape as long shots were sent after her. At noon the *Tecora* was within gunshot and the *Buzzard* fired one of her long bow guns. It struck the water alongside the *Tecora* and McClapp hesitated. The pilot began to curse. After a day and a half chase, during which the British had run her a hundred miles, the *Tecora* was about to be boarded.

McClapp ordered all fires put out, the forecastle nailed shut, all Negroes below, and the gratings over the hatches closed. Then he ordered a supply of small arms and ammunition on deck covered with blankets. The cannons were sponged and loaded with care. The American flag was run up. There was not a breath of air. The brig rolled slowly on the lazy swell. The *Buzzard* did not approach, nor did the *Tecora* advance.

The captain paced the deck for half an hour beneath the awning, now and then seizing a telescope. He mounted the rigging. Then he saw the *Si* fully manned making way with Portuguese insignias flying. And behind her, the distant lightning and thunder and black-handed clouds of a white tornado. McClapp had a choice between the British and the eye of the storm. As the other slaver changed courses, McClapp made for the squall, insignias flying. The blow lasted twenty minutes but to McClapp and his men, it seemed an eternity.

The *Buzzard* seemed to hesitate, standing poised on a shimmering crest, beautiful and regal. Then the *Tecora*'s captain saw the *Buzzard* tack and swerve in pursuit of the *Si*, the slower of the two boats. McClapp was almost disappointed. He could have outrun the *Buzzard* any day. The captain of the *Tecora* lowered his spyglass as the British cruiser disappeared over the horizon.

The *Buzzard* &
March 1839

The black gunner looked down from the shrouds of the ten-cannon, forty-three-ton British brig of war, HMS *Buzzard*, his home. The unfurled upper canvas almost hid the dark, angel-like figure peering from behind the puffed-out sails, their contours rounded like small white clouds snarled in a net as the breeze lifted from the flat, glossy ocean. He listened to the faint, pitched thunder echo off the Sierra Leone mountains in the distance. Then he looked out over the blue waters of the Gulf of Guinea. The peninsula of Sierra Leone, named by the Portuguese for the continuous thunder that clung to its peaks and for the roaring of the wild lions that roamed them, rose in a hump from the ocean like a garland sprung from the sea. Great masses of light and shade projected from innumerable hills heaped one upon the other like man-made monuments. The torpid air had a taste and a smell. The wide open arm of the South Atlantic, which fitted into the angle of Western Africa from the Bight of Biafra, had the hot acid-metallic odor of the pure yellow-gold Guinea coins the Royal African Company had first minted to celebrate the slave trade. The green-tinged, low coastline was hazy, studded with black marshes, mangrove trees and reed-pricked islands. Every time the cannoneer arrived at this particular coast, he fixed his eyes on the exact same place he had first seen as a boy from the captured slave ship *Henrietta* as it was being towed back to shore. The spot had been on the farthermost tip of sighted coastland and stood where the muddy Gallinas River met the clean sea in foamy, choppy waves. On it had risen a sandy black-rock formation. Part pyramid, part giant palm, part lighthouse, part fortress, it forbade the entrance of sea and ship alike, of time and history;

45

the defiant, furious gesture of a forgotten potentate. If it had fallen, he had thought as that filthy, emaciated, hollow-eyed boy, it would have brought down the world.

"Hey there, James. Get your arse down here. Captain wants to see your pretty black face!"

The sun caught James Covey's profile and blackened it even more against the tapestry of the sail's white curves, vaults and half-moons. The thick, chiselled features, high forehead and perfectly shaped head, capped in tight black curls cut close except for a long, thick braid held by a black ribbon at the back of his neck, wavered in the tropical heat like molten tar. His eyes were so large and so black they seemed to have no white at all, though on closer examination one could see that the white was the pearly blue of a newborn, making his gaze disconcertingly candid, fringed with thick, long lashes. The flared wide nose was straight, the lips full and a rich purple. He had not yet, in his twenty-five years, taken a razor to his chin, a fact that greatly amused the crew of the *Buzzard*. The fine features were complemented by a tall, strong body which despite its small bones was sturdy, with full, thick muscles, and the legs of a sprinter. His body was as far as it was human, indestructible and indefatigable. He also had one amazing gift for a sailor—he could see in the dark. In the pitchest black he picked out objects static or moving; he always took night watch since, of all the crew, he was the only one who could spot an unlit ship after sundown. The crew depended on his extraordinary sight, which they considered almost supernatural, a gift given to him when everything else had been taken away.

James Covey was almost twenty-three years old. He was a Mende born in Benderi who had been kidnapped at the age of nine from his parents' house and sold as a slave to the King of the Bulloms at Mani. For two years he had planted rice for one of the king's wives who had treated him kindly, but in the end she had sold him to a Portuguese slaver. He had been taken, along with two or three hundred others, to Lomboko, where he had been put on a Spanish slave ship headed for America. The slaver had been captured by a British man-of-war patrol and, in accordance with the 1814 treaties outlawing the slave trade signed by all the former slave-trading countries, the ship had been towed back to Freetown in Sierra Leone, where the eleven-year-old slave had been liberated. Thus Covey had gained his freedom. He had learned to read and write from the white missionary couple who had adopted him, but as soon as he was old enough, he had enlisted in the British navy and had been assigned to the brig of war *Buzzard*, commanded by Captain Fitzgerald, who, as part of Her Royal Majesty's African Slave Patrol, cruised the Gulf of Guinea, chasing and capturing illegal slave ships and liberating their cargos.

James Covey was not his real name. In Mende his name was *Kaweli*, War Road, which meant "the road dangerous to travel for fear of being taken captive." The bitter irony of his name always made him smile.

The Guinea coast was divided into the windward and the leeward. The former extended from Senegal to Cape Palmas. And the latter extended as far south as white men normally traded for slaves. From Cape Palmas to Cape Three Points the Ivory Coast began, ending at the Gold Coast, 180 miles away. Fine rivers flowed into the sea along the entire seacoast, rivers that penetrated the interior of Guinea or Negroland in great, looping curves, dividing into smaller branches and creeks which communicated with each other like canals. In the interior unchecked forests crowded to the edges of the rivers, their luxuriant vegetation shading against the terrible sun. Because men were so scarce, there was the awful stillness everywhere. In fact, thought Covey, the entire interior of Africa remained as silent and blank as it had been three hundred years before, when the first slaves had been exported, and for the same reason, no white man had ever been there. The brutal terrain, the alien climate, the killing fevers and the belligerent inhabitants continued to block the white man's way inland. But there was another reason for this ignorance—a total lack of interest in getting there. Why should Europeans run the risk of penetrating the continent's interior? he asked himself. They had organized themselves quite efficiently to obtain, from the relative safety of their coastal ports, the only thing they wanted of Africa: her men.

Ten million slaves had thus been landed in the New World in the past cruel centuries, and although the Portuguese, the Dutch, the Danes and the French had taken their share, imperial Britain, the undisputed maritime and mercantile power on earth, had dominated the trade. More than half the slaves taken from Africa had been carried in English ships to English colonies. Slaving had been the first principle and foundation of the empire, the mainspring of the machine that set every wheel in motion. Wheels within wheels, thought Covey, and perhaps because England *had been* the greatest slaving nation, she had become the greatest anti-slavery nation and emancipator, as the greatest sinners, once repented, often become the most fanatical saints. The traffic in slaves and the abysmal ignorance of the African interior were paradoxes in this great new nineteenth century in which the slave trade had been outlawed by all civilized Christian nations. It had begun with Denmark, followed by Britain and the United States, then the rest of Europe. Finally, three years ago, even foot-dragging Portugal had come around. The law, Covey knew, had not halted, or for that matter even reduced, the number of slaves shipped. If anything their plight became even worse, on smaller, faster and more brutal ships. The armed naval squadrons to police the African and American coasts, and the triangle of which he was a part, were nothing compared to the pirates willing to run her blockades so long as the coin of Africa remained her men.

For the Mendian Covey, of all the nations that made up Guinea, Mendeland was the most beautiful. It was covered with the most umbrageous trees. Its soil was the most fertile and fruitful. Large open savannas swept up to cloud-struck mountains covered with wild, coarse grass, long and bent in the wind. Covey always felt in his bones the coursing River Mitouba which crossed Mendeland, then flowed into the Cape where the Sierra Leone mountains, perpetually lost in fog and thunder, began. Covey recalled all he knew of Africa now; its six hundred thousand square miles of rain forest where the sun never shone, the endless desert, ordained by the ancient Arabic name imitating a man's last gasp for water: *Sahara.* Forty years had passed since Mungo Park had first gazed on the waters of the Niger River, yet the lands surrounding it, equal in size to half of Europe, had never seen white men. Liverpool merchants still held forts on the Gold Coast. London and Lisbon companies still traded in Sierra Leone, Gambia and Uganda, but nine years would pass before a European would set foot in what would become Rhodesia. There were majestic, unexplored mountains, highlands, lakes and waterfalls, and, above all, the great African rivers that crisscrossed the continent like the veins and arteries of a godly beast, rivers that already had names like the Nile, the Niger, the Congo, the Gallinas, and rivers yet unnamed or, rather, unnamed on charts and maps of white men. As for his own destiny, ever since Covey had been rescued as a slave of nine, he had dreamed of doing exactly what he was doing now: plying the two thousand miles of Guinean coast, chasing and capturing illegal slavers and liberating their cargos. Covey knew that Freetown was little more than a recruiting station for laborers in the British West Indian colonies of Trinidad, Jamaica and Barbados. The black men he and his captain freed were being persuaded to immigrate to conditions little better than slavery. The French, the Portuguese and the Spaniards, who all indulged in illicit slave trading, accused the British of hypocrisy. God knows, thought Covey, the English *invented* hypocrisy—but even if Great Britain were not the first to outlaw the trade, it was the only nation whose navy maintained any surveillance of illegal traffickers in slaves, pitiful as it was. The warships, with some thousand men that made up H.M. Queen Victoria's African Squadron were old and certainly insufficient. To police the seas was one thing, to patrol the swamps, inlets, branches and intricate labyrinths of waterways of West African rivers was another, thought Covey. Ever since the Congress of Vienna, sixteen years earlier, had pronounced the slave trade (but not slavery itself) illegal piracy and subject to the death penalty, British ships of Her Royal Majesty's Squadron for the Suppression of the Slave Trade had patrolled the coast, boarding and searching ships suspected of being slavers. For, if anything, the trade in slaves had increased with illegality. In this Year of Our Lord 1839, second year of the reign of Her Majesty Queen Victoria, eighty thousand slaves would be illegally exported to the Americas. Only a tenth would be freed by the patrols. And of the remaining, only half would live to see land on the other side of the ocean, and of that half, only a third would survive their first three years of captivity in the New World.

Out of every hundred Africans who left, only thirty would be alive in slavery three years later. He remembered the first

lecture he had had on the subject, given to him by Captain
Gabriel Fitzgerald, master of the *Buzzard*.

"James, the history of the slave trade is the history of a war
of more than two centuries, waged by men against human nature; a war carried on, not by ignorance and barbarism against
knowledge and civilization, not by half-famished multitudes
against a race blessed with the arts of life, softened by luxury,
but as some strange, nondescript inequity, waged by unpro-
voked strength against uninquiring helplessness by the best
nations of Christendom, making the best men the worst. . . ."

Here Fitzgerald had paused, his wind-burned face flushed
with passion. It was said that Captain Fitzgerald had been made
for the sea in his mother's womb, so perfect was he in his role.
He was the right height, the right weight, with the steadiest
hand, the bravest (and cruellest) heart. His voice had been
fashioned to carry over the tumult of any storm, and one quiet
word could make a grown man shake. The captain had the
keenest eyesight on the ship, except for James Covey's. But
the captain could gauge distances to a hundredth of a mile or
the seconds of an hour, his sense of smell recognized unseen
land miles away, his ears heard families of sharks beneath him
or the creak of a fleeing ship, out of sight. For Covey, who had
loved him from the moment he had set eyes on him, he was
perfect. And why not? Fitzgerald was son and grandson of navy
men and the daughters of navy men. He had spent the beginning of his career under Commander Denman, a legend amongst
the British patrollers of the African squadron. Denman was ob-
sessive, ruthless and almost mystical in his pursuit of slavers,
and reckless in bringing them to justice. Everyone knew why.
Denman had been a young lieutenant serving off the coast of
Brazil in command of the *Curfew*, of His Majesty's navy. That
year he had captured the first slaver ever taken off the coast of
South America. He was ordered to take his prisoners and its
cargo of 550 Africans back across the Atlantic to Sierra Leone
to stand trial for piracy. The forty-six days of that dreadful
Middle Passage in reverse had marked Denman as surely as
hot iron branded. The suffering of both slaves and sailors had
been terrible. At Freetown, Denman had failed to secure the
condemnation of the slaver because she had been taken south
of the Equator. The slaves therefore had had to make a third

passage back to Brazil. Denman, half crazed, had nevertheless obeyed the order and had deposited one tenth of the original cargo of men and women on the docks of Rio de Janeiro. Then he had taken to chasing, capturing slave ships like a demon, the British cruisers waiting on the high seas until a suspected slaver was sighted and then giving chase. Even now, Denman was still out there, in his schooner, the *Wonderer,* searching.

The British squadrons had captured 333 slavers and freed almost 65,000 Africans, thought Covey. And he had been one of them. The Netherlands schooner, the *Henrietta,* had carried 306 slaves, including himself, and had been captured by HMS *Aden* on the third of October 1825. It had been his extreme youth, he imagined, that had saved him from death in the slave hold where he had survived twenty-six days, the last two of which he had spent chained to a dead man on one side and a raving maniac on the other.

Then one day the portholes had been shut, the Africans all herded on deck, and the ship had literally flown across the waves, lurching this way and that. He had seen another ship in the distance, following them and gaining. The ship shuddered as it opened fire on the pursuing ship, and almost immediately an explosion smashed into the *Henrietta,* made her tilt and sent her crew scampering up the masts. Some of the Africans, free of their chains, jumped overboard. The sick or dying were thrown overboard with the ship's papers and log, but it had been too late; the *Aden* had borne down too swiftly on the *Henrietta.* Then the deck was filled with other white men who had boarded the *Henrietta,* pistols and muskets cocked, mingling in confusion with the white men on board, shouting. He had understood that these white men were the enemies of the others, and even before he saw the one brown face amongst the newcomers, he knew the reason. The brown man, dressed like a white man, had spoken in Mende. *In the name of the King of England, you are freed.* And he had known from that moment that one day he, too, wanted to pronounce those words to the pitiful remnants of the mysterious misadventure that had taken him onto the waters and shown him the sea where all ancestors and all spirits lived. The tall brown man had picked him up and patiently given him water from his own gourd. It was clear that many of the cargo were still too frightened or too sick to know what was happening to them as the *Henrietta* was towed back to Sierra Leone. Of the three thousand Africans, a quarter were dead, all were nude, and none were capable of walking from the waterside to the dock, except he and two other small boys. The rest, dazed and emaciated, huddled on board the schooner until an English official from the Liberated African Department came aboard to count the living and the dead. With him came other interpreters, who finally convinced the remaining Africans they were free. Distrust, disbelief, then joy, relief and frenzied happiness broke out on deck. Feeble singing and dancing began. People embraced those too numb to realize what had happened to them. He had been taken to a large, square wooden building and there learned that his father and brother had perished in the passage, and his mother, sister, and aunt in the firing of his village by warring neighbors. The surviving Africans had been given new names: John England, William Spain, James Scotland, Wilkes Wales. Some were named by history—August, Napoleon, Wilber Hannibal, John Cesar, Leslie Nelson, Freddy Drake, James Spartacus, John Regent, Willington Sharp—and some by caprice: Ajax, Alabaster, Try John, Afric Charter, Miller Brend. A family of missionaries had given him their name, Covey. James Covey. But he had never forgotten that he had been named by his parents, Kaweli.

"You were one of the lucky ones, lad," Fitzgerald had said, looking at him in surprise when he had asked to enlist on the *Buzzard*. And for Fitzgerald and his crew, Covey became the talisman. A living, breathing symbol of their mission, for *he had been there and had been saved.*

As he hurried towards the captain's cabin, the ship shuddered under him. They were lifting anchor. The *Si*, which they were stalking, must be beyond territorial waters. Covey heard the commands and cries that accompanied a ship under way. He was happy to be moving. He had crossed the Atlantic four times, and four times the *Buzzard* had come back with a prize. The *Si*, a notorious slaver, was carrying seven or eight hundred slaves. Captain Fitzgerald was determined she would not get away this time. Covey's heart was beating faster than usual when he knocked at his captain's berth.

"Come in, James."

Captain Fitzgerald didn't look up from the log book as Covey entered.

"I know how you feel, Jim, but I don't want a repeat of what happened with the last prize we took."

"Sir?"

"You know what I *mean*. I mean someone saw you push a sailor of the *Rita* off the deck. And someone saw you shoot into the crew of the *Rita*."

"They had just flung a slave overboard, *and* the ship's logs."

"You have eyes in the back of your head? You couldn't have seen that! You may see in the dark, Jim Covey, but hardly through the *back* of your head."

"Sir—"

"James, you've been roughing up *prisoners*. I can't have that. Not a British seaman in the Queen's navy."

"Just because a few pirates happen to slip and fall—"

"Overboard," finished the captain.

"I protest. . . ."

"I *said* now that we are going after the *Si*, and I don't want any accidents. I want the whole crew of that ship alive."

"I'm not the only—"

"I don't care that you're not the only one! I care about *you* and your behavior, your forbearance. . . ."

"Why should I be more forbearing than a white sailor, sir?"

Fitzgerald looked up, surprised at the bitterness in Covey's voice.

"Because you are a gentleman," said Fitzgerald, "not a murderer, even of murderers. There are the courts for that."

"And they really do a lot, don't they? When was the last captain of a slaver *hung* as a pirate? You sound like one of those sanctimonious judges in Freetown."

Fitzgerald looked at Covey, surprised and hurt at his tone of voice. He had fine sons at home and a beautiful wife, but Covey was like a younger brother. He loved him as much.

"I don't mean to say you can't or won't have . . . feelings."

Covey willed himself not to speak. Endurance, he thought. Endurance. He had hardened his heart to everything that might attack it: pain, remorse, pity, affinity, love and memory. Covey's handsome head turned and the black eyes surveyed his captain. At sixteen he had begged his adoptive parents to allow him to go to sea. Two years later, which he had spent in

school in Freetown, they had yielded and he had enlisted in
the British navy. At the end of his tenth cruise he had returned
to Freetown to find his missionary parents dead of one of the
illnesses Africa bestowed upon its white benefactors. Now he
was all alone, and perhaps it was better this way.

As if in mockery, Covey's beloved Fitzgerald had the same
white skin, transparent eyes, and a tail that grew out of his
neck that had once terrified Covey. Gabriel Fitzgerald was almost six feet seven, with a frame to match. He sported a rich,
luxuriant, sumptuous, red beard to make him look older than
he was and which was his pride. He was convinced that it was
the reason for his great success with women.

"There is such a thing as sinful pride," said Fitzgerald.
"Taking the law into your own hands."

"Never."

"Never what?"

"Pride is never sinful when it is Justice."

"And who are you to decide when and where and how justice is to be served?"

"Sometimes you just have to make the best of what is at
hand."

"Not an Englishman, James."

"Perhaps."

And not a Poro man either, thought Covey, suddenly remembering the meticulous, elaborately severe procedure of
justice of a Mende trial.

Fitzgerald's deep, rich voice broke again into the hazy afternoon. The lilting authoritative voice of the Irishman was hard.

"Stay away from the crew of the *Si* . . . when we catch her.
That's an order."

"Aye, *aye*, sir."

The spotter announced the *Si* ahoy. Fitzgerald took out his
telescope to see what kind of ship it was. There were two ships
ahoy, the *Si* and a second vessel, the *Tecora*, more than likely
another slaver. Fitzgerald decided to go after this new prize
first. The ship doubled in all directions, changing courses and
zigzagging to avoid the *Buzzard*. Fitzgerald fired five guns and
the brig hoisted the American flag. Undeterred, Fitzgerald gave
chase for a day. The second day, he was about to board her
when Covey's extraordinary eyes saw the dark cloud, not larger

than a man's hand, on the verge of the eastern horizon. It was, he knew, June, the month of storms.

Then, in quick succession, came faint flashes of lightning and distant thunder. Even before the warning bell, the clouds rolled in, becoming dense and black and bulky, so that they seemed heaped upon each other, tripping one over the other like a column of suddenly halted infantry. The ship's crew scurried around tying down everything that moved. They lashed the sails tightly to the masts and closed every porthole. The *Tecora* was forgotten for the moment. It was in the eye of the storm. The thunder grew by degrees nearer and became more tremendous. Most of the sky was wrapped in steel gray except for an awful aura of eerie light to the east. Covey knew that just before the storm's onslaught there would be a light breeze, scarcely perceptible from westwards, and the temperature would drop eight or even ten degrees in two or three minutes. Then the sea would rush like a savage animal, a white foam marking the advance of furious wind sweeping itself into a whirlwind on the water's surface. Covey could still spy the escaping slaver, a tiny speck on the horizon. The sea had lost its glossy smoothness now and had changed into terrible mountainlike bellows and turbulent headwinds. This was a white tornado. No rain accompanied it, which made it all the more violent, like a womanless man. Covey felt the ship shudder then rise and fall sickeningly as the first gales hit. He leaped to his post, elated and ready for it. The *Buzzard,* too, readied itself. The world, even the world of slavery, was forgotten. This elemental war always astonished Covey and filled him with awe. If slavery was a continuation of war, a storm was a continuation of creation, both reminders of man's fragile hold on his existence and happiness.

The crew lashed themselves to the deck. The *Buzzard*'s prow dipped nauseatingly into the deep, and at a burst of thunder, a roaring, stifling wind pushed palm-tree high waves across the deck's surface. Headlong gales rushed the man-of-war forward under the wheeling spires of water. "Let the devil dance," cried Covey into the wind, clutching the lines that secured him to the deck. It was as dark as midnight at two in the afternoon. The howls of winds pirouetted the ship, lit its sides and furled sails with flashes of lightning. The blow lasted for almost twenty minutes, but to the *Buzzard* it seemed an eternity. The brig was old, decrepit and in need of repairs. One of its cannons broke loose from its ropes and danced crazily across the quarterdeck. A dead sea gull crashed upon the deck. No one spoke for no human voice could be heard over the winds. The crew had all heard of old boats breaking in two in the wake of a white tornado, or capsizing, unable to resist the ten-ton waves and winds that reached twenty knots. With the dogged optimism of sailors, everyone prepared for the worst while hoping for the best.

Then, suddenly, it was over. The blackness passed to the west and little by little diminished to the size of a pointing, accusing finger. The finger disappeared over the horizon, where two ships could be seen in the distance.

A black hand appeared in the sea and then a body. The *Buzzard* was surrounded by dozens of floating dead black men or parts of them, men that had been jettisoned or swept overboard. Amongst the bodies circulated the hard, shiny, gun-metal blades of shark fins. It was the *Si* that had left a trail of cadavers they could follow. The chase was on. Captain Fitzgerald ordered full sails and the *Buzzard* struck forward like an aimless blow. Then she righted herself and increased her speed. At the limit of her tack, the helmsman brought the ship around and she turned regally, poised, quivering, seemingly weightless on the crest of a wave, all the exhaustion of the storm she had endured forgotten. Light as air, she rose as if there were not twenty years upon her masts, thought Fitzgerald, and two thousand fathoms of cold, watery grave beneath her hull. The vessel, on a new tack, caught the wind. The sails flapped, unfurled, the booms creaked, the brig straightened. The second ship had disappeared. In delight they realized they were upon the *Si*.

The *Buzzard* swerved into fighting position and the crew unlocked the cannons. Within Fitzgerald's sight the Spanish frigate was jettisoning more bodies overboard. They were trying to hurl the entire cargo into the ocean. Fitzgerald saw the *Si* lower its foresail in preparation for turning into the wind.

"Get the sons of bitches," said Fitzgerald into his loud-hailer, "if we have to chase them all the way to Brazil!"

Covey wiped the sweat out of his eyes. The helmsman bore off to windward and the *Buzzard* began her assault on the *Si*. The man-of-war leaped. She broke through the waves in a rage, an avenging angel. She took the wind full force, keeling over, her rigging singing. The *Buzzard* gained on the *Si*. They chased the slaver for an hour before coming astern.

"Ready to weigh ship," cried the second mate. The men of the *Buzzard* scurried to their posts on the ropes, the cannon, the hawsers, the halyards. Fitzgerald swung the tiller a little crazily. The ship swerved in a semicircle. The yards screeched and strained to leeward and the halyards howled and stretched in the effort to bring the *Buzzard* parallel to the *Si*. Once done, the *Buzzard*'s cannon roared. They tore a hole in the stern of the *Si* and another in the masts, which came crashing onto the decks. In the mind's eye of every sailor were the floating black bodies paving the way to the *Si*. They swept everything before them. Covey heard himself cry, "Spare no one!" Sailor after sailor went down. The Spanish fought tooth and nail, but the long gun of the Spaniard was disabled. A round shot from the launch had unmoored the cannon. Amid the cries and screams of men on deck, the order went out to split the gratings and release the slaves. The Spaniard struck its colors and Captain Fitzgerald, with seven officers from the *Buzzard,* reached the deck of the *Si* and discovered the scene. Fitzgerald's sailors were now bent on revenge. The Spaniards that opposed them were cut down. Then all was over. Here was a hushed and panting knot of victors and vanquished on the slippery, bloody deck, and under his feet Covey knew five hundred helpless, confused, dying slaves were imprisoned. The Englishmen rounded up almost thirty men. The frigate itself listed from the hole in its stern, but it was towable. The worst, he knew, was yet to come. What had happened in the hold of the ship when the *Si* had passed through the eye of the tornado? The sailors of the *Buzzard* knew to expect crushed bodies, broken bones, concussions, even men smothered to death by jammed-up bodies. The chains, too, would have done their work: torn ulcerated flesh, dislocated feet and hands, fractured arms, decapitated heads and broken necks. This was going to be one of the worst boardings of his life, thought Covey.

The *Si* had taken in on the coast of Africa 562 slaves and had been out seventeen days, during which she had thrown overboard fifty-five. When the slaves, dazed and stunned, were let on deck, no entreaties, threats or blows could restrain them from the water that had been prepared in a long trough. They shrieked and struggled and fought with one another for access as if they had grown rabid at its sight.

With the opening of the trapdoors, the stench, putrid and solid, curled into the fresh sea breeze. The slave deck was so covered with blood, mucus and offal that it resembled a slaughterhouse. Rats scurried from the light, leaping over men. The span was so low that the slaves had sat between each other's legs and were stowed so close together that there was no possibility of their lying down or changing their position at all, by night or by day. As they belonged to and were shipped on account of different individuals, they were branded with the owners' mark, under their breasts or on their arms.

The *Buzzard's* men gagging and retching, their mouths covered with handkerchiefs dipped in vinegar, carried the unconscious slaves onto the deck, a dozen moribund, all naked. Then the crew of the *Si* was forced at gunpoint to bring up the rest of the cargo, living or dead, and lay them out on the deck. There were 182 men still alive and four small children. All the women below deck were dead. The crew of the *Si* was locked into the slave deck for the duration of the tow back to Sierra Leone. The captain was placed under arrest. By the time the *Buzzard* towed the *Si* back to Sierra Leone, Covey calculated a third of the Africans now alive would be dead. He heard a hushed voice beside him.

"Look." Covey turned. A cannoneer brought him a newborn infant as if he, Covey, could speak to him. The mother must have died giving birth. He was still bloody. The infant screamed. Covey opened his shirt and laid the baby against his chest, then bound the tails of his shirt tightly around the small body, making a sort of hammock for him. This one, he was determined, would live. It was now his job to find a Mende-speaking captive and to explain to him that the cargo had been set free. Little by little the intelligence would spread amongst those who were still in their right minds. Most would not believe it until they saw land again. Many were too sick or too stunned to believe anything. He began speaking into the ship's loud-hailer slowly, repeating, *"Mu li tei hu ba hua."* You are free! Do not be afraid.

He repeated the words again and again into the silence until small, astonished murmurs of belief began to be heard. He lifted the squealing infant so that the whole congregation of former

slaves could see the miracle. He had only this family of slavery. And his tears were not tears, he thought, but the rivers,
lakes, marshes, waterfalls, springs of Africa itself.

The white tornado which had hindered the capture of the *Si*
had allowed the other slaver, a 370-ton Rhode Island–built
Portuguese frigate, the *Tecora*, to slip by the *Buzzard*. She was
carrying 670 Africans and was headed for the Spanish possession of Cuba. Chained to its slave decks, and still alive, was
Sengbe Pieh.

The *Tecora* had been at sea for thirty days, several days off
the Cape of Good Hope, buffeted by a series of adverse gales,
when the first mate brought the news that several slaves were
ill of smallpox. Of all the calamities that occurred in the voyage of a slaver, this news was the most dreaded, unpredictable
and unmanageable. The captain stared at the first mate for a
minute as if in doubt, then called in his officers. The corpse,
which belonged to Belewa, was quietly thrown into the sea
and the cause of death kept from the crew. But when Captain
McClapp visited the slave deck himself that day, his lantern
struggling to burn in the humid miasma, he found nine infected slaves. McClapp had already decided to rid the boat of
the infected by poisoning them with laudanum, but with nine
already prostrate, it was too late. A hospital was set up in the
forecastle manned by those of the crew that had been vacci-
nated or who had already had the pox. But the sick list soon
rose to thirty. Twelve sailors took the infection and fifteen
corpses were thrown into the sea. Body after body fed the deep,
and when at last the captain ordered the gratings to be removed from the hatches, he found nearly half the slaves dead
or dying. The dead were dragged out by the crew, who, covering their faces with rags and their hands with tarred mittens,
flung the fetid masses of putrefaction into the sea. One day
was as another until death was satisfied. Of the 670 beings who
had left Lomboko, there were now 397 skeletons; a loss of 6,825
dollars.

By the time the *Tecora* reached the Equator, the remnants
of the cargo were unshackled; the dead had left space, food
and water for the living. The survivors began to regain their
strength, if not their sanity. Several of Sengbe Pieh's row re-

covered in body, but their nerves had given way so completely that what fever and delirium had not done, was completed by madness. And they, too, died. At last McClapp saw the arrival of the favorable trade winds that would end a luckless voyage. From deck to royal, from flying job to topsail, every stitch of canvas that would draw was packed and crowded onto the brig. Ships began to be seen daily in numbers, but not until the *Tecora* had reached the waters of Cuba did they spy another cruising British schooner. The captain ordered the helmsman to keep his course, and tautening sheets, braces and halyards, carefully unrolled the insignias of Spain, Denmark and Portugal, each with its own set of papers. He chose the Danish and hoped he would not have to fight another time for his wretched cargo. When the captain reached the deck, he found the cruiser gaining on him. She outsailed the *Tecora*. Escape was once again impossible. The captain kept to his course, fired a gun, and hoisted the Danish signals. A shot from the pursuing ship fell close to the stern; the captain ordered in studding sails alow and aloft. The cruiser persisted. Four hours later she was still within half gunshot of the *Tecora*. The captain loaded, flung open his ports and ran out his mortars. McClapp smiled at the precision of his gunner's well-drilled defiant cannonade, but it had not the least effect on the schooner, which still pursued them. At last within hail, her commander leaped on a gun. "Heave to or take a ball," he ordered.

Captain McClapp answered with a *"no entiendo"*—I don't understand you. Meanwhile the cruiser had shot ahead, sure that she had trapped him. But McClapp swivelled the revolving cannon and, firing backwards, managed to strike the cruiser near the bow, blowing away her foremast and bowsprit. The cruiser's captain was so surprised that he failed to order action until it was too late. Contemptuously the *Tecora* left the crippled schooner in her wake.

A few days later the *Tecora*'s cargo was safely disembarked on the beach of a small village nine miles east of Santiago de Cuba, while the *Tecora* herself was set adrift in the spectacular bay of the same name and burned to the water's edge.

Nine men stood watching their erstwhile prison and torment burn. They had forged a bond between themselves during the voyage of the *Tecora*. Each had helped the other survive. They were now bound together in blood by the Middle Passage even more tightly than by their Poro vows. They were Burnah, Kimbo, Kabba Sei, Sessi, Fabanna, Kaba Kpekalay, Grabeau, Fooni, and the youngest, Sengbe Pieh.

⊸ Havana, Cuba ⊷
June 1839

Dr. Robert Madden stepped out of the United States Consulate into the harsh Cuban sun, his flushed face shaded by a wide, sloping straw hat. Havana was the commercial center of the West Indian slave trade, the extinction of which was Robert Madden's mission in life. The idealistic, hot-tempered Irish physician had spent most of his life not practicing his profession, but travelling throughout the Near East, West Africa, the Caribbean and Australia, driven by his passion to rid the world of slavery. Madden uttered a fervent, elongated chain of curses directed at the American consul and then reached over and took his own pulse. It had accelerated to an alarming degree. Cuba, he mused, was not the healthiest place for a white man. Nor were any of the islands of America. As a magistrate in Jamaica he had barely escaped the fate of his other four colleagues, dead in the prime of life from yellow fever. It was taken for granted that this climate was deadly to European constitutions, but on top of that he had twice been beaten up in the course of his magisterial duties as the Queen's High Commissioner to Suppress Slavery in Jamaica. In his lonely battle for abolition, he had only once succumbed to depression and despair, resigning his post with a letter which ended, "I find the protection of the Negro's life incompatible with the protection of my own."

But now he was back, and if earlier threats and danger had not stopped him, if malaria, typhoid and yellow fever had not brought him low, he had no intention of succumbing to apoplexy over a rude, overbearing, dishonest, third-rate dangler on official life like Nicholas Philip Trist, the United States consul in Havana. The man was a disgrace to the diplomatic corps, a vain, arrogant, bigoted slave-holding Virginian chimpanzee!

Trist was closely allied to the republican aristocracy of America, having married Virginia Randolph, the granddaughter of Thomas Jefferson, and he had established a small colony of that illustrious stock at Havana, fumed Madden. He did and said what he pleased, the people of the United States being far from insensitive to the distinctions of either ancestry or money.

The consul could not have been ignorant of the notorious, blatantly illegal arrival of the *Tecora* which, moreover, had sailed from Havana under American colors. Madden had visited the *Tecora* and was convinced that her papers were of another ship, too old for the trade, which had sailed under many aliases. The doctor had gone to the consul, thinking to ask for the intervention of the ship *Boston,* of the American patrol now in harbor. But Mr. Trist had seen things in a very different light.

"By the Tenth Article of Ghent, you are to use your utmost endeavors to promote the entire abolition of the slave trade," Madden had said to Trist. "The *spirit* of your government's engagement is that they should furnish to the agents of other governments any information which might help that other government to accomplish its common purpose."

"The hell we have a common purpose. You hypocrite," Trist said. "I believe, uphold and encourage slavery. What about the manufacturers of goods in Great Britain *expressly* for the slave trade? Do your manufacturers furnish you with *lists* of their clients? I have *seen* casks of shackles passing through customs here without attracting any more attention than a box of cheese! Can *they* not be traced all the way back to Birmingham or Liverpool? Do that before you start bothering me about clearance papers."

"Trist, you fully lend your own countenance and your office to cover a practice which the laws of your country have deemed piracy—slavers are sheltering themselves under the American flag! The refusal of mutual right of search means that the United States is extending the protection of its flags to miscreants and pirates!"

"You're damn right. And I shall go right on doing it."

"You sign blank forms to be filled up at pleasure by the persons in command of those vessels. I caution you to be more circumspect in the future and to exert all your vigilance to prevent slave traders from screening themselves under the protection of the American flag."

"You dare caution me! Why don't you address yourself to President Van Buren? Let him take fire at these . . . friendly suggestions! Or go to Hell . . ."

"And you," Trist had repeated coolly, "are not working to abolish the slave trade, but to gather evidence against Spain's breaking its treaty, so that England can use it as an excuse to seize Cuba and everything on it!"

"You are a stranger to the truth, sir," Madden had shouted.

"And you, sir, are as wretched a mixture of bigot and religious fanatic I have ever had the misfortune to meet. Malice and envy are mixed with your hellfire and brimstone damnations. And I'll be damned if I'll be damned *or* impugned by the likes of a hysterical nigger-lover like you!"

Madden climbed into his carriage and banged the door shut. He spoke to the driver in a combination of French, Spanish and Congolese, the lingua franca of Cuba. He swayed as the *volante* lurched into the rutted alley that led directly to the slave barracoons of the House of Martinez. The carriage scattered small black children in all states and stages of dress and undress. The wide avenue of the Prado skirted the sea, slashing the narrow, shadowed streets of Havana down the center. The streets were bustling with other *volantes*, mules, parasoled ladies and tophatted men. Wide-skirted laundresses, cooks, and food hawkers sauntered along the cobbled streets. Huge fish, vegetable and meat markets flourished under white awnings.

It was eight, and Madden could hear the bells of Havana's churches over the din of hawkers in the street. He signalled his driver, perched on the shaft horse of his *volante,* to stop in front of the cathedral. He needed Mass; the cool, dark interior and comforting click of his rosary would calm him. He would also go to confession, he thought, to atone for having lost his temper with Trist. A crowd had gathered before the massive white stone facade with its sculpted saints and angels. As was the custom, the slave sale of the day was being announced before Mass began. Madden pushed his way through the crowd of haggard emancipados, slaves, mulattoes, peninsulars or *creoles,* and Spaniards. Only whites and mulattoes were allowed inside the cathedral. A priest would soon arrive to bless the ragged, noisy black multitude milling about the great stone ship anchored in their midst. At least that is how Madden had come to think of this church.

Entering the cool, crowded interior, he knelt and crossed himself. The narrow spaces between the columned naves, and its soaring, cedarwood and goldleaf ceiling, transformed the cathedral into an ethereal galleon. The shaft of light from the dome over the altar seemed miles away. Within each nave the *retablos*—the baroque carved and ornamented shrines holding a painting or relic of a saint—gleamed gemlike, in contrast to the simple brick architecture. A flotilla of lit candles formed two radiant, shimmering canals of lustrous light from the back of the church to the front, illuminating the *retablos,* whose saints had now become, for Madden, a parody of slave names: Antonio, Simon, Lucas, José, Pedro, Martino, Julio, Andreas, Agustino, Viviana, Tomas.

Madden rose and, fingering his rosary, walked the length of the church to the shrine where the ashes of Christopher Columbus, the man who had opened three continents to black slavery, lay in their gold and jewelled reliquary. The American slave trade had begun from east to west when Columbus had shipped home five hundred Carib Indians to save their souls, and be sold in the markets of Seville. But it had been the Dominican friar Bartolomè de las Casas, Bishop of Chiapas, the Apostle of the Indians, son of a companion of Columbus', who had sealed the fate of the Atlantic Trade. Convinced it was evil to enslave the American Indian, he had pleaded that Africans replace the Indians as slaves for the mines and plantations, before Emperor Charles V, king of Spain.

The introduction of Negro slaves into America was one of the first measures that the Spanish kings had dictated for the support and prosperity of those vast American regions, soon after their discovery. As Casas had argued the impossibility of inducing the Indians to engage in different useful though painful labors, arising from their complete ignorance of the conveniences of life, and the very small progress they had made in the arts of social existence, the working of the mines, and the cultivation of the soil, required hands more robust and active than theirs: Africans.

This measure, he insisted, did not create slavery, but only "took advantage of that which existed through the barbarity of the Africans, by saving from death their prisoners, and alleviating their sad condition. Far from being prejudicial to the negroes transported to America, slavery conferred upon them not only the incomparable blessing of being instructed in the knowledge of the true God, and of the only religion in which the Supreme Being desires to be adored by his creatures, but likewise all the advantages which accompany civilization, without subjecting them, in their state of servitude, to a harder condition than that which they endured in freedom, when free in their native country." This same plea had been taken up by every Spanish king, thought Madden, from Charles to Isabella. The result, thought Madden bitterly, was that the Indians, whom Las Casas considered to have souls, had been almost exterminated, while the blacks, who were considered to have none, had been engulfed in the nightmare of slavery.

Madden glanced up at the procession of glittering saints, wishing Monsignor las Casas in Hell. The Church, *his* church, condoned slavery as the best way of bringing Africans to Christianity, but they did little to convert those same slaves except to forcibly baptize them with saints' names. At least the Protestants, thought Madden, believed baptism equivalent to freedom, and knowing how subversive God could be if used intelligently, declined to convert souls.

Meanwhile the Negroes, both slaves and freemen, had so blended Catholic and African religions that processions of Christian saints received the adoration that Africans lavished on their own gods. Madden thought it had something to do with the painted Christs, the gilded and mirrored figures of saints, the incense, the carved dragons and animals, the miracles, the mysterious signs and omens. The slave ships had, after all, carried not only men, but gods.

Kneeling before Columbus' shrine, Madden prayed fervently for his own soul and that of his wife and son. He prayed that Nicholas Trist would see the error of his ways. He prayed for strength to overcome his volcanic temper. He prayed God to spare his life. He knew there were plots against him, and this morning he had made another enemy. But he was determined to carry on his work, and if God called him in the course of his duties, he would rejoice in having served Him well.

The Misericordia Corral was situated directly beneath the windows of the Palace of the Governor-General. A crowd of merchants, plantation owners and traders milled around the gates of the slave corral, waiting for the "scramble" when some slaves, no matter their age or gender, would be sold at the same price and a buyer could purchase any Negro, Negress or infant he could actually lay hands on. Older slaves, women and children, and flawed slaves were sold in this manner, and then false papers would turn these Bozals, wretches straight off the pirate slave ships from the Guinea coast, into Ladinos, slaves born into slavery in Cuba, or imported before 1820.

Madden barely glanced at two Spaniards who stood talking and gesticulating nervously before the corral. As High Commissioner his jurisdiction extended only to treaty violations brought before him by Spanish or British patrollers who had captured a slave ship off the coast. He had no authority over blacks who had already been landed. His thoughts turned once more to Trist. The man was in deep trouble, the doctor thought sourly. A group of Americans in Cuba had petitioned Congress for his removal. Trist was going to have to return to Washington to answer charges.

José Ruiz and Pedro Montez just as studiously ignored the High Commissioner. Don José Ruiz was a tall, cadaverous young man, darkly handsome with a shock of blue-black hair hanging in tight waves around a sharp, determined face. He was dressed not in white, like his companion, but in a blue jacket and pantaloons, loose buff boots with large silver spurs. He wore a white top hat bound with a braided ribbon, and if his eyes had been discernible, they would have been as tawny as his skin. For some reason unknown to Don Montez, the other Spaniard, Don Ruiz even affected a long cowhide whip which was curled and carried under his arm like a baton.

Don Ruiz had his own ideas about the colonial aristocracy. A *criollio* was a man who carried himself with a vivid sense of role, who affected a distance between himself and people of lower birth and servants, that is, slaves and strangers. This posture was cultivated to show off wealth, breeding and authority. Don Ruiz was a crack shot, a fine horse breeder, a good sailor and a decent billiard player. He was a characteristically typical Spanish colonial, ill-tempered, physically courageous and morally and mentally bound by the rigid customs of his caste. He considered swearing, duelling and drinking marks of a gentleman. He had been educated partly in the state of Connecticut and spoke English perfectly with a Yankee accent. He was happy. The week had been spent in playing cards, calling on friends, having clothes and boots made, horse-trading, three cockfights and seven consecutive nights in the brothels, called "*casas*," of Havana. Whoring was also the mark of a gentleman, according to Ruiz. Above all, Don José was a man who measured himself in Negroes. He owned over a hundred fifty.

Ruiz and Montez both had plantations at Puerto Principe, a three-hundred-mile sail from Havana.

The crowd included numerous Cuban ladies shopping for slaves. They wore white like Montez, with white parasols and Ottoman shawls. Their bonnets were fixed with gauze, and mittens protected their hands from the sun. The real women slavers, or mesdames looking for new inmates for their brothels, were more bold. Dressed in dowager black with red parasols, they circulated throughout Misericordia, picking, choosing, taking notes, handling, pinching, prodding both male and female adolescent slaves. All of the women were accompanied by their nannies or governesses dressed in wide blue and white checkered skirts and petticoats, their heads wrapped in white turbans.

Sengbe Pieh, Grabeau and a man named Burnah stood blinking in the sunlight of the Misericordia Corral. It had been fourteen suns since the *Tecora* had debarked its cargo under the cover of night on a desolated inlet miles from Havana. It was not until all the survivors had been unloaded and were safely inside the gates of the slave factory that their chains had been removed. When morning arrived, the crew of the *Tecora* had disappeared. In their place were Spanish and Cuban guards and slaves who initiated the ten-day regime of healing and fattening the captives for the market, so that they would lose their look of hunger and unhealthiness.

"I am Twin," said Burnah, standing next to Sengbe Pieh. "I am Mende. I know some English words. I'm from the river people. I owned a canoe. I also owned a rice farm. I have a wife and one child, a father, three sisters and a brother. I was taken on the War Road and sold to a Spaniard, a Lomboko." Burnah did not mention he had been sentenced to slavery for a crime committed in the small town in which he lived. The two men stayed close together, looking for a chance to escape. But to go where? What country was this? What language? The black guards spoke Spanish, but Burnah had found one who spoke English. Burnah had told him of their fear of being eaten alive. The guard had doubled over with laughter.

"You're the cannibals, not us! You're getting in shape for the slave market of Havana. And what country are you in? Why, in Cuba, the richest colony of Her Most Catholic Majesty, the Regent Queen Christina, who has made a fortune in slaves! You are in the barracoons of the House of Martinez, the greatest company of slavers in the world. And what is Spain? Why, a Christian nation of white men who discovered the New World!"

"Then we did sail off the earth into another world?" asked Burnah.

The guard looked at him in amusement. "If you want to put it that way, *sí.* In what world are you? Why, in the white world! And why are you here?" he laughed. "Because you're stronger, blacker, better than any lazy Indian."

Burnah returned with the news that they would not be eaten and all the guard had told him. Sengbe Pieh begged him for more. How many white men in Cuba? How many slaves? What were the rivers? The mountains? Had anyone ever escaped?

"You try it and you're dead," smiled the guard as he pressed his rifle against Burnah's chest. "There are maroons in the mountains, bands of pirates and robbers. To join them you at least have to speak a real language, not African gibberish."

"Africa?" said Burnah.

"Africa, where *you* bloody well come from—you stupid gorilla. Africa. You are Africans. *Africans.* Africa is a *continent,* a land mass situated between the Atlantic and the Indian oceans as big . . . as big as the whole continent of America!"

"Continent? Not Mendeland?"

"Mendeland? Mendeland is more than likely Africa's asshole. . . ."

"Continent," repeated Burnah, nodding.

Burnah returned with this new information. They were in a

place called Cuba. On a continent called America, in a new
world. They came from a place these people called Africa, which
was even bigger than the New World they had sailed onto.
The black people here were all Africans and all slaves. The
white people were all Spanish and all masters. This was the
law of the land. . . . Sengbe Pieh pondered all this as the two
men waited for their strength to return, the specter of canni-
balism still never very far from their minds.

Slowly the men began to heal in body, if not in spirit. Many
had died in the two weeks they had debarked from the *Tecora*,
but Sengbe Pieh thanked God that the children—Kale, Teme,
Kagne and Margru—were still alive. Practically none of the
women had survived. As his strength returned, his mind filled
with hundreds of plans for escape, each one coming up against
the inexorable barrier of not knowing where they were, not
even in which world, and having no language with which to
communicate. There were mountains, rivers and trees. There
was sky, birds, snakes, ants. There were grass and bushes and
growing things. There were rice and yams, poultry and cornmeal. There were black women and children, white women
and children. But only the black women and children were
slaves. That was all he knew.

Days later all the Africans in the barracoon had been marched
under cover of night into the Misericordia, where they stood
now. Held naked, exposed to the eyes of the crowd, herded
into an enclosure with hundreds of other black men, Sengbe
Pieh found other faces from the *Tecora*. Stoically, Sengbe Pieh
reached down within himself for his last reserves of strength.
What would happen now? Trial by fire? Torture? The corral
was ringed with so many white faces, Sengbe Pieh's head
turned. Here were their women as well, he thought. White. He
marvelled at the pale faces, half hidden in bonnets and straw
hats and holding something shaped like a palm tree over their
heads. Abruptly Sengbe Pieh was separated from the others
and pushed into an enclosure which had a roof and stalls for
animals. There were wooden benches and what looked to him
like chiefs' stools. White men and a few women wandered here
and there, speaking their incomprehensible language and inspecting the captives. Outside the enclosures he heard sudden
hair-raising shrieks and screams as if everyone beyond the

bolted door were being massacred. A cold sweat broke out on his forehead. Grabeau and Burnah were in the enclosure but Kabba Sei was outside! As were the children. He heard the pitiful high-pitched screams of women. Mende words flowed back to him, prayers, screams for help, cries of murder. They were massacring all of them! Or burning them alive, or . . . Oh, Gewo, thought Sengbe Pieh, why the children? And the women. Trembling with rage, Sengbe Pieh began to bellow, but a sudden blow from one of the guards knocked him to his knees and temporarily stunned him into silence. Outside, the screaming never ceased.

Robert Madden stood watching the sickening spectacle. If the history of the Irish people could be traced like a wounded man through a crowd, by the blood, so could that of the Africans, he thought, as the doors of the corral were thrown open. The buyers rushed in and began to seize as many of the Negroes as they could lay hands on. Others tied several handkerchiefs together and encircled them in that way, while still others used a rope. One man used a lasso. The fright and terror of the blacks, the ferocity and confusion of the whites, resulted in violent quarrels. The slave women were especially alarmed, shrieking and clinging to each other.

Even the men cried for help as they were chased around the corral, cornered like animals or caught by the ankle or neck with lengths of cotton cloth or rope. Women laughed, men whooped with joy. Kabba Sei escaped the corral and stark naked, his pants having been pulled off in the fracas, was pursued down one of the narrow alleyways leading away from the Misericordia. Kabba Sei's arms and legs flailed, his eyes popped from his head, his lungs bellowed for air in his emaciated body. Finally a stranger stuck out his leg and tripped the running man. Before he could rise, Don Ruiz was upon him and Kabba Sei was finally returned to the pen.

There was one long final outcry. Then the noise of the scramble ceased. Within the long hollow tunnel of the indoor corral, light filtered through holes bored in the high-pitched, wood-beamed roof. The light fell in tiny islands, leaving the rest of the enclosure in gloom. The men moved and moaned, and before long the hall was filled with a low non-human sound like the noise of cattle, while around them swarmed the whites in their white clothes, luminous in the penumbra, accompanied by the incessant shrieks of their language and laughter. The heat from the bodies under the sun-soaked wooden roof rose to infernal intensity. Sengbe Pieh felt as if something solid were being forced into his mouth each time he breathed. Perspiration gave him dancing visions of the crowd which he assumed were the famous Mende water spirits, for running from one end of the enclosure to the other was a trough of water, wide enough to float a canoe. This must be the river the dead must cross, he thought. Penned into stalls, five or six to a group, Sengbe Pieh, Grabeau, Kimbo, Burnah and Sessi stood huddled together listening to the shouts of the men who seemed to be the overlords and who walked about with scrolls and tablets, followed by gangs of whites, pointing to group after group and shouting, *"Whathavewehere? Finemandinkaspecimenstraightfrom Africa'sshoresnotmorethansixteenyearsold. AmIbidthreehundreddollars? YesthreehundredandfiftydoI hearfour? YessirIhearfourthankyouIhearfourIhearfourfour fiftyfivesixhundredandfiftyoncesixhundredandfiftytwicesold sold. Sold. Forsixhundredandfiftydollars."*

The strange, godlike voice boomed out into the thick yellow air. It filled the cavernous space with its bleating, yet still another voice in another part of the tunnel overlapped it and in the same language began the same litany again. The light seemed to come from no earthly source and became wild and murky with the voices that echoed and reverberated in sequence—in response, it seemed. Sengbe Pieh stood naked in the trough of water while one of the voices hovered near and around him. He was afraid to turn his head. He licked salt from his lips and suddenly heard the crack of a whip. He was greatly relieved. This was the end of earth. It was so different from what he had imagined; he was not even surprised when the voice floated even nearer to him and he saw it was attached to a singular-looking white creature with night for one eye and day for the other. He was not duly alarmed. No one had ever been sure that the spirits resembled the masks and figures sculptors made. Evidently they did not. And no one ever insisted that the spirits spoke Mende. The night-patched face with the blue eye came closer and its hand reached out and grabbed Sengbe Pieh's bicep; another hand ran along his flanks. "Courage," whispered Grabeau. "These are real men, not spirits. We are on earth, neither in the sky nor the spirit waters!" Men pulled at him. A woman touched him. At least he thought it was a woman. Now he was raised higher onto a wood block. The world turned darker. The incantations began. Sengbe Pieh would not have been surprised to have seen his feet lift from the block and his body soar towards the rafters.

"Whathavewehereandwhatdo Ihaveforthisexceptionalboy of Africa. Undoubtedlyfromthefamousmandikatribefamousfor thequalityandstrengthofitsslaves. DoIhearfourhundred dollars? Fourhundred? Four-fiftydoIhearfourhundred seventy-five? Madame? Four-fifty, Madame? Four-fifty, Madame? Fivehundredandfiftydollars . . . doIhear sixhundred? Sevenhundredandfifty? Sold. Sold. Sold foreighthundreddollarscongratulations."

A young spirit in a white conical hat that made him feel taller than anyone else stepped forward determinedly. He seemed to have decided to possess him, thought Sengbe Pieh, and if he had simply walked into Sengbe Pieh's body, Sengbe Pieh would not have been startled. The young spirit was José Ruiz.

Ruiz and Montez took their time in selecting their purchases. In all they selected sixty men, including Sengbe Pieh and his companions. After examining them all, ramming fingers down throats and up the anus, looking for signs of venereal disease and weighing testicles, having men run and jump, running their fingers through kinky hair, over scars and sores camouflaged by oil, Ruiz selected his final forty-nine, which included Kabba Sei, who had been caught in the scramble. They were chained in groups of ten and separated from what they had learned to call their *carabela*, their passage brothers. Men and women wept, clinging to each other. Ruiz was always quite touched by this moment. It seemed to him that the Africans exhibited every noble emotion of humankind, and it always astounded him. He left to pay the 24,050 gold dollars he owed the House of Martinez.

When he returned, he said to the older man, "Let's get these people on the boat before dark!"

Sengbe Pieh began to speak. In the voice he had used at the trial—cunning, elegant, emotional, authoritative—he spoke to the faces he recognized from Don Pedro Blanco's barracoons, or from the *Tecora*, comforting, exhorting, convincing. He held the Mendes spellbound, and the others, who did not speak Mende, were mesmerized simply by the tone of his voice. Ruiz looked around, embarrassed. Other whites were staring as if a dog had begun to speak. The low, lilting Mende rolled off Sengbe Pieh's tongue as slick as the beads of palm oil on his skin. This spirit-world place was called "America," he said, but they all had a home in the real world. It was called "Africa," and it had been created by God for all black people regardless of their nation. They were now only one nation, where pain and slavery were their lot. But not forever. Africa waited for them. One day they would return—see their loved ones, their families, their ancestors. This was not the end of earth.

Ruiz started at the words "Africa" and "America" that surfaced in the swelling unintelligible cadences. How had this Bozal of two weeks grasped the meaning of these words? he wondered.

"Make sure that man is kept in irons twenty-four hours a day," he said to Pedro Montez. But Montez, in the confusion and excitement of Sengbe Pieh's speech, did not hear him.

Don Ruiz and Don Montez marched their coffle of slaves through the streets of Havana to the port where the *Amistad*, the ship Ruiz had bought, lay in anchor awaiting its cargo. The late afternoon sun struck the high white spires of the Cathedral of Havana as the line of men and children passed by. Sengbe Pieh looked up at the first stone architecture he had ever seen. The size astonished him. The endless spires seemed to pierce the sky; fifty men could stand with arms outstretched and not encompass its facade. He studied the draped sculpted figures, marvelled at their bizarre, distorted beauty as if the sculptors, unable to achieve any semblance of the spirit world, had contented themselves with placing real people of stone on the walls and roof. Yet the effect, he thought, had something of beauty. The stone faces looked like the elders. If there was no emotion, there was at least respect. He bowed his head, the heavy muscles of his neck and shoulders twitching in the blue shadows of the cathedral's shade.

A groan of horror and protest rose from the men when they realized they were being led to another house that swam. The suffering of the *Tecora* was to be repeated. Some broke into sobs. Sengbe Pieh allowed none of the despair and desperation he felt to show on his face. Some of the men touched him imploringly. The ship, a sleek black-hulled, green-bottomed, Baltimore-built schooner, sat rolling gently in the harbor's waters, a sinister promise. She had been baptized the *Friendship,* and the captain had simply translated that English name into Spanish: *Amistad.* Sengbe Pieh's heart leaped as he saw on deck a huge copper cauldron bubbling with boiling water. An evil-looking, green-eyed man with thick, kinky blond hair and a fat belly grinned viciously at them.

Besides the cook, on board the vessel were a crew of four and the Spanish captain, José Ferrer, a placid, corpulent, black-bearded veteran of the coastal slave trade between Havana and Santiago. He had even smuggled slaves to the Floridas and as far north as South Carolina. The remainder of the crew was on deck: Antonio Ferrer, a mulatto cabin boy; Celestino Ferrer, the octoroon cook; Rojo, a young sailor whose real name was Jacinto Verdagne but whose nickname "Red" described the color of his hair and the rose of his complexion. There was another older sailor, Manuel Pagilla, who was so dark he could himself have been an African. Ruiz and Montez were angry. Ferrer had promised them more crew. But Ferrer jokingly assured them that, held in chains, no more than two armed guards were necessary to control the fifty-three slaves. It was, after all, only a two-day sail back to Puerto Principe, their destination.

"Well, then, keep chains on them," replied Montez nervously.

"The ship is fitted out and ready to sail tonight," said Ferrer, grinning. There was just one thing more, thought Ruiz, the buying of the Ladino passports.

At Moro Castle the *Amistad* was met by a Spanish customs ship. For ten dollars a head passports were issued for Don Ruiz's slaves. The customs officer began to read off the fictitious names: Joseph! Ruiz looked at the man who was already known by the name Sengbe Pieh. "Joseph Cinque!" called out Ruiz, "Antonio, Simon, Lucas, José, Pedro, Martino, Andreas." Ruiz looked at Have-Mercy-on-Me. "Agustino Grabeau!" he said. "Evaristo! Casimiro!" The officer went down the list until he came to the names of the children owned by Montez. A boy named Kale became Gabriel. A little girl named Teme became Juana.

Another girl, Kagne, became Josepha, and the third girl, Margru, had become Francisca. As for the others, there was no distinguishing of names. They had all been baptized in the name of the saints.

"I will never survive another voyage in the white man's canoe," moaned Grabeau.

"It is the white man," said Sengbe Pieh, "who will not survive. We will kill the *caballeros españoles,* all of them."

Don Ruiz looked around sharply at the Spanish words. Of course, he thought, the man who had dared to speak would be the one now called Joseph Cinque.

❧ The *Amistad* ❧
June 1839

The sailor, Manuel, wielded a scourge of twisted thongs, using its handle to shove the men down into the slave deck. The *Amistad* had been built for light transport and matchless speed. About six years old, she was a two-hundred-tonner of ambiguous beauty. The cargo hold was small, with very little head room, and the men were forced to sit crouched over, one in the lap of the other. Two sailors ran a long chain through the neck shackles of every man, linking them all to one bolt and lock at the forecastle of the ship. The iron links grated against the iron of the shackles, the weight reverberated down the spines of the men into their groins, and the sound struck their ears and craniums like continuous blows. Groans and cries broke out. Joseph Cinque looked up and saw the small brown face of Antonio peering down the hatch.

"*Lookoutforcelestioforheintendstocookyouallfordinneryou cannibals!*" he shouted, laughing and making faces.

"*Cannibalscannibalscannibals.*"

"I understand a little of what they say. *Cannibal* means men who eat other men. Cannibal," Burnah's voice raised in alarm, "means to be eaten!"

Burnah had addressed himself to Joseph Cinque, but now the whole deck began to vibrate with voices, as if a spell had been broken. Each man reached out desperately to the one beside him.

"I am 'Edge-of-the-Razor,' " said Kaba Kpekalay.

"I am 'Have-Mercy-on-Me,' " said Grabeau.

"I am 'Solitary,' " said Kabba Sei.

"I am 'Cricket,' " said Kimbo chained on the other side of Joseph Cinque. "I was born in Maw-ko-ba, the son of a gentleman. When my father died, I was taken as a slave by my king

and given to his son Bagna. When Bagna attacked a village in
the Bottom Country, I was taken captive on the War Road."

"I am 'Big Sun,' " said Fuliwa, farther down the line. "I lived
with my parents. I have five brothers. My town was surrounded by soldiers and burned to the ground. I was taken
prisoner with my brothers but we were separated at Lomboko." He turned his head from side to side, making the chain
rattle. "As God is my witness, I would rather die than endure
another voyage. . . ."

The other Mendes began to speak out.

"I am 'Crocodile,' " said Sessi. "I have a wife and three children. I am a sculptor. I was captured by soldiers and wounded
in the leg. I was sold twice before reaching Lomboko."

"I am 'Python,' " said Fooni. "I have a wife. I have parents
and four brothers and sisters. I was seized by two men, strangers,
while planting rice."

"I am 'Remember,' " said Fabanna, who was a prince. "I
was born in Dzkopoabu. I have a wife and two children. I was
caught in the bush by black men with guns."

"*Sword,*" said Bartu, not wasting any words.

"*Broke,*" said Bau.

"*Twin,*" said Burnah.

The men began to call out their names, their villages and
towns, the names of their wives and mothers, sisters and children. Each man had a capture to relate. The sea rose and
swelled beneath the slave deck as the voices of the men rose
and fell.

Finally, one voice out of the darkness said: "How many Poro
men here?"

"Poro! Poro! Poro!" came back the answers in disembodied
voices and jumbled dialects. Then there was silence as the
Amistad quivered in a wave and sank down, its great sails full-
blown in the swift wind. Instinctively the men waited for one
man to speak: Joseph Cinque.

"I am Sengbe Pieh. Where I was born or when, how many
children I have, or wives, how many brothers or living parents,
how rich I was or how poor, how happy I was or how oppressed, means nothing now, anymore, to you or to me. For
we have all fallen amongst the uncircumcised, *all* equal in
degradation."

A pact of rebellion was quickly made in the sacred incanta-

tions of the Mende Secret Society, the Poro, a pact that bound
the men together in life and death. Wordlessly Joseph Cinque
was chosen to lead. Joseph Cinque named his lieutenants: Have-
Mercy-on-Me, Cricket, Broke and Waterfall. He named Remember as his personal bodyguard. The rear guards were Big
Sun, Big Man, Python and Sword. Twin, the only captive who
had ever been behind the rudder of a ship, was named pilot,
for Joseph Cinque had vowed to sail the *Amistad* back to
Mendeland. Each man swore his faith and kissed the man
chained next to him, on the mouth, the Poro gesture of peace.

Above the slave deck the hot, dry weather continued and the
winds had calmed and shifted subtly as the crew reefed and
furled the sails in response. The voyage would take longer than
Captain Ferrer had expected. The captain decided not to go
ashore for new provisions, and so those stores that he had on
board were strictly rationed out: a banana, two potatoes and a
cup of water per day. On the third day Twin tried to take more
water than his ration. Ferrer had him whipped by Jacinto. The
silent men watched Jacinto lash Twin, who was tied to the
mast. He endured the thirty lashes in the stillness penetrated
only by the sound of his intake of breath in rhythm with the
sigh of the whip. After the whipping, gunpowder was rubbed
into the bloody pulp that had been Twin's back. The men on
deck fell even more silent. Even Jacinto looked around uncer-
tainly. The men would not move.
"Hey, Antonio. Tell the Bozals we're going to eat them. That
should wake them up."
In sign language the cook, Celestino, pointed to the barrels
of beef stored in the cook house. Celestino jumped up and
down, miming the act of killing Burnah, salting him down and
eating him. Remember found a nail on deck and hid it under
his arm. When the men were returned to the slave deck, it was
passed from man to man until it reached the last man chained,
Sessi, the blacksmith. Sessi picked the lock and released the
chain that bound the men together, but they waited until long
after nightfall before making their move. As the moon rose, a
sudden storm darkened it and, in the pitch-black, heavy clouds
burst with torrents of tropical rain. The storm camouflaged the
movements of the men emerging one by one from the slave
deck towards the forecastle, where they found six boxes of sug-

arcane knives. The cutlasses were square bars of steel, an inch thick with a blade two feet long, razor sharp and widening to a width of three inches at its end. The machetes were the deadliest weapons the Africans had ever seen, yet familiar enough. The Poros—Cinque, Solitary, Have-Mercy, Cricket, Crocodile, Sun, Python and Remember padded softly towards the kitchens. Celestino died first, silently, under the machete of Joseph Cinque. The thudding of the machete into Celestino's body awakened Captain Ferrer, who, because of the storm, had slept on deck near the pilot. Now he and Antonio raced to the kitchens, then stopped as they saw the group of slave mutineers bearing down on them. "Throw them some bread," screamed Ferrer. Solitary raised his machete to strike, but Ferrer ran him through with his sword and parried another blow from Have-Mercy-on-Me. Joseph Cinque, seeing his wife's brother go down, leaped on Ferrer and with one powerful blow split his head in two. Joseph Cinque's hands were around Ferrer's throat when he realized that his life had already left him. Turning, he started after the two sailors who had fled, screaming "murder" and "mutiny." The two men fought their way through the rush of captives spilling from the slave deck to the forecastle and then both jumped overboard into the rain-swept ocean.

The squall died and the moon rose and Joseph Cinque knelt by Kabba Sei's side. Now José Ruiz, awakened by the sailors' shouts, appeared brandishing an oar, but seeing the deck swarming with unchained men, he dropped it and raced back to his cabin, locking himself in. Don Montez came topside armed with a club and a knife, but found himself face to face with Remember. One slash of the dark man's machete was only half parried by Montez and gashed his head, almost severing an ear. A second blow ripped open his arm, and the Cuban fled for his life, dropping his weapons. Desperately, he threw himself behind a crumpled sail and pulled Celestino's beef barrels in front of it to hide himself. Joseph Cinque, Remember, and Have-Mercy-on-Me rummaged the decks looking for the wounded Montez. But José Ruiz had already unlocked his cabin door and surrendered to Waterfall on the promise his life would be spared. Ruiz pleaded with Waterfall to spare Montez as well. Waterfall and Twin reached Joseph Cinque just in time to restrain the blow that would have decapitated Montez.

"He can sail us home," whispered Twin. "He is the only one."

Twin's words penetrated the turmoil of Cinque's thoughts, and he slumped to the deck, asking only if any of the other men were hurt.

"One," answered Have-Mercy-on-Me, "run through trying to prevent one of the white sailors from jumping overboard. They cannot catch land. They have swum to the bottom of the sea."

"Two dead, then."

"We are masters of this ship."

But Joseph Cinque knew he was master of nothing. He knew nothing of white men's canoes or how to steer them or keep them afloat or arrange the cloths or tell the difference between one rope and another.

Joseph Cinque looked over to where Ruiz and Montez sat, tied face to face. To one side Antonio sobbed and grasped a slightly wounded knee.

"Twin, tell the boy we will spare him. But he must explain to the white men that we intend to return home to Mendeland. And that they must steer this canoe." Cinque looked up into the sun.

The clouds had parted and the rain had stopped. The ship rolled drunkenly and the rudder turned crazily. Crocodile ran to it and held it steady, but he had no idea what to do next. It was Montez who cried out in a trembling voice.

"Hold that rudder steady, by God, or this ship will overturn."

"The Africans say you must sail them back," shouted Antonio, translating Twin's pantomime.

Montez collapsed, sobbing. "I can't do it, I can't. I haven't sailed a boat in years. . . ."

"If not, we are dead men," said Ruiz.

The First Sun. They choose me as the memory of this voyage because I am the oldest survivor. Sengbe Pieh commanded me to hold this voyage in my head, as a log book would. *Amistad* means friendship. As for myself, I am Shule, Waterfall, fifth in command after Sengbe Pieh, Have-Mercy-on-Me, Cricket and Twin the Younger. I was born at Konabu in the open land. I was sentenced to slavery for a minor crime along with my wife. A man called Momawsu caught not only me and my wife, but my master Maya as well, and sold us all into slavery. I never saw my former master again, and my wife died during the first crossing of the waters a moon ago. Now, as is the custom, I should describe the weather and the winds: the weather is good, the sky is clear, beautiful, blue-washed, cloudless by so much rain, and the wind comes from the east. And I can say as much since it is true. This is the first sun after the war, and we send the bodies of Captain Ferrer and Celestino to the bottom of the sea. Then we send Solitary and First Born to join them; the other white men have already swum to depths. Sengbe Pieh sings the prayer of the dead, and indeed his voice is beautiful and the chant falls onto the sea as the song of a sparrow upon quivering new leaves. Then we wash the decks of blood. The two white men we put in irons and place in the slave deck, saying, "You say irons are good enough for Mende men, then they are good enough for white men!" We give them one cup of water a day, saying, "You say one cup of water is good enough for Mende men, then it is good enough for the white men." We appoint Big Man to care for the children Black Snake, Bone, and Country.

For the first time in three moons we feel free. The salt in the air, the blood on our lips, taste of freedom. The Poro cheer *"Hooyo"* rings out over the waters and up to the sky. It echoes amongst the white cloths. There is much laughing and singing and embracing and leaping. We have won the war against the white men. We break open the white man's boxes and find cloths of every color and design, necklaces of beads. Piles of bound palm leaves which are called books, according to Twin, who worships by a book. There are wooden containers of a bitter black berry that tastes like a nut. Gold disks Antonio calls doubloons are the white man's cowrie shells. Ordinary knives are filed into four points.

The Second Sun. Once more we point the canoe into the sunrise. The sun moves across the sky and our own shadows shrink in a pool about our feet, then lengthen as it passes over our heads. Sengbe Pieh charts our way home by the familiar and changing shadows on deck. He tells Montez to aim the canoe where it must go for he sees that here, as on land, moving is a matter of reading the sun. The sky is fine, but the night of the second sun a storm rises and the canoe pitches and rolls, the cloths of the sharpened palm trees overhead swell and rip and fall to the deck until all that we can bind with ropes around the tall stakes are fastened. Twin cannot control the canoe, which spires in circles. Ropes tangle in one another and one of our men dies, strangled as the ropes he tries to hold unwind and loop around him without warning and hitch him into the air by his neck and hang him.

The Third Sun. The storm is over. The sun rises and there is a quiet breeze. Antonio pleads with us to release the white men, which we do, and when they emerge from the deck, the hanging man is the first thing that meets their eyes for no one has yet cut him down. The old man hides his face in his arms, but the young one simply stares for a long time upwards, his hand over his mouth, until he falls forward in a faint, cracking his skull on the deck. Sengbe Pieh commands the old man to take charge of the canoe and swim it home. He refuses. Sengbe Pieh draws his machete and holds it to his throat. The old man surrenders. The canoe points towards the sun, from whence we have come. We seem to drift, turning in circles with no wind and no shade from the burning sun. Then finally God sends winds and we speed away from land onto the horizonless waters that curve into the sky. Ah, I forget the weather. The white man says there is a mild breeze from the southeast, and in this I can concur. What is strange is that the sea waters run not like a river current in one direction, but Sengbe Pieh and I have seen the water move at times in the direction of the canoe, then move in the opposite direction against its body, and then not move at all. I wonder if this is magic or if the spirits under the water are playing with us. But it angers Sengbe Pieh. It is just one more thing we cannot understand.

A flock of birds fly so low we throw iron rings at them and strike a great many so that we have meat for days.

The Fourth Sun. We sail away into a restless sea and a sun that moves with us, homewards. As the ship turns, our hearts lift. We have escaped from the enemy and from slavery. Only two of us are dead. The house that swims seems detached from earth and spins lonely and swift over the waters like a wheel. And a great circle of solitude moves with her, ever changing and ever the same. Now and again another white-winged object far off in the distance appears and then as suddenly disappears. Mother Sun looks down on us every day, and every morning rises with a burning, round stare of undying indifference. Sun races after sun, moving and musical like a necklace of copper, and it gleams gold on the white curls of black waves. This is what the white man has called fair weather. At night we dream of Mendeland. Except for Sengbe Pieh, who paces the ship at night without sleep or stands mute and watchful, never taking his eyes off Montez.

The Seventh Sun. We do not seem to abandon sight of land. We go in a small canoe for fresh water. Twin, Cricket and Remember are ambushed and have to flee without water. Our supply is almost finished, and Joseph Sengbe Pieh worries that the white man lingers, hoping to be rescued by others. We pass a long island and we anchor at a safe distance and the men go out once again for fresh water. This time they are successful and all the casks are filled. The white man sets the prow of the canoe into the sun and we make for Mendeland, the cloths full of wind.

The Ninth Sun. The Spaniard commands us to change the cloths so many times a day in order to fill them with wind that the men are exhausted and confused. We pull in one and release others. Have-Mercy-on-Me and Python and Remember and Broke spend their days climbing the leafless stakes, tying and untying ropes. This day Sengbe Pieh who has done most of the work, screams at Montez; the men cannot carry out his commands, therefore the cloths must be reduced to two. Montez protests that we will lose speed, but Sengbe Pieh is decided.

The Fourteenth Sun. The sun shines, the breezes are light, the canoe makes way. Several ships pass us but don't notice us. Antonio tells Twin this house that swims is one of many looking for us. Sengbe Pieh calls a palaver. Twin tries to speak with Ruiz, who speaks one language to Twin and another to Antonio. Sengbe Pieh listens and I see him try to memorize words. He shows kindness to the younger Spaniard, but Antonio seems not to know what foot to dance on; he runs between the two men like a dog carrying fleas. But Sengbe Pieh and Remember accuse the white man of treason. The white man falls to his knees pleading for mercy and again his life is spared. Sengbe Pieh puts Remember and Crocodile on each side of him at the great wheel to watch his every movement and that of the canoe.

The Fifteenth Sun. I see that slowly Sengbe Pieh is beginning to love this house that swims. I see him often staring at it from the prow as a man will contemplate a strange woman whom in his fantasy will change his life if only he were acquainted with her. The wind is with us and I, too, begin to think of the canoe as a woman (Antonio has said that these constructions are always female) with her white, billowing train of foam flowing behind her, her black lappa walking on water, her twin white canvas caps winged out and pressed against the winds.

The Twenty-fifth Sun. We begin to lack supplies: food and water. The men complain at the slowness of the return. We seem always in sight of some land. Yet there are still twenty-seven suns by Sengbe Pieh's reckoning before we accomplish a complete crossing. We have met with three storms, but now the wind whistles and long sunbeams fall into our eyes, making us wink and blink. We are not used to sun on water. It burns our eyes, raising high blisters on our skin and driving blades into our skulls. Violence is in the air. Cricket, Sword and Remember suffer more than any of us. Their lips swell and crack; they have given their rations to the children. Sengbe Pieh has imposed rations on all but the white men, and he terrorizes the decrepit, demoralized men. Day after day black seas leap up. The glowing sun sinks slowly and the crests of waves lap at the edge of our ominous, fearful voyage.

Twenty-seventh Sun. The sky is overcast, the winds are swift and another storm is coming. A man has sickened and died. Sixteen times we have dropped the anchor. Our food is almost gone and half the cloths and blankets overhead have rotted and fallen to the deck. Only the will of Sengbe Pieh and his plaited whip keep us under control. He has Python punished for stealing water. We fear to make land, although several times we have seen coastline. Once we dropped anchor near land for fresh water and found fruit and killed a wild pig; once, an albatross fell upon the deck and there was meat. The white men refuse to eat it, as if it were poison or taboo, but Sengbe Pieh forces the Spaniard who is steering the canoe to eat, for he must be kept alive. Once countless flying fish fell on deck. Often we fish from the side of the canoe to avoid starvation. But the men are beginning to despair, and I am beginning to despair of Sengbe Pieh's power to command. I notice that more and more he paces the deck alone or with Have-Mercy-on-Me at his side. His face is drawn and haggard and there is a wild look in his eyes, as if he wills his powerful young body to *push* our canoe home. Once he suddenly leaped overboard, heedless of the man-eating fish that now follow us. Like a madman or a man possessed of the fish spirit he dove under the sea and dove again and then again, thrashing against the waters as if in mortal combat. Again and again he dives now, inspecting the bottom of the canoe. He roams the canoe, tightening ropes or tying them in strange ways. Land is always there. There was no land when we came. An evil white spirit haunts the canoe. But he watches the old white man like a hawk. He watches the old man watch the stars. He who had been so full of life and power when in captivity is hesitant and melancholic in liberty. He screams and yells and chastises the man. He stares in incomprehension at the canoe's instruments as if he can force them to speak to him in Mende. He repeats over and over that the young white man is bad magic, yet he treats him kindly, giving him full rations and extra water. He never directs his anger towards him, as if he—the white man—were the talisman from which we cannot, dare not, detach ourselves.

The Thirtieth Sun. Three men die. The sky is black. The clouds roll in and the wind howls. Lightning strikes out over the dark water, and thunder like the roar of a thousand wild lions rolls through the sky. We huddle on deck. This sun we know is to be our last. No one expects another. The canoe pitches and tilts and it is black as night, although it is day. And now only tattered remnants of the cloths of the house that swims remain attached to the masts. There is no food and water. We are suffering. The white men are suffering.

The Thirty-third Sun. We are still alive. The storm has passed. The skies are clear. The temperature is mild . . . balmy. The winds are swift, and I see Sengbe Pieh with Have-Mercy-on-Me and Remember by his side, staring out onto the endless blue, willing Mendeland to appear. He no longer sleeps, but watches the old crazy white man who steers us, or paces the decks that are rotting under our feet. He carries his whip with him at all times and he has fastened a tiny square of tin around his neck. I believe he is almost as crazy as the old white man. When he does sleep in the middle of the day, he screams or cries out. The more he watches the white men, the more he is sure they are betraying him. But how? Every day the ship points towards home. Towards the sun. Every day the canoe sails in the direction from which we came. Sengbe Pieh asks me how many suns. I counted fifty-four suns from Mendeland to the other world. Soon we will reach the fortieth sun. Fifteen suns from Mendeland. Six men have died since we left. Instead of fifty-three there are forty-two, and the man-eating fish follow the canoe.

The Fortieth Sun. Sengbe Pieh has beaten Sword for stealing water. Water Stick, Second Bone, Put-On and Have-None have formed a group of their own and placed a barricade at one end of the canoe. They demand the death of the white men. But who can sail this canoe except them? A palaver is held while big seas begin to roll across a crimson disk in the sky and the shadows of high waves sweep across the faces of the men. Sengbe Pieh's voice can be heard pleading over the waves which break with a loud hissing like snakes, and the voice of the Spaniard can be heard, its tone that of protest floating falteringly into the wind.

The Forty-sixth Sun. The sky is clear. The day is fair. The wind is calm. The sun is hot. We are all on the deck; some lie, some sit, some sink. The old man sights another canoe. A large canoe with great cloths and ribbons hanging from its masts, of which there are four. It is a shiny white with golden letters and many men on deck. Sengbe Pieh tries to sail away from her, but he cannot get any speed from his tattered cloths and his exhausted men. The canoe is almost upon us. The starved men rush to the masts. The two white men run from below to stand amongst us.

"*Thisisthecaptainofthemerchantseamanthelafayetteofnew york. Iwillbringyourschoonertosafety.*"

We reply with the arrowless bows. The time to fight has come. The shots frighten the commander of the canoe and there is much commotion on board. We see no big guns of iron, and so the canoe turns and flees. But we can be sure it will return. Sengbe Pieh points the canoe away from the strange house that swims but now there is no doubt. Sengbe Pieh has lost the way to Mendeland and he himself has turned into more of a white devil than the white devils we are fleeing. Sengbe Pieh now knows that the old man has somehow conjured the canoe off our course into who knows what new world. We should be in the waters of Mendeland. Oh, the heartbreak of it, I tell you.

The dishonor of it. Sengbe Pieh jerks the old man away from the great wheel. He slaps him. Tears course down his face. His face is a horrible mask of defiance and rage. The old man is a dead man. But so are we all. For where are we? The wind freshens and the canoe increases speed. Sengbe Pieh motions to the white man to put his tiller over. The boat comes around slowly and proudly, pulling like a great black fish, its cloths all tattered, its rudder gone. It stands there quivering, seemingly weightless on the crest of a wave, foamy and light as air, although we all know that under us is the endless depths of the cold, black underworld. The white man puts the house that swims on a new course, the ragged cloths flap in the wind, the booms creak across the deck, the canoe straightens and makes way. We have learned to respect the mysteries and caprices of the sea and the signs which pass between it and the wind. It is the way we have survived until now.

The Fifty-first Sun. Finally we can spare no moment of thought beyond wishing to live, and only wishing keeps us alive. There is water, but no food. Now and again we cross winged canoes in the distance. At night the starlit black dome of the sky revolves slowly above us, huddled below, close together, bearing the pain of existence as we had borne the pain of slavery. At night we see sunshine and rave. In the day we see darkness and fall silent. Some hear voices from the deep, others laugh insanely for hours or roam the confines of the boat, weaving in and out of the rotting, tangled ropes. Others gone blind hear human shrieks from that other ship, claiming it has followed them—but I point out that if we recrossed the same waters returning, we were bound to meet up with those spirits that had descended into the depths again.

The Fifty-second Sun. The torn cloths and the ends of broken masts stream in the wind like wisps of flax. Through the torrid sunshine, over the flashing black turmoil, the house runs blindly, disheveled and maddened, headlong as if fleeing for her life. We all speak at once, but not to one another as men, but rather as animals would bay in a herd. We have the aspect of invalids, the gestures of maniacs. Eyes shine deep and haggard and hunger seems to have dusted our faces with clay. We are all naked. We stamp and clap our hands, ready to jump the rail, ready to do anything to escape.

The Fifty-third Sun. God have mercy on us. Hazy. With no

wind. Wetness in the air. The smell of land. More canoes cross our path but still we sail on, away from them. One canoe hails us and tries to approach. Again their unintelligible gibberish echoes in the distance.

Remember, Twin and Cricket open fire. Yet we all know our time has run out. The ship disappears.

The Fifty-sixth Sun. We travel in circles, hiding from the canoes. We stay out of sight of land, drifting with the tides; our cloths have all fallen off or rotted. We drink saltwater. Another man dies. We have no food. Yet Sengbe Pieh fights on. He calls a palaver. The two white men are sentenced to die for treason. In all this time they could have carried us back to Mendeland but they did not. They tried to murder us all. And the penalty for murder in Mendeland is death. The execution is scheduled for this night. The white men neither cry nor beg for mercy. I doubt if they know who they are or where they are now. Nor do we. Only the children and Antonio resist. Sengbe Pieh takes six men and Antonio to shore to find water and buy food with the gold disks we found in the canoe's boxes. But which land? The land lying so close cannot be Mendeland. We go to the rail and stare at the shore. However, I should tell you, as the memory of this voyage, that much later I was told this place is called Montauk Point, on a long island called New York, on a beach called America.

❧ Sag Harbor ❧
August 25, 1839

This was not, could not be the Gallinas, the land he had promised his men. Joseph Cinque stood on the bridge, leaning slightly forward. The soft, luminous, green-tipped landscape stretched outwards, slightly curving beyond the moody deep waters of the sound. Could there be men here like themselves? "Gallinas, Gallinas," muttered Cinque under his breath as if willing the impossible. For suns and suns they had drifted along this deserted virginal coast, the shoreline appearing and then disappearing for days at a time in the summer mists. Giant black sea monsters had followed them for days. They travelled in numbers, these water animals, and made a high wailing sound and sprayed the ocean with their urine, which came out of their back. They had not been able to rid themselves of these creatures from the underworld.

Gallinas. There was no longer any question of a destination, he thought. The *Amistad* was no longer a ship, but a prison, their voyage no longer a passage but a trial by water, and only the need for water attached them to reality. Thirst made them realize they were still alive and not being escorted by those creatures of the underworld beyond the world and all knowledge.

They were starving and dying of thirst, yet they feared landfall almost as much as slow death. His mouth foul, naked and trembling with the ague, Joseph Cinque stared at the insolent, empty green and white shoreline. He had no choice. He had to go ashore. Where had he led his men? Into what disaster, when he had promised a return to Gallinas? Impotent rage and the sickening lurch of the drifting ship shook Cinque even more than his fever or his fear. The listing ship, its sails in shreds, its paint peeling, its decks filthy and warped, spun rudderless in wide circles, sometimes taking a whole day to turn in on itself. He saw now that the innocent-looking land swells were dotted in places with white sticks and small replicas of dwellings like those he had seen in Ruiz's country. There he had recognized the landscape, for it had not been much different than Gallinas. But this new world was completely different; sweeter, softer, greener, with blue mists, silently menacing with its groves of strangely shaped trees. Whatever this new land was, he would have to face it. There was no water left. The men sprawled listlessly on the decks. From below he could hear the monotonous sobbing of Montez. He would release them, he thought. Even revenge seemed pointless. The voyage was over.

Cinque ordered a longboat lowered. Twin volunteered to take two of the strongest men and the water kegs to shore. If Twin found fresh water and no hostile inhabitants, he was to signal an all clear, and Cinque would follow with another dozen men. Twin and Cinque faced each other. They had come so far together, and now probably death awaited them all. Safety was unthinkable, yet in the back of both their minds was the thought that perhaps there were men like themselves, or at least not hostile to them, on land.

"We can still find home," repeated Twin. "Perhaps we are closer than we know. The white men in the other boats mean nothing. The creatures from the underworld mean nothing. . . ." Yet even as he uttered the words, both men wondered how false they would prove to be. Cinque put a gold doubloon in his hand. Twin clutched the piece-of-eight like a weapon. He knew the value of money. It was their only defense, their only language, yet it was their mortal enemy, for money was what they were worth. The gold glinted in the sunlight, in Twin's palm.

Cinque watched as Antonio and Python stepped into the boat. Perhaps if there were people who spoke Antonio's language . . . Cinque's swollen, red-rimmed eyes scanned the horizon. There was still no sight of life on land. Anticipation fought with fear as he watched Twin's boat become smaller and smaller. For a moment Beyah Bia's face flashed before him in the blank sky. Home. He had kept her face before him through so much darkness that it was unearthly and unnerving to see her face in broad daylight. Soundlessly his lips formed her name again and again, until he realized he was praying. He began to pray in earnest, beseeching God for mercy, for luck, for the safety that had eluded them for fifty-nine suns, for water. He prayed he had not led his men to death. They were young men all. They, as he, wanted to live.

Cinque repeated the prayer for victory as Twin's boat disappeared into the white line of the shore.

Have-Mercy-on-Me came to stand beside him, startling him out of his reverie.

"War Sparrow is dead," he said without emotion. "I would like permission to throw him overboard." Their eyes locked. This evil passage was finished. But the question in Have-Mercy-on-Me's eyes was definitive.

"Montez is condemned to die."

"We don't have to kill him. They are dying just as we are."

Twin, Antonio and Python stepped gingerly ashore. The beach was deserted. Twin knelt and fingered the sandy yellow soil. He sniffed the shiny green foliage; his hand explored the rough bark of the thick tree trunks he found along the footpath they were following over the dunes. Antonio and Python found a small creek and began to fill the water kegs. On the other side of the dunes Twin met a farmer with two dogs and a cart full of potatoes and straw-wrapped kegs of rum. The man was white and was watching him, a shovel held before him like a shield. There was neither fear nor hostility in his face, simply a hard-baked peasant's curiosity about a stranger. Twin's color was not the most imposing part of his foreignness. Twin opened his clutched fist and showed the doubloon. Magically, the farmer's shield lowered. Twin pointed his open palm towards everything edible, the two dogs, the potatoes, the jugs of rum. A silent dialogue began with the farmer nodding, it seemed, more in dismay than anything else. The farmer's name was Macintosh and his small farm reached to the limits of the sand dune. A tough Irish peasant, product of five centuries of serfdom, he had escaped to America. Macintosh had neither the time, the temperament, nor the extra energy to be astonished at anything. As Twin slowly approached, the farmer, immobile, reached out for the coin which glinted in the sunlight. It had left a small red circle imprinted on the orange palm. Antonio put the sacks of potatoes, the water, the rum on the boat.

The dogs followed him excitedly. Before leaving, the farmer lifted his hand and indicated the way to the village of Sag Harbor.

"Well, if I'm not a sperm whale's wife . . . it's her, the *Flying Dutchman!*" For weeks rumors had circulated amongst the fishermen and whaling men of Sag Harbor of a phantom ship in their waters, that had arrived with the pods of summer whales, appearing along the coast for days and then disappearing again. Some Long Islanders swore she *was* the mythical ship, with her tattered sails, no flag and no destination. And there, bobbing in the bay just beyond Culloden Point, her gilt-edged prow to the east, was the low-lying black schooner, so strangely rigged she drifted like a derelict.

Peletiah Fordham turned to the man standing near him. "Henry, I swear to God, we've caught up with that damned pirate ship the newspapers have all been ravin' about."

"And with the pirates as well," said Captain Greene as he pointed his spyglass on the approaching longboat. He sucked in his breath. It was the strangest conglomeration of men and costumes he had ever seen.

"Here, take a look."

"Sweet Jesus!"

"Only if he needs a boat to walk on water."

"Can you make out the name on the schooner?"

"Looks to me like . . . 'Hampstead' or 'Almeda,' or something of that order. . . ."

"What kind of name is *that* for a ship?"

"Well, what the hell kind of sailors are those coming towards us?"

Peletiah Fordham and Henry Greene raced down the sweep of sand dunes towards the place where black men, knee high in surf, were pulling their boat onto the beach.

Joseph Cinque and his men had returned to shore. The two fat dogs, the potatoes and rum had not been enough, and they were returning with more gold.

"It seems," said Captain Greene, slightly out of breath as he ran, "more than two weeks ago the *Emmeline* tried to take her in tow, but the pirates were armed with sugarcane knives and cutlasses, and they cast her off. Then . . . then the coast guard sent out the steamboat *Fulton* to look for her. . . ."

The two captains stopped, rooted to the spot in stunned disbelief. Of the eight men, four were stark naked. One wore a fine cambric shirt and nothing else. Another had a Spanish shawl tied around his loins, and the obvious leader had on a white planter's jacket, a planter's hat, but nothing else. Slung over his shoulder was a canvas belt holding three hundred gold doubloons.

Twin approached the white men silently, searching desperately for words. In sign language the white men asked him if he and the men with him had come from the black schooner. Twin nodded yes. Then he turned back and sought out Antonio. Were there Spaniards here? The white men shook their heads, no. The absence of black men was reassuring; there were no captive black men here. Twin conferred with Joseph Cinque. Captain Greene could make out a word like *galley*. Twin made it clear they meant the whites no harm. He gave them two guns, a knife and Joseph Cinque's hat. Cinque gave Twin a handful of gold which he held out to the two men. He indicated the trunk Cinque had brought on shore. The two white men were dressed as the captain of the *Amistad* had been. That meant they could navigate. Twin began to repeat the word Africa. Africa. Africa. It took the two sea captains a while to understand that Twin was not telling them where he came from but where he wanted to go. The captains knew they were Africans. Yes, they knew how to return, they nodded, as Twin and Cinque pointed to the schooner and then into the sun.

"This here's America," said Captain Greene, "not Africa!"

But Twin continued to shake his head. America, no. Africa, Africa, *si.* He held out the gold, pointing eastwards, making swimming motions.

"Swim?" said Captain Fordham. "Swim on back to Africa? You mean swim that thing out there back to Africa?"

Cinque, with a handful of gold, began to push Captain Greene towards the east.

"Henry, I think they're trying to tell us something. I think they want us to navigate *that* back home to Africa for 'em."

The two captains looked at each other. It wasn't such a bad idea. The Africans certainly had enough gold to pay somebody to sail them home. And they had a ship. A seaworthy ship, despite its damaged state. How many days? thought Greene. Thirty to forty, sailing with the wind. How would they get home once they had delivered the Africans? The ship. The ship in the distance was worth a fortune! Would the Africans allow them to take it back to America afterwards? They might even pick up a few slaves to bring back. Neither of the captains had ever navigated so far.

"Peletiah, they want us to sail their asses back to Africa!"

"Where?"

"Well, I don't know *where*. Africa is mighty big. But most slaves come from the Windward Coast."

Cinque had brought a roll of maps. He handed them to Twin. Captain Greene snatched the maps, brushed the sand level and rolled them out, fixing the ends with pebbles.

"Now, where? Where, you niggers? Where the hell in Africa?"

Captain Greene began to read off the names of the rivers on the maps. When he read the name Gallinas, both Twin and Cinque broke into smiles.

"Gallinas, Gallinas," they shouted.

Fordham and Greene exchanged a look of unadulterated greed. The real prize was that pretty ship offshore. Forty, maybe fifty thousand dollars. It had already crossed the ocean once, and now these poor souls couldn't navigate it back.

"Well, I know Sommers down there in Bridgehampton sailed to Africa once, on a slaver. . . ."

The captains asked to board the schooner, but Cinque signalled a no to Twin. Instead, he offered to return to the schooner for a trunk of gold to show the captains. Greene and Fordham exchanged a look of complicity. By Admiralty Law the schooner was theirs. And they did not even have to sail it to Africa. Just turn the niggers over to the coast guard as shipwrecked.

Whaling men, fishermen and farmers had all arrived at the scene. They poured out of houses down the main street that led from the port to the church. Macintosh had come back from the beach with a good doubloon! The people who began to wander onto the beach were silent, suspicious but not hostile. Everyone wanted to give the impression they had already seen such a sight on land or sea. The wives of the whaling men stayed glued to their second-story windows when word came that naked men straight from Africa were roaming the beaches. Most likely pirates. But if they were pirates, they were a most pitiful sight. They looked more like they had been ship-wrecked.

Macintosh began to show his gold coin around, not letting it out of his grasp.

"John, you done sold your dogs! I thought you loved them dogs!"

"You know what they do to dogs in Africa? They eat them. People too. They're cannibals!"

"Listen, Macintosh'd sell his mother for a Spanish dou-bloon. . . ."

"Looks like these folks are lost. I mean, lost!"

"Hear they got more gold on the schooner."

"Somebody warn the coast guard and the navy."

"Heck, somebody did *that* two weeks ago."

"Well, people been spotting that ship every which way and every few days, calling her the 'Dutchman.' "

"Anyway, last pirates seen around here was in 1750!"

"I'll do it," said Captain Greene. "I'll sail you fellers to Gallinas for all the gold you got on the schooner, minus the rations and supplies for the voyage, plus the ship. Is it a deal?"

Understanding nothing but the sound of the river name, Cinque nodded. There were no signs of slavery here. There was the stink of fish and unwashed white men, but no stench like the Havana barracoons. He raised his eyes towards the village. A road led upwards from the harbor through the village to a large white house of wood, with columns and a tall spire like that of a ship. At first Cinque thought the large house was a boat, except that the edifice was firmly anchored to a stone foundation and had two-dozen steps leading to its doors. There were neither the sights nor sounds of Havana, only silence, propriety and slow-moving people dressed plainly in gray or black. The high, narrow houses were painted discreet colors of beige, gray and white. The town square was dotted with wide, spreading shade trees. Even the white sandy dust which gave the sharp, clear air a haze, added to the impression of peace and tranquillity. Women in wide bell skirts and bonnets, men in caps and smocks, were delineated by great empty spaces, as if in this land of discreet comfort and solidity space, not time, ruled.

The *Washington*, a United States Coast Guard brigantine, patrolled between Gardiners Island and Montauk Point, its trim sails impeccably white against the clear summer sky. Her commander, a certain Thomas Gedney, had spotted something so peculiar he decided to stand in to satisfy his curiosity. In his telescope he could see a crowd of people on shore with carts and horses, and an unidentified schooner about a half mile off shore in the sound. There were two things the lieutenant did not care for: too many people on the beach, and an unidentified ship, badly anchored, showing no colors, in United States territorial waters. Thomas R. Gedney decided to board the ship.

The *Washington* drew abreast of the mysterious schooner and discovered a living nightmare. The horrified commander and his men seemed to have walked into an illustrated myth of Charon's boat ferrying voyagers across the river Styx into the land of the dead. The men on board stood huddled on the littered deck. Some wore nothing, or only a small piece of cloth wrapped around their loins. Others, including several children, were dressed in filthy European finery. But they were so emaciated that they seemed no more than black skeletons draped in the clothes of living men. Some stood staring dumbly, while others fell to the deck. Armed sailors in starched white, their faces aghast in disbelief, filed on board and forced the men into a corner of the starboard deck. Several seemed to be dying, and on the forward deck a cadaver lay under a tartan. Beside it was a spectral man with filed teeth and the most ferocious expression any of them had ever seen on a human face. Pilfered cargo lay about the deck, and the wanton confusion and squalor was mirrored in the eyes of the voyagers. Nails, musket balls and iron bolts lay strewn amid reams of silk and cotton, unravelled and snapping in the breeze, like checkered stepping-stones. In the silence the sailors could hear the slow flapping of the unrigged sails overhead. Open cases of crystalware and a glass chandelier caught the sunlight and cast multicolored reflections onto the white uniforms and sunken black faces.

"My God," Gedney whispered, more to himself than to his first mate.

Now the light changed and became an eerie rose as passing clouds blotted out the sun and shafts of escaping light touched every object with the colors and shadows of hallucination. Out of the penumbra a last apparition stumbled into the light, a young white man, haggard and bearded, his thin arms outstretched, crying, "We are saved. We are saved."

Then, to the horror of the startled men, another white man, this one older, emerged sobbing to add his Spanish to the other's story in English. Don Montez burst into tears now and again as he spoke, giving thanks with uplifted eyes to the Virgin Mary. Don Ruiz, a taciturn and somber shadow, coolly set about explaining to all who would listen that the majority of slaves on board were his and greatly attached to his person. The Americans remarked the glint of madness in Don Ruiz's eyes and his strange behavior towards Pedro Montez. As the men's story unfolded, Thomas Gedney and his second-in-command, Richard Meade, listened at first incredulously, and then with more and more attention as they both realized the importance of their prize. The *Washington* was a large ship, but too small for Gedney's ambitions. This cargo, he estimated, was worth thousands of dollars, and it belonged to him as salvage. The ship itself was of inestimable value and it, too, belonged to him as a prize. If the men on board were slaves, then they were even more valuable than the rest.

"Sir," Meade reminded him, "we're on the wrong side of the sound."

The crowds on shore had watched the *Washington* approach the nameless schooner, their attention drawn from Cinque's gold to the sailors clambering aboard. Cinque looked out to sea, then in panic raced down the beach towards the longboats, gathering up the gold around his waist as he ran. Cursing, he leaped into the boat, the other men scrambling after him, pursued by the townspeople shouting, "The *Washington*! The *Washington*!" As if realizing they would never see the black men's gold again, the fishermen and whalers began wading into the sea or made for their boats as the Amistaders began rowing desperately towards their ship. They could see another longboat being lowered into the water, filled with armed sailors from the brigantine.

* * *

Gedney saw the frantic activity on shore, and watched the boatload of black men rowing towards the *Amistad*. He ordered his men to intercept and capture them. He could not move the *Amistad* until he had all of them, for if they remained free on the wrong side of the sound, they could be witnesses against him. Gedney watched as his men intercepted Cinque's boat. He grabbed his loud-hailer and, as if already before a tribunal judging his salvage claim, and more, to legalize the action he was about to undertake, he shouted:

"In the name of the United States, you are under arrest. I repeat, under arrest. I command you to surrender without resistance."

Yet the black men in the boat struggled wildly with the sailors as, one by one, they were hauled up in ropes aboard the *Washington*. When Joseph Cinque, with the doubloons draped around his waist, was dragged aboard, he began to exhort his men in their own language. From both decks his men shouted and chanted their replies.

"We would have returned but the sun was against us," Cinque shouted. "I shall be hanged! Save yourselves from the white man!"

Lieutenant Gedney listened hypnotized to the sound of the strange, lilting dialogue. Was it a preparation to rush his men? Instinctively he swerved and his men aimed their pistols at Joseph Cinque.

"I tell you," Cinque shouted, "you have only once chance for death and none for freedom! Make the white men kill you by killing them!"

Cinque lunged, and as if expecting his men to follow him, climbed up onto the bridge and, dodging bullets and ignoring commands to come down, plunged into the sea, diving beneath its surface for minutes at a time. Yet each time he rose to the surface he saw that his men had not followed him and he looked towards the beach, or dove beneath the waters, as if scouting a path towards the shore.

"Don't shoot him," Meade called, "he has the gold!"

Cinque swam until his lungs were bursting, his body weighed down by the doubloons. After an hour's pursuit by Gedney's furious men he saw he could not escape. He loosened the belt and abandoned the gold to the sea. The water was so clear, he

could see the belt sink, the coins like flecks of solid light, into
the underworld to join the spirits there. He was dragged back
to the *Washington* by boat hook while the angry sailors spent
more time futilely diving for the gold. More in frustration than
fear, the enraged lieutenants chained the Mendian spectacu-
larly to the deck of the *Washington*. Indifferent to his chains,
Cinque kept his eyes fixed steadily on the *Amistad*. A guard
with a cocked pistol stood over him.

The steamboat *Fulton* was sighted. Gedney sent the *Washington* with the *Amistad* in tow across Long Island Sound to
New London. Boarding the *Fulton,* and after a conference with
her captain, Gedney was speedily brought to Connecticut: There
was the matter of a salvage claim to be entered in his name
before anyone could contradict his story. In New London, at
the admiralty, Captain Greene angrily claimed the trunk of gold
which Cinque had promised him.

"These men are prisoners of the United States," Gedney replied. "Make your so-called claims to the U.S. Navy!"

The United States District Court judge for Connecticut, Andrew T. Judson, had to make an immediate decision. The
schooner could not just lie in New London harbor with its sick
and dying passengers. Obviously a crime had been committed,
but by whom? And what punishment, if any, should be meted
out, and under whose jurisdiction? Judson, a cautious bureau-
crat, was the President's man and a known enemy of the Negro. Connecticut, where slavery was extinct but paradoxically
still legal, was crawling with abolitionists, and he wanted those
black insurrectionists and murderers out of his district before
someone tried to make heroes of them. A judicial hearing ought
to be held immediately on board the *Washington*. The Negroes alone were worth twenty to thirty thousand dollars, and
the cargo another forty thousand. Only one man needed to be
hanged for good form, and that would be this Joseph Cinque.
The others, thought Judson, valuable as they were, would be
returned to their owners without any more to-do. He did not
want to be responsible for that kind of money, or for such an
unprecedented legal case. He and the port's surgeon, Lieutenant Gedney, and several newspapermen, removed to the
Washington and her prize riding at anchor in the bay near the

fort. In the meanwhile, Judson had sent a message to the Secretary of State, John Forsyth in Washington City.

JUDICIAL INVESTIGATION

At anchor, on board the U.S. cutter *Washington* commanded by Lieut. Gedney, New London, August 29, 1839.

His Honor Andrew T. Judson, U.S. District Judge, on the bench, C. A. Ingersol, Esq., appearing for the U.S. District Attorney. The court was opened by the U.S. Marshal.

Antonio, the slave of the murdered captain, was called before the court. Don Pedro Montez, owner of parts of the cargo, Don José Ruiz, also owner of part of the cargo, were heard. Lieutenant Richard Meade acted as interpreter between the Spaniards and the court.

No one appeared on behalf of the Africans nor was any communication held with them, but after this examination, the adults, numbering 38, were committed for trial for murder on the high seas and piracy, to be held at Hartford on the 17th of September. Antonio and the four small children were committed as witnesses. The whole were then transferred to the jail in New Haven, Connecticut.

[Affixed seals and signatures]
[herewith]

❧ New Haven ❧
August 1839

All New Haven was on the green to watch the procession of the first Africans they had ever seen advance from the docked *Washington* to the tavern which also served as the village jailhouse.

Two of the people in the crowd watching the parade led by Judge Judson were a prosperous-looking colored man named Henry Braithwaite, the town's printer, and his daughter Vivian. Braithwaite exchanged a look of resignation with his daughter. This was the same Judge Judson who, as district attorney, had prosecuted Vivian as a "public danger, rendering insecure the persons, property and reputations of the citizens of Canterbury," a small town some sixteen miles away. His daughter's only fault was to have been one of the colored girls enrolled in the abolitionist Quaker academy for young ladies when its headmistress, Prudence Crandall, had opened her doors to Negroes. When the townspeople protested, Miss Crandall had transformed her school into an academy *only* for colored girls as her answer to having been forbidden to mix the two races. The men and women of Canterbury had laid siege to the Quaker lady's students. Traders had refused them provisions. Men had assailed the girls on the streets. The doors and the steps of the school had been smeared with filth, the well filled with manure, and the town doctor had refused to treat any of the sick. Committee after committee had waited on Miss Crandall to remonstrate against the school, but to no purpose. Miss Crandall had held her ground. A town meeting was summoned to consider this awful calamity: black girls learning reading, writing and geography. That was when old Andrew T. Judson had passed his "Black Law," forbidding any person, under penalty of prison, to establish a school in any town in Connecticut for colored people not of Connecticut, or teaching, boarding or harboring Negroes born out of the state. If the same law had been applied to Yale College, thought Henry Braithwaite, it would have had to close its doors! But the Canterburians had gone wild with the news. They had rung bells, fired cannon and marched Miss Crandall off to jail, putting her in a cell that had just been vacated by a condemned murderer who had been hanged.

Miss Crandall was tried three times, in three different courts of the land, but no jury would convict her. The Canterbury townspeople, feeling cheated by the due process of law, had then set fire to the school. The girls had wakened to screams of "Fire!" and, in their nightdresses, the twelve-year-old Vivian amongst them, they had tried to put out the flames. But a mob had attacked the house with clubs and iron bars, and the school had been set afire again, with the girls inside. From the crowd that night had come shouts and screams, especially from the women, that nearly nineteen-year-old Vivian never forgot. "Kill the nigger girls! Kill the nigger girls!" The school had been burned to the ground. If Canterburians could do that to help-less females, Henry Braithwaite thought, what would they do to these terrifying, emaciated black men who had risen up against their master?

Perhaps he should not have brought his daughter to such a cruel display; perhaps it brought back even crueller memories and her fear of white crowds. He saw Vivian draw her breath in sharply, then bite her lip. It would not do to show his an-guish. He already felt guilty about what had happened six years earlier.

Vivian watched the tragical procession stagger past, then, for one moment, found herself staring at the almost immobile fig-ure of the man said to be the leader of the revolt: Joseph Cinque. To march them through the streets half naked! To arrest men who had only risen to secure their God-given liberty! She could tell he was right, just from his hard, indomitable eyes! For a fleeting second their eyes locked; then the procession strug-gled on. Only his scarred back was visible now, followed by the armed marshals and deputies.

Henry Braithwaite scrutinized his daughter worriedly. He had seen the alarming glance exchanged between her and the leader of the captives. And now he felt her trembling beside him. That African had frightened his daughter to death! He had to admit nothing like this had ever, in his memory, happened to sleepy New Haven before: black men without masters, claiming to be free Africans, speaking a language no one could understand, demanding justice, their leader resisting arrest and inciting his men to attack—a foreign warrior prince! Absently Henry Braithwaite began to compose Joseph Cinque WARRIOR PRINCE in Bodoni Bold. His habit was to translate his thoughts into typography whenever he was excited or upset. Braithwaite was a tall, handsome, beige man, over six feet four, with shrewd, round hazel eyes and only the suburbs of long wavy curls that had been the magnificent head of hair of his youth. To compensate he had cultivated a sumptuous moustache and vigorous, fluted side whiskers. His voice was so sonorous that it could and did shake the crystal chandelier in his living room. And when he spoke, he spoke in the typeface he most favored at the moment, or which, in his opinion, suited the occasion. He cast off his speeches the way he cast off his typographic compositions, each letter, syllable, word, sentence, paragraph, the clipped Yankee accent falling precisely like his lead fonts into their type cases, neat, precise, errorless. There was Great Primer, Baskerville, Old English Black, Paragon, Didot, Double Pica, Calson, Bourgeois, and his own favorite, Bodoni. He had even designed a typeface of his own, which he had as yet given no name. Braithwaite could not conceive of any typeface in the world ugly enough for prosecuting attorney Judson's remarks to the jury in the Prudence Crandall case. Judson had said,

There has ever been in this country a marked difference between the black and white men. There is still that difference, and it is impossible to do away with it. Those who claim to be the exclusive philanthropists of the day will tell you this is prejudice. I give it no such name. It is entitled to no such appellation. It is national pride and national honor which mark this distinction. The white men were oppressed and taxed by the king. They assembled in Convention, and at the peril of their lives declared this WHITE NATION free and independent. It was a nation of white men who formed and have administered our government, and every American should indulge that PRIDE and HONOR, which is falsely called prejudice, and teach it to his

children. Nothing else will preserve the AMERICAN NAME or
the AMERICAN CHARACTER. Who of you would like to see the
glory of this nation stripped away and given to another race of
men? . . . The present is a scheme, cunningly devised to destroy
the rich inheritance left by your fathers. The professed object is
to educate the blacks, but the real object is to make people yield
their assent by degrees, to this universal amalgamation of the
two races. And have the African race be placed on the footing
of perfect equality with the Americans.

Blacks are not citizens. The Declaration of Independence does
not apply to blacks: it concerns only the relations of WHITE
colonists with Great Britain and does not speak to their rela-
tions with their slaves. Even the Constitution does not claim
that blacks are equal to whites.

Decidedly, thought Henry Braithwaite, the American Revolution, in which his own family had fought, had changed transplanted Englishmen into Americans. And if a transplanted
Englishman after a hundred fifty years was an American, why
wasn't a transplanted African as well?

Henry Braithwaite made his way through the crowd. The
world did not bode well for the *Amistad* captives—not in Connecticut, not anywhere. Where were the men who would or
could defend them when they had not even a common language? If they had been kidnapped white men who had risen
and taken their liberty from criminal pirates, this procession
would have been a hero's welcome!

"I say, Braithwaite, nothing like this has ever happened to
New Haven before!" The tall courtly man tipped his hat to
Vivian. Braithwaite turned and smiled into the blond, rosy
countenance of Josiah Williard Gibbs, the rector of Yale College Divinity School. Gibbs was both a friend and a client.
Braithwaite had printed more anti-slavery pamphlets for the
good professor than he could count.

Josiah Gibbs could not believe his good luck. The *Amistad*
captives had fallen into his lap like a gift from heaven. The
Anti-Slavery Society, founded by two rich brothers from New
York, Lewis and Arthur Tappan, was floundering, looking for
a dramatic cause to offset the sudden apathy in the North to
their cause of abolition and the recent success and strength of
the South and the slavery cause. The Tappans and their news-

paper, the *Liberator,* would certainly spill a lot of ink about this as soon as he had spoken to them of the captives. This was of course his Christian mission.

"I'm going over to the jail and try to get the story from these men," Gibbs said. "Before we can help we have to know their story."

"It seems no one speaks their language," said Henry Braithwaite. "No one can make heads or tails of what they are saying. They could just as soon have landed from . . . another planet."

"God, Mr. Braithwaite, will show us the way. If they speak in tongues, why, God will make sure his message gets through!"

For Josiah Williard Gibbs, Joseph Cinque's arrival was no less than Divine Providence, planned by Him to encourage the Christianization of Africa. He intended to organize a group of Yale divinity students to begin the conversion and education of the *Amistad* Africans while they awaited trial. He would ask the Reverend Leonard Bacon, Henry Ludlow and Amos Townsand, Jr., to take measures for giving intellectual and religious instruction to these benighted pagans, he mused, during such time as they remained under the surveillance of Christian benevolence. He almost licked his lips in satisfaction as he walked towards the village jail with the eccentric stiff-legged gait that had earned him the nickname "Stork" from his students at Yale.

Upon entering the jailhouse, Joseph Cinque was separated from the rest of the captives, but he was glad not to be with them. The faces of the men who had followed him to their doom were more than he could bear now. He thought back over his useless voyage towards what he knew now to be death, and wondered what he could have done differently. The voyage was over. The destination more horrible and strange than he had ever imagined. The children. His men. His ship. His life. His obsession with freedom had blinded him to an even more horrible fate—death, exiled from one's ancestors, separated from one's family, one's people, without a tongue to speak or an ear to listen or a hand to hold. He strained against his chain, then in exhaustion sat back. He did not want to die. For the first time he gave in to despair. He put his head in his hands and wept while the men, both black and white, who were in the same cell, watched the African with curiosity, too hardened for compassion but human enough for comprehension.

Oblivious of the others, Joseph Cinque removed the strange, tight clothing and draped the blanket that had been given him, Mende style, to cover his nakedness. He put as much space as he could between himself and the men staring at him, squatted tailor style and placed his head against the wall. In the oppressiveness and heat and darkness he dove in and out of his hopelessness as he had the cold waters of Long Island Sound; remaining beneath as long as his breath held and then coming up for air, gasping and thrashing, his head on fire, his lungs bursting. He wanted to cry out. But he could not even call on Gewo, for how could his voice reach Him from this new world?

The next time he looked up, he saw a tall white stork wearing a high conical white hat and carrying an ivory-handled staff, hovering over him.

"Gibbs, Gibbs. Gibbs," it sang.

New York Harbor
September 1839

The harbor lay at the southern tip of New York City, with its
serpentine waterfront, narrow cobblestone streets and alleys
swarming with multicolored crowds and carriages, pushcarts
and platforms. The wharf was a chaos of draymen, wagons,
stacks of merchandise, cartloads of coal, cotton, lumber and tea.
The walk to Broadway was dangerous, for the sidewalks belonged to wheelbarrows, pyramids of loose brick and stone,
and the sandbags of the construction crews of the Manhattan
Water Company. Broadway, wider than the Champs Elysées,
reached four miles north into the city, and when darkness shut
down villages and cities across the nation, Broadway, with its
fine, brick buildings, gleamed by gaslight.

Wall Street was lined with banking houses, exchange brokers, insurance auctioneers, custom houses. Along the quay
bankers, merchants, brokers and tourists mixed with seamen
from the ships in harbor and dock workers in pea jackets, whose
job it was to unload the stream of trade goods which spilled
out upon the quays, along with throngs of businessmen looking for commercial paper and the latest news from Europe.
Lining the noisy quay for four miles, fifty vessels lay at anchor:
brigs and schooners, frigates and sloops sailing under the colors of every earthly nation. The famous *Constitution* was in
drydock with her 1677 tons and seven-hundred-man crew, famous enough to have a nickname, "Old Ironsides," and beautiful enough that every sailor in port went to visit her. Thousands
of masts struck the flat blue September sky and spread themselves along the waterfront in a leafless forest of gray weath-
ered wood and white furled sailcloth. Scalloped reflections
speckled with reflected autumn sun. The bay's soft water swells,

ivory, sienna, bottle green, black, gray, yellow, marine blue, and royal purple, floated, touched with gold leaf and scarlet. Pilot boats scurried in and out amongst them like water bugs. There were no awkward, dangerous and noisy new steamboats among the sleek sailing aristocrats. Sailors scrambled around and over the decks and stern; clambering and cleaning, scrubbing, polishing, mopping and burnishing until the ships glowed. The mariners' cries and commands, a Babel of languages, spiralled up the masts.

Amidst all this noisy confusion the long, rumpled Dr. Gibbs cut a strange figure. Dressed in a cleric's winter clothes of black, the latest vogue, he wore his jacket shorter than normal and cut in the European manner, which contrasted with the more old-fashioned, flared, printed knee-length coats of the merchants and brokers. But what drew the passersby's attention to him and made them laugh was that the Reverend Mr. Gibbs trod the quay, a towering dignified figure in a top hat, and in a beautiful baritone voice, repeated out loud for anyone who would listen:

"Eta, fili, kiauwa, naeni . . . Eta, fili, kiauwa, naeni . . ."

Dr. Gibbs ignored the snickers and rough derision of the harbor loiterers, thinking of himself as a martyr in the long line of Christians that had preceded him throughout history. His daily visits to Joseph Cinque and the *Amistad* captives had resulted in his deciphering the names of the first ten numerals of their language, with the help of coins, fingers and a bright boy named Kale. And now he repeated those few pathetic words in desperate search of an answer that would unlock the solitude and silence of the African men. How, he asked himself, could the word of the Lord be perpetuated if one was ignorant of it? If it had not been so, he reasoned, there would have been no need for Revelation. How could he make good Christians out of the *Amistad* Africans, emissaries of the word of God, if they could not understand the Bible? Was it not true that the Abbé de l'Epée, the founder of *Les Amis des Noirs*, The Friends of Blacks, in Paris, had had to invent a whole new language for the deaf and dumb for the same reason—so that they would not remain for the rest of their lives in a state of original sin? And just as the deaf and dumb had to be lifted from their silence, so his captives had to break theirs—in order to defend themselves and understand the accusations against them. And so he cleared his throat and in a loud voice, continued:

"*Eta, fili, kiauwa, naeni . . .*"

". . . *loelu, weta, wufura . . .*"

A young man turned and laughed at the crazy white man counting in Mende on a crowded pier in New York harbor. He responded with a clear, crisp, "four, five, six, seven . . ." at which moment both voices shouted, "*wayapa, tau, pu!*"

"So, you also read and write the King's English?"

"The Queen's English, sir. God save Victoria." Yes, this language is Mende. Yes, he spoke it. Yes, he read and wrote as well as spoke English. "My name is James Covey," he said, and the candid sailor's eyes met Dr. Gibbs' with that peculiar sea gaze so typical of his vocation. His ship, the British cruiser *Buzzard*, had just arrived with two prizes in tow and was laid up in quarantine. Dr. Gibbs was afraid his happiness was too great not to be considered the sin of excess. Gibbs believed in miracles. He believed in Providence. He believed in the conversion of souls. And he believed that the *Amistad* captives had been sent as a sign that all Africa was waiting.

"I want you to know," said Captain Fitzgerald, "that I consider James Covey a member of my family. I am happy he can be of help to you, for we have read of the case in the newspapers. But I know how you Americans feel about men of color, Dr. Gibbs. I hold you personally responsible for James' health and happiness. I will not have him hurt or insulted or molested."

"Sir! I'll be all right."

"I know you will," said the captain.

"You still think of me as nine years old."

"So I do, James, so I do. . . . James was rescued from the slaver the *Henrietta* by the brig of war *Aden* twelve years ago, and now he's an English sailor."

"I give you my word of honor, sir, nothing bad will happen to Mr. Covey," replied Dr. Gibbs. "And may God bless you for helping us."

"You'll need more," replied Fitzgerald dryly, "than God's blessings."

"Oh, no," said the doctor, "my trust is in the Lord."

James Covey and Dr. Gibbs walked up Broadway towards the warehouse of the abolitionist Lewis Tappan. Covey's hawk eyes darted to the left and right. He could hardly believe such a street existed. From the Battery and Park Row they moved northwards, away from the city and its tumultuous noise, carriages and boisterous population, past the wide, elegant red-brick Federal town houses of the rich merchants and shippers. A foul odor permeated the neighborhood, which had been built above the badly drained Collect Pond. The gentry were abandoning their fine homes, moving uptown to Greenwich Street and Washington Square, and leaving the area to the newly arrived Irish and Germans. Recently, the Native American Society had been formed to protect the white Protestant majority from being overrun by foreigners.

"So, if you go through the newspaper clippings, you will be up to date."

James Covey nodded. The sensational articles about the *Amistad* had made him anxious to set eyes on Cinque and his men.

"Three men have formed the Amistad Defense Committee. We are going to meet them now. They are the millionaire Lewis Tappan and the Reverends Joshua Leavitt and Simeon Jocelyn. Also present will be William Jay, son of Chief Justice John Jay, and Arthur Tappan, Lewis' brother. The Tappans are great-nephews of Benjamin Franklin, who founded the Pennsylvania Abolitionist Society," continued Gibbs. "Arthur Tappan is fifty-four-years old and Lewis is two years younger. Both made fortunes as importers of European and Chinese silks, and both worked diligently to make the money which they now just as diligently give away. The brothers consider the money they possess as belonging exclusively to God. The gentle, pious Lewis is devoted to spreading the Gospel and abolishing slavery. Arthur, who is humorless, colorless, and the Lord forgive me, quite self-righteous, regards himself as the steward of the Great-Giver-of-All-I-Possess. Satan Arthur, he's called. And as money is his passion, to give it away is his security. Yet they are both brave men!" Gibbs shook his head.

"Lewis is the editor of an abolitionist newspaper whose offices have been sacked and burned by mobs. Threatening letters are their daily bread, and physical assault as well. Arthur
has been stabbed, beaten, and dragged through the streets of
New York. His warehouse has been burned, as has his house.
Once, someone sent Arthur a slave's ear in a box. Countless
times Southerners have tried to kidnap them. There is a price
on their heads in every state in the South, up to fifty thousand
dollars, dead or alive. 'If that sum were to be placed in a New
York bank,' Arthur once told me, 'I might possibly turn myself
in.' " Dr. Gibbs smiled.

"But even in the North they enjoy no tranquillity. A few years
ago Arthur bought some land in New Haven to found a college
for free Negroes. But the town decided that the establishment
of a college to educate colored people was incompatible with
the prosperity, if not the *existence,* of the present institution of
learning, Yale College, my own school." Josiah Gibbs continued. "I have never, never understood this . . . this visceral,
irrational fear of the black freedman and of the educated black.
Many Americans, you see, even those opposed to slavery, do
not think abolition is the answer. Most favor colonization."

"To Liberia?" asked Covey.

"Do you think American Negroes can be deported?" Gibbs
asked.

"According to Captain Fitzgerald," said Covey, "using all
the naval vessels and all the merchant fleet of the United States,
it would be physically impossible for anyone to transport all
the Negroes in the United States to the nearest place possible,
say the island of Santo Domingo, half as fast as Negro children
are born. Not to mention that they were born American citizens."

"Yes, well, that *is* the question," said Gibbs testily. "Some
feel that inflexible opposition to slavery would bring about a
worse evil, the dissolution of the Union. They consider us fanatics, dangerous fanatics. But the men you will meet are all
abolitionists and immediate emancipationists. As for the other
two men, the Reverend Simeon Jocelyn used to be the pastor
of a colored church in New Haven, where he endeavored to
apply Christian principles to both black and white. But mobs
and threats finally drove him from the town, and he now works

with the colored of New York City out of an office on Wall Street. The Reverend Joshua Leavitt is a Yale graduate, a lawyer and the editor of the Anti-Slavery Society's newspaper, the *Emancipator*."

Dr. Gibbs' long, scholarly hands gesticulated in excitement, his scant auburn hair lifted by the wind, his flat cheeks pale and clean-shaven. Since he was invariably the tallest man in any company, he had taken the habit of stooping towards the person he was talking to in a way people took for condescension. He was more than a head taller than Covey, and his round spectacles sparkled in the sun.

"The *Amistad* is a godsend. Until now all we could do was hold meetings and recruit members in the North. Joseph Cinque has changed all that. He has become the standard of a whole new battle."

❧ New Haven ❧
September 1839

Vivian Mae Rachel Braithwaite had been going to the New Haven jailhouse every day for a week. Each day she filed by Joseph Cinque's cell, the first in line with hundreds of other New Haveners, Canterburians, Hartfordians and New Yorkers who paid Colonel Stanton Pendleton a New York shilling for a look at the Africans. Vivian came because she was drawn by emotions and dangerous thoughts she had not yet been able to explain or even justify to herself, let alone her father, from whom she hid her visits. Vivian had begun to bring small gifts: bread, sweets, fruit. Her white-gloved hand would slide between the bars of the cell, and with some incomprehensible sentence like *"Herehavethis,"* her light brown eyes would stare at Joseph Cinque with a lingering, infuriating question.

From her first visit, Joseph Cinque had noticed Vivian. She was beautiful, but it was not that which fascinated and stirred Joseph Cinque and made him burn with shame that she should see him so humiliated. It was the question in her eyes, which it seemed that he and only he knew the answer to, if he could only find it. The elusive question had from the first moment perched like a black crow between them. The girl was curious, yes, excited, even a bit terrified, but not *of* him, he realized, but *about* him. There was something she wanted to know, and he was sure he could tell her if only he could find a voice to speak. He was enclosed in the silence of total incomprehension, as if he had fallen into the pit of a lion trap, able to cry out but unable to communicate in any other way his horror, his fear, his disgust at the interminable lines of white faces that passed and peered into his—without modesty, without either decency or compassion. His men and he were being exhibited like wild animals in a cage, and even some of this was in her gaze. Yet though he hated all the others, he forgave her because of that persistent lingering question that always hung there between them. On the sixth visit Joseph Cinque realized that Vivian was taller than he. He had risen when her slim figure approached in the line, and suddenly found himself looking upwards. He could not know that under her long green skirts were soft leather boots that, with their heels, added two inches to her height. It seemed one more of the hundreds of humiliating facts he had had to digest in the past week—his failure to lead his men to victory, his failure to lead them home, his failure to prevent their recapture, on which he had sworn his honor, even his failure to kill himself. Joseph Cinque brooded over Vivian's height for the rest of the day. It was the same day that James Covey arrived.

Mr. Moulthrap had thrown the captives into a state of panic, though he worked as rapidly as he could, given the circumstances. The circumstances were the Africans' terror of the wax he used to make the impressions he needed for the life masks. Although he had patiently explained that it was an utterly painless and scientific operation, the Africans had not, of course, understood anything, and without Professor Gibbs and Professor Day, it was impossible to communicate even the simplest ideas. Moulthrap had had to request the aid of the jailer, Mr. Pendleton, whose great commercial idea this was, and several of his deputies, to hold each man down until he had finished the molds. As it was, he had almost asphyxiated one who would not or could not breathe through the little bamboo tube he used to allow them air. Their cries had been pitiful to hear, indeed. Yet if he were to exhibit the wax likenesses of these Africans throughout the country, from which there was a great deal of money to be made, they would have to get at it. Colonel Pendleton and his partner, Mr. Curtiss, were paying him well to make these masks, and the exhibition by Pendleton and Curtiss of "The *Amistad* Captives" was already, it seemed, booked from Maine to Missouri.

Before Mr. Moulthrap there had been Dr. Fletcher, a phrenologist, who was convinced that mental faculties and dispositions could be judged by measuring and observing the nature and shape of the skull.

"Joseph Cinque is about twenty-six," Fletcher had told Gibbs pompously, "and he is of bilious and sanguine temperament, bilious predominating. His head measures twenty-two and three-eighth inches in circumference, fifteen inches from the root of his nose to the occipital protuberance over the top of his head." He paused. "At the Meatus Auditorius he measures fifteen inches over the head and five and three-quarter inches through the head at the lobe of destructiveness. He has great development of the faculties of firmness, self-esteem and hope. Above normal faculties of benevolence, veneration, conscientiousness, approbativeness, wonder, inhibitiveness and comparison. He has average faculties of amativeness, philoprogenitiveness, adhesiveness, combativeness, secretiveness, constructiveness, caution, language, individuality, eventuality, causality and order. There is only a small amount of his personality of alimentiveness, acquisitiveness, ideality, mirthfulness, imitation." Dr. Fletcher was amazed to find no evidence at all of destructiveness. "The head, however, is an admirable one, well formed, one which evokes the admiration of phrenologists. The coronal region being the largest, the frontal and occipital nearly balanced, and basilar modest; such an African head," Fletcher concluded, "is seldom to be seen, and doubtless in other circumstances would be an honor to his race."

Dr. Fletcher made an analysis of all thirty-nine men. He would later show the sketches to Dr. Gibbs and her Britannic Majesty Queen Victoria's phrenologist, Dr. Combes, of London.

When the doctor and the interpreter reached New Haven they went directly to the jail. It was four o'clock and the combative jailer, Pendleton, insisted on feeding the prisoners dinner before allowing Covey and Gibbs to see them. James Covey was appalled at the circus atmosphere surrounding the men in their cells. Hundreds of people were still standing in line to inspect the captives, but finally, when the last of them had filed by, Covey and Gibbs were allowed to see the prisoners. When Covey greeted the men in Mende, it was as if he had cast himself into the eye of a summer squall at sea. Men jumped, laughed and cried, called out questions, grinned, gripped his hand, thumped his shoulder. Covey was almost borne down under the flood of joy. He noticed that three men were desperately ill and lay silent and motionless on mats in one corner. Several minutes later a tall man, draped in a blanket, arrived and stood in the doorway. Covey's eyes met his and he knew he was looking at the commander of the *Amistad,* Joseph Cinque. Cinque hesitated, his face showing surprise and bewilderment, like a blind man who had suddenly been given sight. For Cinque it was almost this; James Covey had released him from his prison of silence. The two men approached each other, holding out their fists, and then touched knuckles, as was the Mende custom.

Joseph Cinque

"I am," began Joseph Cinque, but he had no time to finish.

"*Sangbei,*" said James Covey. "I am called *Kawoli,*" he continued, using his African name and smiling ironically. "War Road" repeated Cinque and both men knew Joseph Cinque had found not only his voice, but his future. Have-Mercy-on-Me came up to the two men, tears welling in his eyes.

"Tell them what really happened. Tell them we won the war! Ruiz and Montez have lied—lied to everyone—and we had no voice except that of that little wretch, Antonio, and Twin here. Once they hear our story, they will set us free!"

"Tell them also," said Joseph Cinque, "of our sufferings. Of the ship that brought us across the waters. You know of these ships?"

Covey, without speaking, nodded.

For the first time since he arrived in this place, Joseph Cinque heard himself speak to a stranger in his own language, and was himself understood and answered by someone who could transmit his thoughts to the white man. Here was the answer to his prayers, this tall, handsome Mende in white man's clothes. Joseph Cinque embraced Covey tentatively, but the other young man clasped him hard in an emotional embrace.

The gunner of the *Buzzard* had never had any real contact with any of the captive slaves he had freed. Now he would liberate these men, at least from ignorance and prejudice. The rest was up to the courts of the United States.

As the men crowded around, the interpreter began to pick out faces, knowing that he or Joseph Cinque would have to choose amongst the men, those who would become symbols for them all. No appeal could encompass thirty-nine men; for the great public to react to the captives as *men,* they would have to have names, faces, personalities. They would have to live and be remembered. James Covey had already decided on the number, thirteen, a lucky number in Mende, for if the rebellion ever went to a jury, it would be twelve white men plus one, the judge, who would acquit or condemn them. He would learn about Joseph Cinque by listening to him.

Grabeau

"Have-Mercy-on-Me was my first lieutenant, War Road," said Joseph Cinque. "We met almost at the moment of my capture and we managed to stay together in the barracoons and on the *Tecora* and the *Amistad.* Have-Mercy-on-Me's parents are dead. He is married but has no children. He was sold to a Spaniard for the debt of his uncle. He is my age."

Covey smiled at the tall, broad, jet-black Grabeau as he came forward. "Cinque and I have become like brothers," he began. "It was he who kept me alive during the time on the *Tecora.* When I despaired, he revolted against our fate. When I was whipped on the *Amistad,* he again saved my life. Our village had wars, had famines, had plagues, but I never dreamed of what one man could inflict upon another until now."

"Crocodile is the oldest captive," said Cinque. "He is thirty-nine. He was fourth in command on the schooner. Sessi was taken as a slave along with his wife, who died on the *Tecora*. Both had been captured and sold to the Spaniards. Crocodile is our log—he is the memory of the *Amistad*. He has memorized everything that happened. It is to Crocodile that you should truly address yourself, War Road. Far even better than I, he knows its secrets."

Sessi

Sessi was very different from the ebony Grabeau. Sessi was a light brown, with a scarred cheek and back and deep-set, sad brown eyes. His hair even had some gray in it. He was so small in stature, Joseph Cinque, Have-Mercy-on-Me and James Covey loomed over him.

"This is Big Sun," continued Cinque. "He was my bodyguard on the *Amistad*. He is called Big Sun to distinguish from Little Sun, whose father Bia is another of the captives."

"My town was surrounded by soldiers and burned," Fuliwa told James Covey. "I was taken prisoner along with my brothers."

Fuliwa's manner and obvious intelligence impressed Covey. Tall, slim, a walnut brown, he spoke of his brothers,

Fuliwa

naming each and telling of their closeness as a family, with a father who was a village elder. Of the hardships of the *Tecora*, he spoke not at all, preferring to dwell on the revolt and the days and nights of wandering up the Atlantic coast. His manner of recounting had much to do with a sail-

or's way of seeing things: in great detail and minuteness, each
detail patiently placed into the whole fabric. James Covey liked
him immediately.

"My second lieutenant was Cricket," said
Cinque. "He was born at Mawkoba. His
father is a gentleman, and after his death
his king took him for his slave and gave
him to the prince Banga, who lived in
the Bullom country. The prince sold
him to a Bullom man who sold him
to a Spaniard at Lomboko. Cricket
helped teach Doctor Gibbs to count
in Mende. If anyone led us to you, it is
Kimbo here. He is not a Moslem, although there are some amongst us, but he
says there is no book in his country."

Kimbo

Kimbo was tall and very dark, with a moustache and a short
beard, and to Covey seemed older than almost all the others.
Cricket's eyes seemed to hold all the sadness of the world in
them.

Cinque indicated another man. "Twin, the
younger, was from the river people in
Mende country. He was sold for a petty
crime directly to a Spaniard from Lomboko. His father is dead and he lived
with his mother. He has four sisters
and two brothers."

"When my father died," said Burnah, the younger, "my eldest brother
married and we all lived in the same
house. None of the other boys had wives,
nor did I. We are river people who live in
elephant and leopard country. I owned a boat

Burnah

and a rice field. I was six weeks travelling to Lomboko, where they kept me for three-and-a-half moons before putting me on the *Tecora*. I met Sengbe Pieh in Lomboko. I was the only one on the *Amistad* who knew anything about boats or who could speak a few words of English. It was Antonio and I who translated Sengbe Pieh's orders to Ruiz and Montez. I had only navigated on rivers until then, never on the open sea."

Covey listened carefully to Burnah's story. Burnah was jet black and powerfully built. He had a handsome face but one of his eyes had a cast. As he was the closest link to Ruiz and Montez, Covey asked Twin what sort of men they were.

"Not all bad," said Twin, "for white men. But evil in their greed for slaves and incapable of realizing we are men just as they are. Many of our men were afraid of their white skin, but not I. Ruiz is little more than a boy. Montez is an old, weak man. Both are capable of great and inhuman cruelty. I have the scars to prove it."

"A more just man I do not know than Python," Cinque said. "He is our poet. He writes our songs and listens to our complaints, guesses our wildest dreams. It is to Fooni that we reveal our secret selves. He was born at Bumbe, a large town in Mendeland not far from my own village. The name of his king was Kabandu."

Fooni

"I am married," began Python. "I have a family, living brothers and sisters . . . many. My favorite sister has always been Sula. I was seized by two men on my way to the rice fields. I was carried to Benbelow in the Vai country and sold to a Spaniard called Luis who kept me two months before he took me to Lomboko."

He suddenly fell silent. Covey looked up and saw an athletically built man in the prime of youth, with thick hair and a small, well-shaped head. He had let his nails grow in captivity and they were white and shiningly well groomed. Fooni had about him an air of shy gentleness and good humor. He seemed the best-tempered man in the group.

"Waterfall is a sculptor," continued Cinque. "He makes us laugh even when we should cry. It is said that only his *funny* stories number two thousand. And as far as his wicked stories are concerned, they are infinite. He was born in Massakum in the Bandi Country, where his King Pamasa lives. He is a blacksmith, much appreciated in his village. I once hoped to become a sculptor, but a true sculptor has magic in his hands, as Waterfall does. Many nights we have spoken of spirits and the spirits of sculpture. One day when all this is finished, it will be Waterfall who will carve it all in images."

Shule

"I learned my trade of blacksmith from my brother," said Shule, nervously fingering a piece of wood he had been carving, "that of making axes, hoes and knives. As for my sculpture, it was predicted by a Griot. I have carved for King Pamasa. I was taken captive by soldiers and wounded in the leg. Here, you see it is not even now completely healed. And I have a limp. I was sold twice before I arrived at Lomboko, where the Spaniards kept me about a month. I arrived before Sengbe Pieh and Grabeau but became friends with them in the barracoons. By God's will we were put in the same canoe."

Waterfall was tall and light brown with a sly, mirthful face and large, strong hands. He hardly raised his eyes to those of Covey but instead kept glancing over his shoulder at another of the captives, Bartu.

"I am Sword," said Bartu, stepping forwards. "I am of a noble family. I have never worked. I was sent by my father to a village to buy cloth and was captured on the War Road. My king's name is Dabe and he lives in the town of Tuma, where my family lives. There is a great lake there. My captors tied me up hand and foot and carried me to Lomboko. My country is mountain country and rice is cultivated there. People have guns. I know how to use a gun. I was one of the men who fired on the *Grumpus*. My country is also elephant country and quite rich in ivory. If I had had some ivory with me, I might have bribed my captors—but I had none." Bartu shook his head sadly.

James Covey noticed a young man standing apart from the crowd of men.

"Who is that?" he asked.

Bartu

"Big Man," answered Joseph Cinque. "He has already begun to learn the white man's language. Perhaps he could help you with your work and you could teach him to make letters?"

Big Man stepped forward. "My name is Kinna. My parents and grandparents are still alive—at least I hope so. I have four brothers and one sister. I was born at Simabu where my King Samang also lives. I was taken on the War Road on my way to Kongolli by a Bullom man, who sold me to the Spaniard called Luis at Lomboko. I'm beginning to understand a little of what the white men speak. I would like to help you."

Kinna

"You can, Kinna," said Covey. "I sorely need help. I will teach you to write the names of each man in letters the whites understand. That is the first step."

"At your orders, Sire."

James Covey smiled.

* * *

"Twin, the elder," continued Joseph Cinque, turning to Faginna, a man whose face was pockmarked and whose skin was very black, "was born at Tombolu. He was made a slave for infractions of the laws of his village along with his wife. He was owned by a man called Tamu. Tamu sold him to a Mende man who sold him to a Spaniard, the same one who bought Grabeau. His village had been decimated by the smallpox and local wars, and so was susceptible to slave raiders. He lost a young son to the smallpox."

Faginna

Faginna was a fierce-looking man with thick hair and a small moustache. Covey wondered for what crime he had been sentenced to domestic slavery.

"There is another man here from Grabeau's kingdom," said Joseph Cinque. "This is Broke. He is thirty-seven years old."

"We have the same king, Grabeau and I," said the huge, intelligent-looking, sober man with a large round head and tattoos and incisions on his chest. "I have a wife and three children. I was caught in the bush by four men as I was going to plant rice. My left hand was tied to my neck. I was ten days going to Lomboko. I lived near a large river called Wowa. I was a rich man. I paid ten bolts of cloth, one goat, a gun and a hundred mats for my wife. My mother paid for her."

Bau

"It was Bau who prayed over Tua, who died just before you arrived. They buried him in the town after a white man had spoken over him. It was a strange ceremony, but Bau insisted Tua be buried as an African. Bau's family has been dead a long time. His wife and child were taken prisoners in war, and four moons after he was taken, he arrived at Lomboko."

Cinque went on with the introductions.

"Remember is thirty-five years old. He was born at Dzkopoabu in the Mende country. He is the son of a King Bawnge. Fabanna's title is prince. He has a wife and two children. He was caught in the bushes by a Mende traitor, about a ten-day march from Lomboko. He says it was probably a vendetta against his father. His father sent a rescue party after him but they were ambushed by Spanish men and either killed or kidnapped into slavery, as he was. He thinks he should be the one to file suit against Ruiz

Fabanna

and Montez. We met on the *Tecora*. He was chained two men down from me." "We planned a rebellion," interrupted Fabanna, "but never had a chance to organize the men."

James Covey shook his head. Gallinas. Gallinas. It ran like a litany through every story. One day it must be destroyed. Covey cracked knuckles with each man he had been introduced to. He agreed with Joseph Cinque's choices. They had their men. Now the others gathered around the two men.

"This is Sa, Berri, Bagna, Nga honni, Kwong, Gnakowol, Bia, Pungwuni, Tsukama, Ndamma, Kapeli, Yammoni, Moru, Konnoma, Fuli, and Ba Shuma." Covey registered the names: Stick, Gravel, Water Bird, Second Born, Duck, Learner, Water Stick, Put Up, Little Sun, Have None, and Falling Water.

"Where are the children?"

"There are four children," said Cinque. "Teme, Kagne, and Margru—three little girls—and a boy, Kale, plus the cabin boy Antonio, who speaks only Spanish."

"Why are they kept here in jail?" asked the interpreter.

"We are trying to have them released," Dr. Gibbs interjected, "so they are kept by Mrs. Pendleton, the wife of the jailer. If you would like to speak with them alone? I'll get on home." He smiled. "Never in my entire existence have I had such a tumultuous week, spiritually and physically. Of the slave trade, I knew nothing. And now I know too much ever to sleep the sleep of the just again." Josiah Gibbs turned and left, his stiff-legged gait a parody of a man dragging a ball and chain.

Dr. Gibbs signalled Mrs. Pendleton, who, after showing the reverend out, returned flushed and not a little apprehensive at being in the midst of so many mysterious and unpredictable heathens.

"This is Kale," said Cinque as the children filed in, passing Gibbs. "Bone's parents are alive. He was stolen in the street when he got separated from his father. He was taken to Lomboko. He says he is eight years old. Teme is seven. Frog lived with her brother and sister. Her father is dead. One night a gang of men raided her mother's house and took them all prisoners. She has never seen her mother or brother since. She says she doesn't know how long it took her to reach the slave barracoons. Country here is ten. She speaks a little Fai as well as Mende. She says her parents are alive and that she has four brothers and four sisters. Kagne was pawned for debt by her father, for which, not being paid, she was sold."

Kale

Teme

Kagne

"And this is Margru. . . ." Black Snake hung back timidly before the strange man. Her delicate, thin face registered both fear and curiosity. Margru knew that Covey was not one of *them*. And she wondered where he had come from, this handsome man who strangely resembled the white devils. Slowly, a shy smile spread across her face. Quickly her hand flew to her mouth to hide it, Mende style. It would not be seemly to show such joy in front of a stranger. Black Snake needed permission to smile. With the resilience of childhood, she had forgotten most of the horror of the Middle Passage, only the dark still frightened her, and the white man's language with its strange, beastlike sounds.

Margru

The exhausted interpreter   up the beautiful child with the large black eyes, high forehead and perfect features. She put her arms around his neck and clung to him. From her size and weight, Covey guessed her to be about seven or eight. The pressure of her light body, the tiny hands clinging to his neck, the soft warmth, were his only solace for the unending stories of terror and suffering. For it was not so much what the men had said about their homes, their birth and families, but what they had not said. They had not spoken of those who had died. And they had not spoken, as Covey knew they would not, of the Middle Passage.

Covey went over and knelt beside three sick men. He recognized all the signs. These men would never recover. It had happened often with freed slaves on his ships. Men who had held on in captivity, gave up when freed. They had a name for it amongst the sailors—they were called the *Pumui Koe hui,* the walking white dead. "Here are Fa, Kaba, and Welluwa," said their leader gently.

The men fell silent, their curious eyes now on Covey, and Covey realized he would have to explain who he was, his *Nge gbembi*. He had forgotten that to these men, his line of blood relatives was the only thing that mattered. He decided to address Cinque.

James Covey

"My *Nge gbembi*," said Covey slowly. It had been years since he had thought about that. "I was born in the Vi country, the first son of Tsukama. My father and uncle were killed in the battle of the Koama River, and my mother, my sisters and I were kidnapped and sold to Pedro Blanco, in Gallinas. We were put on a ship called the *Henrietta* and after ten days at sea were rescued by the English, who towed the ship back to Mendeland. I was the only one of my family to survive. I was adopted by white missionaries, whom I loved, but they died of the black vomit. Shortly after, I joined the British African patrol, as a seaman. But as for my *Nge gbembi*, there is more, much more." He hesitated. "You see, it has to do with the Triangle."

Cinque watched as Covey pulled a sea chart from his knapsack and spread it on the floor. Cinque shook his head. He could recognize no mark but the shape of the place, Gallinas.

"If a chart of the Atlantic Ocean is spread out," said Covey, "and a line is drawn from Gallinas to Havana, and another line is traced from there to where my ship comes from—a place far in the north called Liverpool—you have the strangest commerce in this world. This is the Atlantic Triangle. Those who navigate it make fortunes. Men in England where my squadron comes from make objects to be traded for slaves at Gallinas, who are then shipped to Havana to be traded for sugar and tobacco and rum, which is then shipped back to England.

"There are twenty important Havana merchants who are the overlords of the slave traffic, and the biggest is the one who sold you, Pedro Martinez. But there is another man, Joaquin Gomez, who owns the first bank in Havana and is a member of a secret society called the Masons, which is like the Poro. His Masonic name is Aristides the Just, and he is in partnership with the Queen Mother of the Spaniards. On the other side of the ocean stands his counterpart, the man you know as Pedro Blanco. Here, also, there is another man, a mulatto named Francisco Felix Da Souza, who has the monopoly to export slaves from Ghezo, King of Dahomey, whose own income from the export tax on slaves amounts to one million three hundred thousand dollars each year. But understand me, brother, the European merchants are only the last station of an immense organization. The white man has never been permitted by African rulers to go beyond the coast. And since commerce and not conquest is their aim, they are content. They know nothing of the complicated arrangements of which they are the final, but not the only, benefactors. Each powerful African king, prince, baron and viceroy has his trading organization, many run by the Aros of the Ibos, whose religious power, based on the Aro Chukwa Oracle, is their medicine to be the middlemen of the hinterland trade. The Efiks are the other slave-trading nation, and they have founded a sacred cult in Havana.

"As for your own king, he refuses to sign a treaty with us outlawing slave trading in his kingdom, despite pleas from our Christian queen, Victoria, who has outlawed slavery, and the efforts of our squadrons, which are commanded by men like my captain, Fitzgerald, and his commander, Denman. The adversaries of my English *Nge gbembi* are the pirates like Mongo John and Theodore Canot, who, like many of their infamous predecessors—John Hawkins, Francis Drake and John Paul Jones—combine slaving with piracy. There is not only one ship, my brother, but hundreds of ships like yours. For three hundred years Africans have made the same terrible voyage as you, under the same terrible suffering. I know what you have endured. I chase and capture the men who ply this trade, and their ships, and try to bring them to justice, and their cargos to freedom. But it is hard. I come now from New York, where our ships delivered two prizes to the United States Admiralty. Perhaps, the crew and the captain will be tried for piracy."

Cinque rotated his powerful neck in shock.

"*You* do this?"

"My ship does this."

Then Covey turned slowly, studying each face. He realized what a nightmarish story he had told these men, and he wondered if they could accept it as true.

"Are you the one who will take us back to Mendeland?"

"No," said Covey, "I am only here to act as your interpreter, to speak your words to the white men, at your trial."

"What trial?"

"There were men killed. You are to be tried for murder and piracy."

"But that was war."

"What is war for you is only the Triangle for them."

"But we even spared the Spaniards' lives, to sail out of your triangle. And even so we failed, for we could not sail the ship." For the first time Cinque said the word "ship" in English, repeating the word he had heard Covey use.

"There were waters under you, but there was a sky over you," said Covey. "That was your error."

"But we followed the sun," protested Cinque, "measuring by the shadows of the masts. The water changed direction and color, there were storms, the winds blew or did not blow, yet each time I followed the sun, measuring by the masts."

Cinque's wide-eyed stubbornness was infinitely sad to Covey. Cinque had done his best. He had used courage and intelligence. It simply had not been enough.

Kneeling down, Covey turned the sea chart over and began to draw the stars and constellations of the summer sky. "These are the stars one must follow from Havana to Gallinas: Deneb, in the constellation of Cygnus, the Northern Cross; Vega, the brightest star of the north, in the constellation of the Harp; and Altair, that sits almost directly above your head in Mendeland, in the constellation of the Eagle." He pointed. "Behind you, as you sailed toward Gallinas, there were two stars you must know well: Arcturus, in the constellation of the Herdsman, and Regulus, in the constellation of the Lion. But you would have lost them beyond the horizon, the second week you were at sea. . . . There is a great river in the ocean, called the Gulf

Stream," said Covey, "which is why the water changed color and direction."

Covey looked up at the silent, uncomprehending Cinque, for whom the star chart was still a piece of cloth lying on the dirt floor. Covey raised his eyes in frustration, then leaped to his feet. Drawing over a small pine table by the window, he climbed up on it and began to redraw the same constellations on the ceiling of the cell. Suddenly Cinque realized that Covey was begging him to follow the stars across the water with him, to navigate. He looked up, searching, and recognized several stars as parts of constellations, but in unfamiliar configurations. He identified the star Covey called Altair; it was directly over his head, and revelation dawned on Cinque's face.

"Altair," he said in awe, "is called Konunqui in Mende. Vega and Deneb are Ndeloi and Sokolequli. How many times have I gazed at them in the night? . . ."

"And these three stars . . ." Covey paused for a moment, and then said, his voice desolate. "And these three stars are called the Summer Triangle. They were your way home. . . ."

Cinque pointed his finger to the line Covey had drawn across the cracked plaster overhead.

"And this?" he whispered, still trying to encompass the enormity of what Covey had told him.

"This is the dividing line between the northern skies and the southern skies. This star is Spica, the Ear of Corn, in the constellation called Virgo, the Maiden, that lies to the south; and even farther is Antares, in the constellation called the Scorpion. This sky was taught me by the English and I had to learn it, I learned it, I learned it, I learned it. . . ." Covey found himself sobbing helplessly, weeping as he had not done since he had watched his mother die on the slave ship *Henrietta.*

Cinque slowly recognized the pain of a *carabela:* Covey had spoken the truth. The other men looked away.

Cinque now knew how Montez had tricked him: While he had steered by the sun by day, Montez had steered by the stars by night. An emptiness gathered in the pit of his stomach. He looked around at the others. He had seen only the obvious, the familiar, the sun; he had been too stupid, or too blind, or too proud, to imagine the more subtle language of true knowledge that might have saved them.

"If I had followed the stars, instead of the sun, we would have made the return. I would have known the Spaniard was tricking me."

Cinque's helpless roar exploded in the silence. "WE WOULD HAVE MADE THE RETURN!" Now it was Covey who looked away from the devastation in Cinque's face, to the line he had drawn on the ceiling. And for the first time he himself felt whole; his two *Nge gbembi's* had finally connected in that fragile line, that line that up until now had divided his soul. The Summer Triangle, and the consciousness that went with it, had truly made him what he was, not just the person who had been given the name James Covey.

"White men use knowledge to trick," said Covey. "I don't say it is good or bad, it simply is; moreover, they change the rules on us all the time. The very basis by which you and your men judge honor or war or dignity does not exist here. I am not only your interpreter in language, but in the learning you need to deal with white men. And you, Cinque, speak not of careless error because you sailed beyond your ken. Your duty now is to recognize that black men are not allowed error, for we are never forgiven, and possibly dead."

"Recite the stars again, from this place to Gallinas," demanded Cinque.

❧ Washington City ❧
September 1839

The diminutive President of the United States stood with his
back to his Secretary of State, the tall, handsome, urbane John
Forsyth. Forsyth had actually heard Congressman Davy Crockett declare that the President could "take a piece of meat on
one side of his mouth, a piece of bread on the other, a cabbage
in the middle, and chew and swallow each in its severalty,
never mixing them together. . . ."

If this were so, thought the Secretary, now was the time for
Martin Van Buren, known ironically as the "Little Magician,"
to do just that. Forsyth had in hand an irate letter from the
Spanish Ambassador, Angel Calderón de la Barca, Minister
Plenipotentiary of her Catholic Majesty, Isabella of Spain, as
well as two plaintive messages from Connecticut District Attorney William Holabird, a threatening self-righteous letter from
three abolitionist lawyers, Theodore Sedgwick, Seth Staples
and Roger Baldwin—hired by the self-styled Amistad Defense
Committee—an angry editorial by the editor-poet John Green-
leaf Whittier, and a sheaf of newspaper clippings from every
part of the country. The President was at this moment gazing
pensively at a lithograph of Joseph Cinque made by a reporter
named Sheffield, which had been circulating along the eastern
coast from Boston to Norfolk.

It was, thought Forsyth cynically, a question of *who* was *what*
in this case. The meat was certainly the captives. The bread,
Spanish-American relations; the cabbage, that smelly mess
called public opinion.

"I suppose," said the President, "that all eyes are on New
Haven." Martin Van Buren usually thought that all eyes should
be on him.

His Secretary of State took a deep breath. "Well," he began,

"the image of the man you have in your hand is the leading
African, Joseph Cinque or Sinqua, or at least that's the name
given to him by the newspapers. Secondly, I have two letters
from District Attorney William Holabird, the first saying that
he *supposes* he will have to bring the Negroes to trial, unless
they are in some other way disposed of. He adds that should
you have any instructions on the subject, he should like to receive them. He also writes to the Attorney General, Felix
Grundy, saying that the abolitionists have already raised a great
deal of excitement on the subject. The Tappans, especially,
seem determined to make capital of it, and have begun to organize public opinion and are employing an army of counsel.
Holabird asks Felix for opinion and instructions. As for the army
of counsel, you have received a letter from the lawyers hired
for the defense—Baldwin, Sedgwick and Staples—who write
that neither according to law of the United States nor of Spain
can the pretended owners of these Africans establish any legal
title to them as slaves. They put the matter on the Spanish law
and affirm that Ruiz and Montez have no claim whatever under the Treaty of 1795. These Negroes, they say, have only
obeyed the dictates of self-defense, and liberated themselves
from illegal restraint. It is, I quote, 'This question that we pray
you to submit for adjudication to the tribunal of the land. It is
this question that we pray may not be decided in the recesses
of the Cabinet, where these innocent men can have no counsel
and can produce no proof, but in the Halls of Justice with the
safeguards that she throws around the persecuted and the oppressed.' "

Forsyth flushed. He was a Georgian, formerly governor of
that state, and sided with the hereditary slave owner, although
as often occurred, he was too poor to own more than a family.

"I have a letter from His Excellency Angel Calderón de la
Barca, the Spanish Ambassador, as theatrical as his name, demanding that the *Amistad* be immediately delivered up to her
owner with every article found on board at the time of her
capture, including the Negroes, without payment being ex-
acted for salvage. He claims that no tribunal in the United States
has the right to institute proceedings against, or impose pen-
alties upon, the subjects of Spain for crimes committed on board
a Spanish vessel and in the waters of Spanish territory. He

demands that the Negroes be conveyed to Havana to be tried by the Spanish laws which they have violated.

"Insurrection, by the way, is a capital offense, punished by breaking the neck, using a 'garrote'—an iron collar tightened by a screw—before being burned at the stake," murmured Forsyth. He resumed reading Calderón's letter out loud.

"Any delay in the delivery of the vessel and slaves should be indemnified for injury accrued to them. In return Her Catholic Majesty agrees to concede that for the protection of United States property, slaves that have escaped to Cuba will be extradited."

"And the newspapers?"

"Oh, damn the newspapers, Mr. President. They have got hold of a wonderful story of a low black schooner, black pirates, a jungle prince . . . or a band of cannibal savages. The newspapers are drawn along the lines of the country: anti-slavery and slavery.

"And what about our friend Whittier, of the Anti-Slavery Liberty Party?"

"My God, the old man calls Cinque a 'master spirit'— and says, 'what a soul,' for the tyrant to crush down in bondage. . . ."

"And what have you done so far, John?" Van Buren's back was still to him, so Forsyth had no idea of what he was thinking.

"Well, I conferred with other cabinet members, who agree that the case is covered by the Treaty of 1795, Articles Eight and Nine. I answered His Excellency Calderón's letter in the affirmative to that effect. That calmed *him* down a bit. I then wrote William Holabird that he make sure that no proceedings of his circuit court or of any other judicial tribunal places the vessel, cargo or slaves beyond the control of the White House."

Martin Van Buren turned to face his Secretary of State, one of his many compromises with the "Southerners" who had elected him. His small hands rolled and unrolled the lithograph of Joseph Cinque. Even in agitation, Van Buren's pale, longish, delicate-featured face was incapable of sending out any strong message. Forsyth still could not tell what he was thinking, even with eye contact. Van Buren pulled himself up on his tiptoes to his inconsiderable height and then rocked back upon his heels. Also known as "Red Fox," he had come to the presidency as a compromise candidate, a Northerner with Southern sentiments.

"Men or property, uh?"

"Or Executive or Judicial, as you like."

"We must keep this under control. . . ." He tapped the rolled-up lithograph against his high glossy forehead.

"The Southern press has been keeping as quiet about it as the Northern press has been noisy. For obvious reasons. We don't want any word getting around that black slaves have killed white men and tried to sail back to Africa! Think how this could incite our slaves! Another Nat Turner!"

"Well, slaves aren't supposed to be able to read anyway, John. That's your law."

"Well, there are lots of ways to get around the law . . . as you well know."

The irony was lost on Martin Van Buren. If he understood his Secretary of State correctly, they had promised that they would interfere in their own judicial system *in favor of* an alien power over this . . . that stupid ass Holabird.

John Forsyth studied the round little man. The remnants of his carefully waved red hair surrounded a white skull of impeccable smoothness perfumed with *Double Extract of Queen Victoria*.

He had once believed that the presidency of Van Buren would be that of a "little magician"; instead it had become that of the sorcerer's apprentice. President Jackson had left Van Buren a nation in crisis: bank notes without guarantee, land without buyers, towns without inhabitants, canals without traffic, mortgages without interest, stocks and bonds artificially inflated. Wild spending on the part of speculators had constructed a house of cards which had now collapsed. A deficit balance of payments and bankruptcies in England had brought the country to panic in 1837. Mismanaged banks had issued too much paper and dozens had failed. Merchants had even printed their own money: *This ticket is good for a tongue of beef and two biscuits.* But Martin Van Buren had remained calm through it all, thought Forsyth, and stuck to his argument that government intervention would only aggravate the panic. "The government," he had said, "should not prop up a paper money and nourish the illusion that its value can be created without work." The President's inertia had infuriated the business world. Van Buren, who had never been loved by Americans, was now detested. And the *Amistad* might be the last nail in the coffin of his dreams of reelection, thought his Secretary of State.

Martin Van Buren knew he was a mediocre president. Uncharismatic, unimpressive, adept at intraparty politics, he was at a loss on great issues. And the whole United States seemed to be engaged in debates on great issues, he thought irascibly. Transcendentalists, Mormons, Shakers, Fourierists, members of the Oneida, members of the Skaneateles, perfectionists, supporters of women's rights, and abolitionists; all fanatics! Yet this energy, dedication and passion had no parallel in history. Every man you met in Boston—for Boston was the capital of the reform movement—might pull out from his waistcoat pocket some petition, some protest, some call for a convention, some plan for a Utopia to revise the social structure, the State, the school, religion, marriage, trade, science . . . to try to rid the Church of dogmas and return it to transcendentalism, to create public schools, to educate girls, to improve the conditions of the working class, to do away with private property, to campaign for women's rights, to lead a crusade on behalf of the insane, or the reform of the penal code, or the lot of street urchins. . . . There were hundreds of temperance societies, hundreds of women's conversation and sewing groups, hundreds of schemes for universal peace, while the most dangerous man in America, William Lloyd Garrison, had invented something called non-resistance, and Charles Sumner had announced that there was no war that was honorable and no peace that was dishonorable. There was even a movement to limit the authority of the State by civil disobedience. And all of these forces were moving together like a dark cloud towards the main and overwhelming issue of slavery and abolition. Van Buren continued to rock back and forth on his heels.

After a long silence he addressed Forsyth again. "I realize the strength of Northern aversion to the Constitution has been recently very truly stated on the floor of the House by Quincy Adams. In the South the feeling is very different because of culture, dispositions, and the force of habit. This incurable di-

versity of opinion and feeling should beget a spirit of con-
iliation and inculcate mutual forbearance in speech and
action. . . ."

There he goes again, thought Forsyth, fence-sitting, or as they
said on the Hill, fence-shitting. This wasn't solving the problem of the *Amistad,* only of Mr. Van Buren's pretensions to
another term as President. Next year was an election year. Forsyth sighed. Would he ever get a straight answer out of Van
Buren?

Davy Crockett was right. And here was some piece of meat,
some piece of bread and some cabbage for Van Buren's presidency to swallow.

The former First Lady of the United States walked up Pennsylvania Avenue to the Capitol. She needed the fresh air, though
it was hot and humid and malodorous, and she needed the
time to think. Besides, it would save the quarter for a hack.
She had spent all week going through the hundreds of anti-
slavery petitions that poured into her house on F Street. The
plain, modest, rather shabby brick edifice seemed actually to
be collapsing under their weight. Louisa Quincy Adams had a
headache from the ink and she was sixty-five years old and she
owed the butcher forty-two dollars. It was September and
summer recess was over. She and John Quincy Adams, sixth
President of the United States, had had to sneak into Washington to escape their creditors. As he had so many times before,
John Quincy had put his ambition, his overbearing pride, his
excessive largess, at the service of total strangers. Now they
were being dunned for unpaid bills for coal and firewood, gro-
ceries, and even their pew rental at St. John's Church. The
roof was leaking and the back porch had collapsed. Louisa
fought back tears. One day, she thought, Mr. Adams' enemies
would gain enough power to censure him in Congress—perhaps even expel him. They always tried to silence him on points
of order. "Put him down!" they cried. "Shut the mouth of that
old harlequin!" But he went right on introducing petition after
petition against slavery, while slave holders gathered around
him and glared, Mr. Adams glared back, and the galleries hooted
and cheered, hooted and cheered, hooted and cheered. She
closed her eyes against the vision of his impending stroke.

*   *   *

The House of Representatives was a spectacular semicircular room hung in fine red brocade and ringed by massive marble columns. It had two very fine fireplaces, a handsome crystal chandelier, a high-domed ceiling, and it was filled, thought Louisa, with men, intelligent or stupid, virtuous or immoral, elegant or uncouth, and most of all, Southerners or Northerners.

The Speaker's dais was elevated high above the floor, like a preacher's pulpit, and had a canopy of crimson silk like a cardinal's, trimmed in gold fringe and supported by four posts, with draperies that fell to the floor behind the chair. It was very hard to hear. Not that anything the Speaker said had anything to do with the ladies listening, Louisa thought. But still the ladies came, wearing wide skirts, billowing sleeves with shoulder ruffles, tight corseted waists, large broad-brimmed hats and cashmere shawls. They sat in the front rows and came and went as they pleased, as if they were watching a play or a pageant.

She sat down in the visitors' gallery. This was where her husband had lived his life for the past nine years. And there was nothing she could do about it. At least it wasn't the President's house anymore. Or Berlin, or St. Petersburg, or London. Louisa nodded to Mrs. James K. Polk, wife of the House Speaker, a Tennessee slave holder, who nodded in return but did not smile. Mrs. Polk, thought Louisa, wanted to be First Lady. Well, she could have it, and with the birds and the bees. Mrs. Adams never wanted to see the inside of the White House again.

Like his father before him, John Quincy had suffered the ultimate humiliation of being turned out of the White House after only one term as President. The 1828 campaign between her husband and Andrew Jackson remained for them unforgotten and unforgiven to this day. . . . The scandal-mongering, fear, envy and calumnies that had perhaps killed General Jackson's wife, had almost killed her. But failure to win reelection had been for John Quincy a terrible vote of censure by the people, not only on his presidency, but all his past service to the nation. To suffer without feeling, her husband had said, is not in human nature . . . and they had suffered, thought Louisa. The President's house had been a prison and a lonely existence. Her memories of that house standing bare and unshaded on open land—with its lean-to sheds and stables and neither running water nor indoor plumbing—she had happily put behind her. But John, like his father before him, had refused to attend the inauguration of the President who had succeeded him. She had never believed that defeat was a disgrace, but her husband had and did.

Yet now, over all her protestations, John Quincy had returned as a lowly Representative from the state of Massachusetts. She had been so beside herself with rage, she had threatened not to come at all. He had promised; promised to retire from public life, take care of his family and their pitiable fortunes after that humiliating presidential campaign. And yet the people of Massachusetts had only to crook their little finger and John Quincy had come scurrying back to swampy, malarial Washington and its Bull Bait politics. Louisa sat in the red velvet Visitors Gallery, thoroughly weary of being beaten about in a stormy world. She had been married nearly forty-two years ago in the Church of All Hallows in London, and, at most, only a few more years of married life, or any life, remained to them.

Louisa Adams had lived a life of severe stages and little pure satisfaction, and had survived a marriage to a hard-driving, hard-drinking public man who put God, country and public service before wife, family, love and comfort. John Quincy now was the last of his generation, the last link to the holy "framers" and his father, the great John Adams. But the flaws in the Adams dynasty—improvidence, lunacy and liquor—had pursued them clear across time. Two grown sons had fallen victim to their curse, and now, of their own sons, only Charles Francis was alive to become the next generation of Adamses. To live longer than one's children, thought Louisa, was the hardest thing, like being trimmed from a wide oak back to a sapling. Since George's suicide she and John Quincy had grown both closer and yet further apart. Her grief made her feel like a child.

Louisa Johnson Quincy Adams had always been almost beautiful. Traces of the delicate-featured, hazel-eyed Southern belle still lingered despite her sixty-odd years. She was small, under five feet, and her curly hair was still the light brown of her youth. She had had the reputation of having the most tantalizing, enchanting smile in all London, but in fact she had developed her flashing smile to hide her bad teeth. Born into a slave-holding family, she had grown up along with her five sisters in London, loved and protected by a rich indulgent father who had been American consul under George Washington.

Louisa Johnson had been disappointed in love and had married John Quincy not knowing that he, too, had not married his first choice. She had been an heiress who promised her husband a substantial fortune and splendid dowry. A week before their marriage, to her everlasting shame, her father had suddenly declared bankruptcy. Despite her persistent feeling that she had cheated her husband, John Quincy, an honorable man, had never once reproached her. Yet poverty haunted him, and he saw himself as a man not unjustly, but fatally poor. Moreover, her mother-in-law, Abigail, had not approved of her. She had always considered Louisa too frail, too spoiled, and too Southern to be the wife of the scion of the Adams dynasty.

Louisa's still beautiful hazel eyes lowered to the stout, black-clad figure of her husband. He was at this moment attacking before the House committee, the nation and the world, the principles of Henry Wise of Virginia, whose wife was sitting behind her. John Quincy Adams' waspish, New England voice broke onto the inert air. He was on his feet, his short, pudgy body twirling and practically dancing on small, neatly shod feet to the rhythm of his own words. Louisa called it the Congressional shuffle, but it was really more like that of the little pickaninnies who performed for their masters. John Quincy hopped and skipped, shifted his weight from one foot to the other, his shoulders now hunched in sarcasm or creased with indignation or slumped in disgust, while he kept up a steady stream of rhetoric, ironic abuse, righteous debate, cajoling legalistic deductions, Latin quotations, operatic scales of brilliant language or long-winded redundancy that had earned him the title of Old Man Eloquent. Louisa sat back. John Quincy was pleading for ten of the hundreds of petitions in his possession. All contained three prayers: the abolition of slavery and the slave trade between the states, and the denial of admittance to any state whose constitution tolerated slavery. Mr. Polk was saying that only the prayer concerning new slave states could be laid on the table.

"Well," said John Quincy, "then you'll have to cut the petitions in three. . . ."

"I object." This was Representative Black from Georgia.

"You object to cutting them in three?" asked John Quincy.

"I object to your misconstructions, Mr. Adams." This was Wise from Virginia.

John Quincy pirouetted and again addressed the Speaker. "Sir," he said in his high, cracked voice, which made Louisa smile, "My old petition that I presented the other day," he said, "being presented under the old rule, was adopted and so does not come under this new rule."

"But it does," said the Speaker.

John Quincy turned upon the House, gave a sly look up at the Speaker's chair and said, "Give me back my old petition then!" Louisa began to laugh. The Speaker sent a boy to fetch it. John Quincy reread it again: "Lydia Lewis and one hundred fifty women of Dorchester praying for the abolition of slavery in the District of Columbia, Rachel Newcomb and one hundred thirty women of Braintree praying for the abolition of slavery . . ."

"Order!" screamed the Speaker.

"Mary Perry and eighty-two women of Plymouth; Abigail M. Emmons and three hundred fifteen women of Franklin; Phoebe Weston and one hundred fifty-six women of Westminster . . ."

"Point of Order," someone shouted.

"Impressed with the sinfulness of slavery and keenly aggrieved by its existence . . . Ann E. Hildreth and ninety-five women of Derry, New Hampshire; Eliza Tower and seventeen women of Waterville, New York; Esther Chase and sixty-four women of Kirkland, New York; two hundred ninety-five female citizens of Westmoreland County, Pennsylvania . . ."

"Order! Order!" shouted the Speaker.

"For Liberty!" the House budged a little. *"The human race,"* the House budged even more, *"to relieve the wrongs of the Africans!"*

"Order! Order!" House members shouted.

"Take your seat!" Polk shouted at Adams.

Adams walked backwards to his seat. "I've finished my speech." There was an exasperated buzz in the House. Louisa blushed. John Quincy had had his way, even with the opposition two hundred to one! Louisa raised her head proudly, daring anyone to meet her cool hazel eyes with derision or pity.

* * *

The House rose. The session was over. Louisa made her way through the crowd towards her husband. She still moved like a young girl. Her tiny figure had taken on weight, but not enough to kill the illusion of lightness and slimness. She was the only one in the chamber without a trace of perspiration on her face or a telltale stain. She had even kept on her white gloves. She liked the heat. She had been born to it.

Louisa looked down at the gnarled, clasped hands of her husband, slumped in his seat. It seemed to her that all the years of battles and disappointments had found their resting place in those two clenched fists.

Her white-gloved hand came to rest on them, waking him from his reverie.

"Well, my dear," she said as he looked up, "you certainly made a fuss today."

"Louisa! What in the world are you doing here? You never come here!"

"Then who copies and brings the anti-slavery petitions you so diligently try to introduce in the House despite Pinckney's Gag Rule?" she answered.

"I liked your speech," she went on. Louisa kept her hand on Quincy's as much to calm him down as out of affection.

"You shouldn't have walked—you *did walk*, didn't you?"

"I like the heat," Louisa said. Her face dimpled and she flashed her famous smile at the man who was incapable of a pun and missed the point of every joke.

John Quincy's deep, black eyes, piercing and provocative under their quizzical eyebrows and neat triple furrows, met hers. He was short when he stood and looked short even seated, and his gnomelike baldness was relieved only by ferocious, luxuriant, white side whiskers.

His eyes held belief in humanity as passionately as his heart held a grudge. Sometimes, Louisa thought, their whole life seemed one long grudge: intense hatreds, neat lists of enemies, both eyes on History, a half-hundred portraits John Quincy had found time to pose for, fast walks, overwhelming ambition and every position of any importance in the United States. Stern, gruff, egocentric, scrupulous, her husband was a moralist: first and foremost duty to God, to country and to Duty itself. A smile looked positively out of place on him. But Quincy Adams did his best to smile at his good-looking, elegant wife. He loved

her, though his passion had been reserved for another. And
they were so different in temperament, had such a different
outlook on everything including life itself, that he wondered
how they had ever gotten through married life. The only thing
they really had in common were their respective fiery tempers.
One Southern. One Northern. Even to that they were section-
alists! Well, all they could hope for now, he thought, was rec-
onciliation with what life had dealt out to them. He could not
complain. He had sacrificed ease, pleasure, wealth as he had
been taught to do in defense of justice, benevolence and the
service he owed society. It made life hard, he thought, even
for an Adams. He had forgotten how to laugh. And he had forgotten what peace and quiet was.

The couple stood quietly for a moment while the crowd ed-
died around their private circle of complicity. Moments later
friends and acquaintances would interrupt with polite if not
effusive greetings. The Adamses had few friends in the House.

The war between John Quincy and the United States of
America over slavery had been going on for nine years.

✍ New Haven ↣
September 1839

Increase Braithwaite's steady, glossy eyes surveyed the long, immaculate length of her Sunday dinner table. She smiled in satisfaction, youthful dimples breaking out on each cheek. Her hand, on which glinted a wide wedding ring, hovered over the white napkin before she lifted and unfolded it. It was an uncharacteristic gesture, for normally Increase was not inclined to unnecessary movements. She was naturally still, her oval face expressing calm, her dark eyes a kind of watchful restfulness.

Increase had Indian blood, which had given her magnificent, abundant straight black hair that reached her knees. Her eyebrows were dark gashes over even darker tilted eyes. It was her form and size that made her memorable, her weight adding to the notion of permanence her husband so adored. Her magnificent scale was a straight and direct appeal to his senses, like the weight of his lead fonts.

Henry Braithwaite was saying grace, his solid wide-shouldered frame filling up all the space between his oldest daughter Vivian and his youngest, six-year-old Honor. His soft vibrating intonation instilled a strangely penetrating power into the most familiar words, as if they were meant to be seen rather than heard. Increase was glad that Vivian had come out of her sulks after being forbidden to continue her visits to the New Haven jailhouse.

Braithwaite usually spoke to his women, Increase, Vivian, and Honor, in Calson, all sweetness and light. But his thunderous Great Primer Bold was enough to bring Vivian running and reduce his wife to tears. Mostly his boys heard the lithe and elegant Paragon or Didot spoken in even lines, the words marching one after the other across space and falling neatly into justified paragraphs. There were as few flourishes and decorations in Henry Braithwaite's speech as there was in his typesetting. Ordinary Great Baskerville, with nice wide margins, seemed to him appropriate for most things. Energetic and fatalistic, Braithwaite believed that in typography as in law, it was difficult to specify the qualities that constituted justice, balance and excellence, which to him meant perfection. The productions of typographical artists, he knew, varied as much as the figures of Canova varied from a Wanted poster or an advertisement for a fugitive slave. True perfection, like real justice, did not depend upon inflexible principle but on creative interpretation, and it was therefore difficult to point out every particular which it was necessary to combine in order to accomplish a masterpiece. Yet, he thought, it was not so intricate, for when Braithwaite saw a beautifully uniform typeface bestowed upon a faultless selection of dazzling white paper, displaying all its proportions with a just degree of luster and harmony, his conception of typographic beauty as well as his notion of justice was satisfied. He had learned from his ancestors in an era when black freedmen had enjoyed the best of times: in colonial America. Colored subjects of the Crown and, after the revolution, citizens of the republic had lived, worked and married where and when they pleased. They had owned property, traded, invested, sold, bought, paid taxes and voted. Braithwaite, therefore, was a man of property, descended from men of property. His great-grandfather had bought his first printing press from his former employer in 1756. His grandfather had added another, so that his father had inherited a lively, reputable establishment with two printing presses, a binding press, two apprentices—not counting his sons Jasper and Jefferson—and three typesetters, two of them his elder sons, Jacob and Cotton. He owned the property in which his presses were housed, and lived in a large white shingle house on the same land behind his publishing house. He also owned a large farm and another house outside of Westbury, Connecticut. His greatest struggle in life had been to marry the girl of his choice, Vivian's mother, the fourth and youngest daughter of the minister of the First New Haven African Baptist Church of the Apostles. The courtship had been long and nerve-racking, opposed by his wife's father on the grounds that he had printed and published "anti-Christ" literature. He, an atheist, had been

saved from rejection by the most beautiful, luxurious, illustrated, leather-bound and embossed Bible in the village of New
Haven. Increase Braithwaite's father had succumbed to brib-
ery and exchanged the hand of his loveliest daughter for Henry
Braithwaite's hand-printed Quarto Bible in two volumes printed
upon yellow weave royal paper on one side only. The Bible
had evoked the speechless, furious, un-Christian envy of the
rector of the Yale Divinity School when he saw it.

Henry Braithwaite, standing at the head of his table, even
had the stance of a compositor: perfectly upright, yet without
stiffness, his feet firm on the ground, heels nearly touching,
toes turned out to form an angle of forty-five degrees. He held
his head and torso perfectly steady without any time-wasting
or superfluous motions.

The Braithwaite house was a mile outside of town, set on a
sixty-acre parcel of land. The printing press and office, a red
clapboard affair, stood downslope of the house, and the sign
bearing Henry Braithwaite's insignia hung out over the town
road: a brown bear rampant, holding a large scroll upon which
was imposed a Gothic B for Braithwaite, and beneath it his
name with the words PRINTERS and TYPESETTERS lettered in
gold. The town liked Braithwaite's sign. It reminded the people of New Haven, all fishermen, of a ship's masthead.

The house was a comfortable shingle and stone building large
enough for a family of at least twenty, if one considered that
none of the Braithwaite boys had as yet brought home a wife.
Cotton and Joseph worked the land, and the three younger boys
helped out with the presses and were taught at home by Vivian and a tutor. In a grove behind the house Henry Braithwaite had two barns. One held his second printing press, his
inventory of paper, his casks of ink and acids, his metal plates
for engraving and an indoor water pump. There was also a
sleeping attic for travelling journeymen and salesmen. In the
other were the stables for the plow horses, the buckboards and
the Braithwaite carriage and carriage horses.

Braithwaite loved the smell of ink, which was like the odor
of pitch in the bottom of a ship. The depot was all in wood,
and he loved everything that was wood, and the place itself
was as neat and clean and scrubbed as the decks of a sailing
vessel.

"One cannot be a printer in disorder or filth," he was fond

of saying. "Everything must reflect the printed page: pristine black on white."

But then there was a hollow floor in the print shop and a secret door disguised in the barn walls. Henry Braithwaite's printing depot had another function than that of storing textbooks, pamphlets and anti-slavery tracts. Braithwaite's house was a stopover on the famous underground railway.

"It's a scandal," said Henry Braithwaite in the more emphatic Bondi-Roman instead of his usual Baskerville, his great curled wavy sideburns trembling with indignation, "exhibiting men like caged animals . . . charging admission! Taking life masks! That old ruffian Pendleton would sell his own mother! The talk in town is that he has a scheme for a travelling wax museum. I heard the sculptor he engaged almost asphyxiated one of the Africans. And now a Dr. Fletcher who claims to be phrenologist from New York, taking their head measurements and reading their character by it! It's true we don't understand their language, but it is obvious they have one—it means an interpreter must be found without delay! Without it, they are wretched curiosities, and not even human curiosities. Imagine . . . an exhibition travelling all over the east and the *territories!*"

Increase Braithwaite exchanged glances with Vivian. *Territories* had come out in Old English Black Letter, which meant that Mr. Braithwaite was getting worked up. She hoped that Vivian, whatever her fascination with the *Amistad,* would hold her tongue. But she had wished too late.

"It's not unhealthy curiosity on my part, Papa," said Vivian stubbornly, "and not lack of modesty either. Day after day it seemed that if only I had had the . . . key to unlock the speech of those poor men, to unlock their terrible heathen muteness, then I would have the answer to the question. . . ."

"What question is that, daughter?"

"I don't know what the question is," said Vivian. There was a yelp at her side. Vivian turned to her eight-year-old brother, Jasper.

"Jasper, you know you *can* have a question and not know what it is, just as you can have an answer and not know the question."

"My sister's crazy."

"All I know," said Jacob Braithwaite, "is that Papa's right. So long as those Africans are locked up in the town jail behind the town tavern, no self-respecting young girl should be visiting them."

"Well, if we can't visit them, what can we do to help them?"

"I hear say there's a professor of the deaf and dumb called Day, who's come from New York to try and speak with them in sign language, and a professor from Yale College went to New York by steamer and found some African on the docks who speaks their language."

"Wonderful! Now we can get *their* story," said Henry Braithwaite to his second son, Cotton. "We need the truth. Then we can start working for justice for those men."

Jefferson Braithwaite, the fourth of Vivian's brothers, interrupted.

"I think Vivian was right to go. All those evil-looking faces. Imagine if *you* were white and landed in a place where everyone was black and all you longed to see was one friendly white face. . . ."

"There is no such thing as a friendly white face, Jefferson—a friendly white face is like a ghost. Have you ever *seen* one?"

Everyone laughed. Jeremiah, the eldest Braithwaite, had the knack of making everyone laugh.

"I think every colored family in New Haven should visit the Africans!" said Jacob.

"Lots of them have," said Jasper, "but not young girls, is what Papa's trying to say."

"Young girls, young men, what's the difference?" said Vivian. "I can shoot and ride as well as you, Jacob."

"Your father is just trying to protect you from ugliness, low-class people, speculators," said Increase, brushing crumbs of Sunday biscuits from her splendid lace bosom.

"Well, it's not the *Africans* who are ugly, low class or speculators," answered Vivian. How could her father speak of protecting her from ugliness after Miss Crandall's fire, the mob and the trial? she wondered. What was more ugly than burning a house down around frightened children and a lone woman?

"Well, Mother," said Henry Braithwaite, reverting to his calm and elegant Baskerville, "most people in this town have never ever seen an African. The village claims it has nothing to do with the slave trade, but I can personally point out three man-

sions right on the Green built by New Haven slave traders.
How many ships have the New Haven dockyards built for the
slave trade? I ask you. And Gedney and Greene and Meade
claiming salvage, including the men as cargo! Chattel! Beasts!"

"Reverend Sullivan says that the slave market has tripled
since 1812. Reverend Sullivan says those Africans are worth
from one thousand to two thousand dollars apiece in Georgia!
That's forty to eighty thousand dollars Lieutenant Gedney is
after!"

"There are three million slaves in the South, Mama, worth
sixteen billion and a quarter dollars," replied Cotton.

"That's the actual national deficit!" said Jefferson.

"How did you know that?" Henry asked his son.

Before he could answer, the whole table fell silent. The
serving girl, who was white, came in from the kitchen and set
the roast on the table in front of Henry Braithwaite.

"Well," said Increase, after she had left, "Reverend Sullivan
has taken up a collection for clothes, extra food and legal defense for the Africans. The money will be turned over to the
Amistad Committee."

Increase Braithwaite looked around her table, anxiously surveying her nine children. She had thought slavery and all its
dangers far from her family. Now all the fears of every free
black family in Connecticut had been revived by the arrival of
the Africans. The hatred and incomprehension they had learned
to push aside or slough off had come back with all its terrible
force. Increase's fears for her sons, their safety and happiness,
had reappeared in her dreams of late. As she lay beside her
husband these days, she imagined Cotton or Jacob abducted
by slave kidnappers and sold down south to Georgia or Mississippi, never to be heard from again; and Henry, moving heaven
and earth to find them, but having no redress to the police or
any court of law. Cotton or Jacob claimed by some white man,
any white man, as his slave, and nothing they could do or say
to prove otherwise.

She thought of the danger Henry ran, printing anti-slavery
pamphlets, of having his printing press attacked, his house
burned, his body mutilated or exploded by a bullet in the chest
like the abolishionist Lovejoy, in Illinois. She thought of their
station on the underground railroad for fugitive slaves, which
even their younger children didn't know about. Increase ab-

sently dished out the yams and red cabbage her husband adored, then the baked beans and cornbread Jasper would hang around the kitchen just to smell. She had made gingerbread and pies from William apples from the orchard for dessert. She had sent three over to the jailhouse. But all she really wanted was for Cinque and his men to free themselves and return to that mysterious far-off country they had all sprung from, but which now had no more meaning to them, the Braithwaites, than the Bible's Ophir or Sheba's kingdom. Her family thought Increase, was descended from the freedman Lemuel Haynes who seventy-six years ago fought in the War for Independence, endured the battle of White Plains and the bitter winter of Valley Forge. He was long dead, survived by almost fifty grandchildren. The Braithwaites were an even older family. For two hundred years there had been prosperous black Braithwaites in Massachusetts and Connecticut, and for seventy years they had been printers and typographers. And now, she thought, a skeletal, forlorn little band of Africans from the "old country" were the talk of the United States of America, the bane of existence of its President and the cause of an international incident between the United States and Spain. The Amistaders had also become the dangerous rallying call the abolitionists had been waiting for: Joseph Cinque, kidnapped African who had liberated himself and his men by rebellion, only to be claimed as salvage by the likes of Lieutenant Gedney.

"What does *amistad* mean?" asked Honor.

"It means 'friendship' in Spanish," replied her father. "What a name," said Henry Braithwaite in English Primer, "for an insurrection."

"When I was a child," said Joseph Cinque to James Covey, still staring up at the Summer Triangle traced on the jailhouse plaster, "I always imagined myself in dangerous situations where only my cleverness and my courage could save me. There was always an exit because there was always a method and an application, because the world of men and of spirits, even the animal world, was governed by certain rules. But here the world is round, as you say, and not flat, therefore ungraspable and without limit. Men say what they don't mean and mean what they don't say . . . they look at me like an animal—but can't conceive that they are as repulsive to me as I am to them. Have they no imagination at all? Is there no confederacy at all in the intercourse between black men and white? If not, War Road, all your translations are of no avail. If we are not to be considered human and understood as men, well, then we might as well speak in Mende—since it makes no difference."

Joseph Cinque fingered the blanket thrown over his shoulder and chest. There was one other thing he had observed these last days. Since Covey's arrival the tall brown girl with the honey-colored eyes had not been seen in the lines of spectators. Perhaps she had indeed sent War Road, or had *been* War Road all the time, in different guise. There had been something of the boy about her despite her skirts. She had been supple, lithe, straight like a palm tree. There had been an upwardness in her appearance like a young plant ready to bloom, buoyant with life. He was sad. The girl was gone. For Joseph Cinque the appearance of Covey and the disappearance of Vivian became permanently and mysteriously linked. He turned his attention back to what Covey was saying.

"Habeas Corpus means 'you may have the body,' " said James Covey slowly and carefully, for it was not long since the Africans' lawyer had explained it to him. They had petitioned the presiding judge of the future trial in Hartford to release the children Country, Bone and Black Snake as not being party to the charges of murder and piracy and therefore of being imprisoned illegally.

"It is a written order directed to some person who has detained another, commanding him to bring the body of the person in his custody at a specific time to a specific place in order to judge if he is being illegally held prisoner. The purpose of Habeas Corpus is to prevent a person from being unlawfully deprived of his freedom . . . and the Americans regard this privilege very highly."

"Habeas Corpus," repeated Joseph Cinque slowly, trying to relate it to something in his own experience of trials, but it corresponded to nothing he had ever heard of. It was like the ever-changing Paramount Chiefs, every four years Covey had told him about.

"The judge demands that the marshal bring the prisoner to court, where he gets a hearing. If the judge finds he is being unlawfully detained and deprived of his liberty, he must be released."

"You think they will release the children?"

"I should think, yes," said Covey. "After all, it is, according to Mr. Baldwin your lawyer, a fundamental right guaranteed by the Constitution of the United States, drawn up by their revolutionaries. It guarantees the right of Habeas Corpus except in cases of rebellion . . . or threat to the public safety," continued Covey.

"And are Black Snake, Country and Bone rebels?" asked Joseph Cinque.

"No."

"Do they threaten the public safety?"

James Covey laughed. "That's a grave question a lot of Americans are asking," he replied, "and Judge Thompson will have to decide. It seems," said Covey pensively, "that this is the first time in America that a writ of Habeas Corpus has been invoked for the protection of an African's freedom."

Both men fell silent. So many alarming, strange things had happened since they met. For Covey, Joseph Cinque had become a part of him; he could anticipate his questions, the way his mind worked, his fears and obsessions, his stubbornness and pockets of total ignorance on one hand, and salient brilliance of his native intelligence and deductive powers on the other. He was a clever, beautiful, hard-nosed African tyrant, quick to anger, sure of his physical and mental superiority, arrogantly stoic as befitted his role. He had been hardened but not crushed by his suffering, and he was less cynical than Covey, who had been taught the value of life by seeing so many die.

Cinque was more of a mystery than the interpreter had imagined. Despite the best efforts of the good divinity students and professors of Yale College, Joseph Cinque remained intact, Covey believed, untouched by the frenetic religiosity surrounding him. The men of New Haven saw Cinque as a convertible heathen, a new warrior for Christ. Did he not believe in one God, Gewo? Did he not believe his God was God to all men?

But Cinque saw himself as a prisoner of war. The fear of whiteness and its evil connotations had not altogether left him. He thought of himself as being in the *palihun*, the deep—neither here in the "new" world nor home in his own. The sole emotion he truly felt was deep, abiding fear, and an even deeper shame of this fear. War Road knew this, he was sure; or guessed at it. But Cinque felt helpless to control it. It was as if he were a child, and he was no child. Too often now tears of frustration welled up. Even the name of his mother rose to his lips. That he should die was one thing. That he should die despised, a criminal, a prisoner in a strange and hostile white world, was another, this world in which he could not even protect his children. They needed a . . . a Habeas Corpus for that. Cinque walked away from Covey and sat down in the farthest corner of the cell and pulled his blanket tightly around his body.

Cinque had taken to watching and studying whites as scrupulously as they did him, in their endless, odorous, noisy lines that filed by his cell each day, with their strange costumes, their strange sky eyes, their coughing and spitting and chewing.

He missed the girl. He finally asked Covey about her, as if he could somehow conjure her up, but Covey had laughed in surprise. He knew no girl like the one Sengbe Pieh described. . . . As a matter of fact, said Covey, there could not possibly exist such a wondrous creature. And there had been no magic in his own apparition here except, perhaps, the magic of Dr. Gibbs' baritone.

Slowly, it dawned on Joseph Cinque that he was prisoner in a country where nothing he had ever learned or ever done in his entire existence would help him.

On the third of September, Fa died. On the eleventh of September, Tua died. On the fourteenth of September, Welluwa died. The jailer, Pendleton, decided there would be no funeral. Even Dr. Gibbs could not convince him to change his mind.

By the end of the third week James Covey was exhausted, his voice gone, his throat raw. He sat now, dejected and silent, facing Joseph Cinque, who had also fallen silent. Each man was wrapped in his own thoughts. Covey had questioned all the men himself, translated their stories and questions to their Yale mentors and then translated the questions the white men posed. Some of the men, he had discovered, were Moslems like Python, but when he had recounted this fairly banal fact to Dr. Gibbs, he had cried out in alarm:

"We thought we had to do with heathens, not infidels!"

Joseph Cinque had turned out to be an eloquent speaker,

mesmerizing and powerful. It was this power and fervor that Covey struggled to transmit to the Yale men. He had in fact become Joseph Cinque—imitating in English his voice and manner, his repetition of certain phrases, his emphasis and turn of thoughts. Covey knew that to pose a direct question in Mende was as impolite as to answer a question directly. So the two Africans would spend hours circumventing a certain point somewhere in time and space until they arrived at the question, leaving an embellished cloth of words and silences behind them. It was hopeless to insist or become impatient. And besides, the interpreter had fallen under the Mendian warrior's spell. Had fallen, in fact, in love with him, his intransigence, his courage, his dignity, his pride, his native intelligence. It was a powerful personality which burned like a touchstone deep within him, sending out sparks that surprised and delighted and astonished Covey.

All the Braithwaites watched as the string of three bay horses, one behind the other, pulled the barge. The boatman's horn reverberated in the chilly morning air, and Vivian watched her own breath turn to vapor as the barge slid by. The horses moved slowly, tugging the barge of blanket-draped Africans. At each drawbridge and village silent crowds had gathered to watch them pass. The trial of the circuit court was tomorrow in Hartford, and when the barge stopped at Plainville, there would be wagons waiting to take the Africans the remaining fourteen miles to the Hartford jail. Although Henry Braithwaite had forbidden Vivian's trips to the New Haven jail, today this procession seemed to him a special occasion.

The boat pilot's horn sounded again, and as if in answer, a high, resonant voice, strange and eerie, glided over the water. The call came from Waterfall, and as it gained strength, some of the men began to answer him. The crowd, hitherto amused, fell silent. Now Waterfall's lament collided with the crisp New England atmosphere like tropical heat, causing the turbulence that was answered by a chorus of thunderous male voices. So extraordinary was the cadence that even the occasional murmur on the bank ceased as the crescendo of sound spilled out uninterrupted, an anguished, agonizing supplication.

For Joseph Cinque, his men's chant was a subtle challenge to his authority. He had incited them to revolt, led them astray on the sea, shipwrecked them in a land of slavery and brought them to prison and trial. His brave speech and brave actions on the *Washington* had been to no avail. Cinque struggled against a desire to dive over the side of the barge and swim until he sank or the rifle of one of the guards killed him. The men around him continued to sing while he stood, leaning his weight into one bent knee. He was angry and he was afraid, and he could show his anger and fear to no one.

People watched the flatboat move slowly. Covey with his unnatural eyesight could read the faces of the people lining the canal. Children ran between the silent adults, shouting the taunts and insults they had heard from their parents. Covey saw a tall, black-clad figure leaning on a cane throw back his head and heard the short harsh laugh, the hoot echoing. Several people near him, including a small dapper man who appeared to be a companion, turned curiously, smiling as people will when there is a joke they have not understood. The configuration on the flatboat had provoked in the painter John Trumbull an indelible and hilarious vision of his own rendering of George Washington crossing the Delaware.

"This is no performance we are watching, my friend," Trumbull said to his companion, whose first name was Washington. "It is a prayer for deliverance. Everything is there: revenge, rage, melancholy, shame, a message home. Listen. This is not the easy, comprehensible Negro spiritual of the gospels. This song comes from beyond time . . . a spiritual of archaic spirits; earth and rock and water and sky. Spirits these yet unbroken men have brought here with them not from the Old World but from a third world."

"Are you thinking what I'm thinking?" asked the other man, "that the men of the *Amistad* have frightened the pants right off these New Englanders with that war chant?"

"Well," said Trumbull, "I was thinking what a metaphysical distance separates that song from this canal bank."

Washington Irving shifted nervously. A rotund, world-weary cosmopolite whose writer's curiosity and friendship with Martin Van Buren had brought him to New Haven, he was ill at ease with the provincial philosophical musings of the painter. If anyone recognized a good story when he saw one, it was Irving. But the world-renowned chronicler of the *Legend of*

Sleepy Hollow and the Knickerbocker stories was more comfortable with the burlesque than with the melancholy scene he was witnessing. He was here to see the trial and, incidentally, report back to the President.

Farther down the canal, out of sight of either Irving or Trumbull, a tall, blond man of about thirty stood bareheaded, his hands deep in the pockets of his Redingote staring gloomily at the passing barge. Like the excellent lawyer he was, Nathan Langdon of Tidewater, Virginia, was mentally reviewing the complexities of the *Amistad* case with an intensity that was much more than legalistic.

Vivian's face was rosy in the sharp air, the brim of her riding hat and profile in chiaro against the hushed winter landscape. A small dimple flashed as she pressed her lips together against the cold wind, a loose tendril of hair thrown across the soft curve of her cheek as she reined in her brother Jacob's chestnut gelding. Her father reached over protectively. People around them were drifting away, gathering in the reins of buckboards and carriages and pointing them towards the town. Nervous ripples of conversation from those on shore carried on the air like the crackle of fall leaves underfoot, for long distances.

Only Vivian noticed that standing beside Joseph Cinque had been a tall, handsome young man in Western clothes who somehow resembled him, and who had looked neither to the right nor to the left.

T R I A L

OF

THE PRISONERS OF THE AMISTAD

ON THE

WRIT OF HABEAS CORPUS

BEFORE THE CIRCUIT COURT OF THE UNITED STATES, FOR THE DISTRICT OF CONNECTICUT, AT HARTFORD;

JUDGES THOMPSON AND JUDSON

SEPTEMBER TERM, 1839

CIRCUIT COURT OF THE UNITED STATES: DISTRICT OF CONNECTICUT

Hon. SMITH THOMPSON, Circuit Judge.

Hon. ANDREW T. JUDSON, District Judge.

ᦙ Hartford ᦙ
September 1839

Wednesday, September 18, 1839

Visitors and tourists had swarmed over the placid town of Hartford for days. Rumor had it that a mass hanging was to take place. Lines of people had formed outside the Hartford jail to file past the cell of Joseph Cinque, for the last time.

That morning Yale Divinity students, top-hatted and cloaked, led by New Haven's richest, most belligerent and fiery abolitionist, Amos Townsand, staged their theatrical escort of the prisoners across the square, from the jail to the courthouse. Townsand had deployed the captives and theologians like operatic extras, against the russet-draped backdrop of linden trees and gray-columned, red-brick Greek revival facades. They marched past a monument to the town's Revolutionary War heroes in the center of the green. The dramatic atmosphere, thought Seth Staples, one of the three lawyers for the *Amistad* captives, was perfect. And the spectacle of a U.S. armed marshal escorting three small Negro girls weeping with terror up the steps of the courthouse was worth a dozen abolitionist newspaper articles.

The presiding judge, the Honorable Smith Thompson, Associate Justice of the Supreme Court of the United States, was the last of the "old court" appointed by James Monroe, and was seventy-three or, by some counts, seventy-four years old. His origins were as mysterious as his politics, although his earlier ambitions for the presidency of the United States, and his bitter anti-slavery views, were not. He had been appointed to the court when the boiling controversy over Missouri's admission to the Union as a slave state had been at its peak, and public opinion had run high over Jackson's invasion of Spanish Florida. Moreover, a third great controversy had centered upon the Monroe Doctrine, conceived when John Quincy Adams had been Secretary of State, defining the country's relations with its neighbors in the American hemisphere and with Spain's former possessions. Behind the mild, bespectacled countenance was a man who had renounced his ambitions for the presidency in a political deal that had placed him on the Supreme Court, for which he was, according to everyone, as eminently qualified as he was unfit for political life. His enigmatic character made it impossible for men like Seth Staples to decide whether he was a man of stature whose devious traits had arrested his full development, or whether he was simply a lucky mediocrity.

It had been a long time since Hartford had seen such a panoply of powerful lawyers, all celebrities of Washington city. There was Governor William Ellsworth, the lawyer for Greene and Gedney; Ralph Ingersoll and William Hungerford, the lawyers for Ruiz and Montez, who were not present in the courtroom; Theodore Sedgwick, Seth Staples and Roger Baldwin, who sat at a table on the opposite side of the room from where they could see the faces of the six defendants huddled in the dock: six black monks, spectral and silent, in a mass of draped blankets and shawls.

Twelve rough Hartford males took their seats in the jury box, their faces grave. The grand jurymen were all between twenty-five and fifty, several dressed in dark frock coats, but others, farmers, in sturdy homespun wool. All had managed a cravat or a tie and white shirt for the occasion. In the courtroom sat their wives, as well as the wives of the lawyers and judges.

It was now up to Baldwin, Sedgwick and Staples to convince a hostile judge and a grand jury that there were no grounds for Cinque's indictment for murder and piracy.

At the defense table Seth Staples ran his hands through his hair, then began to chew on his glasses nervously as he spoke to Baldwin and Sedgwick; Amos Townsand and James Covey stood nearby.

"The problem is not only the Habeas Corpus," Staples said. "I can't believe we have five libels on our hands, but it's true.

"Lieutenant Gedney, the commander of the brig *Washington*, has filed a libel in the district court for the schooner, the cargo and the Negroes as salvage. Secondly, the captains Green and Fordham, alleging *they* had captured the Negroes and held them on shore until the *Washington* made its capture, have presented a second libel. Thirdly, Ruiz and Montez have filed claims to the Negroes as their slaves, and the cargo. Then some Cuban merchants called Tellineas and Aspe claim certain merchandise which was on board the *Amistad*. And, fifthly, the Minister of Spain has claimed the slaves and cargo under the treaty between the United States and Spain."

"This isn't a trial about men, by God, it's a trial about greed," said Townsand bitterly.

Baldwin rose and filed his answer to the libel of Lieutenant Gedney for salvage, that Ruiz and Montez claimed the Negroes as slaves, and also to the intervention of the United States on behalf of the Minister of Spain.

"The respondents," said Baldwin, "being treated on board ouid vcssel by said Ruiz and Montez and their confederates with great cruelty and oppression, and being of right free as aforesaid, were incited by the love of liberty natural to all men, and by the desire of returning to their families and kindred, to take possession of said vessel while navigating the high seas as they had a *right to do*, with the intent to return there into their native country, or to seek an asylum in some free state, where slavery did not exist, in order that they might enjoy their liberty under the protection of its government."

The lawyers focused on the two most notorious observers in the courtroom: the most famous artist in America, John Trumbull, and the most famous writer in America, Washington Irving. They sat, shoulder to shoulder, as if balancing one another on an invisible scale of justice. Everyone knew John Trumbull's anti-slavery, pro-abolitionist views, but the presence of Washington Irving was more intriguing. Known as a friend of the President, it was as if Van Buren himself was in the room; and Irving's passion for Spain and the amount of time he had spent there made his sympathies evident. And, if Trumbull was used to painting the rich, famous and titled, Irving was used to associating with them. The fifty-two-year-old New Yorker had become an overnight success twenty years ago with his *Sketchbook* and his immortal character, Rip Van Winkle. Now his plaster bust sold by the thousands and was as much an icon for the living rooms of the American middle class as the busts of Socrates, Beethoven and Benjamin Franklin. Irving had deliberately sat on John Trumbull's blind side so that the artist could not read the notes he was taking. As a result, Trumbull had a crick in his neck from trying to spy on Irving's notebook with his good eye. Trumbull's efforts underlined the differences between the two men: tall, aged, severe Trumbull, a participant in the revolution of the idealized republic, and the short, blond Irving, the satirist of what the republic had become.

"Ah, I'd like you to meet a friend of mine," said Washington Irving. "Mr. Nathan Langdon, one of the brightest legal minds in Washington."

"Colonel Trumbull and I have met."

"Well, Mr. Langdon, it's been six years. Very nice to see you again." But Trumbull didn't look overjoyed to see the pale, handsome specter from the past—his past. Yet once his discomfort had passed, he realized he was glad to see Langdon, glad to have this reminder of life's terrible contradictions that could humble the proudest of men, as it had Joseph Cinque. It was only fitting that the Virginian should be witness at this particular trial. Trumbull glanced at Washington Irving, wondering if he should tell him a love story worthy of a novel. . . .

"Is she still alive?" he asked abruptly, turning back around to focus his good eye on Langdon like a beacon.

"No, sir."

Trumbull turned back to the trial, ignoring Irving's inquiring, quizzical glance, while in his mind's eye composing "The Trial of Joseph Cinque" in his usual pedantic, historical-tableaux style, after the manner of his *Resignation of Washington,* now hanging in the Rotunda of the new Capitol. He took Irving's whispered comments about the chances of Joseph Cinque with a grain of salt. Irving might have once served as secretary to the Legation in London, thought Trumbull, but he carried seventy years of American history around in his one eye. If anyone was the definitive observer here, it was the painter of the heroic, not the burlesquer of the common man.

Judge Thompson stared across the high mahogany bench into the cluster of black faces below him. It was as if his courtroom had been invaded by another world. This was certainly no ordinary trial, as he had told his wife, who was young enough to be his granddaughter, that very morning. He would be confronted with momentous issues—property versus men, the law of nations versus natural law, North versus South, slavery versus abolition, rebellion versus liberation. Despite his former ambitions, the judge would not have wanted to be in the President's shoes at the moment.

Everyone stood as the court was gavelled to order. The most dramatic trial of the decade had begun.

The first problem was the separate writ of Habeas Corpus for the three girls. The strategy decided upon during innumerable discussions between the lawyers, Townsand and the Tappans would force the prosecution either to dismiss the children or bring criminal charges against them. And if he could prove that there was no legal basis for holding the girls, he could expand the argument to all the captives. The writ was the test of the Africans' right to a personality. It would establish the captives as human beings, and not chattel property. And no one would dare claim salvage on human beings, or so Townsand believed. Seth Staples looked up at Judge Thompson.

"On the affidavit of Thompson Sedgwick, Junior, Esquire," he began, "I move for a writ of Habeas Corpus, directing the marshal to bring before the court three African girls—names Teme, alias Juana; Kagne, alias Josepha; Margru, alias Francisca—now confined in the jail, in the city of Hartford, and to show cause, if any there be, why they should not be released."

"These individuals are persons claimed by two Spanish gentlemen as their slaves," Hungerford argued. "In addition, there is a libel pending before the district court, on these persons as part of the cargo of the *Amistad*, in behalf of Lieutenant Gedney, for salvage."

"I would suggest that all these matters will come up on the Habeas Corpus," said Judge Thompson. "The affidavit states that these persons are imprisoned without any cause. If any reason is shown why they should not be discharged, the court will not discharge them."

The marshal brought Margru, Teme, and Kagne into court, all of them weeping and clinging determinedly to the hand of the jailer, Mr. Pendleton.

A wave of sympathy went through the courtroom. Staples intended to use this righteous indignation to remove the girls from the trial. He began as if he were summing up instead of opening his argument:

"We are placed before this Honorable Court in a singular

position. Here are certain parties concerned in vindicating the right of property in third persons; and they wish to take these persons and confine them till this litigation is closed. Here are the unfounded claims of the Spanish owners, and others claiming liens on their property, equally unfounded. And under all these cases the rights of these persons are left entirely out of the question; and they are left to be incarcerated in prison, till these litigants settle their rights. In this situation these children come and ask the interference of this court, so far as their personal, their civil rights are concerned.

". . . . Go on with your litigation as to the *Amistad* and her cargo to your hearts' content, but take not these children and deprive them of the Habeas Corpus under pretext of a question of whether they are brutes and property or human beings.

"The question here is, Who are these children? Whence came they? On this subject we have an African, the interpreter James Covey, who has been with these children and examined them; and he says they are native Africans. He gives their ages, and the reason for his believing them to be native Africans: their language is a dialect of Mendingo. They have no knowledge of the Spanish language. This, at their tender age, is decisive— it is the best evidence we could have.

"If these children were born in Africa, they are not old enough to have been brought into the island of Cuba before the law abolishing the slave trade. If the African question is settled, they must have been brought to Cuba since the treaty of 1827.

"Now, as to the claim of the district attorney:

"One, he acts here in some manner in *aid* of the movements of the Minister of Spain. How, we know not.

"Two, he acts for the Executive of the United States, on the supposition that these Africans may, in some respect, fall into his hands. On that subject the law is perfectly clear. If these slaves were not brought in here by American citizens, or in American vessels, the President of the United States has nothing to do with them.

"But what are the presumptions? That every person who is not proved to be a slave is free—everywhere, except in certain quarters, where they find it convenient to presume that every man of a certain color is a slave."

This conclusion, thought Trumbull, as Irving took notes furiously, would not please Irving's good friend, the President, at all. Irving had been scribbling both words and images and now noticed Trumbull's good eye glaring at him. Smiling diplomatically, Irving said:

"Staples is good, but the Amistaders don't have a chance. Spain is entirely within its rights. He'll never get a Habeas Corpus from Thompson no matter *what* he says."

Staples decided now was the moment to introduce his first witness, Bau. Bringing in the testimony of one of the accused would have little effect at his summing up.

Broke rose and came forward trembling and wide-eyed. He stood quietly while Covey explained to him that the story Bau had told him of the origins of the little girls was now to be presented as evidence in the form that Covey had written down and that Bau had signed with his mark. Broke was sworn in on the Bible and asked to recognize his mark:

"I, Bau, of Bandaboo, in Africa, being duly cautioned, depose and say that I knew Margru and Kagne, two little girls, now in prison at Hartford; they were born in the same place I was, which was Bandaboo, and further saith not."

"Do you recognize your mark?" asked Staples.

"I recognize my mark," answered Broke.

Covey's precise English trailed the lilting Mende of Broke like a fisherman's net.

Broke returned to his seat. Covey saw Joseph Cinque stir nervously, but he signalled that all was well.

Both Trumbull and Irving studied the sad, heavy bulk of Broke with something akin to pity. For Irving, Broke aroused the kind of horrified compassion one would feel for a great beached black whale.

"The testimony," said Irving, "of a defendant cannot carry much weight, although the captive certainly does. . . ."

But Trumbull was thinking of how Cinque and his men seemed to cast a long, oversized shadow on the proceedings, weightier than even the black-robed Thompson. In some ways it seemed as if Cinque and his men were the judges instead of the other way around.

Staples, hoping to give the impression that Broke's testimony was definitive as far as the three girls were concerned, suddenly shifted the whole argument on to the question of jurisdiction.

"I ask," demanded Staples, "what right has the District Attorney of the United States to file a libel in the District Court of the State of Connecticut, and cause to be apprehended as slaves, or to be held subject to further proceedings, these persons, simply because the Spanish minister has thought proper to make the demand for their restoration? And why in Connecticut where slavery is nominally legal, rather than New York where it is illegal and where the *Amistad* actually landed? Moreover, what treaty imposes an obligation on our government to be slave catchers for Her Majesty's subjects? The laws of Spain forbid the traffic—the laws of Portugal forbid it—the laws of the United States declare it piracy."

Judge Thompson was becoming progressively unhappy. The proceedings were going awry. Instead of a narrow argument on the liberty of the three Negresses, the issues had degenerated into a morass of generalities that could only lead to uncomfortable political questions, rather than questions of strict legality. Could he really allow that? Where was Staples trying to lead the trial? Thompson took one last look at the dark, indecipherable and indistinguishable faces and dismissed the court.

As Irving rose he studied the sad faces of the men so far from home. He understood homesickness. Despite his tour of the American prairies and his new upstate New York house, Sunnyside, he was homesick for Europe. Turning to Trumbull, he invited him to lunch. It would be much more amusing to discuss the case with him, who knew the ins and outs of politics, than it would be to give his opinion to the journalists and reporters waiting outside in the square. The two men left by the prisoners' exit.

John Trumbull was a little awed by Irving. The eighty-four-year-old painter had often pondered that state of grace called genius that had eluded him all his life, yet kept him always on the threshold of other men's greatness. He had painted great men, from Washington and John Adams to Jefferson and Lafayette, yet he understood greatness no better than if he had painted horses and dogs all his life. And Irving was certainly a genius, the recognized master of the essay of manners and stylist of humor, which were communicated with a facility of expression, the precise nature of which, like all great technique, remained part of genius' mystery.

"Well, what do you think?" he asked.

"About Cinque as a subject for an essay? Or about the trial?"

"Well, I was thinking that Nat Turner was captured less than fourteen miles from home, whereas Cinque is approximately six thousand."

"You thought of the trial of Turner as well . . ."

"Of course. How could one not?"

"That was eight years ago, and Turner was a Virginia slave . . . and his pitiable revolt failed. . . . And Cinque, too, is doomed, having wandered onto that stage of American history that allows no other issue for blacks. It is not even cruelty, it is simply the way this country is running. The entire nation is in a state of political agitation over the approaching elections. Inflammatory harangues engulf the country, spoken by the likes of Henry Clay and Daniel Webster, before groups of six or seven thousand people! The Cinque controversy is being discussed not in the Halls of Justice, or by members of Congress, but by mobs of ordinary people. And what can't an orator like Webster do with charges that Spain, a foreign nation, is influencing the judiciary over something as decisive as slavery, which is so overwhelming it may just open up and swallow the bloody Union. The Africans are black, and therefore, if not slaves, potential slaves, if they are not under the protection of the white man."

"The white man!" said Trumbull, "You sound like—"

"Trumbull," interrupted Irving, absently scribbling on the tablecloth, "I like Cinque, I feel for him, as I do for the native Americans. But I side with Spain and international law."

"You are not translating the half of what the lawyers say!" Cinque was furious. "When shall we be allowed to speak?"

"I'm not translating their mumbo-jumbo legalities because I don't understand them myself. They have nothing to do with us. So far, it's simply sparring for position."

"The judge has been bribed. I feel it."

"Perhaps," said Covey. "I would not vouch for anyone involved in this trial."

"But it is a *trial*. We are to swear on medicine. How can you not vouch for it?"

Covey looked at Cinque strangely. Cinque really believed

in justice. "I'd vouch for the jury," he said. "Northerners, fishermen, farmers . . ."

Cinque began pacing up and down. "I want, I need to be
able to speak, to defend myself and my men. I shall not be
treated like a child."

"Nobody's treating you like a child," said Covey unconvinc-
ingly.

"*You* are, my friend."

"I'll translate every single word *I* understand, Okay?" said
Covey, using the phrase Van Buren had made famous by signing his documents *Ordered by Knickerbocker,* "O.K."

"Translate everything," said Baldwin to Covey as the lawyers entered the guardhouse where Cinque's men were being
given their supper. "You have every right to know what's being
said," he said, addressing Cinque. The face of the African was
a study in rage. It hovered like a cloud, an odor in the room.
For the first time Cinque appeared to the white men as para-
doxical, difficult and complex, even menacing. He had been
giving orders to Covey; he had been acting, thought Staples,
as though *he* were conducting this trial. Storm clouds were
gathering, thought the two lawyers, and not only on the bench.

That afternoon Judge Thompson addressed the jury, and to
the surprise of the entire courtroom, reversed his original stance.

"According to my judgment upon the merits of the case, the
offense was committed on board a Spanish vessel, with a Spanish crew and commander, and Spanish papers, as a mere coast-
ing vessel, off the island of Cuba," he began. "The question
arises whether this court has jurisdiction of an offense committed on board a Spanish vessel of that character. It must be either
an offense against the laws of the United States or the law of
nations. . . .

". . . The courts of the United States have jurisdiction of
offenses committed against the law of nations. But, in reference to that, though there is nothing stated in the facts, even
admitting that this vessel was a slaver, the courts of the United
States have decided over and over again that the slave trade is
not a trade against the law of nations. They have endeavored
to get it so arranged as to consider it piracy to be concerned in
this trade; but this has not yet become so universal to be con-

sidered as the law of nations. I have no hesitation in telling you that, under the state of facts presented, this court has no jurisdiction; and that there is not enough by which you can find an indictment. . . ."

There was a wave of excited murmuring. The first victory belonged to the Africans. Joseph Cinque and his men would not stand trial for murder and piracy. There would be no hangings in Hartford.

Judge Thompson had avoided ruling on the Habeas Corpus. But Seth Staples knew this was only the preliminary to the real battle.

"At least," said Trumbull to Irving, "the United States of America won't kill them."

The next day the prosecution attacked.

"The question here," said William Hungerford, "is if these persons are to be considered as property. Whether it be morally wrong has nothing to do with the case. If these persons or this property have been brought into New London and landed, it must be libelled there, for it cannot be taken anywhere else."

Ralph Ingersoll, Ruiz's and Montez's lawyer, afraid that the interest of his clients were being forgotten in abstract and political questions, interrupted:

"We are not now talking about *whether* these persons were property or not. The court has decided that under these libels, the question as to property *may* be made. The case stands, then, as if it had been decided that the Africans *were* property. . . . These persons are libelled in the district court as the property of Spanish subjects. . . . They are also libelled on the part of the United States, and, by existing treaties, it is the duty of the American government to restore them to their owners!"

The trial had now entered Baldwin's territory. He jumped to his feet, interrupting Ingersoll:

"May it please the court . . . if the district court has issued a warrant against these persons as *property*, the marshal has no right to seize them . . . the warrant of the district court is only directed against the *cargo* of the vessel; yet under this warrant the marshal has seized persons. . . .

"No, before the district judge can issue a warrant to take

these individuals as part of the *cargo* of the *Amistad,* it is incumbent on him to find judicially that they are in the condition of property. . . .

"Now, I claim that, by none of the acts that have taken place since the Habeas Corpus was issued, can these persons be held in custody. They were within the limits of the state of Connecticut, a *free* state. . . . The Admiralty has no power to arrest human beings as property, within the limits of the state of Connecticut. . . . I ask on what pretense this Don Pedro Montez can come into this court and ask us to reduce these persons to slavery? They have been brought here in violation of the laws of Spain and the laws of nature, by an act which, by the laws of this country, is considered as piracy.

"There is a provision in the law of the United States that, when any persons shall be brought into the United States in an American vessel, as slaves, the President of the United States shall be at liberty to send them to Africa. . . . But these powers are confined to those cases where the *slaves* are brought in in American vessels, but this is entirely inappropriate to this case.

"They cannot be held as property, for they are *not slaves,* and for the United States to interfere and reduce them to the condition of property would be a violation of good faith with Great Britain. . . .

"Our government knows very well that Great Britain paid Spain two million dollars to induce them to give up this traffic; and the United States has agreed to cooperate with Great Britain in putting an end to it; and yet we are called upon by an officer of the United States to become auxiliary to persons engaged in this foul traffic. I say Great Britain would have good ground to complain of us."

Covey struggled to interpret the complicated concepts and legalistic language to Cinque and the men who sat silent and brooding, radiating defiance, malediction and passive resistance. They all looked in the direction of Ingersoll as he rose, realizing he was the speaker for their enemies, Ruiz and Montez.

"Again we are being told that these persons cannot be considered as property, because this is a free country," said Ingersoll. "But we are a peculiar kind of government. In a part of these states, slaves are recognized as property. It is idle for the gentleman to stand here and say they are *persons* and therefore not *property*. The very case cited shows that there may be slave property belonging to foreigners as well as citizens of the slave states. . . ."

Ingersoll was about to continue when William Holabird, District Attorney for the United States, who had been absent all morning, reentered the courtroom with his greatcoat still on. He passed a note to the standing but silent Ingersoll, who flushed deeply. Holabird undid his scarf and, still in his overcoat, began to speak.

"Your Honor, I, uh, wish to present some views that have occurred to me since yesterday," Holabird said. "I stand here to contend that *these blacks are free men*, brought within the jurisdiction of the United States by force"—Holabird's voice was higher than usual with embarrassment—"and, if found to be, as I suppose, native Africans . . . may be sent to their native land. . . ."

The surprised courtroom broke into applause and cheers, and Judge Thompson was forced to gavel for order. At least one man was not surprised: John Trumbull's good eye found the expression on Washington Irving's face anything but astonished; instead it held a self-satisfied smirk.

The commotion continued in the courtroom. "Fantastic," murmured Baldwin. "The United States attorney has completely reversed himself. *Paul Revere* must have ridden all night for Van Buren's about-face to have arrived so quickly."

"What now, what now?" said Staples. "The President is planning to turn the Africans over to the Spanish minister as murderers, that is, as *persons*." He rose angrily. Holabird had received instructions directly from the White House! It was written all over his face! Realizing that Judge Thompson would lean towards the defense argument, the President had decided the safest course was to rid the country of Cinque!

"The argument of the district attorney," Staples said hotly, "reminds me of the saying, 'Save me from my friends, and I will take care of my enemies.' In claiming the prisoners on behalf of the United States as free persons, I can hardly believe the district attorney to be serious. . . . I only wish to know if the district court has jurisdiction of the vessel and cargo. If not, all pretense that the district court has jurisdiction falls to the ground. . . . If the principal libel fails, the incidental ones fall also. If Gedney's libel doesn't stand for want of juris-

diction, nothing can be done here. In that case, the Court of
Admiralty here is powerless.

"The defense rests its case."

Seth Staples and Henry Baldwin listened stoically to the
summing up of the United States case and to Ingersoll's plea
for his clients. They were unable to read any expression on
Judge Thompson's face. Cinque and his men listened impassively, some drawing their blankets closer around them. Finally, the courtroom heard the words:

"The United States rests its case."

Judge Thompson rose to his six-foot height and adjourned
the hearings until the next Monday.

Monday, September 23

The grand jury, the six lawyers and the courtroom rose as
Judge Thompson entered, his robes flapping about his tall, lean
body.

"The case has not been placed before the court on the abstract right of holding human beings in bondage, or on the
general question of slavery," he began. "The court is not called
upon here to determine this abstract question. It is sufficient
to say that the Constitution of the United States—although the
term 'slavery' is not used—that the laws of the United States
do recognize the right of one man to have the control of the
labor of another man. The laws of this country are founded
upon this principle. They recognize this kind of right. Whatever private motives the court may have, or whatever may be
their feelings on this subject, they are not to be brought into
view in deciding upon this question. They must give the same
construction to the laws of the land, sitting in this state, as they
would were they sitting in Virginia.

"The Constitution also provides for the recovery of persons
that may escape from one state into another where service is
due. It goes even beyond this, and interdicts the states from
passing laws that oppose claimants from taking fugitive persons in the free states. Should any state pass such laws, they
would be absolutely void. We must look at things as they are.
*The court feels bound, therefore, to say that there is no ground
upon which they can entertain the motion under the writ of
Habeas Corpus.*

"As we perceive there are note takers present, we hope they

will be careful to make a true representation of the decision. The court does not undertake to decide that these persons have no right to their freedom, but leave that matter to the district court, subject to appeal."

Judge Thompson had glared at Washington Irving when he had mentioned "note takers." Then, without showing any reaction to the groan that rose from the audience, he hammered the trial to an end.

"The Court is then adjourned sine die."

As Judge Thompson left by the side door, District Court Judge Andrew T. Judson entered. The two judges passed each other like ships, their black robes billowing out saillike, not exchanging one word. With no interruption or further ceremony, the district court was opened in the same room. The audience rose: "The District Court of Connecticut is now open," intoned the short, mild-mannered, bespectacled Judson. He then directed the district attorney, Sedgwick, Baldwin and Staples to return to Montauk Point to determine where Gedney had seized the *Amistad*. He adjourned the hearing until the third Tuesday in November, to meet again in Hartford. He offered to release the captives on bail, but Baldwin objected. Bail would tacitly admit Joseph Cinque and his men were persons libeled for murder. Cinque would remain in the New Haven jail.

All through the days of the trial, Joseph Cinque and his men had sat impassively while their fate was argued. And, even now, they were being ignored. Cinque understood immediately that his men were still not free.

Covey's head was bursting with pain. He felt as if a sledgehammer were striking at his chest. The long endless days of translating, cajoling, editing and writing the affidavits of the men had drained him of all energy. His face was an ashy gray and his eyes red and swollen almost shut. For weeks he had had a persistent cough, and now a pain seized him that almost brought him to his knees. With his last strength he explained the worst to the men, who received the news without emotion, as if they had never expected a different verdict. Their stoicism made James Covey even more miserable. They had won a small victory, men over property, but they may have simply postponed the inevitable.

Outside, reporters and journalists milled about excitedly, talking to themselves or each other.

Covey stepped out of the dimness of the court, his mind in a turmoil. Lewis Tappan came to stand beside him.

"Well, James, I have long thought that the heart of this nation would never be effectively touched except through the power of sympathy—be it for the martyred abolitionist or the murdered slave—but I never anticipated such mysterious Providence as this," he said, his gesture taking in the excited, gesticulating crowds and the newspaper reporters who had come from every city and were now rushing off with their notebooks and sketches in hand. "Such mysterious Providence," he repeated to no one in particular, for James Covey had already started down the steps.

The weather had remained the warmest of Indian summer temperatures. Vivian Braithwaite and her father had shed their outer garments, as had everyone milling around the steps outside the courthouse. There was unexpected, riotous color everywhere, as bright and as fierce, it seemed to Covey, as the tropics. The trees held African colors, orange and magenta, blood red, burnt sienna, tawny yellow and the russet brown of the earth of Sierra Leone. Walking down the courthouse stairs, Covey took a deep breath to ease the pain in his chest, then stopped short. His pilot eyes had caught sight of Vivian Braithwaite. The crowd melted away in a haze of light, leaving only the girl in his line of vision. She had removed her hat and veil to let the sun touch the mass of luminous light brown hair, twisted so high on her head it might have been a silk turban. Her head turned slowly to one side while her eyes narrowed against the bright daylight outside the dim courtroom.

Two wisps escaped from that great wavy mass long enough to sweep the floor, so thick, strong and abundant that merely to envision it brought a heaviness to Covey's chest. Vivian carried its weight as a woman would a light basket, on the strong cylinder of a perfect neck. The curls on either side framed her face, which was oval, its shape delineated by wide-set light hazel eyes under long lashes and heavy straight eyebrows. Her eyes darted back and forth, weighing the boisterous crowd, intense, questioning, yet with just a hint of fear.

Covey's strange gift of vision focused on the most minute details spellbound. Vivian's simple dress under the flung-back coat was violet. Her whole allure shimmering under the dappled light filtering through the tall trees elicited a radiance all its own. At that precise moment she lifted her arm to open her parasol, and the slender wrist and tapering fingers shot up in a magical gesture. She stood, holding her parasol as one did in Africa, the arm free of its cape, the violet sleeve slashing through the dazzling colors aerating around it. A rain of yellow and orange rays streamed over the girl's face and arm and dress like marquetry. The face gleamed like the polished brass of the *Buzzard,* its contours lost in the shadowed spaces between the glints of mottled light. Covey felt an unreasoning jealousy. At the same time he yearned for the moment that had just passed, for he would never again recapture the first surprised emotion which had begun with the delicate caress of light and ended in a sudden storm of passion, its unexpectedness working its way into his heart, awaking a sense of wholeness filled with God-only-knew what hopes and fears. The girl seemed to send him a sidelong glance. And in the perfect serenity of that glance, Covey felt the uncanny conviction that his own fear had been vanquished. That one look seemed to him the perfect assurance that the trial would end in victory, if for her sake alone. Her aura of invulnerable innocence and self-possession gave her the right to expect justice. He had no need to know her name; he knew it already. She was his luck come home, his living amulet. His guardian angel. The courthouse steps had become his home simply because she was standing on them. Covey's whole life suddenly spread out before him like the ocean, tomorrow and the day after and the day after that, and all the years to come.

❧ New York ❧
November 1839

Lewis Tappan was not satisfied as he sat amongst the captives in the Hartford jailhouse. He had received word that a new minister from Spain had arrived and was putting so much pressure on the President that their friends in Washington, including John Quincy Adams, were afraid Van Buren would give in to the demands of the Queen of Spain. They had to find a way to neutralize the new envoy quickly or the case might simply be dropped and the *Amistad* captives surrendered to the Spanish and certain death. "James," said Tappan to Covey, "ask Cinque and Big Sun if they would like to see Ruiz and Montez in prison just as they are."

Tappan was thoughtfully fingering an envelope with a large red seal. He rose as if deciding something, and conferred in the corner with Covey.

"This," said Covey, showing the paper to Cinque, "is called an affidavit. The gentlemen who defend you, Mr. Sedgwick and Mr. Staples, have prepared this for you to sign. It accuses Ruiz and Montez, in the district of New York, of kidnapping, assault and battery, violations of your rights and illegal imprisonment. If you and Big Sun make your mark here," continued Covey, "they promise that the Spaniards will be arrested and sent to prison just like you."

Big Sun looked at Covey in amazement. That small fragile white leaf could say and do all that? He seized the paper in one hand and the quill Covey held out to him with the other. He signed "Fuliwa" as best he could.

"Ruiz and Montez," said Tappan, "are going to have a sorry surprise."

"I want Ruiz and Montez dead," said Joseph Cinque without emotion. "They killed Big Man, they killed War Sparrow, they killed Water Place. Fa, Tua and Welluwa have died in this place because of them."

"With this suit," said Tappan, "we will shift the proceedings from Connecticut, where slavery is legal, to New York, where it is not. We are also suing them for three thousand dollars in damages."

"That is less than what we are worth," snorted Cinque after Covey had translated the lawyer's words.

On October 17 a New York deputy sheriff, John Keen, accompanied by Lewis Tappan, knocked on the door of the rooms Ruiz and Montez had taken at the Spanish Hotel on Fulton Street. They were armed with an affidavit, and a warrant for the arrest of the two Cubans. The sheriff was a tall, powerfully built Scot with piercing, lambent blue eyes, a booming voice and carrot-colored hair.

"You are under arrest," said Keen, "on charges brought against you by Mr. Cinque, Mr. Python and Mr. Big Sun for kidnapping, false imprisonment, assault and battery."

"What!" screamed José Ruiz, turning the same color as Keen's hair. The two Spaniards leaped to their feet, imploring the Mother of God and their Sovereign. Sheriff Keen was a Protestant and a republican, and neither the evocation of the Virgin Mary nor the Queen of Spain had the least effect upon him.

"Your bail is one thousand dollars, set by Judge Inglis of the New York Court of Common Pleas. You can arrange it now, gentlemen, or I escort you to jail."

"I'll burn in hell before I'll pay a cent of bail," screamed Ruiz. But Montez shook his head in mute disbelief. What was the world coming to when Negroes could send white men to jail? He felt lost, old and vulnerable as he looked up into the cool eyes of the robust young sheriff. But he detected neither connivance, equivocation, nor sympathy.

"My clients will go to jail," said John Purroy, their lawyer. "They will enlist behind bars at least as much sympathy as your Negroes. Their voices will be heard ten times as far from 'The 'Tombs,' as you call it."

Sheriff Keen smiled. The new state prison, an ornate, Egyp-

tian-inspired building on Centre Street, had been renamed The
Tombs by its occupants.

Benjamin F. Butler, the District Attorney for the City of New
York, was astounded but impressed. If there was a way to
maintain public interest in the fascinating case of the Africans
and put the President of the United States in hot water, the
arrest of the two Cubans was it. He had not been surprised to
receive a message from the President and the Secretary of State
to assure the immediate release of said Cubans. Butler, a corpulent, high-living, ambitious man who would one day run for
the presidency, leaned back in his chair. He was a Van Buren
man and he intended to do exactly as he was told. He would
advise Ruiz to post bail and free himself, but not escape.

Later in the day he visited the Spaniards in jail. Their excit-
able lawyer, Purroy, was present.

"Nearly forty other blacks can bring suit against my client!"
screamed Purroy.

"One more already has," said Butler dryly. "A certain Pungwuni, or if you like, Mr. Duck as it is translated, has brought
similar charges before the New York Circuit Court."

"Does this mean," said Ruiz, "that if a master from the South
claims his slave in New York, the slave can procure an affidavit
asserting his freedom as a kidnapped man and claim damages?
And the master can either put up bail or go to prison and await
the verdict of a prejudiced, fanatical Northern jury?"

"The only recourse is to go ahead with the trial," said Butler. "A jury will acquit you, and if it doesn't, I have orders
from the Secretary of State to appeal even to the Supreme Court!
Good God, man, we are *all* on your side, but there are appearances to be kept!"

"The devil take your appearances. The 'appearance' is that
a white man has been clamped into jail by your government at
the demand of a black savage who can't even read his own
affidavit! It is the duty of the American government to secure
my release. It is a national—nay, an international—matter. Remember Pinckney's Treaty of 1795," Ruiz shouted.

Butler said nothing. If Ruiz chose to stay in jail, at least that
would deprive the abolitionists of their accusations of collusion between the President and the Spaniards. Forsyth had told
him that the President's hands were tied, that Butler could not

release Montez and Ruiz without causing a public outcry amongst Americans sympathetic to the captives and hurting his chances for reelection.

"If the *Amistad*'s mutineers had been white," said Purroy, "the United States would have observed our treaty and ascertained the facts of the murders for a Spanish court. I don't understand the privileges enjoyed by Negroes in this country! Since when does a black have civil rights? The blacks have admitted to their state of slavery by confessing they have been sold! I demand a writ of Habeas Corpus!"

Martin Van Buren, the first President to have been born an American citizen, was, outwardly, the only calm man in the room. Silently he gazed out of the window of his office on to the rolling cow pasture beyond Pennsylvania Avenue. It was true, he thought, that he had had his fill of fugitive Negroes. For five years he had waged a long, expensive war against the Seminole Indians for refusing to give up escaped slaves that had taken refuge with them in Florida. And now, in an election year, he had to deal with mutineers, insurrectionists, and colored men claiming to be Africans and free. He had already consulted Attorney General Felix Grundy, a slave holder from Tennessee, who had assured him that legally he could turn over Cinque and his men to the Spanish.

The sixty-two-year-old eighth President of the United States, who had already been blamed for the panic of 1837 and the hard times that followed, decided to allow himself to speak with the voice of his Southern cabinet, which in any case he could not desert, and by which he had reached the White House. That is, if the Chevalier Argaiz would allow him to say a word. The new Spanish ambassador was arrogant, overbearing, and had an inflammable temper and a royalist's scorn for judicial procedure.

"It is lunatic," fumed Argaiz. "The whole farcical situation of blacks suing whites!"

"Do the abolitionists intend to make blacks the masters?" asked Secretary of State Forsyth perfidiously.

The President continued to look out his office window, down the half-macadamed Pennsylvania Avenue towards the Capitol Building. The lower part of the avenue was a rutted dirt road that ran into the cow pasture. After eight presidents, he thought,

the White House still overlooked somebody's damned plantation and the President's house had become that place where
perfectly sane, healthy, successful rich men incarcerated themselves for four and hopefully eight years, disrupting their families and their fortunes at the call of the People, only to be
insulted, reviled and, if not careful, assassinated, and not only
figuratively speaking. Washington was still a Southern frontier
town, duelling was tolerated, and the slave block was only five
hundred yards away. Van Buren was worried about public
opinion. Accusations of his interference in the *Amistad* case
were running rampant in the press. Charges of collusion between the United States government and Spain, between Spain
and the State Department, and even of mistranslating and
tampering with official documents as evidence, were falling
about his ears, and he did not like it. Judge Thompson's decision had astonished Van Buren. He had a long and distinguished record not only of tolerating but encouraging the
pro-slavery interests. Moreover, as Vice President it was he
who had cast the deciding vote to break an eighteen-to-eight-
een tie in the Senate supporting the bill to censure the press
for all discussion of slavery in the Southern states. It had won
him, a New Yorker, sixty-three electoral votes from the South,
and had put him in the White House. The three million slaves
in the South represented sixteen and a quarter billion dollars
in capital. He was not going to tolerate anything that would
disturb that sixteen billion dollars, even if he had to use the
presidential office to do it.

"John Quincy Adams is making another ruckus down at the
House again, trying to present petitions," said Forsyth.

"He is, I believe, the most extraordinary man alive," said
Van Buren. "I have seen with my own eyes slave holders literally quake and tremble in every nerve and joint when Adams
harangued them for their political and moral sins. His power
of speech exceeds all conception of what I had always believed to be the power of words."

"As a debater, apart from Webster, he has no superiors. Certainly there is no one else in the House to compare with him.
He is literally a walking encyclopedia, ferocious in invective,
matchless at repartee, and insensible to fear."

"Can't anyone shut up that old man?" said the President
petulantly. John Quincy Adams, Van Buren thought with envy,

owed his place to no official party. He was therefore absolutely free, probably the freest man in Washington, and as one absolutely free, could do what he damned pleased.

"They just hunt me like a partridge upon the mountains," said Quincy Adams. And it had just made him more stubborn, thought Louisa.

"But no one else will undertake it!" John Quincy said bitterly to his wife, the one person who was always there to listen to him. "They count their slaves as three fifths of a man in order to pack the House with one hundred bogus Southern representatives, who would crucify me if their vote could erect a cross! Another forty members who are in league with slavery would break my legs on the wheel if *their* votes could turn it, and the other hundred and twenty are so lukewarm they would desert me at the hammer of the first nail in the palm of my hand!"

Louisa finished copying the last petition of the day. Her palms were black with ink, as black, she thought, as Prince Cinque. Exasperation and pride mingled as she listened to her husband. Oh, God, she prayed, don't let them kill him. And don't let them expel him from the House.

When they had returned to Washington, and public life, John Quincy had made himself a stalking horse and a sacrificial target for that gang of duellists, nullifiers and man-merchants, putting his own career and that of Charles in danger. She hated being surrounded by slaves. In Washington Louisa herself used hired-out slaves occasionally. The buying, selling, transporting, hiring and imprisoning of black men and women thrived in the capital. Lines of chained men passed down Pennsylvania Avenue on their way to Alexandria. Newspaper advertisements offered twenty-five dollars for a slave captured in Washington, Virginia, or Maryland. A white worker who captured a slave in Pennsylvania could earn his yearly salary.

Because John Quincy had refused to be stopped by the Gag Rule, they were awash in petitions, over half a million of them at last count.

The universal opposition to John Quincy's efforts *had* a reason, Louisa thought. Even John Quincy admitted that if Washington City became a free island in the hostile white ocean of Virginia and Maryland, it would become the center of black insurrection against all the surrounding states.

At first it had been only the abolition of slavery and the slave trade in Washington, but now it had become a question of Constitutional freedom of speech, and Americans were beginning to petition for themselves. And so, like a madman, every petition that came into his hands Mr. Adams presented to the House: prayers for his own expulsion, aid to crack-brained inventions, shelters for the insane, the annexation of Canada, the protection of maniacs from their delusions, the honoring of the Indian treaties; and when an objection was raised, he simply replied that the right of petition for the redress of grievances was an extension of the right of free speech, and any curtailment of it was unconstitutional. He was waging a war, his personal, private and solitary war against the Gag Rule. It was lucky that the Adams name and John Quincy's age kept them relatively safe. Even so, she never knew if Mr. Adams would return home at night on his own two feet, or carried in on a stretcher, dead of exhaustion, or smashed to pieces.

❧ Hartford ❧
November 1839

It was the middle of November when the trial resumed in Hartford. The lawyers and men of the *Amistad* rode this time in stagecoaches. In the first was the United States Marshal, the jailer and seven of the Amistaders including Twin, Have-Mercy-On-Me and Joseph Cinque. In the second, fearing that the Africans might be kidnapped on their way to the trial, rode Amos Townsand and a group of armed men, including James Covey. In the third rode Lewis Tappan, Roger Baldwin and Robert Madden, who had arrived directly from Cuba to testify in favor of Joseph Cinque's men. The law was not on their side, thought Baldwin, who sat facing the indomitable doctor and Lewis Tappan in the rolling stagecoach. They had failed to convince the public of the validity of natural law and natural rights inherent in the law of nations. Race riots in several Northern cities only underlined the long-abiding racism in America. President Van Buren wanted the whole issue buried before the election. Ruiz was still stubbornly in jail. Montez, a beaten, bewildered old man with failing health, had already sailed for Cuba on the same boat that had brought Dr. Madden to New York.

Robert Madden had already decided what he must do: He would personally visit the President of the United States before leaving for England, where he would take the case of the *Amistad* to the Queen herself, and her Prime Minister. Surely the presence of Victoria would balance that of Isabella . . . white queen against black queen.

Henry Braithwaite and his daughter were amongst the small group of people clustered around the courthouse when the stages arrived. A notice of libel had been posted on the court-

GENTLEMEN—*That said schooner AMISTAD sailed on the 28th day of June AD 1839 from the Port of Havana bound to a port in the Province of Principe, both in said Island of Cuba under the command of Ramon Ferrer as master of that schooner (now deceased), had on board and was laden with a large and valuable cargo consisting of and amounting to the Libel believed to be:*

10 dozen glass knobs	200 feet of rods
39½ thousand needles	11 boxes of crockery and glassware
48 bolts of iron	20 sides of sole leather
45 bottles of rum	10 iron drums
45 maps of the City of Puerto Principe	86 guns
13 maps of the City of Havana	1 box with 200 wedges
8 cog wheels	3 iron kettles
25 bags of Spanish beans	14 packages of French linen
500 pounds of jerked beef	4 packages of Holland linen
50 pairs of shirts and pantaloons	4 dozen parasols or umbrellas
200 boxes vermicelli	30 pieces of Muslin 10 yards each
1 box containing books	21 Ingots
20 boxes of Castile soap	14 pieces Muslin
2 bags of rice	4 pieces Rouen silk
5 boxes containing ribbons house equipment	1 dozen shawls, fans, gloves, 50 shirts, tapes, thread, towels
10 dozen Morocco skins	16 woolen shawls
5 dozen calf skins	4 silk ditto
5 saddles	15 rug saddles
75 pieces striped cotton	70 sheets
18 blankets	50 demi Johns olive oil
800 yards striped linen	6 kegs olives
60 volumes books	11 dozen Ladies' hose
2 dozen bits	

a large quantity of silks, linens, hardware and provisions to the amount in all of $40,000, and also money to the sum and amount of two hundred and fifty dollars, and also fifty-four slaves, to wit, fifty male slaves and three young female slaves who are worth $25,000.

house door, listing the articles found on board the *Amistad.* Vivian's heart beat faster as she read it. The Africans had been listed as property.

"Imagine, twenty-five thousand dollars," murmured voices in the crowd. "More." "I hear prime Negro slaves in South Carolina selling for fifteen hundred to two thousand dollars." "What about all those gold coins, the Spanish doubloons?" "At the bottom of the sea, it seems." The crowd reading the posted libel shifted and buzzed with misinformation. Vivian felt her stomach turn. To be listed so—as merchandise along with twenty-five bags of Spanish beans and olive oil—yet her eyes went back again and again to the list, questioning. The sky was full of January sun, and the people shaded their eyes in order to read the list more easily. They began to trickle inside, hoping, having arrived early, to obtain the best seats, which were already taken by newspaper reporters and artists.

A little before ten o'clock Vivian, Henry and Cotton Braithwaite took their seats as close to the front as they could get. They studied the faces of the Africans, already seated in the courtroom. They knew by sight the interpreter, Covey, and the *Amistad* lawyers. At another table sat the Spanish consul from Boston, Antonio Vega, and a New York lawyer for the Cubans, John Purroy. There were two other lawyers seated, Governor Isham for Lieutenants Gedney and Meade, and Governor Ellsworth for Captain Greene.

Lieutenant Meade had brought suit against Lewis Tappan for slander for having implied in a newspaper article that he had stolen the famous gold doubloons "supposedly" found on the *Amistad.* The courtroom rose. The clerk read the notice of the session:

"The United States of America, District of Connecticut, Circuit Court, holden at Haverford in said district on the nineteenth of November the Year of Our Lord 1839."

"The Honorable Andrew T. Judson, Judge who of the Circuit Court of the United States in and for the District of Connecticut declares: This court is in session."

Roger Baldwin began by saying: "The captives pray that they may be set free, as they of right are and ought to be, under the process of this honorable court, under color of which they are holden as aforesaid. I deny the court has jurisdiction in this case. The Africans of the *Amistad* were captured in New York State and not liable to trial in Connecticut. I further deny they are slaves. They are free men. There were seized on shore and therefore entitled to trial by jury."

To no one's surprise, Holabird replied that upon careful examination he found that the schooner was lying clearly and decidedly upon the high seas.

Judge Judson agreed the question before the court was solely one of jurisdiction and invited Baldwin to call his witnesses.

After Captain Greene stated that the schooner was not more than thirty rods from shore, Peletiah Fordham took the stand. "The niggers were on shore. Joseph Cinque lifted one trunk full of money rattling. Me and another nigger lifted another and heard some more money. So Captain Greene and me, we were determined to have the vessel at all hazards, forcibly if we could, peaceably if we must."

The court burst into laughter. Judge Judson demanded silence.

"Mr. Fordham, how many Africans were on shore?" asked Baldwin.

"Twenty."

Baldwin knew he was lying, but he did not insist.

"If the court please, I call Robert Madden."

Madden took the stand and sat there like a brooding angel. His black hair and blue eyes gave his pale skin a luminous quality enhanced by the weak winter sunlight that struck his face in a shaft of light that came from the high windows on one side of the courtroom.

Permission having been asked and granted, Madden proceeded to read his deposition.

"I, Richard Robert Madden, a British subject, having resided for the last three years at Havana, where I have held official situations under the British government, depose and say that I have held the office of superintendent of liberated Africans and still hold it; and have held for the term of one year the office of British Commissioner, in the Mixed Court of Justice. The duties of my office and of my avocation have led me to become well acquainted with Africans recently imported from Africa. I have seen and had in my charge many hundreds of them. I have seen the Africans in the custody of the marshal of the district of Connecticut, except the small children. I have examined them and observed their language, appearance, and manners; and I have no doubt of their having been very recently brought from Africa. To one of them I spoke and repeated a Mohammedan form of prayer in Arabic; the man immediately recognized the language and repeated a few words of it after me, and understood it, particularly the words *'Allah akbar,'* or God is great. The man who was beside this Negro I also addressed in Arabic, saying—*'salaam ailkoem,'* or·peace be to you; he immediately, in the customary Oriental salutations, replied—*'aleckoum salaam,'* or peace be on you. From my knowledge of Oriental habits and of the appearance of the newly imported slaves in Cuba, I have no doubt of those Negroes of the *Amistad* being bona fide Bozal Negroes, quite newly imported from Africa. I have a full knowledge of the subject of slavery—slave trade in Cuba; and I know that no law exists, or has existed since the year 1820, that sanctions the introduction of Negroes into the island of Cuba from Africa for the purpose of making slaves, or being held in slavery; and that all such Bozal Negroes, as those recently imported are called, are legally free. Such Africans, long settled in Cuba, and acclimated, are called Ladinos, and must have been introduced before 1820, and are so called in contradistinction to the term creole, which is applied to the Negroes born in the island. I have seen, and now have before me, a document, dated twenty-sixth June, 1839, purporting to be signed by Expeleta, who is captain general of the island, to identify which I have put my name to the left-hand corner of the document, in presence of the counsel of the Africans; this document, or *'trasspasso,'* purporting to be a permit granted to Don I. Ruiz, to export from Havana to Puerto Principe, forty-nine Negroes, designated by Spanish names, and called therein Ladinos, a term totally inapplicable to newly imported Africans. To have obtained these documents fraud would have to have been committed, the payment of the necessary fees to corrupt officers would be required. I further state that the above documents are manifestly inapplicable to the Africans of the *Amistad*. They have been obtained illegally and are frauds and forgeries. I swear this under oath."

An outraged exclamation from John Purroy was seconded by Vega banging his cane on the floor, but it was Holabird who addressed Dr. Madden.

"Are you, Dr. Madden, acquainted with the dialects of African tribes?"

"I am not acquainted with the dialects of the African tribes, but I am slightly acquainted with the Arabic language. Lawful slaves of the island are not offered for sale generally, or often placed in the barracoons, or man marts. The practice in Havana is to use the barracoons 'for Bozal Negroes only.' Barracoons are used for Negroes recently imported and for their reception and sale."

"Is not the native language of the Africans often continued for a long time on certain plantations?"

"I should say the very reverse is true," replied Madden. "The native language of the Africans is *not* often continued for a long time on certain plantations. It has been to me a matter of astonishment at the shortness of time in which the language of the Negroes is discarded and the Spanish language adopted. Rebellion, revolt, or insurrection is immediately and cruelly punished by death by garrote or burning at the stake. I speak this from a very intimate knowledge of the conditions of the Negroes in Cuba, from frequent visits to plantations and journeys in the interior; and on this subject I think I can say my knowledge is as full as any person's can be."

"Please state how many barracoons there are at the Havana," asked Holabird.

"There are five or six barracoons within pistol shot of the country residence of the Captain General of Cuba. On every other part of the coast where the slave trade is carried on, a barracoon or barracoons likewise exist. They are a part of the things necessary to the slave trade, and are for its use only. I repeat, any Negroes landed in the island since 1820, and carried into slavery, have been illegally introduced. The transfer of them under false names, as Ladinos, is, necessarily, a *fraud.*"

"Indeed it is."

"Thank you."

Dr. Madden returned to his seat. Covey leaned over to congratulate him. Madden smiled but noticed that the interpreter was visibly trembling and his eye movements were erratic. Madden touched Covey's hand, and it was cold.

"My boy," said Madden. "Are you ill?"

"I don't know," said Covey, his head swimming. Instinctively he turned and saw the girl sitting to the left of him several rows back. There was a flash of recognition, and then the courtroom seemed to move under his feet.

Madden leaned over to Baldwin's chair.

"Covey's ill. I don't know what's wrong with him; we should ask for adjournment."

"But I must call him," said Baldwin. "His testimony is essential."

Hurriedly the lawyer rose to his feet and called Covey to the stand. After eliciting Covey's history and background, Baldwin said:

"Mr. Covey, could you tell us what you know of Joseph Cinque and the others?"

Shivering with ague, James Covey said, "All these Africans are from Africa. I can talk with them. They can speak the same language. I can understand all but two or three. They all have Mende names and their names all mean something: Kale means bone; Kimbo means cricket. They speak of rivers which I know. They sailed from Lomboko. Two or three speak different languages from the others; the Timone language. They all agree as to where they sailed from. I have no doubt they are Africans."

Baldwin bowed to the court and took his seat.

Holabird rose.

"James," he began, "how did you learn to speak English?"

"I am a British subject from Sierra Leone. And my name is Covey. Mr. James Covey."

"Yes, yes, James," said Holabird, "but you must understand in this country we call Negroes by their first names."

"I am a seaman on Her Royal Majesty's man o' war the *Buzzard*, on which I am addressed as Mr. Covey, sir."

"Who is paying you, James?"

Covey was now trembling, not only with ague, but with anger.

"Did you understand the question, James? Who is paying you to interpret for the *Amistad* captives?"

"Your Honor," protested Covey, staring at Holabird, "I have the right to be addressed in this court by name and surname. Unless I am addressed so, I refuse to answer. I cannot answer to a first name that could be any person's."

"Your Honor, James is wasting the court's time," replied Holabird. "It is irrelevant as to how I address a Negro."

"Please answer the question," the judge ordered.

"No one is paying me. My commander offered my good services to the Amistad Committee as a gesture of solidarity between the British navy and the captured Africans," Covey paused, "William, sir."

There was laughter in the court at William Holabird's discomfiture. Vivian looked around nervously, as if for help. It was obvious to her that James Covey was ill.

"May I add that the British Court of Mixed Commissioners has no jurisdiction except in cases of capture on the sea and that Mr. Covey's *Buzzard* did not capture said *Amistad*. He therefore is entitled to no special consideration as a witness. Witness dismissed."

Returning to his seat beside Dr. Madden, Covey stumbled. Beads of perspiration had broken out on his forehead. A low groan escaped his lips.

"I call Joseph Cinque of the *Amistad*," said Baldwin.

"Will Joseph Cinque please take the stand," ordered Judson.

Joseph Cinque approached the bench majestically, because it was so slowly done. But it was trepidation, not pretense. His blanket was draped Mende style, and beneath that he wore high leather boots and flannel breeches and a white shirt. The light struck his youthful face as he sat in the box, as it had struck that of Madden, and his eyes roamed the silent courtroom as if scanning a battlefield. He swore on the Bible, murmuring a hesitant "Yes," but then he was unable to understand Baldwin's first question and looked imploringly towards Covey, who remained slumped in his seat.

Dr. Madden saw Covey make an effort to rise, but he fell back suddenly with a groan, clutching his chest. His eyes had glazed and his sudden gray pallor so alarmed the doctor that he leaped to his feet, catching Covey as he fell forwards. A buzz of alarm and a feminine cry filled the courtroom as Madden bent over Covey and tried to revive him.

The young interpreter had already sunk into a stupor.

Two marshals carried him from the courtroom.

Joseph Cinque and his men were on their feet, their faces dark with alarm. Had someone worked magic on War Road, their only hope, their only voice in this white world?

"Is there no interpreter?" asked Justice Judson.

William Holabird leaped to his feet. "It is the duty of the

government to cause this property to be restored to the true owners . . . without delay as required by the treaty stipulations with Spain. I pray the court to make such order of the disposal of the vessel, cargo and slaves as would comply with our obligations to Spain and preserve the faith of the government. . . ."

"Your Honor, I protest. I pray for a short postponement until Mr. Covey is recovered sufficiently enough to serve as interpreter. These men . . . must be heard through Mr. Covey. . . ." Baldwin shouted.

"Your Honor, for imperative reasons the prosecution accedes to the request for a postponement of Mr. Baldwin." Holabird retorted.

"Dr. Madden's deposition will stand, its admissibility to be decided at a later date. This case is adjourned until the next meeting of the District Court of Connecticut in New Haven on January seventh, 1840," Judge Judson intoned.

Dr. Madden rushed from the courtroom to tend to James Covey, who lay on the floor of the anteroom, his cravat open, his frock coat under his head. As far as Dr. Madden could discern, he was in a coma. He looked around for help and saw a young colored girl approaching in great haste down the corridor, escorted by an older gentleman, probably of her family.

❧ New Haven ❧
November 1839

It was dark in the room, but Covey's extraordinary eyesight could clearly trace the contours of her face. He did not know how long he had been here, drifting in and out of consciousness, but he preferred anything to the disappearance of Vivian Braithwaite's face hovering over him. He had been afraid he invented her, and now she was beside him. He felt his muscles relax, and a profound sense of security and happiness engulfed him. An essential part of his life was there, shadowy and delicate. It was as if she were one of those Mende fetishes of good fortune, as if her body contained all the magic he needed, all the medicine necessary for success and safety.

He studied her soft, rounded chin, the full lips, the elegant modelling of her cheek, the long eyes so absorbed in their fixity that she seemed to be staring at her own reflection.

Her beauty had the same perfection of sculpture, the same severity, serenity and inevitability of shape and form. Covey was sure her soul was that way too; as clear, as functional, as life-nourished, as the season of rains. He, Covey, had died and been reborn.

Vivian wondered when she had fallen in love with him. Had it been the first time she had seen him, that day on the flatboat with the *Amistad* men? Or had it been outside the courthouse, when she had felt his eyes on her and turned to meet his brooding, uncanny gaze? Or had it been in the courtroom, when he had swayed and crumbled to the floor and her own body had leaped forward, as if from a sprung bow, to catch him? She sighed. It hardly mattered now how it had happened, but that it had happened. She thanked God first for saving him, and secondly, for leaving him helpless in her care. Not even her

father questioned her long visits at his side. Although it was
her mother who bathed and changed him, she was free for the
rest of the day to fondle and handle him and touch and admin-
ister to his needs for hours on end. She caressed his cap of
tight curls and every part of his face. She held his hands and
squeezed his feet. She brushed her lips across his forehead
and held his shoulders. She had even touched him *there* over
the coverlet, and insistently enough to provoke a hard lump
underneath, mysterious, astonishing, frightening and hopelessly poignant. Her slim hand slid down the length of him,
her face flushed, her heart beat against the stuff of her dress,
her throat drew together in inexplicable tenderness. Vivian flung
her arm across the covers just below Covey's waist, ready to
withdraw it at a second's notice should he stir or her parents
or brothers walk in.

The young man pretended to sleep so as not to disturb the
exquisite weight of the arm flung across his body. A happiness
he had never thought possible engulfed him. He was sure he
was getting well. Each day he felt stronger. But it would be
stupid to renounce such beatitude merely for good health. The
beautiful, insistent vision would be there when he opened his
eyes. It must have been weeks ago that he had awakened in
this room, his head on fire, a pain in his chest, a heavy, suffo-
cating inability to draw breath. Terrified, he had not been able
to move any part of his body.

"Don't try to move," the girl had said, "and don't be afraid.
You are with friends. My name is Vivian Braithwaite."

Then, one day, it was over. He had opened his eyes and
seen not the girl's face, but Increase Braithwaite's lustrous black
eyes searching his. At first Covey thought he had dreamed the
other, but a few minutes later she appeared at the side of the
woman. Of course, he thought, mother and daughter. It was
the mother who bent down and kissed his forehead.

"Dear boy," she said quietly. "You have been so very ill, we
feared for your life. But now you need only rest. The doctors
say you will recover completely. It is only a matter of time."

"What . . . what did I . . ."

"It was pleurisy. Oh, your Captain Fitzgerald was here and
you didn't recognize him. He was beside himself with remorse. He had his orders to sail for the Bahamas, leaving you
behind. He was so afraid you were going to die, he carried on

something terrible. We have already sent a letter by steamer, hoping it will reach him in time in New York City, and another straight to Jamaica, his first port of call, informing him of your recovery. . . . Dearest boy, three more of the Africans have died. . . ."

Mrs. Braithwaite strode over to the window and with a large gesture opened the curtains, then stood by the open window. As she turned to the bed the interpreter took in her calm, un-ruffled expression, the smooth bands of jet-black hair which had the sheen of precious metals, and the eyes, so black she appeared to look at him with the empty candor of a statue. She was far more than handsome, thought Covey. The opulence of her form, her imposing stature and the sense of unquenchable life that surrounded her made her worshipful.

The daughter, too, had the same virginal earth quality. But whereas the mother was constructed, or rather, erected, with regal lavishness and a staggering expenditure of material, the same fine materials had been pared down in the daughter into exquisitely slender dimensions. Her waist in its corset was no more than a hand span, her neck and shoulders even child-ishly thin, although her bosom was voluptuously fine. Her pale eyes were like amber set into the face of a bronze statue, her skin only fractionally darker than her mother's olive complex-ion, as if it had been temporarily darkened by the summer sun.

Vivian's hair, like Mrs. Braithwaite's, was plaited tightly into one single tress that fell over her shoulder, touching below her waist. Her nearness brought back all of his memories of her, fleeting sensations of cool caresses, scent of jasmine, the pres-sure of a soft, narrow hand, even secret, tormenting touches when she thought he was asleep.

"I've kept all the newspapers for you," said Vivian. "There are dozens and dozens of them, and letters from your aboli-tionist friends. Even Kinna and Kale have written you: imag-ine! They have learned to write in an amazingly short time. There are get-well messages from the Yale divinity students who are teaching all the men to read and write, and religion. There is a letter from a Mr. Robert Purvis of Philadelphia, who intends to commission a portrait of Cinque. The trial has been postponed to January, and the *Amistad* revolt is the talk of America!"

* * *

James Covey began to mend. The past being done with, and the future not yet arrived, the present could be lived and felt without comment since the state of love that had sprung up between Vivian and Covey spoke for itself for everyone to see, and with touching precision. Covey had awakened to a sense of order that was strangely familiar to him. The New England house of the Braithwaites was like a ship, both in its tightness and simplicity, and its insularity and independence. Each object had a place and function that served, as in a ship, as a bulwark against the unknown, the unexpected, the hostile, the ever-present possibility of sudden destruction. There was no excess; each object was necessary, its use evident and unchanging.

There was beauty, too, in the stately, pale yellow curtains of the sitting room, over venetian blinds with their thin, regular strips of wood regulated by cords; the high-backed mahogany chairs, polished into sculpture, which sat serenely around the long English table; the wide-planked bleached floor covered with colorful handmade rag rugs, and one precious Persian carpet glowing like a jewel in the parlor. There were portraits on the wall, and books on the shelves. The shimmering windowpanes and perfect sphere of the chandelier were softer reflections of the adamantine New England light without. The scent of the house was of beeswax and bayberry soap, apple wood and lavender. It was a house with music, as there was a pianoforte and two flutes in the sitting room, and a violin in a glass-panelled cabinet in the parlor. Covey would never know to whom it belonged. Everything looked as though it had been there forever, steady and solid and peaceful, a habitation that had been constructed much as a thought might be: carefully and well-turned; its place a decision rather than merely a selection.

It was Increase Braithwaite's kitchen that Covey loved more than any other place. Since by habit he avoided the cook's galley, he had been hesitant to cross the threshold of Increase's gleaming sanctuary. Yet she had welcomed him, and afternoons she allowed him out of bed to sit at the long table and watch her and Vivian bake, clean vegetables, polish pewter and lay the table with such capable, spare and beautiful gestures of domesticity that Covey's heart ached. Yet communication existed in that light silence, and unspoken affection.

Becalmed, Covey allowed the cleanliness, propriety and security of the house to lull him into happy defenselessness. Contentedly, he lined up the boots in the mud room, stacked the linen, carefully laid logs in a crosshatch pattern in the woodshed, lovingly cleaned the guns and tools and hung them in their place.

The house itself had high, narrow windows, open beams and an attic that spanned the width of the house, which was square, as tall as it was wide. There was a center staircase, with four rooms on each side on three floors. There was a back door and back stairway, which Henry Braithwaite used to go to and from his print shop.

Covey knew how dangerous his state of mind was, not only for a man of the sea, a man trained to search and kill, but for a man who had so long buried his feelings. In good health he had been a sick man, and now as a sick man, wounds deeper than he had imagined had begun to heal. He sighed. The past weeks had been more than just falling in love. After a life of hardship and suffering, of abysmal loneliness and the brutality of the slave trade, love, at last, had come; a recognition of his humanity, his worth, and a seal on his wholeness.

So, he simply loved. Silently. Obstinately. Perhaps shamelessly. It was love as the Africans understood it: an irresistible and fateful impulse invented by the gods.

Vivian, too, found herself in the throes of a mysterious forgetfulness. She clung to Covey, determined not to release him from the protection of his illness. Soon he would return to the courts, to the outside world, to Cinque and his men. Meanwhile, let him seduce her with his stories of the sea and Africa.

"Mendes have another name for white men," said Covey. "They call them the smooth-haired ones." Vivian smiled and instinctively touched her temples, patting them into neatness. Her woollen dress fitted the irreproachable roundness of her arm like a skin, and the elaborate lace stretched across her bosom like the living tissue of scarification Covey dreamed of having under his fingers.

As the days wore on into Christmas, he and Vivian began to play games with his phenomenal eyesight. In the pitch dark Vivian would hold up an object or point to an unfamiliar cor-

ner of the house, and each time Covey would correctly identify the object or describe the room. He made her laugh, and
therefore made her love him even more, and they began to
speak to each other in a different language, a language of possession, of pauses and smiles, of unguarded glances and secret
movements, of long, charged silences and bursts of unpro-
voked laughter.

"Remember," said Vivian softly, "how you told me your African name was Kaweli, War Road, the road dangerous to travel
for fear of being taken captive?"

"Yes," said Covey.

"Well, I shall call you War Road, for you have made me your
captive."

Slowly, Covey's admiration grew for the man he considered
in his secret heart his father-in-law. Braithwaite, Covey realized, was more than the town printer. As deacon of his father-
in-law's church, he was one of the group of men who formed
a bridge between the black community and the white. His faith
in the printed word made him a succor for both. Faith, for him,
meant only one thing: continuity and coherence in a hostile
world.

"Without family," he was fond of saying, "we blacks have
no foundation in the world. It is the one thing America has
offered us, not without a price, but since we are paying that
price, family is ours: family, justice and the American Revolution." He occasionally had long conversations with Covey, but
Covey's real education came from the community surrounding
the Braithwaites, simple men who seemed to him very much
like men of the sea, for the white world was to them a hostile
ocean, and these men were responsible for the watertight community of blacks that survived through discipline, self-suffi-
ciency and a code of honor reminiscent of that found on
shipboard. Carelessness, wastefulness and any act that placed
the group in danger was not tolerated. Drinking and swearing,
as on a well-run vessel, were permissible only on land, which,
in this case, was a society far from white scrutiny. Unsocial
behavior was promptly and severely punished. The rule was
that one took care of one's own, and for Braithwaite and his
friends that included Joseph Cinque and his men. When Covey
innocently questioned Vivian about the underground railway,

she told him of what she knew, not guessing that the slave chaser had already divined what her father's second depot was used for.

"Sometimes my father prints up advertisements for the very slave . . ." Vivian hesitated, but Covey finished her sentence: "that has just passed through his print shop, in flesh and blood."

Vivian and Covey were sitting in Increase Braithwaite's sunny kitchen. "Why don't you children take those newspapers out to Mr. Braithwaite's print shop instead of getting ink all over my table," said Increase, who was crocheting a new rug, her knees covered with multicolored ropes.

Increase also took the precaution of not leaving the two young people alone together for too long. She knew about men from the tropics, and her own passionate nature and her strong, self-willed daughter made her guess that it would be Vivian who would take the lead in any seduction, if seduction there was to be. She loved and trusted Covey, but physical desire could break the strictures of the most careful upbringing.

Covey and Vivian looked at her, surprised at the mild note of disapproval in her voice. "But, Mother," said Vivian, "it's too cold out there for James. Besides, I thought you might like to hear some of this."

Vivian's hands were black with ink from the packets of newspapers Lewis Tappan had mailed from New York. Seeing Vivian's black palms, Covey thought of the hands of aristocratic Mende women who dyed cloth. Covey had been reading the dozens of newspaper articles on the Amistaders, and Vivian had been cutting out the articles and placing them in two piles, one in favor and one against. "The New York *Express*," said Covey, "in favor. It says the abolitionists have secured enough legal ability to delay anything to the ends of the earth. If the Spaniards can match what the Africans have, we shall have about as brilliant a tournament *in curia* as has happened in a long while. The New York *Globe*, in favor. They talk about a new nautical melodrama called *The Black Schooner* which has just opened at the Bowery Theater in New York and in its first week has taken in one thousand six hundred and fifty dollars. Boxes cost seventy-five cents, the pit thirty-seven-and-a-half cents, and the gallery a quarter. The principal roles are *Zambra Cinques—Chief of the Mutineers, Lazarillo—Overseer of the Slaves,* and *Inez.* I wonder who *Inez* is?"

"In any case," said Vivian, "she is a white, painted in black-face."

"The New York *Advertiser and Express,* is against," read Covey. "Mischievous consequences may follow this ridiculous fraternizing with the barbarians, who would probably eat them if they could catch them in their native country! It goes on to say that the poor fellows are hardly above the apes and monkeys of their own Africa and the language they jabber is incomprehensible."

"I find the sound of Joseph Cinque's language pleasing," said Increase.

"Joseph Cinque and his men speak the language of several nations fluently—Mende, Sherbro, Kissi, Temne," said Covey, "which is more than I can say of our good Dr. Gibbs. Here, the Long Island *Star* is for. They say they are the lions of the day and will probably eat a good many dinners before they return."

"Against," said Vivian, coldly. "They are writing in an ironical vein."

"Well, the New London *Gazette* says, 'The more we learn of Cinque's character, the more we are impressed with a sense of his possessing the true elements of heroism.' I trust that is not irony."

On Christmas day the sun's hazy orange touched the quiet, rolling white-frosted hills, with their black clones of tall ghostly trees erasing forever those tropical Christmases Covey had spent with his adopted parents. Hot winds had blown, and palm leaves and bird-of-paradise flowers had served as decorations as his parents, sweating in black serge, blessed a meager guinea hen. The succulent turkey Mrs. Braithwaite brought out of her kitchen at noon must have weighed, calculated Covey, fifty pounds. The long table groaned under the mincemeat, sweet potato and apple pies, plum and corn puddings, yams and white potatoes, cabbage, turnip greens and Boston-baked beans, cranberry sauce, mint jellies and orange marmalade. There were, thanks to the Braithwaite boys, wild pigeon, rabbit, squirrel and venison. There was store-bought peppermint and home-made fudge, Madeira plum wine, cider, birch beer, milk and tea. At midday all the Amistaders were marched over to the Braithwaite's draped in their blankets and cast-off clothes, their feet ill-shod in shoes or boots either too large or too small. The Christmas tree astounded them, draped as it was in silver garlands, red ribbons, and alight with dozens of candles. There was a roaring fire in all the fireplaces. As they looked out of the small, paned windows decorated with pine and holly, pressing their noses against the mysterious glass that separated them from the white landscape beyond, they were a pathetic sight, confused and disoriented, a dark, almost sinister mass of disbelief and waiting.

Frog, Country and Black Snake played with Jasper and Honor, climbing up and down the stairways and sliding down the bannister. With Covey's help, Increase had attempted some African dishes, rice with bits of lamb and black-eye beans, flat cornbread, yams and roasted snake. The Abyssinian Church had donated hats, scarves, warm socks, woollen underwear, gloves, flannel shirts, leather belts, old pants and waistcoats. The little girls were, for the first time, prettily dressed, with new smocks, stockings and ribbons by the Braithwaites. The Africans were allowed to remain only a few hours, and then they had been marched back to the jailhouse. Only the little girls were allowed to stay for the carols.

At Christmas Joseph Cinque realized that Covey's beloved Vivian was the girl in the jailhouse line, the girl who had reached out and touched him with the question in her eyes. He had sat for moments in shocked disbelief. If Vivian and Covey had not been one and the same person, they were now so. And if the girl had not sent Covey, she had at least, through her one act of impulsive pity, brought him back to a sense of his own humanness. He remembered how her gloved hand had reached out and touched his arm and her other hand had offered a simple gift as one would in Africa: a kind of pomegranate called an apple, burnished and polished, its taut, reddish skin glowing. *Herehavethis*, she had said, her eyes glowing with that unasked question. It had been the first recognition of him as a person, and more than that, it had been the recognition of a woman for a man, with all its courage and fearless tenderness. Bayeh Bia was like that, he thought, and he had a passion for fearless women.

But for Joseph Cinque, the day was still a pagan affair. He yearned for African gods and ceremonies. When the captives returned to the jail, Waterfall conducted a ceremony in honor of the Poro Secret Society, substituting objects and offerings taken from the feast. Broke called on Gewo for help against the grief the white man could cause, his violence, and above all, his hypocrisy. The subtle pain of betrayed trust, which the divinity students might have called civilizing, had begun to shape the mind of Joseph Cinque. An overwhelming loneliness had settled upon him from the leaden sky and the moons without sunshine. And he felt himself living in a silent underworld, overshadowed and oppressed by the lack of any knowledge of the physical and material appearances of the things surrounding him. The bitter cold, the unending lessons, the Christian Book, the sickening stream of curiosity seekers and visitors, the unending torment of having no authority, had rendered him unarmed and disconcerted. He could see contempt for the color of his skin, even in his so-called friends and protectors. Arthur Tappan would die for his right to be free, but hated and despised his race and the idea of *amalgamation*, which, as far as he understood, meant the mixing of the white and black races. But who wanted that? he wondered. In his broken English, which he himself realized resembled the speech of a young child, he told Dr. Gibbs that he was a full-grown man, sanctified by Poro ritual, who was being treated as if he were an infant. Dr. Gibbs smiled and said, "We are all children in the eyes of God."

But the arrival of Covey, restored in health and radiant with love, his white smile flashing, helped alleviate the sense of despondency surrounding the men. Bone and Big Man had made amazing progress in reading and writing, and all the men had been coached in lines from the Bible, only Joseph Cinque remaining locked in his prison of silence, expressing himself in a kind of anxious baby talk, but always with that singing, soft, vibrating Mende intonation that instilled a strangely penetrating power to even the simplest words. He would end his comments with many an emphatic shake of his head and the terrifying sensation of his whole being melting into mindlessness. Until he and Covey spoke again in Mende, he remained in this childlike state, irreparably diminished.

One day Covey and Cinque overheard Professor Gibbs say to one of the seminarians:

"Like all sinful men, the African needs faith. But they have never had a Socrates to talk wisdom to them, nor a Cyprus who was not a slave merchant, nor a Pythagoras to teach that truth is a virtue. Hence the difficulty which the Christian missionary has with them is to satisfy their minds as to the miraculous phenomenon of the existence of good. The civilized as well as the savage need the example of the missionary. The experiment in respect to this race is essentially a new one. The nonsense about Hannibal and Cyprian and Augustine being black should have been out of the heads of people long ago. These men spoken of as black were white! The African has never reached—in fact, until the new settlement of Liberia—a higher rank than a King of Dahomey. No philosopher among them has caught sight of the mysteries of nature, no poet has illustrated the heavens or earth or the life of men; no statesman has done anything to lighten or brighten the links of human policy. In fact, if all that Negroes of all generations have ever done were to be obliterated from recollection forever, the world would lose no great truth, no justifiable art, no exemplary form of life. The lot of all that is Africa offers no memorable deduction from anything but the earth's black catalogue of crimes for which they must repent and be saved!"

Cinque and Covey realized that these missionaries dreamed of a whole continent of black people, neatly dressed in New England calico, each carrying a Bible, each with a Christian name like those they had given the prisoners of the *Amistad.*

Gewo, save us from them, Covey thought.

⤙ New Haven ⤚
January 1840

As far south as Washington the Potomac was blocked with ice. Connecticut birch groaned under garlands of snow, roads were blocked and the leaden sky zoomed by in dark, swift clouds filled with ice slivers. It was the worst New England winter in forty years. Lieutenant John S. Paine stood on the prow of the schooner *Grumpus* and read in disbelief the secret orders of the President.

The Marshal of the United States for the District of Connecticut will deliver over to Lieutenant John S. Paine, of the United States Navy, and aid in his conveying on board the schooner Grumpus *under his command all the negroes late of the Spanish schooner* Amistad *under process now pleading before the Circuit Court of the United States. For so doing, this order will be his warrant.*

Given under my hand, at the city of Washington, this 7th day of January, A.D. 1840.

By the President's hand,

M. Van Buren

For so doing! For so doing! thought the captain of the *Grumpus*. He looked up helplessly at the sky, then out to the ominous, gray turbulence of a sea in dead winter, lethal, angry, merciless. The *Grumpus* was one of the smallest ships in the U.S. Navy, and not having any concept of the stacking of a slave deck, he had already pointed out to the Secretary of State that it would be impossible to accommodate all the prisoners below, and if the men stayed on deck, they risked being washed overboard by the violent winter storms of the Atlantic. But Forsyth had been adamant. "The order of the President is to be carried out." Discretion was not a strong point of Van Buren's Secretary of State.

But, unknown to either the President or the captain of the *Grumpus,* an armed black yacht commanded by a group of abolitionists had slipped into New Haven harbor under cover of night and dropped anchor only yards away from the *Grumpus.* Everything on board was ready if the marshal attempted to put the *Amistad* captives on the naval vessel. The men, all armed, were under orders from Amos Townsand, whose ship it was, to fight to the death for the kidnapped Africans, rescue them from the navy and set sail for the Bahamas. The President's plan had been divulged by a nervous and frightened Holabird, who had then taken to his bed with acute colic. Townsand thought the Bahamas were far enough, but he was ready and had provisioned the boat with enough supplies to sail clear to the Indian Ocean if necessary. Not even Baldwin was aware of the contingency plan Townsand and his men from Yale College had secretly devised in less than thirty-six hours.

Their blankets covering their heads, that same morning nine men of the *Amistad,* accompanied by armed guards, crossed the New Haven Green through two feet of snow, Have-Mercy-on-Me and Joseph Cinque leading the procession. Big Sun was coughing. Flakes of snow caught in the beard and moustache of Cricket; Twin's eyes watered with the cold; Crocodile's nose was running and Sword had trouble catching his breath against the sharp blast of rough wind off the sound. Broke was ominous in a black overcoat. Remember and Python walked apart, holding hands.

In the overheated, overexcited courtroom, Vivian, Covey, and her father sat together for the few minutes it took the prisoners to arrive. The two young people avoided each other's eyes, not daring to touch in the presence of Henry Braithwaite, who looked away in complicity. It was as plain to him as Gothic Bold that Covey and Vivian were hopelessly in love. But, thought Braithwaite, until Covey actually declared himself, he needn't cross that bridge. He turned his attention back to the trial in which Covey was now the key.

"God bless the United States of America and this Honorable Court!"

James Covey's hand touched Vivian's gently as he rose and started down the aisle toward the defense table where the *Amistad* lawyers were already seated. He was thinner, thought Vivian, which made him look even taller, and in his well-cut black frock coat and white cravat, his long legs encased in dove-gray breeches and black boots, he was the handsomest man she had ever seen. I'm his, she thought as she looked around the noisy courtroom proudly. Excitement filled the room since Joseph Cinque was expected to testify and no one wanted to miss that. Students from Yale Law School and the Theological Seminary had been given the day off; the press was out in predatory gangs; people from other states, New Yorkers, Bostonians, Washingtonians, were all present. The courtroom rose as Andrew Judson took his place. "Members of the grand jury," he declared, "I am fully convinced by the arguments already presented in this case that the men of the *Amistad* are recently from Africa, and it is idle to deny it or take up the time of the court in establishing that fact."

A stunned courtroom filled with murmurs. In one sentence, thought Henry Braithwaite, Judge Judson had ruled in favor of the most important argument the defense had made. The blacks were not slaves! They were not property! They therefore could not be returned as such to the Spanish. Now it was up to the defense to show that Cinque, as a kidnapped free man, had acted in self-defense to gain his liberty and save the lives of his men.

"Are you ready to proceed on the capital charge of piracy and murder?" asked Judson.

"The government is prepared to proceed," said the District Attorney.

"The defense is ready and will argue self-defense," Baldwin stated.

"I call Antonio Ferrer," said William Holabird.

Cinque looked at Covey in surprise. "Why is Antonio testifying for them?"

Covey held Cinque's eyes. "Don't judge him too harshly. He is the only slave amongst you, and as such he will be returned to Ferrer no matter what, although he doesn't know it. Perhaps he believes he can buy his freedom this way."

"Ramon Ferrer was my master, the captain of the *Amistad*," began Antonio. "I was there when the blacks came on board.

It was eight o'clock in the evening. Señor Ruiz brought all but four. Señor Montez brought the children. We were bound for Puerto Principe. The blacks were loose, not chained. Cinque killed the captain with a cane knife. I saw it with my eyes. I don't know who killed the cook. The cook was killed first, killed with a cane knife. The captain was standing. He was killed at night, and thrown over the side in daytime. Cinque took the master's watch."

"Were the captives badly treated?" asked Holabird.

"They were fed on rice, potatoes, bananas, crackers and meat. They had plenty to eat," replied Antonio. "But the cook told them we were going to kill and eat them. I don't know why he told them that. They didn't know it was in sport. The cook couldn't speak African. He just made signs with his hands."

"Who killed the captain?"

"Cinque killed the captain."

Baldwin stepped forwards to cross-examine. "Didn't your master have the captives whipped?" he asked.

"I did not see the blacks whipped," said Antonio. "After Señor Montez was wounded, Cinque, Grabeau and Burnah took command. They tied me to Señor Montez and Señor Ruiz. Cinque was going to kill Señor Montez and me, and Burnah, because Burnah took Señor Montez's and Señor Ruiz's part. Cinque didn't want to go back to Havana. I was tied to the anchor of the schooner, but Burnah cut me loose. I was in the schooner's boat that landed on shore—Cinque, Burnah, Grabeau, Faginna and me. Seven went with me. There were others on shore; I think there must have been twenty men on shore. I didn't count them. The brig's boat was a big one, maybe ten Africans were on board it, and eight in the schooner's boat."

"Did you see Captain Greene?"

"I saw Captain Greene. Burnah could talk a little; he couldn't talk Spanish. Burnah talked with Captain Greene."

"If no one could speak African, how did the cook tell the Africans he was going to eat them?"

"The cook made signs when he told the black men they were going to eat them."

"Had the *Amistad* carried slaves before?"

"Every two months they made the trip. Señor Ruiz had carried slaves before."

"Why was Burnah whipped?" Holabird interjected.

"Burnah was whipped for stealing water," said Antonio.

"Didn't you tell me that you did not know who killed the captain?" Baldwin insisted.

"I didn't tell you."

Baldwin turned away in disgust. Holabird rose: "Your Honor, I introduce the depositions of James Ray and G. W. Pierce, sailors on board the brig *Washington*, giving a detailed account of the capture of the Africans. I also introduce as evidence the papers of the *Amistad*."

"Will Cinque, known also as Sinqua, take the stand," Baldwin called.

Joseph Cinque drew himself up to his full height. He tried to remember the things he had learned since he had been in this place: that the world was round, that Gewo was called the Lord Almighty by white men, that the color of evil was not white, as he had been taught, but black. His eyes surveyed the packed, sunlit courtroom. Face after white face pursued him with their eyes full of malicious excitement. All the faces looked alike to him, he still had trouble distinguishing one white face from another, yet each held that peculiar expression with which they viewed a black man: hatred, indifference, incomprehension, fear, amusement, empty diversive curiosity, pity, superiority. Not one face he saw showed the only relationship that truly mattered: respect. For respect, thought Joseph Cinque, like love, was one of those affections of humankind that was most intensely felt and understood when it was absent or denied.

Joseph Cinque thought of the trial so long ago in Kawmendi. He saw his uncle and his father and the Paramount Chiefs assembled under the great canopy of the veranda. He heard the buzzing of crickets, the hiss of sand lizards, the crack of a bird overhead. His grandmother was there and so was Bayeh Bia and Gewo; the tall palm tree which gave no shade sang in the constant wind that swept the plains of the Vi country, the flowering bushes burst with magenta and indigo, russet, rose, violet and verdure, thirty shades of green. In his imagination he saw the white man plant his stake measuring the distance between them as he had that day. Except that now America was the adversary and the stake was his life. The young Mendian blinked in the brightness of the courtroom. The snow outside reverberated with the noon high sun and flooded the curious, suspended faces with light.

There were more women in the courtroom than men. They stood out against the dark bulk of their men like African birds, their eyes bright, their heads turning to and fro on their thin necks. They wore every color Joseph Cinque had ever seen and some he hadn't. Their hats were festooned with ribbons or feathers and veils, and their shoulders covered with multi-colored shawls and dense animal skins.

The clerk held out the Book to him as Covey rose from his seat.

"James," Andrew Judson said, "please explain to Cinque what an oath is and ask him if he understands that if he lies, he will go to Hell."

"Mr. Covey, sir."

"*Mister* Covey, then."

"Sengbe Pieh, do you swear by Gewo and on the white man's medicine to tell the truth, the whole truth, and nothing but the truth?"

"I swear by Gewo."

"He swears by God," said Covey.

"Tell him to go ahead," said Judson.

"I was taken on the War Road," Cinque began, "the road between Menni and Kalumbo. I never sold myself. I am married and I have a son. And now perhaps a daughter or another son. We all came in the same house that swims, from Lomboko to Havana, except for the children. We first saw them on the *Amistad*. The children are Mende. We belong to six different nations but can converse together in our dialects. We are not related to each other, though there is amongst us a father and son, and my brother started out from Lomboko. We were kidnapped separately, many by black men, some by Spaniards attacking town after town. We remained in Lomboko two moons, until seven hundred of us were collected. Then we were put on the ship. We were kept in irons, hands and feet together like this."

The Africans watched as Joseph Cinque stepped out of the box and placed his hands before him as if they had chains holding them to his feet. He laid down on the polished oak floor in this position, evoking a shocked sigh from the courtroom. The Africans had been following the testimony of Cinque, each reacting in his own manner, but all nodding in agreement with his words. To the curious in the courtroom, each seemed to be praying to some unknown God, bowing in agreement with Covey's translation, although they could not understand it.

"In this way," Cinque continued, "all the women died, most children died, most men died of sickness, but also many died of suffocation, suicide and jumping overboard, by beating and wounds, by melancholy, by madness. The man that brought us from Lomboko was with Ruiz in Havana. First came Ruiz in Havana prison house to feel of me. He said, 'Fine, fine.' "

Covey paused. There was no need for translation. Joseph Cinque felt himself with his own hands, his arms and limbs, repeating, "Fine, fine." He touched the hair on his head, he pulled back the lids of his eyes, he bared his teeth, he pulled open his mouth. Then he touched his chest, his biceps, his flanks, and between his legs, repeating: "Fine, fine, fine, fine, fine.

"On the *Amistad* we had only half to eat and half to drink. We suffered. The cook made sign with his hands to say they carry us some place, to kill and eat us. Ruiz told the sailors to beat us, and they beat us."

"Did Pedro Montez beat you?" interrupted Holabird.

"No, he did not," Cinque answered. "The captain and Ruiz whipped us. Montez did not whip us. They whipped Kimbo, Sessi, Burnah."

"What about the night of the revolt?" Holabird demanded.

"In the storm we broke our chains. We leaped on deck, we found weapons, cane knives. I killed the cook. The captain killed two of my men. He wounded two more. There was blood everywhere. Two sailors jumped overboard and swam to the bottom of the sea. I took command of the ship. I put Sessi to the wheel. Then I fed everyone. I left Ruiz and Montez in the slave hold. They cried, they begged, but I told them fetters good enough for black men, good enough for white men. They asked for water. I gave them as much as they gave us. Ruiz and Montez cried all the time, they cried. I let them out. Ruiz gave me a letter for a boat that spoke to us, but I could not know what was in it."

"There are no letters in Mende," Covey interjected.

"I took some string and some iron and tied them to the letter and sent it to the bottom of the sea. There might have been death in it. I had counted three moons from Mendeland to Havana, so there must be three moons from your shore to Mendeland, but by trickery we travelled three-and-a-half moons from Havana to this place."

And Cinque raised his forefinger to trace a meandering line in the air. "This is how we sailed from Havana toward Mendeland by the sun and back to captivity in the night. I, Grabeau, Bartu, Burnah, Kimbo, Fuliwa, Fabanna, Fooni, Sessi, Shule, Kinna and more were on shore and encountered these men," Cinque pointed to Captain Greene and Lieutenant Meade, "although I remember the names only of those I have numbered. We were going back to Mende country, which you call Africa, and I told Captain Greene that we wanted to go back. Grabeau and Sessi carried two trunks of gold to shore. We wanted to know if the Captain Greene would carry us back to Africa for this. I told him I would also give him the ship. Burnah spoke with Captain Greene. I whistled for our men to come to him. The white men ran for their guns. Then we gave them our knives to explain we only wanted to go home."

Suddenly Joseph Cinque rose in his seat, making that particular gesture of planting an imaginary staff before him, and began speaking too quickly for James Covey to interpret. His voice rolled out upon the audience like summer thunder, the incomprehensibility of his words an attraction to the auditor, who was mesmerized by these incommunicable phrases, softly guttural and lilting like the tap of rain on a tin roof. The whole courtroom, including the surprised Covey, fell silent as Joseph Cinque concluded,

> "So ha a guli woklch, i sihan;
> yey Kpanggaa a lolohhu lee.
> So ha a guli wohlch; ndi lei; ndi, kaka
> So ha a guli wohloh, i sihan; kuhan
> ma wo ndayia ley. . . . E longa koe hui Lomboko."

The Africans began to weep. Covey remained stonily silent. The Africans no longer moved their heads but swayed their bodies in a seated dance of lament. The hushed courtroom seemed almost to hear the sha-sha-sha of the chains of iron, the lash of sea, the protest of a simple man trying to articulate the unspeakable.

"Order, order in this courtroom," said Andrew Judson. "Mr. Covey, please tell Mr. Cinque to sit down and to stop speaking in tongues! Mr. Baldwin, your client is out of order. Out of order. Shall I clear the courtroom?"

Before he could bring down his gavel, Covey took hold of the pleading Cinque as Baldwin jumped to his feet.

"I should like to introduce as evidence these fraudulent passports," said Roger Baldwin. "When the said Africans were shipped on board the said schooner, by the said Montez and Ruiz, the same were shipped under the passports signed by the Governor-General of the island of Cuba." Baldwin began almost as a continuation of Joseph Cinque's litany in Mende, the litany of the Saint's names of the captives.

"These passports do not truly describe the persons shipped under the same, as Dr. Madden testified earlier.

"Now, Your Honor, I wish to introduce as evidence precisely that the decree of Spain of 1817 prohibits the slave trade after 1820 and declares *all* slaves newly imported from Africa *free*. With this, I rest my case. Shall the clerk read the decree out loud, please."

> *"Your Majesty prohibits forever all your subjects of the Peninsula, as well as America, from purchasing Negroes on the coasts of Africa, enacting that voyages for that purpose may not be undertaken to the coasts north of the Equator after the twenty-second of November, nor to those south of the Equator after the thirtieth of May 1820, under the penalties specified.*
> HER MOST CATHOLIC MAJESTY ISABELLA OF SPAIN
> [affixed seals]"

With which Andrew Judson declared that the presentation of evidence was closed, and he retired, Joseph Cinque's oratory still ringing in his ears.

For fifteen days New Haven lay expectant, snowbound and seething with rumors that Andrew Judson was awaiting instructions from the President of the United States. In the harbor, aboard Townsand's yacht, the plans to kidnap the Africans

Description	Havana, June 26th, 1839
Size — — Age — — Colour — — Hair — — Forehead — — Eyebrows — — Eyes — — Nose — — Mouth — — Beard — — Peculiar signs	I grant permission to carry forty-nine black Ladinos, named Antonio, Simon, Lucas, Jose, Pedro, Martin, Manuel, Andres, Eduardo, Celedonio, Bartolo, Ramon, Agustin, Evaristo, Casimiro, Melchor, Gabriel, Santorion, Escolastino, Pascual, Estanislao, Desiderio, Nicolas, Esteban, Tomas, Cosme, Luis, Bartolo, Julian, Frederico, Salustiano, Ladislao, Celestino, Epifaneo, Tibureo, Venancio, Felipe, Francisco, Hipolito, Benito, Usidoro, Vicente, Dionisio, Apoloneo, Esequiel, Leon, Julio, Hipolito, and Zenon, property of Don José Ruiz, to Puerto Principe, by sea. They must present themselves with this permit to the respective territorial judge.

Havana, June 22nd, 1839

I grant permission to carry three black Ladinos, named Juana, Francisca and Josefa, property of Don Pedro Montez, to Puerto Principe, by sea. They must present themselves to the respective territorial judge with this permit.

ESPELETA.

Duty, 2 seals affixed
(Endorsed) Commander of Matriculas.
Let pass in the schooner *Amistad*, to Guanaja, Ferrer, master. Havana, June 27th, 1839.

MARTINEZ & CO.

if Judson bowed to the pressures symbolized by the schooner *Grumpus,* laying at anchor and icebound nearby, were rehearsed. Henry Braithwaite had alerted the underground railway all the way to Montreal, and a group of vigilantes had been organized to keep watch on the jailhouse in case the prisoners were spirited away during the night.

All through the trial Joseph Cinque had sat stone-faced, listening to Covey's translation of the various testimonies and depositions. Only when the decree of the Queen of Spain had been read had Cinque showed any emotion.

As Joseph Cinque waited for the fate of his men to be pronounced, he thought of how everything was a matter of color. What if there had not been the legends of his childhood of white devils and white spirits? What if death itself was not white? Would he now be so afflicted, certain that these judges in this alien white world held no justice for him? Had not every white man he had ever known betrayed even the simplest notion of honor and reciprocity? Why should this court be any different? he thought. He had to use all his power of self-possession to erase this instinctive, visceral fear of that color—a fear that had in the end given the white man his lordship over Mendeland. For even the kings feared them—their Speakers and their ministers feared them.

The smooth-faced young man, not yet twenty-six, had never even thought of himself as a color until now. Yet he remembered the horror of the young white sailor his own age, at the sight of black men, had been exactly the equivalent of his on viewing *his* first white man. Cinque glanced at Covey, so comfortable with these men, able to converse with them in their own language. He loved Covey, had loved him on sight, but could he really trust a man who dealt with the Devil? Fear radiated from all the men. Twin, Waterfall, Python and Sword. They sat like dark angels, the shadow of every face he saw around him. He, Cinque, had reconciled himself to white men, but never to their power over him, to their cruelty, assumption, arrogance, greed and lordship; never. Awe had been transformed into fear, fear into melancholy, melancholy into rage. He tried to rise; he tried to cry out but was unable to make a sound, though his mouth moved. His pulse beat; the saliva gathered in his mouth as the sweat gathered under his arms and in his groin. There was no question of if, only a matter of how, they would die.

On the twenty-third day of January, an exhausted, pale, forebodingly silent Baldwin came to fetch the Amistaders. This time there was no Amos Townsand to escort them across the square. Townsand and his men were hiding with blackened faces aboard the yacht, anchored directly alongside the *Grumpus.*

Vivian and Henry Braithwaite had ridden their saddle horses to town so as not to risk their carriage in the ice and shoulder-high snowdrifts that blanketed New Haven. Many others had done the same, so that the square seemed a parade ground on which maneuvered a somber and careless cavalry.

John Trumbull had arrived alone at the courthouse, hoping to avoid yet one more exchange with Washington Irving over Andrew Judson's integrity.

The United States Marshals led the Africans through a back street and into a side entrance to the courthouse. They would have to wait a full hour for the Honorable Andrew Judson to open the proceedings.

When the court had quieted, Judson began to read:

"On the twenty-third day of January A.D. 1840, upon the an-swers of the Negroes and the representations of the District Attorney of the United States, this court, having fully heard the parties, do find that the respondents, severally answering as aforesaid, are each of them natives of Africa, and were born free, and ever since have been, and still of right are free, and not slaves; that they were never domiciled in the island of Cuba, or the dominions of the Queen of Spain, or subject to her laws thereof; that they were severally kidnapped in their native country, in violation of their own rights, there unlawfully held as slaves; that the respondents or some of them, influenced by the desire of recovering their liberty and of returning to their families and kindred in their native country, took possession of the schooner *Amistad.*

"And this court doth further find that since the Africans were put on board the schooner to hold the Africans as slaves; that at the time when Cinque and others, here making answer, were imported from Africa into the dominions of Spain, there was a law of Spain prohibiting such importations, declaring the per-sons so imported to be free. This law was in force when the claimants took the possession of the said Africans and put them on board said schooner, and the same has ever since been in force. Therefore, in behalf of the United States, by virtue of the process issued from this court, I decree that they may be delivered to the President of the United States to be transported to Africa. It is so decreed that the Africans libelled and claimed (excepting Antonio Ferrer) be delivered to the President of the United States, to be by his agents transported home to Africa."

They stood like tall black mangrove trees in the swelling sea of white faces and bodies that surrounded their little island with unintelligible words of congratulations and felicitations and meaningless questions. The Amistaders accepted the gestures of friendship and admiration. Python, Have-Mercy-on-Me, Waterfall, Sword, Broke, Crocodile, Big Man, Cricket, Big Sun, Twin the younger, Twin the Elder, and Remember rose, pulling their blankets around them, as much for protection against the excited public as to cover themselves. It had not been so different from a Mendo trial, they thought, as Covey had translated it, and now they could go home.

The crowd poured out of the courtroom and the local reporters raced to file their stories. Covey, Vivian and her father allowed themselves to be jostled by the crowd, so weary and happy they let themselves be moved along by the surprising and unexpected verdict. Why, thought Covey, did he feel like crying? The Africans were to be sent home by the President; he could now face his own future as free as they were. Covey glanced down at Vivian, who leaned deliciously on his arm. Yet immense anguish seized him so violently he nearly cried out. Where was Baldwin?

Twin the Elder noticed it first, and followed the movements of the lips of the players without being able to penetrate the wall of sound surrounding him or to cry out a warning. He could only signal his alarm to Joseph Cinque, who tried to guess what was happening.

At the bench Baldwin and Judson were in heated parlay. "The United States," said Holabird, "is claiming in pursuance of a demand made upon them by the duly accredited minister of Her Catholic Majesty, the Queen of Spain, to the United States, move to appeal from the whole and every part of the said decree, except part of the same in relation to the slave Antonio, to the Circuit Court of Connecticut."

"I move for the Africans," replied Baldwin, stunned, "by their African names, that so much of the decree of the district court as relates to them severally may be dismissed; because the

United States does not claim them, nor have they ever claimed any interest in the appellees, respectively, or either of them, and have no right, either by the law of nations, or by the Constitution or laws of the United States, to appear in the courts of the United States, to institute or prosecute claims to property in behalf of the subjects of the Queen of Spain, under the circumstances appearing on the record in this case; much less to enforce the claims of the subject of a foreign government, to the persons of the said appellees, respectively, as slaves."

"I refuse the motion," said Judge Judson waspishly. "I affirm the decree of the district court, pro forma."

"I then hereby claim in pursuance of a demand made upon me by the minister of Her Catholic Majesty, the Queen of Spain," William Holabird demanded, "to move an appeal from the whole and every part of the decree of the court to the Supreme Court of the United States, to be holden in the Supreme Court of the United States."

"Allowed."

Lewis Tappan came racing towards Covey with more speed than he considered safe for his years or his physique. When he reached Covey he let out a string of curses, prayers and angry evocations of the Devil in Hell, which made Covey stare at Tappan as if the mild-mannered editor-millionaire had lost his mind. He was in tears.

"What is it? What's wrong?" cried Covey.

"They're over there," said Tappan, "undoing the trial! Holabird has appealed the decision to the United States Supreme Court on behalf of the President! He had the appeal already written out and registered!

"And Judson has allowed it!"

"He's turned down Baldwin's appeal to dismiss the case and has allowed the appeal!"

"But what does it mean?"

"It means, James, that the story is not over," said Lewis Tappan. "It means it has just begun."

"I refuse to translate that," said Covey angrily. "Someone else will have to tell him."

"There is no one else," said Tappan. "Do your duty, my boy."

Covey turned and saw that Joseph Cinque already knew, for he had unwrapped his blanket and let it fall to the floor at his feet. And faintly, from across the courtroom, and yet from much farther away, from the slave deck of the *Henrietta,* he heard *"Elonga Koe hui, Elonga Koe hui."* We are dying, We are dying.

The *Grumpus,* hearing of the verdict, lifted anchor and left New Haven harbor.

BOOK II

❦ ❦

He has waged cruel war against human nature itself, violating its most sacred rights of life and liberty in the persons of a distant people who never offended him, captivating & carrying them into slavery in another hemisphere, or to incur miserable death in their transportation hither. This piratical warfare, the opprobrium of INFIDEL powers, is the warfare of the CHRISTIAN king of Great Britain, determined to keep open a market where MEN should be bought and sold. He has prostituted his negative for suppressing every legislative attempt to prohibit or to restrain this execrable commerce, and that this assemblage of horrors might want no fuel of distinguished die, he is now exciting those very same people to rise in arms among us, and purchasing that liberty of which he deprived them, by murdering the people of whom he also obstruded them; thus paying off former crimes committed against the LIBERTIES of one people, with crimes which he urges them to commit against the LIVES of another.

—*The Declaration of Independence, 1776*
Thomas Jefferson (Excised from the final draft by consensus)

❧ Joseph Cinque ❧
1840

The *Amistad* blacks exercised their natural right to liberty by conspiracy, insurrection, homicide and the capture of the ship . . .

—*John Quincy Adams*

Nobody pays any attention to us. The judge has disappeared. Whispering amongst ourselves, we stand here like a flock of ravens in a savanna of shoving, gesturing white bodies and faces. There rises from all of this a kind of dusty cloud of confusion, carried upwards by excited urgent voices, the cry of the speaker: *Thiscourtisadjourned!* and the echo of the Paramount Chief's hammer pounding on oak. Even Covey, for I have begun to think of War Road by his English name, abandons us. I see him near the courtroom door, his dark figure outlined by the streaming sun, shaking his head vigorously and gesticulating angrily with Lewis Tappan. Suddenly I realize I can walk straight out of the courtroom without anyone stopping me or even noticing. I spy the lawyers deep in conversation. The guards have their muskets laid upon their knees, everyone's back is turned. I look around for something to use as a weapon as I inch towards the back exit. I brace myself for a wild sprint, my muscles tense, when suddenly a voice speaks and the cold iron of a shotgun presses into my ribs.

"You ain't going nowhere, Cinque, except to jail."

We go back to the farm the same way we came. The flatboat moves slowly up the canal, the people stare and shout on the banks. We squat on our haunches, our blankets pulled around us. Waterfall's battle lament is once again answered by a chorus of voices that rise then sink softly into the high-banked snow-drifts and the mist rising from the waters.

As I come in sight of Pendleton's barracoons, I can see the men who have run outside wrapped in their blankets that totally cover them, transforming them into strange, virile shadows that dot the prairie beyond the barn. Now and again one moves with strange jerking movements outlined by the colorless landscape. Now a head or a hand emerges and the configuration, like Sande mask dancers, move as their blankets fly around them or make wings of their arms as they raise them in greeting. Behind the men are the leafless trees, the naked shrubs and the falling snow dust. I begin to hear shouts, and here and there a hat, a scarf, a greatcoat changes the form of one of the creatures, making him two-headed or two-winged. My own lips are immovable with cold. When I try to shout, a pain clamps my teeth shut and sets me shivering. If Hell for the white man is, as they say, fire and brimstone, Hell for me is ice. Stiff-legged men limp towards the barge, then stop as they read our faces. Their pitiful forms shrink even farther into their woollen tents. I cannot look them in the eye. Where is my victory if we are to remain captives? That means we have lost the war.

Remember moves forwards with some of the men as an anguished stumbling explanation begins to pour from me. When I finish, Covey says: "I swear to you, Remember, we were freed by the judge and placed under the protection of Van Buren, the Paramount Chief, to be returned to Mendeland." Then he repeated the judge's decision word for word.

"All at once the United States of America appealed. An appeal to a higher Council of Paramount Chiefs that must be respected. It is called the Supreme Court and it is the symbol of . . . the entire nation of these people. Our Speakers defended our cause as best they could. The public applauded, they cheered . . . and then nothing. The whole victory dissolved like a dream, and we were back in chains. Lewis Tappan says we will win this next trial—for beyond the Council of Paramount Chiefs there is no place to go—but when?"

I look into the faces of Remember, Cricket and Sun, which protrude from the hoods of their woollen clothes like horn owls, the whites of their eyes as white as the snow on the ground and the rest of their features screwed up into a knot of cold. Then, questions and exclamations pour from them in Mende, interrupted every now and again by phrases in English which they now use. But the harsh sounds are smoothed by the gliding accents of Mende. It gives the English words an unreal quality, and Remember, Cricket and Sun stand there, their eyes downcast, their arms hanging limply at their sides, their blankets flapping violently around their bodies. There is nothing Covey or I can say to them.

We huddle around a small smoking fire in the center of the barn. I know we can easily burn the barn down, as well as ourselves, but the alternative is to freeze to death. The fire lights our faces and clouds the room. Everyone waits for me to speak, but it is Edge-of-the-Razor who speaks.

"Our teachers have taught to us about the road underground that leads to freedom in the north. I say we should escape by this road and steal ourselves. Who would stop us? Pendleton and his wife?"

Edge-of-the-Razor is a short, stocky man, almost fat, the opposite of his name. His light brown skin glows in the reddish light and his eyes are wild and hard. His teeth are filed to sharp points, so that when he speaks he seems to be spitting light. The vast surface of his body is covered with meticulous, elaborate scars, which in the beginning the white men took for writing. His round head bobbs up and down, the syllables roll thickly and melodiously from his lips.

"What other hope do we have now?"

"It is not so simple," I reply. "Without the help of friendly whites and blacks, we wouldn't last two suns from here, in this cold."

"With snow, we have nothing to eat, there is nothing to hunt," says a voice.

"There are those called Chippewa who live such," says another voice.

"They themselves have been driven beyond the mountain range."

"We are not slaves to steal ourselves. We are warriors, taken out of our knowledge. . . . We have memory and we have courage and we are kidnapped free men. Through our revolt," I continue, "we acquired fortitude, patience, endurance and dignity. Remember we seized ourselves forever on the *Amistad*, it is the part of us that no one can erase or imprison or deny or destroy." I pause. One day during the trial I cut out the image of the *Amistad* from a newspaper Covey had shown me. I folded it and placed that exact likeness inside my shirt. I have carried it there ever since. Now, I think, because I pos-

sess the image of our ship, we can never lose it. I have folded
and unfolded the fragile parchment so often, it is already beginning to wear at the creases. I take it out now and hold it up
for the men to see. "The *Amistad*," I say, "is our only home."
One by one I study their reactions to my amulet. I scrutinize
each face, weigh the desire for victory or death in each pair of
eyes. And I repeat to them as I had a hundred times before:
"The condition of lordship is the opposite of what it pretends
to be—it pretends to be invincible, self-satisfied and eternal,
but I know that all lordship is temporary, weak and conquer-
able."

It is Covey and Vivian who explain to me what I have come
to mean to the people who now hold me in captivity and argue
over me. Covey explains that I will be prosecuted from now
on, not by Ruiz or Montez or Gedney, but by the United States
of America. It is America that demands that the old verdict in
our favor be revoked. It is America that would not let me go.
From murderer and cannibal, I have become liberator and revolutionary. Yet I, myself, am exactly the same man. I have made
war for the same reasons. Yet my every action is now the anxious concern of every white. Like a whirlwind the printed word,
lithographs, posters and pamphlets swirl around me and my
men. My name and image is everywhere, my face reproduced
in portraits and wax, my skull measurements tour the entire
countryside. Debates break out between white men who believe all black men should be slaves and white men who believe no black men should be slaves. I am the cause.
    "You can choose to be whatever you want," says Covey. "It
makes absolutely no difference to them, for they see only what
they wish to see: your color. Nothing more. This country is
obsessed with it."
    Then, he told me about the strange and terrible rebellion of
Nat Turner, a slave who had paralyzed and terrified the entire
American nation. A man who in my country would have been
a Poro Gbeima, had, in the season of harvest, in Jerusalem,
Virginia, nine years ago, risen and, with twenty-eight warriors,
had killed fifty-five white masters and fired their plantations.
He had been betrayed, captured, tried and executed without
ever confessing to a crime. And the slave masters had retal-
iated with hangings and whippings that had taken a hundred

innocent black lives, slave and free, and intiated a reign of terror. Nat Turner had been hung and quartered, soap made of his carcass. America still remembered and feared even his spirit, and his name was legend.

"You are an idea," says Vivian, "much greater than merely Joseph Cinque. You have been thrown into the great divide of America: the slavery question."

"A man," says Henry Braithwaite, "can never be a slave if he doesn't *know* he's a slave. You are a man apart for this country because you are not lost: you have brought the essence of another continent with you intact, undiluted, pure, free. You frighten. You are frightening because you are still attached to your ancestors. You have an identity, a lineage, you are specific. Not like those of us who are brotherless, sisterless, fatherless, motherless, wifeless and childless."

It is hard to understand and even harder to endure. I begin to doubt myself. I begin to fail to keep discipline amongst the men. They become restless and resentful. I lose all idea of time and place. I am again in *palihun*, suspended on a nape of fear in a universe of hostility. I sit day after day, empty-headed and empty-handed, waiting for I know not what except the new trial, while the lines of curious, repulsive white faces appear again, like an attack of locusts one can only wait out, hiding, as they ravage everything one has worked and lived for. I become morbid and sentimental. I think of marching in the procession under the large cloth, my body smeared with palm oil, surrounded by my parents and kinfolk, being led to the *barri*, being taken to the Kameihun for the farewell, drinking the sacred wine, hearing the Gbeima pray for me. I think of the Mabolesia imploring the sacred stones and invoking the spirits of the Poro on my behalf, praying, "Father Siaffa, let it reach you; let it reach to Kanga; let it reach the summit of the great one. This is what Levi brought down long ago. These children, whom we are pulling from the Poro today, let nothing harm them; let them not fall from palm trees; make their bodies strong; give them the wisdom to look after their children; let them hold themselves in a good way; let them show themselves to be men!" I think of standing bound with thread and moss to the other initiates so that I may be as strongly attached to my society as I am to them. . . . I feel a surge of affection for the men around me. We are one in spirit and flesh. I will never desert or betray them nor they me. That is Poro law.

I vow to spend my days building the morale of soldiers. I vow to continue the war of the *Amistad*. I begin to substitute military words for our everyday actions; I impose military discipline. I forgive no failure of nerve; I abhor all sentiment; erase all memory. I fight the men's homesickness with cruelty and derision. Men cry, but I refuse to listen. For if America breaks our spirits, saps our will, perverts our memories, we will never make the Return. So I become cold and unfeeling, masking my own despair in order to kill it in others. I relent only for the children. But we are allowed to see them rarely, and slowly they become strangers to us, little brown rag dolls in their layers of clothing and pinched faces. Until now, I have disbelieved as much as feared. Until now, I have regarded myself as immune not only to death but to tragedy. But more and more I begin to see that man is such a dangerous creature that there is no limit to his cruelty nor escape from it.

The men long for their women. Often in the night the dark barn suddenly becomes warm with familiar scents and breezes, embracing me from an imaginary, distant savannah, springing like an ambuscade off the river Kalwara. I am home, I think. My eyes roam the farthest recesses and a slim figure, her naked form perfectly outlined in the moonlight, always approaches me. She glows like a firefly, her breath a haze in the smoky air. Dazed but not alarmed, I rise and follow her, stumbling amongst the mattresses of the other men. I reach an opening, an unequal circle that pierces the tangled undergrowth of a riverbank. The circle's moss is soft underfoot and spongy, and the crystal river swallows us both silently. I slide under her floating form, my arms embracing the wetness of the palm-oiled flesh, my hands groping her dark triangle and her illuminated breasts, which break the surface like tiny pyramids. Her thousand plaits fan out around her head, the multicolored cowrie shells reflecting the moonlight. Her lynx eyes open and her breath laps my face as she twists over, half swimming away. But I always catch the weightless body and carry her downstream, caressing her limbs, flanks, thorax, as she turns and turns in my arms. I dive under the surface, taking her with me, and plunge into her rotating body, carried even deeper by the tepid undertow. The current always runs counter to our movements, and we struggle down to the slimy bottom, locking and unlocking in violent spasms until, with a sigh, she releases me and all of me flees into her nest, my snake reaching her innermost parts, commanding both our cries of pleasure at the same time, while her body still swivells in my arms. I enter her again, churning the turbid waters as we grasp and ungrasp like wrestlers, her arms above her head, her body bent like a bow, her breath whistling through her, love kisses and cries that split the air as we rock, locked in an arc, still in motion, sinking onto the bed of the river shimmering with filtered moonlight. Rushing downward blindly, her body smashes against mine, I burst inside her, a roaring in my ears as my throat explodes with her name.

Then Remember is perched beside me like a night owl hooting, "Sengbe Pieh! Sengbe Pieh!" the sound ejaculating into the night like my last convulsions.

The marshals find Edge-of-the-Razor's frozen body two days after he escapes, curled up upon itself like a river snail, the gray face as smooth as glass and covered with hoar. He was twenty-three years old. Edge-of-the-Razor follows Yammoni's death. Six moons have passed and six men have died in captivity.

I am taken back to the jailhouse in New Haven. To my surprise, José Ruiz is not in prison, but standing in front of my cell in his reassumed lordship, wearing the inventory of a master; his well-pressed black suit, his demeanor that of a viceroy, his hand resting on an ivory-head walking stick, a long fur cape and fur hat, the curl of smoke from his cigar. I understand at once that he has come to use his old weapons on me: terror and tyranny. He wants to make sure I know that he is destined to win and that we are destined to lose. He isn't angry because he has lost but because we have won. Yet I notice his hand, the hand of a young man, trembles. It is at that moment that I raise my eyes. I understand that his fear is still alive. And it is still here. You are free and I am once again a captive. You have recovered your identity as buyer and seller and stealer of men and I am again out of my knowledge. But I haven't forgotten the sobbing, cringing Ruiz of the *Amistad*, pleading for mercy, urinating in his pants. And if we had arrived in Mendeland, I would have taken your skin off your bones and made a flag out of it.

Deposition of José Ruiz before Judge Andrew T. Judson, on board the cutter Washington, *August 29, 1839.*

I never understood the revolt. I have always treated my negroes kindly. I whipped only under the severest provocation or for obedience. I tortured hardly at all. I never used irons or branding. I have never raped or murdered. The prisoner was never cruelly treated. . . . I am a planter and a gentleman. I bought forty-nine slaves in Havana and shipped them on board the schooner Amistad. *We sailed for Guanaja, the intermediate port for Principe. For the four first days everything went on well. In the night I heard a noise in the forecastle. All of us were asleep except the man at the helm. I do not know how things began; was awakened by the noise. I saw this man Joseph. I cannot tell how many were engaged. There was no moon. It was very dark. I took up an oar and tried to quell the mutiny; shouting "Socorro." Then I heard one of the crew cry "murder." I heard the captain order the cabin boy to go below and get some bread to throw to them, to pacify them. I went below and told Montez to follow me, and begged them not to kill me; I did not see the captain killed. They called me on deck and told me I should not be hurt. I asked them as a favor to spare the old man. They did so. After this they went below and ransacked the trunks. Before doing this, they tied our hands. We continued our course—don't know who was at the helm. Next day I missed Captain Ramon Ferrer, two sailors, Manuel Pagilla, and Jacinto—and Celestino, the cook. We all slept on deck. The slaves told us next day that they had killed all; but the cabin boy said they had killed only the captain and cook. From this time we were compelled to steer east in the day: but sometimes the wind would not allow us to steer east, then they would threaten us with death. In the night we steered west and kept to the northward as much as possible, hoping to reach some southern port in the United States. We were six or seven leagues from land when the out-*

break took place. Antonio is yet alive. They would have killed him, but he acted as interpreter . . .

Thirty times we dropped anchor, a dozen times ships spoke to us. But in spite of all our efforts, no one came to our rescue. We lost count of time, of direction, rations ran out, water ran out. The negroes began to sicken and die, seven in all. We were slowly starving to death. Violent disputes broke out. Some negroes were punished. Joseph Cinque became a tyrannical dictator, harsh and intolerant. The Amistad began to rot under our feet from lack of care and cleaning. Sails ripped and fell to the deck, so that I wonder why no passing ship recognized we were in the hands of pirates. After the first month, I lost all hope, the schooner drifting aimlessly, endlessly nowhere, never making land, never speaking to another boat, I lived with the despair of being murdered by savages. Joseph Cinque was sometimes fierce, sometimes melancholic, sometimes as cruel as a demon, sometimes generous as a prince. Some mysterious unyielding secret commanded obedience, despite everything. Meanwhile, my wound festered. I was in terrible pain. Fooni nursed me. I swear the prisoner before you treated me harshly, and but for the interference of others, would have killed me several times every day. I kept no log or reckoning. I did not know how many days we had been out, nor what day of the week it was when the officers came on board. I had no wish to kill any of them. I prevented them from killing each other.

"Why come?" I say.

"I came to check the conditions in which my property is being held before I go back to jail."

I bare my teeth, understanding what he says, and I force myself to hold Ruiz's eyes until his smirk turns into a crazy grimace, as if my gaze has cut off his breath. But I continue to stare until, like a magician, I have conjured up the gleam of the cane knife, and with a sudden spasm I see it splash into the gray, putrid iridescent flesh of Raymond Ferrer.

Ruiz's hand goes to his crotch and grips his genitals in a gesture of contempt. He stands there, his hands between his legs, as if waiting for something from me. I begin to laugh. I throw back my head and let loose all my rage. It rushes forwards like molten lead and spurts out, delicious and potent. I take down my white man's trousers, take out my snake and shake it at him. Then I piss on Ruiz's boots, on the bottom of his trousers, on his grave. I stand there, watching the vapor from his trousers begin to freeze.

A rich black man, a Republican and an abolitionist, according to Covey, whose name is Robert Purvis and who is from Philadelphia, commissions the brother of Reverend Simeon Jocelyn, Nathaniel Jocelyn, to reproduce me in the white manner on cloth. Waterfall is not impressed. He says it is less good than the white man's mirror. That there was nothing in it of the idea of me or of my spirit, which is of the sky world— certain hawks or night owls. Yet I like the "portrait," as it is called. It portrays me in the form in which I exist—a man, not a spirit—and it is beautiful. Anyone who meets beauty and does not look upon it says the Mende, will soon be poor. So I look. But nothing can change Waterfall's mind. Crocodile tries to explain Waterfall's disapproval to poor Nathaniel Jocelyn, who nods and nods, but I can tell he doesn't understand anything Covey is interpreting. For Waterfall, a portrait is not a portrait, it is a secret. In reality, it is Covey's portrait that Jocelyn the younger is painting, for *he*, War Road, is their *idea* of me. He has become my twin, sharing every word and fraction of my thought. He is obligated to speak with my voice, as I am obligated to answer with his. "I cannot believe all the men of America are against me," I tell him.

Covey explains that the portrait is the black man's idea to present me to the people of the United States, who are so against me. But I have my doubts. If it is such a good idea, why are we still in prison? And why are our protectors so afraid? Why has the new trial surprised them? They have no strategy I think. They do not know where to plant their stakes.

"I can't believe that all the men of America are against me," I repeat. And Covey shakes his head that it is the exact truth.

✌ John Quincy Adams ✌
February 1840

The sympathy of the Executive government, and as if it were of the nation, in favor of the slave-traders, and against these poor, unfortunate, helpless, tongueless, defenseless Africans, is the cause and foundation and motive of all these proceedings.

—*John Quincy Adams*

"I swear, Louisa, Van Buren gives me a fit of melancholy for the future of the republic! Cunning and duplicity pervade every line of it. What is Mr. Van Buren's claim to fame? I'll tell you— the sacrifice of the rights of Northern freedom to Southern slavery! The purchase of the West by the plunder of public lands! That is his only claim to fame—along with being the swineherd henchman of Andrew Jackson with a new coat of varnish, and the swineherd henchman of papist, royalist Spain to boot."

The abusive words withered the air like sparks from the roaring fireplace which spit and snapped back at him. John Quincy performed his little shuffle hop and moved himself closer to the flames. He put his fists behind his back and moved the thick, stubby, aching fingers, warming them.

"The White House is directly involved in the *Grumpus* affair. The White House is offering aid to slave owners and traders and volunteering influence on behalf of foreigners. There is an *abominable* Executive conspiracy going on against the lives of the Africans."

"I can't believe a real presidential conspiracy, John." Louisa was shocked. Martin Van Buren was the President, after all.

"Louisa, everybody in Washington knows Van Buren dispatched the *Grumpus* to New Haven in anticipation of a rigged trial. Joseph Cinque and his men were acquitted by a United States court and jury, but the President has decided otherwise. If that's not a conspiracy, my dear, I don't know what is."

John Quincy looked out of the window. The snow had begun to mantle everything, shimmering over the grounds and
outbuildings, it weighed the limbs of the surrendered trees,
their blackness reminding him of the flesh-and-blood men at
the center of the controversy: thirty-nine lives. A parcel of Negroes like the grove of dark trees he stood staring at this very
moment. The limbs pointed upwards as if in supplication, while
whiteness rained down on them, deforming their true silhouette. . . . Braintree, the estate of the Quincys and the Adamses
stretched for forty-seven acres. The low rolling hills were buried in snow that was almost Russian-winter depth; the land
had been his father's and his father's father's, going back two
centuries. He thought of how often he had absented himself
from it to find himself a stranger in a foreign country. But he
himself had never been *torn* away. How would he feel about
that? he wondered.

"Not only is there a conspiracy, Louisa, there is fraud, forg-
ery, withheld evidence, false testimony and perjury. The
Amistad's papers, as Dr. Madden has pointed out, are fraudulent, false documents obtained illegally from the American
consul, Trist. The passports of the *Amistad* men are forgeries—forged to make it seem as if the men were *Ladinos.* The
President has defied the Congress by authorizing secret and
illegal sailing orders to the *Grumpus,* a United States vessel.
He has failed to uphold the Constitution by trying to influence
the Judiciary in violation of the Constitutionally decreed separation of the Executive powers from the Justice Department.
Then, there is the matter of corruption. The witnesses are lying
for money—the salvage of the *Amistad.* Why do you think Van
Buren is glowing and stinking, and stinking and glowing, excuse the vulgarity, my dear—at the very *thought* that all this
may come out? And in an election year? The president's afraid
of the South, but he needs the North. Let's make it clear, Louisa,
the decision in favor of Joseph Cinque is a good one. Cinque
has already won his trial. What must be defended now is *this
decision,* and not the abolition of slavery. And this is what I
have to make clear to these fanatic abolitionists. Joseph Cinque
considers himself at war with the United States. And he is. He
doesn't have to acquire his liberty. He possesses it already. He
has defended it already. Don't confuse the right to liberty with
the gift of liberty. This is not a case of emancipation but self-

defense. Don't confuse slavery with skin color."

"And does Joseph Cinque understand all this?"

"I would think he understands nothing. If he had, he would have realized that his real enemy was Ruiz and not the captain he killed. And Ruiz wouldn't be around to testify today, and perhaps the captain could really have sailed them back to Africa. Cinque doesn't understand to this day that he killed the wrong man. . . ."

Adams paused. The issue of Joseph Cinque had been nibbling away at the edges of his life for more than a year now, he thought, and it was finally crossing his path. The abolitionists Tappan and Baldwin were on their way to Braintree. He didn't have to ask why. He wondered what manner of man was this Joseph Cinque, who had so disrupted the final chapter of his own tumultuous life. He had read some of the newspaper stories about him that painted him as everything from saint to a savage, from the symbol of liberty and self-defense to a gibbering ape, a heathen straight out of the jungle. Was he a noble prince or a cannibal who dealt in slaves himself and had been sold by his own people for debt?

Tappan and his little band were going to ask him to defend him, he thought, when, at seventy-three, his eyes were failing him, his teeth were dropping from his head, his hands trembled, his memory had deserted him. His imagination had fallen into sere and yellow leaf, and his judgment was slowly sinking into dotage. And for his trouble, he could look forward to even more threats and letters, mud-slinging and ostracism. But he had never feared any of these things. With Abigail Adams as mother and John Adams as a father, he had long ceased fearing anything.

Lewis Tappan, Joshua Leavitt and Roger Baldwin were determined to be persuasive:

"It appears to me that your mind is in a quandary on the subject of the people of color in this country," Tappan began. This was not true: John Quincy knew perfectly well where he stood, but he listened. "Permit me to inquire, Mr. President, if this does not arise either from an unwillingness to look the subject in the face, or the simplicity of the remedy? One of three things must take place: a geographical separation of the white and colored races, amalgamation, or the coexistence of blacks and whites on a footing of social and political equality. Let us contemplate the subject philosophically.

"If slavery continues many years more, will not an amalgamation of the blacks and whites be effected by the present course of things? Or if the maxim of the civil law *partus sequitur ventrum*—the condition of the child shall follow the condition of the mother—should be changed to the old common law doctrine, *partus sequitur patrem*—the condition of the child to follow the condition of the father—and prevail in all the slave states, and throughout the United States, what becomes of American slavery? As to a geographical separation of the white and colored inhabitants on this continent, Thomas Jefferson, as you know, predicted, fifty years ago, that this would measurably take place.

"Now, sir, as one of these three things I've mentioned takes place, and in that not distant day—and as it now depends upon the Anglo-Saxon race in this country to make a choice—is it not wise to inquire which is most desirable? I am acquainted with a Mr. Braithwaite, a worthy man who predicts that in five hundred years all the inhabitants on this continent, white, red and black, will be one complexion; and that the comingling of the Anglo-Saxon, the Indian and the African shades will produce a complexion unique and surpassing in beauty anything that has appeared on earth since the creation of Adam and Eve. *De gustibus non est disputandum.*"

"*Foenum habet in Coram,*" replied Adams. If the man wanted to puncture his tirade with Latin quotations, he would accommodate him, but the gist of what Tappan was saying was so horrible, he could hardly think. Tappan must have seen it in his expression.

"Mr. President, you nor I do not expect to see such a result, neither now nor in another age. Nor do I contemplate the existence of both a white and black government on this continent with any satisfaction. You see then, that I, at least, am for the coexistence of the whites and blacks on a footing of social and political equality. Is it not wise to choose, and that speedily, what must come sooner or later, and probably under more disadvantageous circumstances? It is the least of all the evils that environ us on this subject. Declamation, ridicule, 'calling names,' have no place anymore. The subject is too grave and momentous. With Daniel Webster I can say, 'I am an American,' and with the weal or woe of my country I must abide."

Webster and he were good friends and rivals for the title of the most eloquent speaker in the United States. Together, almost ten years ago, they had formed the American Lyceum Society, the first debating society in the New World.

"You know Mister Webster?" John Quincy asked Tappan, a bit maliciously since he knew Tappan had asked Daniel Webster to defend the Amistaders before he had asked him. But he underestimated Tappan's honesty.

"The Amistad Committee actually approached Mister Daniel Webster to lead our defense before the Supreme Court. But Mister Webster declined."

"What reasons did he give?"

"Well, he said he did not wish to extend his practice any further in that Court and that our lawyers were all very eminent and talented and didn't need any help."

It was no surprise to Adams that Daniel Webster had declined. Though from Massachusetts, he was moderately anti-slavery but ferociously States Rights even if it sanctioned slaves as property and slavery. He was also arguing another slavery case before the Court, that of Groves *vs.* Slaughter, in which the question was, could the transfer and sale of slaves from one State to another be regulated by Congress under its power to regulate commerce. He had no use for people like Tappan and little rapport with them. Daniel Webster wanted to be President of the United States and he would make a great President of the United States, but being connected with abolitionists was no way to the presidency. On the other hand, he, Adams, had already *been* President of the United States. Moreover he was a President's son.

Adams sighed and looked at the tabernacle owner from New York City, the abolitionist lawyer from Massachusetts, and the editor of the *Emancipator* from Yale. What did this Joseph Cinque think of all these strange, eccentric men? Weren't they as curious to him as he was to them? Mr. Day, the deaf-mute professor? The Yale Divinity students like Whittier? The lawyers like Sedgwick? The preachers like Leavitt? The Irish doctor Madden? Did Cinque have any idea what a bastard Forsyth was? Or what a yellow-livered coward Van Buren was? Or that Justice Taney of the Supreme Court was Van Buren's lackey and owned slaves himself?

Tappan squirmed under John Quincy's penetrating and troubling survey, not understanding. Had he gone too far? He looked around the comfortable but sparse sitting room. A sense of history seemed to be everywhere, a part of the decor of the room, from the pale yellow walls, hung with European paintings, to the draped bust of John Adams, the writing table of Abigail Adams: the souvenirs from the many posts in which the Adamses had served.

The chandelier glowed, silver gleamed, silk and chintz warmed, paintings and sculpture spoke. John Quincy seemed as much a part of the room as its furniture as he sat Buddhalike, stubbornly mute. John Quincy could be, thought Baldwin, as taciturn as the Libyan desert when he wanted to.

"The *Amistad* captives seem to have no chance at all before the Supreme Court." He didn't add: If you, Mr. President, don't defend them.

"If the White House or the Judiciary had any respect for *legality* instead of guns," said Quincy Adams, finally breaking his silence, "they would have accepted the point of view of my old friend Thompson and we could have avoided the dirty undeclared war we're in against the Seminole nation and their leader Osceola to recover fugitive slaves. . . ."

"Isn't this the same issue as Cinque?" said Leavitt eagerly. "If the United States can fight Osceola for not—as a sovereign nation—returning fugitive slaves, well then, the Southern states can fight the Northern states for the same reason, and eventually the blacks can take the occasion to fight the whites."

"And Cinque can fight for the return of himself," said Tappan.

"Why," asked Adams, his dark eyes brooding, "should we consider Joseph Cinque a slave simply because he is considered a slave ad hoc by the people who captured a black skin they intend to hang?"

"Not if *you* have anything to do with it."

Adams whistled under his breath, avoiding the question in the statement and in the eyes of his interlocutors. They were convinced that he was their man. Well, was he? Out loud he said, "It seems clear that Cinque and his major lieutenants all belong to a secret society back in Africa called Poro. Of course,

I could never accept the morality of a secret organization like that of Jefferson and Franklin and ever so many more. But I recognize the great moral efficiency of a secret society. After all, forty-nine of the fifty-one signers of the Declaration of Independence were Masons . . . and look where it got them. . . ." Adams even managed a smile, his old quarter moon, which looked very odd indeed on his face. But his intentions remained a mystery to the three men as they rode their diligence back to New Haven.

Quincy Adams paced up and down the length of the white-panelled study with increasing agitation little short of agony. The fire cast long black shadows, and the deep snow outside shouldered the glazed double doors as if it would have liked to come in. It isolated her husband even further from the world, thought Louisa, who had sat down at her card table. As far as *inside* her own house, Charles Francis Quincy Adams was accusing his father of trying to ruin *both* their political careers by even considering defending Joseph Cinque.

"He's being selfish. He's not thinking of anyone except himself!"

"He's thinking of Cinque's men, Charles," Louisa answered.

"It will kill him!" Charles replied.

"Is that selfish?" she asked.

"He ought to have more consideration for my position in the state legislature and my election!"

"My dearest, I'm sure he's taking into account your feelings. He has not decided yet."

"You know what this country does to men who love Negroes. . . ."

"Too much," said Louisa coldly.

"Yes, too much. Defense in the Supreme Court of Joseph Cinque will break out every enemy, every opponent he's ever had, and—"

"And your father has never wanted for enemies or opponents." Just sons, she thought silently.

"Is his pride of abolitionist oratory not glutted, Mother? Is he going to spend the rest of his days producing a civil war single-handedly? Does he want to ruin the country just because he lost his reelection to the presidency?"

"I forbid you to speak of your father in those terms, Charles."

Would he sacrifice the happiness of this son too? For an idea?

Louisa gathered her tarot cards together. She was a talented and sought-after fortune teller. She had intended to leave because Charles was spoiling for a fight with his father. But now he blocked her way. She decided to remain seated.

"I'm sure your father has no intention of harming your chances at reelection, Charles."

"Of course, not *intentionally*, Mother. He just hasn't gotten around to thinking or feeling what it will do to me!"

"Well, it won't do to you what it will do to those poor men."

"You, too, Mother!"

"I only know that the Amistaders must be delivered from the machinations of an entire administration that has been set against their freedom for purely political reasons. They are free men and deserve to go free!" said John Quincy from across the room.

"And we are interfering in the affairs of another government—Spain. We are charging that Cuba is not complying with its treaty with Britain, thus giving her an excuse to walk in and annex it. The Amistaders are the property of Spanish nationals," replied Charles.

"Really? The *property*. Since when are men the property of anyone?" said Louisa. "Or women," she added under her breath.

"Mother, you make me sound like I'm *for* slavery and against eventual emancipation, which you know is not true. That isn't fair!"

"Neither is Joseph Cinque's trial. When he has already been set free twice by the Circuit Court of the State of Connecticut and a jury!" stormed John Quincy.

Louisa Adams looked up at her last son, Charles Francis. He alone of twelve pregnancies and seven miscarriages had survived his perilous birth, brief kidnapping, all the epidemics and accidents of life. He alone was the next generation of Adamses. Of the three sons who had become men, she had never allowed Mr. Adams to separate her from this one.

"I know how you feel. I, too, have felt—how many times— the scorpion tongue of political slander. It has assailed your father . . . me . . . for no reason except the envy and ambition and duplicity of other men. But this time I cannot, will not, preach for a different decision."

John Quincy looked surprised. He had not told Louisa he intended to defend Joseph Cinque. . . .

The delicate, small woman with light brown eyes, the graying but not yet gray hair, and the bewitching enigmatic smile, willed herself to calmness. The house, she knew, belonged more to her mother-in-law Abigail Adams than it ever would to her, even now. She was resigned to it. She was resigned to everything concerning the Adamses. It was Abigail's voice she listened to these days. That quintessential puritan woman, frugal, independent, diligent, courageous, self-righteous, ardent in love, who had only yearned for a *room of her own* and for the men of the Constitution *not to forget the ladies.* For months she had been discovering a woman she wished she had known better. She and John Quincy had been going through her mother-in-law's letters, searching for a clue to their own dilemma. Louisa read and reread the passionate, intelligent, urgent words of the woman she had so feared when she was alive: clues to happiness, dignity, femininity, farming, child-raising. This was, thought Louisa, the American woman before being somehow left behind in the rush to form a nation of white men. Abigail had pleaded with John Adams, but John Adams had found the very idea of female equality laughable.

"And what about me!" cried Charles. "The elections are now. And my term is up. Father will unseat me with this."

Lost elections and bitter feuds, thought Louisa.

Louisa looked up at what was left of her family. Two grown sons had fallen victim to the flaws in the Adams dynasty; her father-in-law always said that they had been visited upon his progeny for the sin of pride. His grandson and namesake had died of fever, drink and the strain of having to squeeze a profit from his father's mills to stave off bankruptcy. Her poor George had died a suicide, drowned in the Potomac River.

"Charles, you know as well as I that this has gone beyond simply the freeing of Joseph Cinque and his men. Even beyond the abolition of slavery. One hundred ninety-six thousand seven hundred and twenty petitions opposing slavery and thirty-two thousand opposing the Twenty-first Rule of the House sit accusingly in a room in the Capitol. Where the issue *was* the abolition of slavery, it *now* is the right to petition, and the right of free speech. By not allowing the American people to petition Congress on the issue of slavery, and by not allowing any discussion of slavery in Congress, we are in direct violation of our most precious treasure, the Constitution of the United States. If the House can refuse petitions concerning slavery, why, they can refuse petitions on *any* issue it wants! Free white Americans are now the issue, Charles; for the first time they are asking if any among us is enslaved, are the rest of us free? As for Cinque, if the White House can interfere with a verdict of the Judiciary, then where is the separation between the two branches dictated by the Constitution?

"If the Supreme Court doesn't defy him, where are we?" asked Louisa.

"A slave-owning Chief Justice will *never* defy a slavery-loving President. But this doesn't help *me* much."

Louisa stared down at her tarot cards. She had often been haunted by fears of insanity, fears that returned so often they now kept her company, and she often imagined sliding softly into a nether dreamworld, or slipping quietly out of her skin and her life, into another.

I was presented at the Imperial Court in St. Petersburg in 1809, only a week after arriving in this capital with Mr. Adams as the new American Minister. My sponsor was Potemkin's niece, a handsome fat girl who helped me to rehearse for the ceremony. I wore a heavy silver hoop skirt and a crimson robe with a long train trimmed in white. As I stood in the center of a vast hall completely empty, completely alone, facing two gigantic double doors, two tall negroes dressed like Turks in splendid uniforms took positions on each side of the door and drew their swords. The Czar was Alexander, who was very fond of black men. When the double doors opened, I saw a corridor of at least a quarter of a mile long, lined on each side with identically dressed black men with sabers.

The Grand Marshal, the Czar and the Czarina marched towards me like three gilded automats followed by the innumerable ladies and gentlemen of the court. I curtsied slowly, as I had been taught. Alexander had been young then, only thirty-one, tall, fair, strong, handsome and radiating the apo-

*gee of his power. I liked him. He would rule Russia for an-
other twenty-five years. It was an unreal world, his court, filled
with gossip and rumors, charming perfidy, espionage and ci-
phers. I danced until four, rose at eleven, dined at five, took
tea at ten and went out to supper at midnight. I belonged to
the most futile, amusing, immoral society in the world. I filled
my days with ceremony and banquets, polonaises and cham-
pagne, caviar and sweets. The French Ambassador spent
350,000 rubles on entertainment and maintained a household
of sixty-five people and fifty-six horses. Our salary was 9,000
dollars plus 9,000 in expenses, more than the President of the
United States earned. I made my own dresses, lived in a hotel
full of rats and watched bankruptcy stare my husband in the
face, knowing I had brought him no dowery, so that every
economy was a burning slap in the face. I became the poor
the rich always had with them. Only the Czar understood how
poor we really were. In 1811 I gave birth to a baby girl. I had
been married fourteen years. My child died in Russia just as
Napoleon's armies crossed the Nieman River. I found no affection or comfort or gentleness in Mr. Adams. During that winter of 1812 and 1813 I buried my sorrow in reading. I read
seeking answers for a troubled mind. Since that winter, I have
never been sure of my perfect sanity.*

Lost elections and bitter feuds. Louisa watched the last
two men in her life in quarrelsome conversation. She looked
out of the window, over the landscape, her tarot cards still
in hand.

*In the winter of 1815, being left alone by Mr. Adams, who
had gone to Paris to make peace, I was ordered to close our
embassy and house and to join him, and so I set out with
Charles, a baby, and three servants unprotected by any man
across the frozen wastes of Russia and Poland, on the coat-
tails of Napoleon's retreating armies.*

*That journey is the only event in my life that defined me as
a person. I relied only upon myself. I demonstrated that under
such circumstances, a woman is equal to a man at least as
long as one holds a cocked pistol, the great equalizer. I was
attacked by soldiers only twice. The rumor was that I was
Napoleon's sister on her way to Paris, which I encouraged with
smiles and waves of my handkerchief. When I arrived in Paris*

at the Hotel du Nord on Rue de Richelieu, Mr. Adams wasn't
home. I have survived life's calamities, long separations, voy-
ages, illnesses, dark winters, fears of insanity, melancholy
loneliness, disappointed love. For the first time I am the only
and most powerful woman in Mr. Adams' life.

Louisa had began a journal which she called *The Adven-*
tures of a Nobody.

"Mother!" Charles burst into her thoughts. "Father has really
decided to do it! Despite my wishes. Despite my warnings. It
will kill him!"

"My dear Charles," sighed Adams, "while a single remnant
of physical power is left to me to write and speak, the world
will retire from me before I shall retire from the world. But I
don't intend to have anything to do with the trial of Joseph
Cinque. . . ."

Louisa turned over the card which represented Joseph
Cinque. It was the Hanged Man.

The Secretary of State was finding it hard to concentrate on
the President's words. His mind was on the *Amistad,* anchored
less than fifty miles away in the estuary of Long Island Sound.

"I do not suppose it necessary to investigate the question
whether, in point of morality, slavery is justifiable or not," said
the President of the United States for the hundredth time.
"There is very little doubt the more reflecting portion of society would like to see the system abolished. But, it is quite too
late to raise the question whether slavery is consistent with
the laws of nations or not. And it being the case, either by
principle, comity or treaty, that these Spanish citizens are entitled to hold these slaves, *I am bound to devise a method by*
which they can obtain possession of them!

"If there has been any arrangement made between the
Spanish and British governments, it is nothing to us. But you
tell me, Forsyth, that there is a treaty between us and Great
Britain; and by that we are bound to use our best endeavors to
put an end to the slave trade. What does that contract mean
between our two nations? If we are under obligation, by the
treaty with Spain, to return these slaves to the Spanish claimants, that obligation must be discharged, and we cannot plead
our treaty with Great Britain against it."

"The authority of the President can only interfere," said Forsyth, "where vessels have violated the laws of the United States; and this gives you authority. But I must warn you, Mr. President, it is as far from the spirit as from the letter of the law, to authorize any armed vessel of the United States to interfere without the authority of Congress."

"Forsyth, I depended on you to keep us out of this quarrel. Instead, in your presumptions of Southern amenity, you have involved us both deeply."

"All this over a handful of bad niggers," Forsyth fumed. "All over that Negro Joseph Cinque. You would think he was Hannibal himself come to march through Virginia with a hundred thousand men, like Nat Turner was supposed to have done! How irrational can a country get?"

"The Spanish minister has correctly pointed out," said Van Buren, "that if the *Amistad* insurrectionists go unpunished, there will be further slave revolts. It is not only your South that lives with the specter of Nat Turner."

"I've asked for more documents to support the Spanish side of the case, other than the *Amistad*'s papers," replied Forsyth, trying to control his legendary temper, "but the Spanish minister simply does not understand the workings of a democratic Congress and the separation of the Executive and the Judiciary. He demands you overrule the verdict without delay. I've done my best in private meetings to point out that the wishes of a President can be thwarted by an obscure judge, some busybody private citizens and a gang of savages. He does not believe me. It is simply incomprehensible to him!"

"I know," said Van Buren. "Washington Irving has had no better luck. More interestingly, he learned in Hartford, from the painter, John Trumbull, that the Tappans are frightened enough to have asked John Quincy Adams for help with the appeal. Adams is advising them, but our friend says he has refused to do further on the grounds of age, infirmity and, no doubt, drunkenness."

"God, sir, he is like one of those old cardinals who, as quick as he's chosen Pope, throws away his crutches and his crookedness and is as straight as a boy. That old roué cannot live on slops, but must have sulfuric acid in his tea."

Van Buren's small eyes shifted nervously. "In other words,"

said the President, "it would please him to embarrass me on this. Adams can lose me the reelection, Forsyth."

"So can the South, Mr. President."

"But not on the grounds of obstruction of justice. My presidency is in the hands of a pack of Negroes and their henchmen lawyers!"

❧ Joseph Cinque ❧
April 1840

The words slave and slavery are studiously excluded from the
Constitution. Circumlocutions are the fig leaves under which
these parts of the body politic are decently concealed. Slaves,
therefore, in the Constitution of the United States are recognized only as *persons* . . .

— *John Quincy Adams*

"Cinque!"

As I turn, I discover how many moons have passed. Spring
has arrived and Covey's captain has returned for him. It makes
me feel old, as if much more than a year has passed.

"The rebellion of Joseph Cinque," says Captain Fitzgerald,
"is famous! You are a celebrated man; in plays, pamphlets,
portraits, doctor's opinions and the abolitionist press!"

The new trial is more than five moons away, and more than
that, it is sure to return us to Cuba and death. The bitterness
of the trial at Hartford remains with me. It blights the bond
that had grown up between the men and their teachers. There
persists a pall of distrust and even contempt for the white man.
I oscillate between moods of intense elation and depression. I
am never happier than when we have outwitted some foolish
white man or mastered one of his skills. And I am never more
melancholy than when brooding over the impossibility of ever
being free. We cannot help but react to the incentives and prizes
of this new world, each according to his temperament; the oppressive atmosphere spawns the blind rebellion of Big Sun and
the submissiveness of Remember. The younger men like Bone,
Cricket, Twin and Sword do better in instruction than the older
Waterfall and Have-Mercy. From our child's speech of a year
ago we have progressed to a certain awkward fluency in English. I have learned to decipher the black marks that dance
across the pages of the Book until I can now arrange them into

245

the words and the sounds they represent. Thus I have become literate in a sense, a condition I consider magical. Indeed I do like to see my name standing, independent of me yet completely mine. I begin to write, and I understand everything. Yet instead of making me less lonely, the very act of communication seemed to reinforce my sense of isolation and futility. I have forgotten Mende ways and wish I did not have to live this way. There is a wild, intense longing to belong, to feel I am alive as others are, instead of being caught up forgetfully in rancor and waiting. The shadings and nuances of life in the New World are filled in by observing the lives of the whites, their way of thinking and most of all their knowledge. I look at things with a painful and unwarrantable nakedness which is my way of escaping intolerable captivity and aimlessness. And so I hover unwanted between unwanted worlds—the United States and my own humiliated place in it. For our teachers, the delay between the trials is a godsend. For they think we have appeared uniquely and solely in order that our souls be saved by Yale College.

Covey's great preoccupation is his courtship of Vivian Braithwaite. He still hopes for her father's permission, but to me it has always seemed a hopeless, melancholy proposition. Marriage to a girl like Vivian means months of negotiation, a family, a bride's wealth, a powerful intermediary. Covey has none of these things. One can not just go and kidnap a girl like that. When I try to explain this to him, realizing he has been away from Mendeland too long, he merely laughs and said this is America.

"But she wants her father's consent," I say.

"Of course," replies Covey. "I am patient."

No bride money. No marriage contract. No family broker or matchmaker; what kind of betrothal is this? I wonder.

"And the slaves of this country. Are they allowed to marry?"

"They are allowed to procreate. But a father can be sold away from his children and their mother. Mothers can be sold away from their children. And children can be sold away from their parents. And there is no law which recognizes marriage between slaves."

"And marriage between slaves and freedmen?"

"If you mean between blacks and whites, it is a felony in all the states in the Union. If you mean between a black slave and a black freedman, the free one can always buy or attempt to buy the bound one."

"And this occurs often?"

"Not so often, but it happens. A man allowed to work a few hours for himself saves enough to buy himself. He then works to pay for his wife and children one by one. Some men have taken decades, but they have done it. Some women too. Then there are the fugitive slaves, runaways who once free themselves, return South for their wives and children. One man made seven trips back to rescue his whole family, each time at the risk of death."

"Then there are heroes as well as slaves."

"For me, all slaves are heroes. If they remain alive . . ."

And so little by little I put together a picture of slavery in the New World, as I put together a picture of the white and black men who inhabit it.

Covey's captain is a tall, young white man with red hair and a gentle expression. He expects Covey will leave with him to Mendeland, but it doesn't take him long to realize Covey is landlocked, probably forever. The captain has already met Vivian, speaks of her as one of 'a new generation of young women' who think and act as young men of the same age would. She is feminine, he adds, but there is a directness and lack of wiles about her that he greatly admires. He, too, like me, has decided Vivian is fearless. He, too, like Covey, describes her voice as one that solitary sailors dream of on long cruises. As his captain sings the virtues of his love, Covey and I listen, even a little jealous. But I am the one who has the idea of asking the captain to speak to Vivian's father, Mende style, substituting himself for the family Covey does not have. To his delight, Captain Fitzgerald agrees.

"Well," he says, because he doesn't know what else to say, "an old uncle's help is worth something, at least!"

I smile, for in Mende fashion, it is one's uncle, not one's father, who commands unquestioning obedience. For Mende believe that one can only be sure that one was born of one's mother, but never absolutely of one's father, so that it is the brother of one's mother who may indeed be one's closest male blood relative with certainty, and therefore worthy of total respect.

Everyone respects Vivian Braithwaite's father in a manner which is more than esteem. It reflects on his whole clan as it would have in Mendeland. Cotton and Jefferson, the oldest of the sons, are already considered part of the village community. They are unusually tall. I, for example, barely reached Cotton Braithwaite's shoulder, and I am not a small man. Jefferson is shorter but more massive. And both have the amiable disposition of their father and sister. They venerate their mother and sisters in the Mende fashion. And they obey their father unquestioningly.

Braithwaite is our link to the free black men of New Haven, of Montauk, Hartford, Canterbury and many of the other villages surrounding our prison. These men and their wives astound me. It is like a meeting of the elders. Instead of Poro or Sande secret societies, they have their churches. Each village church links in brotherhood with the others, all standing together in a crisis or a disaster. I am the subject of many of their worried conversations.

They speak and think like white men. They had once been African, but nothing of that has remained. Their churches sit, built in white wood like ships with high roofs under a cross, not a tree or a stone. Gewo exists, but none of the other gods. Instead, they worship saints, saints that according to the famous Book have been living men. So, I believe, they continue to worship ancestors. Summer comes and the wheat ripens. I am lonely for my own fields, and for a meal of rice. In Mende there is a saying, if one has not eaten rice, one has not eaten. The restless, unhappy men long for a break in their humiliating routine. From heroes we have become wards and paupers; children white boys ride out to harass and taunt. In the village Have-Mercy-on-Me and Python have been set upon and beaten by a band of these adolescents. When I think of it, I am more and more ashamed to face any woman, especially Vivian.

Vivian Braithwaite reminds me more and more of Bayeh Bia, except that she dresses as white people do: covered from head to foot. This day Vivian is all in white, wearing a wide-brimmed straw hat trimmed in flowers, with a blue veil against mosquitos. She wears mittens on her hands, shoes on her feet—even white stockings—yet she seems cooler in the heat with all this than Bayeh Bia in her lappa. When I tell her this she laughs, then looks at me quite strangely for a long while, silent, pensive. It is hard to read her face, shaded as it is by a large hat, but the splendid eyes gaze out at me, burning.

"You know more about War Road than I do," she says accusingly.

"Co-vey," I say gently.

"We belong to the same nation," I continue. "Our clans are not far removed, our villages either. We are like twins. Co-vey gave me a voice, a language to defend myself and my men. He gave us the only chance we had to speak the white language, to be understood and listened to by white men. Without Covey we would be as mute as mountain lions, unable to do anything except growl and strike out blindly at our enemies."

"Which is a good way, Mr. Cinque, to get killed in this country."

"And what is good way to survive in this country?" I ask.

"There is no good way," she says without rancor, "or rather, there are many ways, few of them worthy of human dignity."

"Will you go with Covey?" I ask her, "after we are free?"

"Will Covey stay with me?" she replies accusingly.

I do not know what to say. I know that War Road loves her; that she is, above all, lovable, of this I have no doubt, but I know he detests Americans, loathes their ways with black men, fears their laws and their slavery. He suffers from keeping his temper here. He claims he has not had a good night's sleep since he had left his ship, except when he was ill and in the arms of the creature now looking at me so belligerently. I know War Road is not a man for this country, the way that Vivian's father is. Mende ways made it difficult to believe in good fortune or good works. The black man here is obligated to believe in goodness. That America is good. Mendes detest violence and resort to it only when provoked. Vivian's father is a violent man, a New World man who believes only in action, who believes man's goal is perfection, not compromise. Mendes believe in fate, that all is written, all is destiny. Our actions, our punishments and our rewards have been written long ago by the behavior of our ancestors. If they have been just men, then we can call on them for help—many the night I have done so— but the great force, Gewo, is the final judge, and he is, by the nature of having to deal with men, cruel, undecipherable and unforgiving, much like the God of Abraham: an eye for an eye. People here believe they have convinced God that being born American they are different. That they of all people were born just.

"You will win, Cinque," she says. "I believe in God."

"Then *you* did send War Road to me?" I ask. "For when you disappeared from the jailhouse, he appeared."

"But I always believed *you* sent *me* Covey!" Vivian exclaimed. "Imagine finding the other half of your soul appearing suddenly from across the sea."

"Perhaps both are true," I say. "You imagine Covey came all this way for me?"

We both sit, smiling shyly. The words I have spoken in her language had been a great effort for me. The sharp, ugly sounds of English often catch in my throat. But this time something else has me by the throat: fear for Vivian and Covey, fear of what might be written, and above all, a premonition of all our deaths, far from home.

"Let's believe," she says, "that we sent each other War Road. It is so very beautiful that way."

Ꮛ Vivian Braithwaite Ꮛ
May 1840

War, conquest and force, have produced slavery, and it is state necessity and the internal law of self-preservation, that will ever perpetuate and defend it. Is it the principle of that DEC-LARATION? That DECLARATION says that every man is "endowed by his Creator with certain inalienable rights," and that "among these are life, liberty, and the pursuit of happiness." If these rights are inalienable, they are incompatible with the rights of the victor to take the life of his enemy in war, or to spare his life and make him a slave.

—*John Quincy Adams*

Again and again Covey and Vivian returned to the cliffs opposite Montauk Point and the sea. The great whales and their harems had not yet returned. So they watched the empty sea sweep by them, dreaming upon it. All around them was the spare, economical, prudent, benevolent New England landscape. Covey thought of the swift, violent squalls and tropical storms of Sierra Leone; the hot winds of the harmattan, the years of the locust, the sunless rain forests and the treeless steppes where men and beasts roamed freely. Yet even here in this domesticated landscape, Covey felt an echo of all that danger beneath the order, the serenity, the clapboard houses and white picket fences, the fields of corn and potatoes. He wondered if he had brought it with him, all the violence of his former life, and if it lay there, coiled like a viper, in this exceedingly safe and peaceful harbor. Now it was his home as well, thought Covey. It offered him land which was rich, bountiful and beautiful even to his sailor's eyes. Six months ago he had been an orphan with an affectionate attachment to a young English sea captain and a newborn loyalty to a man called Cinque. Now his emotions were so tumultuously engaged that he wondered if he could still find room for the meager attachments of his past life. In the spring of long and secret reverie, while their love for each other slowly subjugated all their faculties to its own unique end, Vivian and Covey lingered at Culloden Point, lying length to length in the splendor of high grass, gazing at the sea that had brought them together. Covey strove over Vivian's face as he would have climbed an unconquered mountain, not content until he had placed his mark on every facet, stone, crevice, rock, to snatch, hold on, grasp, in an embrace of mysterious and powerful desire, leaving him stranded in a whirlwind of sensation, battered like an ensign. Again and again he pulled Vivian into his arms and held her, clinging to her like a reefed ship in a storm.

It was also the beginning of a morbid jealousy. Covey grew so jealous he saw jealousy everywhere. Even Cinque was not immune, although he knew this was unjust. His love had produced a great, restless discontent, and he found it took all his strength to hide it from Vivian. This and the anguish of not knowing if Vivian's father would consent to their marriage tormented him. Did he really wish to remain in this country? If not, where would they go? Vivian had grown so large in Covey's heart that often emotion surprised him and happiness suddenly took him by the throat, like an enemy. Covey knew all this to be common to all lovers. For it was an old Mende saying that a lover had eyes only for the scrutiny of that one human form that belonged to him because it was written, and that contained the core of the world.

"In Mende," Covey said to Vivian, "one's uncle is one's ambassador in matters of marriage, if you have not already been betrothed as a child. The American custom of confronting your father face to face makes me feel like bursting into tears. What if he refuses? Elopement is the only other solution."

I shall call you War Road, for you have made me your captive.

Elopement, kidnapping, thought Covey. It was unthinkable. It was bride-stealing, punishable by death under Mende law.

Henry Braithwaite stood silhouetted by the dull oil lamp, his desk littered with papers and pamphlets, ink samples and boxes, his large hand stretched across the long worktable to greet Gabriel Fitzgerald.

They were very similar in height and build, and for a long

time spoke standing. It was only after Captain Fitzgerald had stated his business that Braithwaite invited him to sit down.

"I know," said Fitzgerald tensely, "you are aware of the love that has developed between Covey and your daughter. I have come to ask you to consider a match between them."

From the look on Henry Braithwaite's face, Captain Fitzgerald saw that despite everything, the request had shocked him. Fathers, he thought. They were all the same. He thought of the five generations of Braithwaites, all freemen. How had they gotten here? Surely they had not dropped from the sky. There must have been another James Covey somewhere, back there.

"A foreigner," said Braithwaite tremulously.

"An African son," said Fitzgerald.

"But an Englishman, nevertheless!"

"And a gentleman," replied Fitzgerald. "He is the apple of my eye. He is one of the bravest, most honest and most tender men I know. I believe it would be a marriage of great felicity, and after all, there is little of that in this world."

"He asked you to speak for him."

"I am his family," said Fitzgerald.

"*We* are Americans," Braithwaite said pathetically. Fitzgerald's heart contracted at the pathos of the words on which this man had constructed his whole life. "And let me tell you what that means. We are Americans, and rich and respected, but are we really free if my sons cannot set foot beyond Philadelphia without running the risk of being kidnapped and sold down to Georgia, for want of a pass, a slip of paper, a letter from a white man stating they are spoken for? Where I cannot set foot in Washington City without risking the same? I read the advertisements for fugitive slaves I print! Fifty dollars for a runaway caught in Virginia, Maryland or Washington. Two hundred dollars for the same slave caught in Pennsylvania, Massachusetts or Connecticut! The South claims the Negro as property, but the North holds him pinned down to the earth as with the point of a bayonet!"

"Are we discussing marriage, Mr. Braithwaite, or war?"

Braithwaite's hands dropped wearily. "You know why I can't let Covey have Vivian," he said, not unsympathetically but in a definite uppercase typeface. "What can he offer a girl brought up like mine? Does he have the ground under his feet? Does he have a roof over his head that is not in the middle of the

Atlantic? Money in the bank? How much has he saved as a seaman? Not much, I'll wager." Fitzgerald started to speak. "Never mind, never mind. Black men can't be expected to be rich," Braithwaite continued in a more conciliatory, Calson Bold face. "It's a hard life, the sea. The wife of a mariner is the loneliest woman alive, unless she's a captain's wife who can sail with him. Does James intend to leave Vivian alone, each shore leave with another little one until . . . until what? Does he intend to give up the sea for her?" Fitzgerald nodded and began to speak, but Braithwaite gave him no quarter. "Well, all right. But to do what? Where? Think he can farm? Trade? Preach? He will take her far away from me." He eyed Fitzgerald paternally. "You think I'm being hard, Fitzgerald, don't you? Or cruel. Or selfish. Believe me, I'm not. Covey has not grown up with the rules of the game we must play here. Have you noticed James' eyes?"

"Of course," said Fitzgerald.

"A black man who has eyes like that is a dead man here. And I don't want my daughter a widow. It took me thirty years to earn the reputation of being an 'uppity' Negro; Covey has done it in only six months. And you know why? It's his Argus eyes, his sailor's gaze. Just like yours, Captain. Straight ahead because you've *got* to see; not the damn planks of the deck, but the far, far horizon. But that look is not for black men in America, in 1840. People think black men should look at the ground, or to heaven as a last resort, and anything in between is against the law, Fitzgerald. When addressed, a black man should look to the left of a white man's ear. I've lost many a client, looking a man in the eye. A man will walk into my printing shop for the first time and call me Henry, call my wife Auntie, call Cotton boy. Perfect strangers ask me where I hail from, what I'm doing wherever I find myself, as if I needed their personal permission. They think the state of slavery of some of us gives them rights over all of us. You own one black man and you have a master's rights over *all* black men. Every black American must endure that powerlessness. This shapeless, nameless conspiracy determines the lives of the whole colored population. A transplanted Irishman, German, Englishman is an American in one generation. A transplanted African is not one in five!

"It becomes Covey as a black man to consider and to fully

understand who his enemies are, where they are, and what they are before he takes on the responsibility of a family.

"Well, we have gone a long way from a profession of love, have we not, Fitzgerald? Don't think I don't understand. I have known such passion that I played the Devil to win Increase, and tempted her father with a holy Bible he coveted." His eyes burned into Fitzgerald's.

Where had all this tempestuous anger and emotion come from? Fitzgerald wondered. "You mean, you, too, are going to punish Covey for being black?" whispered a shocked Fitzgerald.

But Braithwaite seemed to be speaking more to himself than to the captain, and Fitzgerald knew that Braithwaite would not accede either to his daughter's happiness or to Covey's passion.

"I love Covey, Fitzgerald, but my answer has to be no. Unless," Braithwaite laughed, "he can tempt me with a Bible."

And Fitzgerald wondered why it was that blacks had learned to laugh in the face of the destruction of dreams.

Increase Braithwaite held the silver brush in suspense over the gleaming blackness of her hair when she saw Vivian, barefooted and in her nightgown, outlined in the doorframe of her bedroom, reflected in her dressing table mirror, her oil lamp casting a faint yellow pallor over her features. Silently, Vivian padded over to where her mother sat and without a word, took the hairbrush from her hand and kneeling, began to stroke the long undulating mass which fell to the floor. Methodically and efficiently Vivian's hands swept down the splendid silk highway, smoothing with one hand and brushing with the other.

"I love him," she said, not raising her eyes from her mother's hair. But Increase could see her face in the mirror.

"I know," said Increase.

"Then why is Papa doing this?"

"Oh, Vivian Mae," said Increase, "you are so young, you have so much time. . . ."

"Why do people always say that?" replied the young girl bitterly. "Is it only because we haven't lived as long as you? But who is to say that because we are young, we have time? We may not have any more time than a seventy-year-old! What if something happens to James? What if he returns to the *Buz-*

zard and takes a bullet in his chest or a bowie knife in his ribs,
or loses an eye or a limb to an exploding cannon? Who says
we have time? If," said Vivian, her eyes cold, her face stony,
"something happens to James before I'm his wife, I will never
forgive Father."

Increase was shocked at the tone of Vivian's voice. Guiltily,
she glanced at her wide four-poster bed. Henry's side was
turned down, although she knew he wouldn't be to bed until
almost morning, when he had finished the work that had to be
done in the depot; fugitive slaves were passing through.

"If you knew," said Increase, "how many times my father
turned down your father . . ." but Increase knew how feeble
it sounded in the face of her daughter's rage and disappointment. She turned suddenly, meeting Vivian's eyes, the two
heads almost touching, the two undone skeins of hair reaching
the floor.

"I am eighteen," whispered Vivian into her mother's shoulder, "old enough to have a life of my own. Women are not the
slaves of their husbands or their fathers. I swear, Mother, I
will run away. I'll leave with James when and where he goes,
if he'll have me, married or unmarried." Vivian's stubborn jaw
clenched and Increase felt the tremor of her fragile shoulders.
She isn't so strong as she thinks, thought Increase as her arms
went tightly around her daughter, but she is strong enough to
hurt us by leaving.

"I never said that time was the prerogative of youth or its
curse. It simply is. Your father only wants your happiness as
did mine. Sometimes fathers can be wrong."

"But Papa will never admit it."

"I wouldn't misjudge or underestimate your Papa. That famous 'time.' Why don't you give him some of it?"

Vivian stared at the wide, white-hung matrimonial bed of
her father and mother reflected in the dressing-table mirror.

"Because I'm lost, Mother," she said. "Because I think I'm
going to die if I don't make love to James; I can't breathe. I
can't sleep at night. I dream of him at night. I want him so
badly I think I'm even capable of giving myself to another
man—any man—pretending it's him. I have terrible thoughts.
No one has ever felt this way before. I never dreamed desire
could be such pain or love this terrible longing. I should be
happy. I should be happy to know that James exists, that I am

the cause of his happiness, but I'm not, for I don't want him happy except with me. I am a selfish, harping harlot with indecent thoughts, a deceitful jealous bitch, worse than a whore. I look at myself in the mirror naked, I touch myself, I yearn and yearn. I think about it. I'm a wicked, evil, impure girl and I can't help myself," sobbed Vivian. "What is time to me when I burn . . . ?"

Covey's hopeful, desperate, passionate, clinging, hurtful, unending kisses were Vivian's secret and her torment, just as the touch of Covey's hand or the pressure of his shoulder, or the glance of his ship-pilot eyes were. It was true, thought Vivian, he could see in the dark. How often had they played games with his sight. Covey would amuse her by sitting in a strange, darkened room and describing in detail each object that he had never seen before. His eyes would bore into her very soul—each time his glance struck her, she felt more unclothed than even now. But she couldn't explain all this to her mother. God in his beneficence had sent her the cannoneer Covey—full of mystery and strength, tenderness and ferocity, alien yet as familiar to her as her skin, her breath, yet totally distant from any man she had ever known. She felt in him the same yearning, not more powerful than her own, but more vulnerable, having survived so many dangers, so much madness, death. And his tenderness was the predatory tenderness of a solitary man, an enraptured outcast, those single navigators whose solemnity knows no limit. Vivian was in the habit of returning his vain look with all the willfulness of her soul and recklessly plunging into it, voiceless and terrified like a daring mad diver taking a desperate leap from the masthead into the ocean where so many men and women had died of loneliness. He had grown in Vivian to the dimensions of a rapture that filled her with those sobs from which she would emerge in a trance of defiant illusions and distraction. She could take existence in her arms—all the suffering in the world—and console it, and that power had found its way into her heart and stirred there some deep response which was something more than love—it was more like a fatal enchantment for an entire unexplored continent.

Increase, shocked, clutched Vivian even closer. Her own placid eyes had a wild look as if some savage beast were in the room, stalking her child. He own heart pounded with Vivian's self-punishing anguish. She had thought her daughter still a child, without those awful yearnings, that immortal pain. What had Covey brought into Vivian's safe little world? But she should have realized that no one had the power to detour Vivian from her own sensuality. She was, after all, her mother's daughter.

"I've felt everything you feel, child, for a man. Such feelings are not a sin in God's eyes since He made such feelings. They are a blessing, not a curse. They bring pain, but they bring happiness. When two young, full-blooded people love, that's how they feel. There is nothing impure in love's desires, only the satisfaction of carnal appetites without love. If you love Covey, you won't put him in the situation of dishonoring you or himself by improper actions."

"You said there was no dishonor in love, so how can there be dishonor in its satisfaction?"

"Outside of marriage, outside of your family's sanction, it's a sin."

"And did you, Mother?"

"Did I what?"

"Did you give in to Papa before you were married?"

"He never pressed me," said Increase slowly.

"And if he had?" insisted Vivian.

"But he never did and Covey won't either. Control your own nature and the man will follow."

"Is that what you did?"

"That's what I did," said Increase even more slowly.

"And that's what you expect me to do?"

Increase hesitated. "Yes."

"Are you lying to me, Mother?"

Increase looked her daughter in the eye and lied.

"Yes. That's what I expect."

"So it would be a terrible disappointment to you if I didn't."

Increase bit her lip. How far should she push her beloved daughter? How much should she lie? She expected love to sweep away everything. She would forgive Vivian everything for she had traversed that desert of desire. But Increase dared not tell her this. What would Henry think with his pristine black-and-white soul? That his daughter's own mother had pushed her into fornication? And perhaps, for who knew what men really thought, into Covey's contempt? Increase contented herself with silence, the better part of virtue, she thought.

But did she really believe virtue the better part of love?

Increase rose, helping Vivian to her feet. Then she stepped back, surveying the tear-streaked face. Lord, what a creature! More beautiful than she had ever been. A rich man's bride, made for jewels to set off her skin and expensive clothes and pampered security. She hesitated, asking the question with her eyes, and then led her to her parents' bed. Increase washed Vivian's face and braided her hair and tucked her into Henry's side of the bed. She went to her room and brought her back her favorite doll. Gently she stooped over and placed a kiss on her forehead. Vivian was asleep before she could see Increase's tears. Her mother took up the oil lamp and went from room to room in the quiet house, checking on all her other children. She opened seven doors and peered down on seven sleeping faces, each time closing the door softly. Only the door of Covey's room in the attic was locked, from the inside. Increase smiled. When had he begun to lock himself in or Vivian out? She returned to Honor's room, where she lingered, contemplating Vivian's face as a child in that of her baby sister. How grown was grown? thought Increase. When did it stop, a mother's vexation?

At four in the morning, Henry Braithwaite entered his bedroom and found his wife and daughter interlaced, asleep in his bed. For a long time, he stood over them smiling, loving them, adoring them. All had gone well this night and the excitement had left him drained and empty. He crept out softly, without waking them and, fully clothed, threw himself on the sofa in the living room and fell into happy, dreamless sleep.

⤙ Robert Madden ⤚
June 1840

But it was from religion or policy, not from national humanity, that the blow was received. . . . The horrors acted in St. Domingo opened the eyes of Government to consequences that it became political to guard against. From that time, philanthropy, like the pent-up vapor, began to diffuse itself, and extended even to the British Court of Admiralty.

—*John Quincy Adams*

The high iron gates swung open and Robert Madden considered how far removed he was from the jail-behind-the-tavern in New Haven. Lord Palmerston, the new foreign minister of Queen Victoria, had invited him to give a first-hand report on his Commission for the Suppression of Slavery while he was on home leave. Madden intended to bring the case of Joseph Cinque before the Queen. His carriage followed the road, edged with green velvet sward rolled to the smoothness of a carpet, that led to the castle. The winding avenue lengthened away before its forests, which spread their green foregrounds and mauve distances under the June sky. A sudden curve in the road brought the country house of Broadlands in view—it loomed against the sky, like a broad-decked stone ship, all gray and rose, with its castellated wings and three hundred windows, turrets and chimneys. It was the modern red-brick architecture that Edward, the father of Victoria, had brought into vogue, elaborated by the latest and most ingenious inventions of the rich, industrial, colonialist England of the middle of the century. The carriage advanced to the row of footmen waiting before the castle's stone steps who addressed Madden by name. He followed a servant through the hall lined with Roman antiquities into a large suite looking onto the park with its lawn and woods, through which a deep, rapid river called the Test ran to the edge of the horizon.

It was a bright afternoon, warm for the season, and the soft English light, so different from the harsh African and Antilles sun, poured into the windows. From the castle the lawns lapped down in smooth levels as bright as emerald, studded by clumps of shrubbery like flowers in an elegant tapestry, and across it, miles away, deer occasionally raced, or a pheasant fed, or a lady with a flowing riding dress and shiny top hat dashed by on her pony. Madden knew this closed world of pleasure, luxury and beauty was the elysium of one man, and a day's journey from the estates of any other human being. This, not just Liverpool, Birmingham and Nantes, was the world slavery had built, thought the doctor. The ruling class owned the land *and* the cities. And they had grown rich before they had discovered a conscience. Carefully, he outlined to himself the arguments in favor of Cinque and his men. Cinque seemed to sit there in the corner of the elegant salon, squatting on his haunches, his blanket drawn over one shoulder, laughing at the decor. Indeed, it was a ridiculous place to discuss the *Amistad* insurrection.

The doctor began to dress for the seated dinner for ninety titled aristocrats and diplomats in the portrait-covered formal hall. Most of them he had only heard of. Lord Palmerston himself was a stranger to him except through the letter of invitation lying in his baggage. Carefully he took out the Boston lithograph of Joseph Cinque.

As administrator of one of Lord Palmerston's pet projects— the Admiralty's African Squadron—he would be listened to.

The doctor stopped dressing to look out the window. What seemed like hypocrisy, he thought, was only the Englishman's ability to wake up each morning and believe the impossible. And surely here in Broadlands it was almost a necessity.

England's Minister of Foreign Affairs knocked and entered. He was a tall, handsome man with a dark, round face, a high, wide forehead, and overly groomed hair that hung in short salt-and-pepper ringlets over a receding hairline. Known to be vain of his personal appearance, he had been nicknamed Cupid, but the force of his personality had made more than one opponent more concerned with an arrow in his back. The smiling figure was quite necessarily unscrupulous, adroit, resourceful and entrenched in the favor of the young queen, despite all opposition from his colleagues. He soothed Victoria's fears, steered her policy and generally monitored events at home and abroad. The cool, aristocratic and distinguished Palmerston delighted the man in the street as much as he irritated his colleagues. He was high-handed, high-minded and determined above all to maintain the prestige of England abroad. He stood firmly on the side of constitutional liberties and the immediate emancipation of all black men.

Lord Palmerston had gone far beyond propriety, it was believed, in his efforts to rid the world of slavery and England's deep-rooted disbelief in profound or sudden change. In fact, the abolition of slavery had drawn him so passionately into a long series of treaties at the Foreign Office that government circles were accusing him of being quite unaccountable for his actions, as far as the black man was concerned.

Dr. Madden hoped that in this unexpected moment of intimacy he might broach the problem of the American President's refusal to meet him, and his interference in favor of Spain against the captives, in a word, the war of the *Amistad*.

"You may not know, sir," said Lord Palmerston in a tone which Madden did not know whether to take seriously or not, "Mr. Combes, Her Majesty's phrenologist, having delivered four lectures at Yale College, examined the *Amistad* Africans. I must say his opinion of the Africans is much higher than that of Americans, whom he finds peculiarly sensitive to criticism from foreigners, especially Englishmen; indifferent to sanguinary outrages, too much characterized by an inordinate love of gain and mania for speculation. They use inflated language, read trifling books, have a nasal tone, excessive vanity and are instilled with violence . . . but then they *are* colonials, after all, and a good deal of the coarseness and dishonesty of America can be charged not to slavery but to its equalitarianism and the absence of classes. Our cousins live in a primitive land which still clings to an institution that Great Britian abolished in its colonies eight years ago—and would have abolished in the United States too *if* it were still a colony. . . .

"I hold," continued Lord Palmerston, "that the real policy of England is to champion justice and right, pursuing that course with moderation and prudence. Of course, she should not become the Don Quixote of the world, but she should give the weight of her moral sanction and support wherever she thinks justice is and whenever she thinks wrong has been done. Your audience with the Queen will be a plea for the Amistaders in view of the attitude of the American President."

"No First Lord and no Board of Admiralty," he said, "have ever felt any interest in the suppression of the slave trade, or taken of their own free will any steps towards its accomplishment. Whatever they have done, they have done in compliance with my prodding or the insistence of Parliament, and grudgingly so. Those old tubs they send out to the coast to catch fast-sailing top-sail schooners are a joke. Nevertheless, we have almost twenty cruisers out there and the fights between the cruisers and the heavily armed slavers have taken on all the aspects of a naval war. Moreover, they are hiding under the American flag."

"I know," Madden said, "there are calls in Parliament to bring home the African Squadron."

"Dear Madden, it is considered a costly failure, a deadly farce, a cruel, hopeless, absurd experiment that dispatches our best and bravest navy officers and men on an idle and mischievous project . . . but I still hope to force Portugal to sign a treaty permitting a vessel to be seized as a slaver if she is equipped to carry slaves, even if there are none on board. This I hope will discourage mass homicide on pirate boats that are chased. We have also begun to sign treaties with the African kings. But they pay as much attention to their treaties as do Spain, Portugal, or the United States."

Madden took a deep breath. "The traffic has neither been extinguished nor diminished; on the contrary, the numbers exported have increased. The Rhode Island merchants and General de Wolfe have retired, but new capital is coming in from New York, the home base of the slavery fleet, as well as from Boston and Portland, Maine. It is general knowledge that several respected New York merchants who are part owners of a slave-smuggling cartel connected with leading Spanish mercantile houses have put pressure on the American President in the case of the *Amistad*. Americans are even part owners. . . ."

"I have," said the foreign minister, "the impression that war is inevitable. But it is hardly conceivable that the United States would go to war to protect the slave trade, is it, doctor? When my predecessor, Lord Channing, asked John Quincy Adams, then Secretary of State, if Adams could conceive of a more atrocious evil than the slave trade, he answered yes, admitting the right of search by foreign officers of American vessels upon the sea in time of peace, for *that* would be making slaves of themselves. . . . Odd, these Americans. Very odd . . ."

"Slaving," Madden added hopelessly, "has increased from a hundred thousand a year when it was *legal* to two hundred thousand a year now, and two thirds of the slavers claiming American nationality have been provided sea letters by none other than the American consul in Cuba, who is married to the granddaughter of former-President Jefferson, if you can imagine such a thing. After all the efforts that have been made, and are being made, the slave trade is more vigorous and profitable than ever. Shares in slave vessels are sold in Havana for as little as a dollar each, and the insurance on the voyage is only fifteen percent, with a profit of two hundred percent! Will not cupidity continue to laugh at the effects of the *Buzzard*, the *Dolphin*, and the few other British cruisers, when the profits are so enormous? But abolish slavery, and the slave trade comes to an immediate end. Annihilate the market, and the supplies instantly and forever cease. How strange that this self-evident proposition is not at once seen and believed!"

"As I said, Madden, I can hardly conceive of the United States going to war over the slave trade . . . but the price of our attempt to suppress this trade has been very high, even for the richest country in the world. . . . Fifteen million pounds we've spent, Madden. Fifteen million pounds."

Queen Victoria fixed Robert Madden with her slightly prominent soft blue eyes and smiled until her gums showed. Her mouth was her worst feature, showing small, short teeth. The Queen was not beautiful, but she was known for her spirituality spiked with young high spirits and an innocence not yet ravished by her enormous responsibilities. She had literally stepped from the nursery to the throne and Madden was much more intimidated by a Queen dressed as a young girl in Manchester-striped cotton and no jewels than he would have been had she been in ceremonial robes. Victoria had already learned how to use both her youth and her innate severity to her advantage. On her left stood her Prime Minister, Melbourne, and to her right, Palmerston. Victoria had enough ominous official concerns without the Amistaders. She had her hands full with the poppy interest in China, French designs on Morocco and the awkward tendency of missionaries to invite martyrdom in the Pacific. Madden, had a great deal to convey to this small sovereign with her sleek blond hair and the protruding azure eyes, and he did his best to describe the case of Joseph Cinque and the *Amistad* to this strange, vivacious young woman who glanced constantly and nervously at Lord Palmerston, who smiled his support. When she picked up her declaration and began to read, the sheet trembled slightly.

"My Lord Palmerston has informed us that our government has reason to know that the *Amistad* Negroes were illegally imported into Cuba on a Portuguese slaver and, on account of the fact that Spain renounced the slave trade for a valuable consideration given by Great Britain, we take a particular interest in the fate of these unfortunate Africans who have been illegally and feloniously reduced to slavery by subjects of Spain. We have instructed our ambassador to advice the President of our former colony that these infelicitous Africans have been thrown by accidental circumstances into the hands of the authorities of the United States; and it depends upon the action of the United States government whether these persons shall recover the freedom to which they are entitled or whether they shall be reduced to slavery.

"It is under these circumstances that we anxiously solicit the President of the United States to take measures in behalf of the Africans to secure them their liberty, to which, without doubt, they are by law entitled."

The Queen glanced at Palmerston, who nodded appreciatively. Victoria, who would soon exhibit an indomitable will of her own, depended almost entirely on him now. But, thought Madden, if she proved to have even an ounce of head or heart, it would count for much more than if she had been born a prince. Victoria was immensely popular; she was doing the best thing that she could do for her royal court in these anti-monarchial times—making it fashionable. Victoria's England was more powerful and more ambitious than at any time in its history since the great Elizabeth. England had imposed emancipation on its own colonies, in the interests of its own

progress and prosperity as well as that of the world, thought
Madden. The defense of Joseph Cinque had now become part
of that concern.

Victoria smiled. She liked Madden's temperamental, fan-
tastical reputation. And it would be just as well to have a Catholic Irishman to do the dirty work of an Englishman.

"We appoint you, Dr. Madden, to serve as our Commissioner of Inquiry into the affairs of the British settlements in
Africa to protect our emancipated Negroes."

Madden's heart leaped with both dismay and anticipation.
He would now have to fight the wealth and power of British
merchants as he had fought the Spanish and American ones.
He sighed. Perhaps it was his destiny to fight greed.

"Your Majesty does me great honor."

Victoria, who would reign for sixty years and eighty days,
held out a miniature hand. Dr. Madden bowed low over it and
presented the Queen with the lithograph of Joseph Cinque.
Victoria drew her fair eyebrows together in a frown and studied the dark face dutifully.

Madden stood on the deck of the *Fair Rosamund*. It crept
down the Thames past the fields and villages, the moors, the
great country houses, the swelling recent towns, the congested
manufacturing districts and seaports that comprised the changing, rich, philanthropic England. The tracks of new railroads
passed the new steamboat station at Waterloo Bridge and an
enclosure hid the recent construction of the Nelson monument
in Trafalgar Square. The gaping foundation for the New Royal
Exchange, which had burned two years ago, and the scaffold-
ing of the new Houses of Parliament, emerged from darkness.
Each view reminded him of what his Catholic, republican,
equalitarian heart held most sacred, that only a country liberated from slavery and enriched by the labor of free men could
achieve a modern, prosperous society that had room for hu-
manitarianism. Young Victoria was the beginning of a unique
era, and not only for England. Down Constitution Hill the gray
mass of Buckingham Palace took shape in the dawn, but Victoria, Madden knew, was renovating Windsor Castle because
she preferred it. The dome of Saint Paul's Cathedral turned
gold. Light crept past the forest of the crowded masts of the
hundreds of sloops, brigs and schooners of London port as the

Fair Rosamund left the Isle of Dogs and moved slowly out to sea. Once again Dr. Madden was on his way to the green-, gold- and white-striped shores of Sierra Leone, where the coin of the realm remained the black man.

Such, thought Madden, was the world.

Joseph Cinque
August 1840

On the 8th of February, 1815, at the Congress of Vienna, Austria, France, Great Britain, Portugal, Prussia, Russia, and Sweden, issued a Declaration, "in the face of Europe, that considering the universal abolition of the slave-trade as a measure worthy of our attention, conformable to the spirit of the times, and to the generous principles of our august Sovereigns, we are animated with the sincere desire of concurring in the execution of this measure, by all the means at our disposal, and of acting in the employment of those means with all the zeal and perseverance which is due to so noble a cause."

—John Quincy Adams

It is wonderful to lift my face to the sun and let it burn. The men have shed the gray skin of the long winter and taken heart with the coming of the reaping season. Now, corn and wheat stand high in the fields while blackbirds swoop overhead and the horizon cuts like a knife of indigo across the sharp curve of bright, rustling gold. A year has passed almost to the day of our capture.

On the first day of August, we sit curled up in the sun like snails surveying this new tribe of Africans, the Americans.

All around us a special feast is going on. On the wide field Black Snake and Country run and play hide and seek, a Mende game, with the children of the town. Musicians play string instruments and Big Sun and Little Sun drum on an old wooden barrel, much to the embarrassment of the colored ladies. The older boys along with the Braithwaites play a game called cricket with stakes and a large ball; the women cluster in groups, gossiping and preparing food. Couples stroll across the scorched grass. Cotton Braithwaite is speaking earnestly with his girl, Clementina. Jefferson, too, has a sweetheart. The old people sit in the wagons under umbrellas or tents like those we saw so long ago in Havana.

Some of the Amistaders have been allowed to come. Others are held in the barn as hostages against possible escape. It has been agreed that later in the day these men will be taken back and the others will replace them. Long tables have been placed outdoors under the occasional trees. They are covered with white cloth and food of every description: hams and roasts, chickens and rabbits, salads and puddings, sweet potatoes and corn. Pitchers of milk are on the tables, while barrels of cider stand nearby. Gaily dressed black people from the churches of New Haven mingle with the somber costumes of the white Quakers, who look as if blackbirds had come to rest amongst a congregation of wild-flowers.

The fragrance of meats and cakes floats upon the air, each household striving to outdo the next in abundance or invention, while Mother Increase outdoes them all as the governing hostess. The sweets fascinate and delight the men, who have not seen anything like them since the Christmas spent at this same farm more than nine months ago.

An orchestra tunes their instruments at the far end of the field, where a mowed clearing has been prepared for dancing. The crowds, wagons and carriages and buckboards are drawn up in a circle around the clearing, and snatches of greetings and children's laughter rise on the still air and carry across the whole field.

Horses still fascinate me. I keep going back again and again to the corral. Enviously I watch them, unyoked from their wagons and carriages, the riding horses still bridled yet roaming free in the adjacent field. These creatures mingle together, yet each is marked by a brand so that his owner can always claim him. Unconsciously I rub my own flesh. I have not allowed it to grow soft with prison and winter. My body is as hard and fit as if I were going to war tomorrow. It is my only satisfaction that my men are as conditioned as wrestlers.

I look over at Python, who is greedily watching the strange, sweet objects he so covets. Python has developed the most passionate sweet tooth of all the men. Like his namesake, he will gorge himself endlessly, then hibernate in the sun all day. Pure honey will never satisfy him again. . . .

My thoughts roam as freely as the unfettered animals I watch.

Summer has lifted my spirits but not my soul. I sink slowly
into my own melancholy and anger, as I often do. Even so, I
hear Vivian's father's voice calling the assembly to order. A
stake has been driven into the ground, and atop it flies the
thirty-star American flag, Columbia. Under it a second flag flut-
ters—the bright red flag of slavery.

"Brothers," begins Henry Braithwaite, "ten years ago Great
Britain freed our brethren in the Antilles. We can only eject a
fervent prayer that next year will be emancipation and abolition for all American slaves! Next year emancipation!"

"God illuminate the United States of America!"

The small crowd applauds and cheers. Henry Braithwaite
stands, his hair caught up by the breeze, his words hanging in
the air like inky black marks which slowly rise upwards to join
the free creatures, circling high above the fields. Every year
for the past ten years, according to Covey, Henry Braithwaite
has celebrated British Emancipation Day, as he celebrates his
own country's Fourth of July.

I draw close to Covey and Captain Fitzgerald, who are listening to Braithwaite's speech. The captain turns to me suddenly, saying, "For the first time, Mr. Cinque, I can speak
to the men I have been rescuing from captivity for fifteen
years. This day has given me faces to go with black cargo.
Voices, names, everything. It is a strange and wonderful gift."
He shakes his head as if trying to digest this new way of looking at us.

Vivian comes and stands beside me. "I saw you looking at
Cotton's chestnut gelding in the meadow. He's beautiful, isn't
he? What were you doing, roaming around the horses out
there?"

I look at her, not understanding until she gestures to the
pasture. I nod, unable to express more than my admiration.
She frowns. "Wait," she says.

I see her enter the corral lugging a heavy saddle and move
with rapidity amongst the creatures. She finally places the saddle on the most beautiful of them all, then leads the animal
towards me.

When I can, I reach up and touch the smooth, burnished
magnificence of its pelt. Vivian seems to understand.

"You," she says slowly, "want to ride this horse?"

I turn to Covey, but Covey and Fitzgerald stand there grinning in silence. I nod.

"Come," she beckons. "I'll show you. Put your foot here, and your hands here, and now throw your other leg over."

My first reaction is to reach for the hair on the back of the neck of the animal, but it is so much like the hair of white men, I recoil. So I put my hands on the edge of the saddle as she demands. She takes the long leather strips and slowly walks me around the meadow. And one thing is unforgettable: the world from my elevation becomes a different place. I discover another of the white man's masteries, like the sea, the house that swims, the revolving, hollow one-eyed bronze column, the gun and the doubloons. But this, this I think, is the best of all. I watch the earth glide by. I am twenty-four palms tall. I can see farther than I have ever seen in my life, except upon the sea, but this time it is not an empty line of two blues, but life itself: Sky, horses, fields, hills, smoke, people and animals far in the distance. Distance itself shrinks before my eyes. I know now how the white man comes by his arrogance, for this is like walking seated on another man's shoulders. No wonder they believe in their lordship. I quickly dismount, while Covey and Fitzgerald laugh for the wrong reasons. This is the most corrupting creature alive, the deadliest weapon of all, and I want no more to do with it. But for weeks afterwards I will yearn for that feeling of what Vivian calls "horseflesh" beneath me.

I yearn and Vivian delightedly promises to teach Covey how to ride. The guests leave in their carriages and wagons. Night falls. An immense bonfire is lit in the field. There are still some of the Amistaders left, but many of them have started the trip back to the Farmington prison. The Braithwaite family have spread themselves around the veranda, their light brown skin glowing in the light of the fire. Vivian, Braithwaite and Covey take over the swing. The twenty-eight-year-old Jeremiah stands beside his father, who, with his hands in his pockets, his gold watch strung across his ample torso, his light white jacket unbuttoned and his white shirt glistening, is the picture of self-possessed serenity. Mother Braithwaite sits on a lounge chair, her white skirt spread, her white shawl crisp against her dark shoulders and bosom. Her magnificent hair is in a long thick braid caught in a net to which are attached tiny beads of coral, a present from Covey. The other boys sit, their knees drawn up, while Honor flits from one person to the other like a nonchalant butterfly. Fitzgerald studies the high forehead and deep-set eyes of Twin, with his powerful neck and sloping shoulders. Have-Mercy-on-Me, with small eyes set close together, combined with a stubborn jaw and a rather cruel mouth, seems to fascinate the captain, although, having spoken to him, he knows him to be the most gentle of men. Increase Braithwaite's yellow draperies are closed against the outside world. Vivian rises and soon her voice fills the air, which is suddenly very quiet, with a song called "The Ballad of Gabriel Prosser." I breathe in her special, inexplicable charm, her voice filled with disturbing passion and straightforwardness and purity. I am, in the most banal manner of a brother, jealous of Covey. Vivian begins to sing:

> *There was two a-guarding Gabriel's cell,*
> *And then one in the jail about*
> *And two a-standing at the hangman's tree*
> *And Billy was there to get Gabriel out.*
>
> *There was musket shot and musket balls*
> *Between his neck bone and his knee*
> *But Billy took Gabriel up in his arms*
> *And he carried him away right manfully.*
>
> *They mounted a horse and away they went,*
> *Ten miles off from that hanging tree;*
> *Until they stopped where the river bent*
> *And there they rested happily.*
>
> *And then they called for a Victory dance*
> *And the crowd they all danced merrily;*
> *The best dancer amongst them all*
> *Was Gabriel Prosser who was just set free!*

"What's that song?" I ask.

"Why, it's the legend of Gabriel Prosser's rebellion. The slaves of the South sing and dance to it. Southern masters, too, dance to this tune without knowing the words. One day they will sing about you, Joseph Cinque, mark my words . . . they'll sing!"

Joseph Cinque from beyond the waves
Came to freedom's shores a slave
But one dark night in storm and strife,
He broke his chains and took a life.

The wicked Negrier he slew,
And seized his ship as storm winds blew.
He changed its course and pointed it,
Into the sun which rising lit,

The way back home return he must,
For days and nights he voyaged thus,
But in a harbor strange he landed.
The African's mutinous ship lay stranded.

In letters of gold, the Amistad's name,
A symbol of heroes' rebellion became,
But Cinque's men hostage to greed,
Stood trial for murder and piracy.

The trial was long, friends scarce, indeed,
But Cinque's men at last stood freed.
The Amistaders will soon prevail,
And back to Africa they'll sail!

Everyone breaks into loud applause. Cotton and Jasper stomp and cheer. Braithwaite leans over and kisses his daughter. She had written the music and the words as a surprise. Vivian's voice illuminates our faces as if she had lit a dozen candles. Her radiant smile grows and grows under our adoring eyes until it becomes beauty itself. At that moment I can think of nothing more wonderful than not to die. . . .

❧ Louisa Quincy Adams ❧
September 1840

We see in the whole of this transaction, a confusion of ideas
and a contradiction of positions, from confounding together
the two capacities in which these people are attempted to be
held. First, they are demanded as persons, to be delivered up
as criminals, to be tried for their lives, and liable to be executed
on the gibbet. Then they are demanded as chattels, the same
as so many bales of cotton . . .

—*John Quincy Adams*

Louisa smiled, remembering Abigail's words:

*We have it in our power not only to free ourselves, but to
subdue our masters, and without violence, throw both natural
and legal authority at their feet.* Certainly natural and legal
power were sitting in her parlor this day.

Louisa was distinctly uncomfortable because she knew why
Angelina and Sarah were here: to persuade her husband to defend Joseph Cinque against the United States. Tappan, Baldwin and Leavitt had already tried. But John Quincy had pleaded
age and infirmity. Now, here they were again, sitting in her
front room, friendly yet arrogant in their conviction that because it was right, John Quincy would never refuse. Of course,
they didn't think she counted for much in his decision, but in
this, they were wrong. She, Louisa, could make or break John
Quincy's decision to defend Cinque. Nevertheless, Louisa was
flattered to have Angelina and Sarah Grimké, the first female
abolitionists in the United States, to tea. The sisters were the
daughters of a South Carolina slave owner and had spoken for
the cause of anti-slavery in more than a hundred towns. Their
appearance always caused a furor. No women spoke in public,
and no one spoke as Angelina did of such a radical idea as the
equality of the sexes along with emancipation of the slave.

Louisa had met the other sister, Sarah, three years earlier,

during her tour to rouse New England abolitionists, and knew
her well. They had been writing to each other for years, Louisa
Adams pouring out—even a bit indiscreetly, and perhaps dis-
loyally—her feelings about the oppression of her sex, of being
left behind in history's course, of her own ignorance and her
bitterness at the arrogance of men.

Louisa had never met Angelina, who was younger and more
beautiful than Sarah. She had been the first woman in the
United States to have spoken in public. Both sisters had been
disowned by the Society of Friends, Angelina for marrying
outside her faith and Sarah for attending the wedding. Louisa
thought of her own wedding, in which she, too, had been ex-
communicated from everything she had ever known to join the
hard, puritan Adams clan.

"My husband's redoubtable tongue can curl itself around
every tone of passion from vindictive spite to the noblest heights
of feelings," Louisa continued out loud. Hadn't she been the
victim and object of them all? And his sons as well?

"Well, I always remember the matter of the nine ladies of
Fredericksburg, Virginia, when he tried to present their petition. . . ." Angelina laughed.

"And they were mulattoes."

"And *infamous* prostitutes, according to Senator Patton."

"As Mr. Adams asked, 'Because they happened to be mulattoes, or because the gentleman knew the women personally?' "
Louisa allowed her voice to slip into irony.

Angelina snorted. "How Senator Patton went on and on that
he didn't *know* them! And he kept on saying it as though
someone had accused him of consorting with prostitutes. . . ."

Louisa laughed, but she flushed at the word "prostitute."

"They *were* free mulattoes," said Louisa.

"The same thing to Mr. Patton, I suppose," replied Angelina.

"Well then I remember Mr. Adams said, 'I'm glad to hear
the honorable gentleman disclaim any knowledge of them, for
I had been going to ask that if they were infamous women,
then who had made them infamous? Not their color, but their
masters!' " Angelina laughed. " 'In the South there exists such
great resemblances between the progeny of the colored people, literally because they are *colored*, and the white men who
claim possession of them. . . . Thus, perhaps the charge "in-

famous" can refer to those who make it, as originating from themselves,' " quoted Angelina.

"The House exploded with shouts and accusations and cries of 'Order' " interjected Sarah.

"But, dear ladies," said Louisa, "not Mr. Polk nor anyone else can make order out of the harems of the South. . . ."

"Then your husband said something wonderful," continued Sarah. " 'The word 'woman' is an expression much dearer to me than that of "lady.' " That's what he said" concluded Sarah, settling back comfortably.

Louisa secretly wished he had said that to her rather than on the floor of the Senate. But Louisa realized her husband was only reflecting his mother's fervent wish that *there not be a slave in the province . . . that it was a most iniquitous scheme to fight ourselves for the thing we were robbing the Negroes of, who had as good a right to freedom.*

Louisa knew that by defending Joseph Cinque, Quincy Adams championed the demands of his mother; by liberating him, he honored her memory.

"My dear Louisa, women and slaves might have achieved equality in a single document: the Declaration of Independence that began our revolution," said Angelina.

"I weep when I think of the long hard road we must travel now, for that one error," murmured Sarah. "Our goal will come, slowly and painfully, and at every step thrown back one. . . ."

"Yet when I asked your husband whether women could do anything to abolish slavery he said to me, 'If it is to be abolished, *they* must do it,' " said Angelina.

"You live in Washington" said Sarah. "Slaves are jailed and auctioned in our capitol. Not ten minutes from your house, there is a slave market. There are unnumbered wrongs inflicted on a million of our black countrywomen. Have you ever visited a black slavewoman in jail? Have you been down to the Washington jail, Louisa? Have you? Have you ever listened to the tales of sorrow a female slave can tell you, of the unbridled passions of a master? Have you ever cried with a black widow torn from her assassinated husband, or the black mother sold away from her children? Can you feel the wrongs of these women and sisters and not hate the system which degrades them to the level of beasts? Can we feel as we should for these unhappy women and not ask in the presence of God, what would thou have me do in the great work of rooting out slavery from our land? Joseph Cinque's only one part of God's plan. That slavery has begun to fall is plain, but its fall will be resisted by those who cling to it with energy and desperation and fury as only fiends can summon when they know their hour has come. The end will be slow. Woe to the abolitionists if we dream that our work is well nigh done. . . . But whatever comes, the cause of anti-slavery and the cause of women's rights are one and the same."

The servant greeted John Quincy at the door as he turned the key. Despite bullying letters and threats upon his life, he still insisted on walking the streets of Washington day and night unattended. The hats and cloaks also announced visitors, and Quincy Adams flushed as he entered his parlor, as if he had been surprised skinny-dipping in the Potomac. There were the Grimké sisters, in all their glory, without Angelina's husband, Theodore Weld. Louisa was blushing. Had she invited them? he wondered. Or had they invited themselves? For a moment there was a stony silence. Louisa braced herself, trembling inwardly. Her husband was not a violent man, but he could have violent reactions. He had exerted violence on her only once during their married life, when he had forcibly wiped the rouge off her face that evening in Berlin almost thirty-five years ago. A box of rouge had been given to her by the Queen, who had probably thought she looked pale simply because her complexion was not revived by the brilliancy of diamonds. The first time, John Quincy had ordered her to refuse the gift, which she did, twice. Then during the carnival ball of that year, when the Queen offered her rouge again, and still having no diamonds, she accepted. When John Quincy saw her pink cheeks, he went into a rage that had no bearing on the smallness of the crime, she thought. He had grabbed her by the collar, dragged her to the washbasin and with a wet towel washed her face clean. Why did she think of this now? she wondered. In the end she had had the last word, for a year later she had defied him again and refused to remove the offending rouge. John Quincy had fled her effrontery in a panic, racing down the stairs and out the door to court without her. She had been trembling and sick to her stomach, but she had actually frightened John Quincy Adams. . . . Louisa slid down in her armchair. Defiance: a little went a long way with her. Now he looked exactly as he had looked that night in Berlin. But instead of a sarcastic outburst or rude sulkiness, John Quincy began to speak to the two women in the most cordial and charming way, even including Louisa in the conversation. He loved his wife and he was proud of her. He had no intention of embarrassing her in front of her friends.

"Angelina! Sarah! You've come at the right time! I need some protection from the Virginians, and you are just the fearless, intrepid ladies I need. Except for arson, riots, a lynch mob, catcalls and threats of tar and feathers and a bull whip, how did your last speaking tour go, Angelina?"

He smiled at the two sisters. One of his rare quarter moons. Louisa, he noted, was as red as rouge. Strange. Louisa, he mused, always underestimated how much both she and her opinions meant to him. She thought he still thought of her as his mother had, as his *English* wife—too refined, sophisticated, snobbish for the hurly-burly of American politics.

Abigail and Louisa had been rivals and enemies while his mother was alive. But now, going through her letters, Louisa had come to admire the old lady and regret they had not been closer. But to him, Louisa was American womanhood personified. Her spoiled, dangerously undisciplined youth in London had been tamed and tempered by the demands and hardships of public life and motherhood, until under that velvet surface, he knew there existed forged steel. There was and always had been something of the captive in her, and this he loved, too, a deep, provocative, untouched center—of anger? he wondered. But she had openly defied him only once in their married life— over that damned rouge. Well, there was something indefinable, a grace, an honor, a loveliness that made up for her unwomanly temper and stubbornness that was always at war with her lack of confidence. He had never forgotten the time she had proved once and for all that the English wife, the Southern belle, had the stuff of the Adamses. February 12, 1815, on her fortieth birthday, with seven-year-old Charles Francis, a maid and two manservants, Louisa had set out from St. Petersburg, across the frozen wastes of Russia and Poland, to join him in Paris. For fifty-two days in an unheated carriage she traveled frozen dangerous roads in the wake of the desolation of Napoleon's armies and Napoleon's wars. She had been dumped in the icy waters of the Riga, submerged so deep in snow peasants had to come and dig her out with shovels and pickaxes. In Poland the two servants had walked before the carriage, sounding the ice with prods to find a passage that would hold. She had slept in hovels and filthy villages, threatened by Napoleon's marauding, unemployed soldiers and deserters, cheered as Napoleon's sister, besieged by drunken imperial guards on their way to meet their general, and had finally passed the gates of Paris safely while he, John Quincy, had been ignorantly and happily at the theater. The journey had been so harrowing that the governess, Mrs. Babet, had been struck with brain fever, and when they left Paris two months later, had still not recovered. All that while he had been sleeping on feather beds in the Hague and Paris; all that while he had performed the most important task of his life, peace for the young republic. That journey had come to mean a great deal to both of them. He had almost lost her and Charles, and she had lost forever the fear of relying only upon herself. His wife had proven herself to herself: resilient, courageous, even foolhardy—the equal of any man. John Quincy looked from one woman to the other. Angelina was brilliant, bold, Sarah tenacious and courageous, but he would take his own Louisa over them and any others. They had lived, he thought, as man and wife, in a continual bustle, a succession of Chinese shadows, banquets, receptions, late and early hours, political excitement and conflict which had stretched their minds and souls and bodies to the extremities of fatigue, despair, exaltation and pride. All the journeys, the ships, the harbors, hotels, houses, land scapes, carriages, cities, steamboats, mounts, palaces, courts, diligences, and now, railroads—all converged into that unforgeable distance that separated them from that young couple that had dreamed of only one thing: public service.

The arguments of the women washed over him like fluttering flags—every party color, every nuanced stripe, every star of language, every shade of politics undulated in the soft breezes of the sisters' insistent belief. John Quincy endured their intrusiveness meekly, while for some strange reason he covertly studied his wife's face: the girl from London, the disappointed, neglected bride, the proud, fragile, unloved daughter-in-law, the grieving mother burying her only daughter in St. Petersburg; who had buried two sons in the Quincy cemetery,

along with all the Adamses, who had buried her own heart in
Washington when he had returned to politics, this same woman
who still believed herself so weak was stronger, stronger
than he.

And what had his father said? mused Adams.

*I never expected pity . . . for fifty years I have lived in an
enemy country.*

Louisa quickly hid her journal as she heard her husband's
steps stop in front of her bedroom door. It was four in the
morning and she had read until now, when she had decided
to jot down some notes in her *Adventures of a Nobody* in preparation for writing a long letter to Sarah Grimké. But now Quincy
Adams tried the doorknob and finding it unlocked, entered.

"Louisa, what are you doing awake at this hour? I saw the
light under the door and thought you had fallen asleep with
the lamp on. . . ." He was still in his street clothes Louisa
noticed, so that he had not been working at home, but in his
office at the House.

"Why, you're not even in your nightdress," he exclaimed,
then flushed with the intimacy of this remark.

"I was just getting ready," replied Louisa as she loosened
her hair. John Quincy watched as the light brown chignon un-
looped to her waist. She hesitated a moment, then handed him
the hairbrush.

"Unless you're too tired," she said.

"No, I'm not tired," said Adams. He began to brush his wife's
hair. It was a chore he had adored at the beginning of their
marriage and it's sudden reappearance for no discernible reason suddenly filled him with elation and tenderness. The soft-
ness under his hands was balm to his soul and he began to
hum faintly.

"Where were you?"

"At the Congress Library. I walked home. It's a beautiful
night, warm and filled with magnolia. I ran into Nathan Langdon while I was working. He was at the Amistaders' trial in
Hartford last year. He even took notes. He was quite helpful.
Kept harking back to the Nat Turner trial." Adams paused. Despite the seven years he had known Nathan Langdon and despite his swift rise to the top as a sought-after Washington

lawyer, he still thought of him as the Virginian census-taker who had, by his own confession, turned Thomas Jefferson's slave wife, Sally Hemings, white in the census of '30 for the sake of history, a felony, and the Constitution.

"I do imagine that Nathan is as fascinated by Joseph Cinque as he was obsessed by Sally Hemings," said Louisa. "He went to her funeral, you know," said Adams. "And to think, it was her own brother, James Hemings, who betrayed them to Callenger and then hanged himself."

"That is speculation on the part of Langdon, John. Nathan never proved it, any more than he proved that Callenger *or* James Hemings was murdered. Sally Hemings is dead and buried. And has been for four long years. Her children—their children are scattered to the four winds as white as snow as far as the last census of our population is concerned. It's all ancient history, my dear, except to him. Don't rattle ghosts. You have enough on your hands."

"I'm not the one rattling ghosts, or seeing them either."

"I know," said Louisa. "As father Adams said, the fault is that damnable institution, chattel slavery. But why didn't John Trumbull tell you that Langdon had been in Hartford when you spoke to him in New Haven?"

"Trumbull doesn't know I know Langdon. And he doesn't know I know Nathan Langdon because of Sally Hemings. We have never spoken of it—either of us," said Adams slowly.

Louisa looked at him strangely. She now realized what John Quincy had been humming under his breath:

> *Let Dusky Sally henceforth bear*
> *The name of Isabella,*
> *And let the mountain all of salt*
> *Be christen'd Monticella.*

"Aren't you going to bed at all?" asked Louisa.

"Well, it's hardly worth it now, is it? I think I'll go down to the Potomac for a bath."

John Quincy was famous for his skinny dips in the Potomac ever since, as a prank one day, some young men who had spied him bathing had stolen, or rather hidden, his clothes. But the amusing outrage hadn't deterred him, and his early morning

swims had become part of Washington City folklore. Louisa
smiled. Since John Quincy took only cold baths anyway, it
hardly mattered if he bathed in the Potomac or at home. But
she still believed he would catch his death one day.

"I'll heat a bath for you if you like," she said, "there's no
sense in waking up the servants."

"It's a warm morning. I prefer the river," said John Quincy.
"Unless you'd like to come," he added playfully.

Louisa looked up. "No thank you, sir, if I'm going to drown
. . ." At once, a cold chill ran up Louisa's spine. Drown. Potomac. She almost screamed, then added lamely, "I prefer the
Mississippi. . . ." John Quincy's eyes filled with sudden tears
as he contemplated the vulnerable nape of his wife's neck where
her hair had fallen away.

"Never mind, Mother," he said gently.

"Stay," said Louisa.

"In the middle of the morning?" uttered Adams.

"It's eleven o'clock at night in London," replied Louisa,
miscalculating.

Quincy Adams walked down to his favorite place for bathing
along the river. There was a rock on which to fold his clothes.
There was a hedge of briar which offered him privacy. There
was a hundred-year-old Acacia which gave him shade and a
place to hide if need be. He stripped and dove into the clean,
cold, slow-moving fleuve. He dived and surfaced and dived
again, staying under longer and longer. He swam in circles,
wheels within wheels, he thought, as the question of Joseph
Cinque, which he had wanted to raise with Louisa but hadn't,
kept turning in his head. Swimming beneath the surface, his
eyes open, his body translucent, his limbs as buoyant and supple as a young man's, Quincy forgot for a moment, all the years
he dragged behind him in the current. He had the fins of three
quarters of a century and this was the only place they were
weightless; ethereal. He could stretch his arms and legs out of
the shell of his years like an old two-hundred-year-old tortoise,
while on land he had to drag around their humiliating burden
for everyone to see. When Adams emerged as Adam grown
into Methuselah, he sat on his rock and let the sun dry him
and thought about the millstone of one more broken promise
he would drag back to Louisa's house.

Did it really matter at this point what his living family thought?

His country would remember.

Not long after that Louisa wrote herself out a pass, signed her husband's name to it, took a basket of biscuits, a Bible, and fifty pennies and set out on foot for the Washington jail. The jailer was so flabbergasted to see the former First Lady enter his jailhouse, he nearly fell scrambling to his feet. Louisa showed him her false pass. He addressed her as Madame President and his mouth fell when she explained to him what she wanted. She would visit the Negro women inmates first and then the men. She wanted him to explain to her why such and such a prisoner found herself in jail, how many were to be sold on the block, how many hanged. The Bible, she announced, should be for the use of the women.

"But," sputtered the jailer, "these people can't read."

"Never mind," Louisa said, "they can look at it."

Of the fifty cents, twenty-five ended up in the jailer's hand along with her best jam. Louisa by her own hand, distributed the rest. Most of the men and women in the jail were fugitive slaves to be returned to their masters. Many were wounded, or had cuts, brands, and whip marks and other mutilations. One woman had an R branded on one cheek, another on her forehead. Louisa had often read the advertisements for fugitive slaves, but until now they had meant nothing to her: two hundred dollars dead or alive, runaway with one ear missing; runaway with brand on his chest; twenty-five dollars reward for proof of death of Ned; man with wife and child, woman pregnant of seven months, scars on back; young girl branded on cheek; young boy with limp, another missing a foot. She peered into face after face. The jail itself was little more than a stable, filthy, crowded as a slave deck, the sick with the healthy, the sane with the insane, the criminals with the fugitives, for after all, hadn't they stolen themselves? When Louisa left the women's quarters, she left the Bible on the table in the corridor separating two rows of cells. She still did not have the answer to the question that kept turning in her head, *What does this have to do with me?* but there was a kind of germ of an answer, no more than a fluttering leaflet lifting in the turbulence of her mind. Louisa knew it was humiliating to be on the other side of freedom. She was shocked at her inability to pronounce anything but the worst banalities, embarrassing even to herself to realize how poor any gift was when the only gift, the only thing that would make them smile, was liberty. She refused to be accompanied by the jailer since this would have conceded the guilt of the prisoners, yet she was more afraid than she had ever been. The prisoners never answered her questions nor looked into her eyes. It was worse than a funeral. She wiped a stupid smile off her face. When she reached the men's section she fell back for a moment, assaulted by the rancid air and the low rough male voices. On either side of her were two long rows of chained men behind bars. As if in a dream, the closed double doors had opened and she had glimpsed a corridor a kilometer long lined with identical black men, their swords drawn, between which she had marched slowly in a silver hoop skirt and a crimson robe, eyes ahead, knees trembling. It had been the same respectful, terrible distance that she had walked to her presentation at the Court of St. Petersburg thirty years before.

The czar's moors with their rich, exotic livery were no more foreign to her than these black American criminals, convicts, fugitives, thieves, or whatever time, destiny and the law had made of them. Louisa wondered if she had passed a face like Cinque's or Grabeau's. Or were real Africans different, not like this wretched puddle of humanity?

Have you been down to the Washington jail?

Now she proceeded along the lines of black men, peering into faces, searching for she knew not what, a question without an answer in her eyes.

Have you been down to the Washington jail?

"You have great heart, Madame President, and courage."

"The only courage, sir, is not to come, but to remain . . . with them." Louisa blinked back frightened tears.

"Mrs. Adams," the jailer said, unnerved at her obvious emotion, "let me take this. It will be distributed amongst the prisoners, I assure you. Now I think you should go home. I can't imagine that your famous husband required you to do any more than deposit your charity at the jailhouse door."

Louisa, again lacking the quarter for a hack, returned home on foot. She felt nauseous, weak. She was in her rooms when her husband returned. He was so shocked to find her in her bath that he began nervously conversing with her, forcing his eyes back to her small form hidden in a chemise and draped with sheets. He felt tenderness, and Louisa felt the same, contemplating the aching, livid, tired old face and body of her companion of forty-three years.

"I ought not to have reflected on his situation, education and customs in our sense of the word," Louisa said. "He is a man, unfortunate, illiterate, unprepared, unknowing of society's laws, but a man with an inalienable right to liberty and justice as a free man."

"But who, Louisa?"

"Why, Cinque, of course."

John Quincy Adams blanched. His affectionate wife was sitting naked, speaking of a black man.

"Mrs. Adams, I don't think your bath is the place to speak of Joseph Cinque."

"But what do you mean, Mr. Adams?" Louisa almost laughed. *"He's* not here. Only the idea of him."

But Adams was staring at his wife's bare arms as if he had never seen them before.

"We will discuss this when you are dressed, if you insist."

But they never discussed it. And Louisa never told John Quincy about the visit to the Washington jail.

As they went in to dinner, Louisa felt the tremor in her husband's arm. The ex-president was older and more tired than he admitted. And he was cold. Louisa vowed never to economize on firewood again. They might be in debt, but the United States *owed* John Quincy Adams a fire.

"What are you thinking, Louisa, staring off into space like that?"

"I was thinking of the hatred of black men and women and the dangers any white man risks in defending Negroes or freeing them or loving them."

"My dear Louisa, I may defend Cinque and I hope to free him, but I assure you, my dear, I am *not* in love with him! Oh, I didn't show you this," he said. "It came just before we left Quincy."

John Quincy handed Louisa an engraved portrait of himself. It was attached to a letter. There was a bullet hole in the head and it was signed "a friend of white supremacy." Louisa Adams did not flinch. He never would have shown her such a letter if he had not made his decision. It was his way of preparing her for the worst.

Louisa thought of a letter she had read only yesterday, signed Abigail Adams.

Don't you think me a courageous Being? her mother-in-law had written. *Courage is laudable, a Glorious Virtue in your Sex, why not mine? (For my part I think you ought to applaud me for mine.) Exit. Rattle.*

"Oh, Mr. Adams. Mr. Adams," she whispered, and Louisa felt a moan, or was it a sob, rise in her chest. She suppressed it, as she had learned to do as an Adams, for all of her married life. . . .

❧ Joseph Cinque ❧
November 1840

If this principle is sound, it reduces to brute force all the rights of man. It places all the sacred relations of life at the power of the strongest. No man has a right to life, or liberty, if he has an enemy able to take them from him.

—*John Quincy Adams*

"My name is Sengbe Pieh, Joseph."

"And mine is Quincy Adams, John."

So this is the man I have been waiting for all these months, I think. The President, as they call him. Wordlessly, I deliver the letter into his extended hand. He is surprised. He expects me to shake his hand, but I am afraid to touch him. Fighting my nervousness, I manage to pronounce his name.

"Mr. President."

He is taken unawares, as if he had never heard himself called thus, or had forgotten. Afterwards he neither smiles nor scowls. He simply waits. Almost at once I discover an antipathy he seems to have for Covey; a kind of repulsion resembling physical fear. He shies away from him instinctively and gives signs of restiveness positively like an ox about to rear. As far as I am concerned, I feel towards him a kind of neutrality. We have no quarrel. One does not quarrel with natural forces, and that is what he seems to me. Neither would I argue with a boulder falling on my head. He listens, sitting sideways at the table placed between us, so that the sunbeams break his face into chunks of radiance and darkness like cliffs and caves. And the more I see of him, the more I see into him. His pale face, creased to the eyes, seems to alternately flicker scarlet or vanish. I study the high cheekbones, the massive forehead steep like a slope, bare at the top, covered at the temples with two white wings of ruffled whiskers like two offended coxcombs.

Something in the shape and setting of his black eyes gives them a peculiar, provoking intensity. Perhaps it is their smallness. Or perhaps it is because they are not blue. This face has seen a thousand battles. It is furrowed, sunken, worn beyond age into the rough bark of a tree to which his gnarled hands, resting on the table, are its companion roots. The body wants to be lean under the plumpness that stretches his black jacket across his chest and belly. The sour smell of age, damp clothing, and an unfamiliar odor I do not recognize hover over him. I stare at the black stain on his forefinger and thumb which looks like some kind of permanent dye. I ask Covey if it is a kind of ritual mark or the sign of a Paramount Chief. He explains that it is from the constant use of the pen and ink of writing. He must have been writing for a hundred years, I think, for that then is the odor that hangs over him: ink. Covey tells me that there have been only eight presidents in the whole history of this powerful nation. And I laugh. The history of Mende is measured in fifty-six Paramount Chiefs over eight centuries. This President, who was only number six, is like meeting an ancestor from the beginning of time. I have never met a white man so venerable: his white brows, his white whiskers, his white dome of a head with its few white strings of hair combed over it. He looks up at me once, then he sits down, gestures to me to sit. He takes out his spectacles, and before reading the letter out loud, reads it in silence. Then he reads it out loud.

"The fifteenth day of November,
"New Haven

"Dear Friend Mr. Adams:
"I want to write a letter to you because you love the Mende people, and you talk to the grand court. We want to tell you one thing. José Ruiz say we are born in Havana, he tells lie. We stay in Havana ten days and ten nights, we stay no more. We are all born in Mende—we don't understand the Spanish language. Mende people been in America seventeen moons. We talk American language little, not very good; we write every day, we read all Matthew, and Mark, and Luke, and John and plenty of little books. We want you to ask the Court what we have done wrong. What for Americans keep us in prison. Some

people say Mende people crazy; Mende people dolt, because we don't talk American language. American people don't talk Mende language; American people dolt? Some men say Mende people very happy because they laugh and have plenty to eat. Mr. Pendleton come, and Mende people all look sorry because they think about Mendeland and friends we no see now. Mr. Pendleton say Mende people are angry; white men become afraid of Mende people. The Mende people don't look sorry again—that's why we laugh. But Mende people feel sorry; O, we can't tell how sorry. Some people say, Mende people no got souls. Why we feel bad, we got no souls?

"Dear friend Mr. Adams, you have children, you have friends, you love them, you feel sorry if Mende people come and carry them all to Africa. We feel bad for our friends, and our friends all feel bad for us. Americans don't take us in ship. We on shore and Americans tell us slave ship catch us. They say we make you free. If they make us free they tell true, if they no make us free they tell lie. If American people give us free we glad, if they no give us free we sorry—we sorry for Mende people little, we sorry for American people great deal, because God punish liars. Dear friend, we want you to know how we feel. Mende people think, think, think. Nobody know what we think; Mende people have got souls. We think we know God punish us if we tell lie. We never tell lie; we speak truth. What for Mende people afraid? Because they got souls. If Court ask who brought Mende people to America? We bring ourselves. Sessi hold the rudder. All we want is make us free.

"Your friend,
"Kale"

The old man takes off his spectacles and places the letter carefully on the table. "How old is Kale?" he asks.

"Kale is fourteen years old."

"Where is Kale?" the old man asks gently.

"With the Pendletons, sir."

"Well, thank him, thank him for his letter. I will try to live up to it, somehow. At his age, one still believes . . . in justice. It is very, very hard to accept anything else. . . ."

Then he says almost inaudibly, so that Covey has to strain to hear the words:

"But the *Grumpus,* I assure you, was not the *only* ship in New Haven harbor that day. There was another vessel ready to receive you and your men in case of an adverse decision and take you to a friendlier shore. I thank God your friends didn't have to break the law. But they were ready to kidnap you all. . . ."

The room is full and buzzing with voices. I am looked at with curiosity by everyone, but I cannot describe the sensation produced by John Quincy Adams. Here is an opportunity and I must seize it; choose my words, lean on confidences, explain by innocence, take advantage of misconceptions, desires, weaknesses. I contemplate my fate without this man. All these things I do—the explaining, the listening, through Covey. I force myself to speak; it is easier than touching him.

"If I could have freed all my men by killing all the white men, I would have done it. And if I could have freed all my men by killing none of the white men, I would have done that. As it was, I had to kill two, save two, and leave the rest to swim to the bottom of the sea."

"We thought the voyage was ended with the capture of the *Amistad,* but it continues even now," I say.

"Why do you say your voyage continues even now?"

"Because we are not saved. Ruiz and Montez are saved. The sea is now here. When the sea was finished with us it left us by trickery in a land in which we were as helpless, despised and captive as on the waters, and we sojourn here. Nothing has changed except the earth under our feet. For all I see is rejection and unfeeling hardness, as smooth and careless as the sea from which we rescued ourselves. Here men circle us like sharks and would eat our hearts if they could. I see it in their eyes. And they fear us as well. And we fear them. This land of yours, Mr. Adams, is worse than a typhoon for a Mende, sweeping away all his knowledge, his dignity, stripping the very skin off his back, cutting off his language as surely as if you cut out his tongue. It demands more than mere labor or slavery, it demands the death of his soul, giving him not one spot where he can rest, where he is not destructible. And now this trial continues our voyage with the appearance of law and order, but beneath its surface is a world of hatred, of rejection, of denial of our humanity, and contempt of everything about us except our price. The only safe harbor is death itself—a grave in it or a ship to sail beyond it."

"But surely you have found friends—the Tappans, Mr. Baldwin and Gibbs, Mr. Townsand and Mr. Staples. Your friends are legion. When the *Amistad* first came within the territorial waters of the United States, acts of violence passed between you and the Spaniards. It must be proved on which side these acts were right and on which side they were wrong. It is clear to me, to any freeman, why you revolted, but was it a *feeling* or a *plan*? Was it circumstance and chance, or was it reasoning? I don't look on what you tell me as a confession but as an illumination."

"How can you speak of a confession? A confession of what? How can you speak of right versus wrong or law and lawlessness to someone who has been taken by force, beaten by force, transported by force, sold by force? A man without force is without honor. Human nature does not honor a helpless man, although it can pity him; and even that it does not do for long. Do not speak of illumination to a man at war. The war I wage now in the great court is the same as I waged in Mendeland, on the waters, on the *Amistad*. I have enemies able to take my freedom and my life; I only tried to defend both. I am a prisoner of war."

And for the first time, the Paramount Chief lifts his head and looks at me with wonder and incredulity. I have tapped a spring. A light sigh escapes him. He draws his hands down his face, which emerges incredibly worn but unchanged in expression.

"The sea betrayed us; shall the land also betray us?" I shout.

The President's black eyes never leave mine. Not once does he turn towards Covey for an explanation or a question. It seems to me that it makes no difference to him what I say or how my story goes. I am being weighed upon a scale for which I know not the measure, not knowing how or why or what he judges as he does, being taken out of my knowledge; I can only return the black gaze and try to calm the alarmed pounding in my ears like the strange sea we discovered. Most white men have thoughts as transparent as their eyes. This man has eyes that reveal nothing: cold, frigid, unfathomable. And his face is the face of a man whom death has already warned. Which of us will cross the waters to the other side first is a question of no coincidence. This old man has no more time on his side than the executioner has on mine. I continue to speak until I have nothing left to say. My eyes slide past the now familiar face of John Quincy Adams. They shift to the falling bits of sky outside. Even I, in all my rich brown, have turned an ashen gray in this country. I squeeze my eyes shut and try to think of a real color: magenta, fuchsia, indigo, sassafras. I listen to James Covey's impudent remarks, a smile playing for a fleeing second around his lips. Did Covey really think I would tell this or any white man the *truth*? I and my men have taken a sacred Poro vow to reveal as little of ourselves as possible and as little of our lives before this place as we can. We have vowed to tell the white man only what he wants to hear. When they ask of our religion, we tell them we were too young to have participated in the sacred rites. When they ask us about war we say there had been peace. None of us would tell a foreigner who we aren't even sure is a *human being* of our Ki'aya, or our mother, or our sister, or the secret society of the Poro or the smooth, tattooed skin of our wives. Could I imagine telling a stranger about Bayeh Bia and her beautiful black-dyed hands? Or the Poro marks of the "Spirit teeth" on my back?

My own hands form a circle, my fingers touching as if I still held the sugarcane cutlass that had cleaved the *Amistad*'s captain's head in two. I remember only that the eyes of the man I killed had reflected the sky, as if pure daylight had been poured into them with a dipper, even as I gazed into them. And I remember that the sea had washed over my clenched fists and bloody knife and the dead white face of the captain and had made me hold my breath while the tumult of sea and storm that swirled around me in a salty vortex swept back out to infinity. And it had seemed to me that there had been some fierce purpose in those violent waves that had stung my eyes and choked my throat and filled me with terror while I gazed into the mirror of the sky in the eyes of a dead man. Even now, brain, brine and blood seem to crash upon the plank table that separates me from the old man. Under the table my knees shake, and upon it my hands tremble. Not in fear of the life I have taken, but of the spirit of that angry sea. The noise and chaos they had made! Ferrer, caught unawares, crying out "Socorro!"

"Socorro," I shout.

John Quincy Adams' face suddenly vanishes in an opaque wall of darkness, rain and wind. He slumps away from the silvery knife and lies upon the tilting deck, his face battered with rain and waves which rise higher than the ship and sink, hooking the boat and pulling it towards the deep. "And if, up to that time," I say, "I had merely been snatched away from everything I had ever known or loved and thrown into the abysses of slavery, it was then that I emerged into a new world which had nothing to do with mine. I became a new person never to be the same again. I can never return to that state I have left, *even if I return.* For I may have killed, but I have also died."

I stare out at the snow falling and the ice clinging to the rectangle of light.

If I have not always known there were white men in the world, I have also underestimated the immensity, the power, the overwhelming legion of whiteness that exists. White people are as multitudinous as the bits of cracked-off sky that begin to fall again. White people fall on nations like that; hard, cold, numbing specks of destruction.

Fifty miles by river and canal lies my ship. The ship that should have sailed me back to Mendeland.

Then I think of something quite different. I have been trained from childhood to rule, I know how to read men's faces. It is knowledge passed from Elder to Elder, from my uncle to me. And I study the black eyes gazing steadily into mine, I find a passionate nature. It is not the fanaticism of the teachers, the abolitionists, the missionaries, all of whom want something more than mere justice for me, but the devotion of an aristocrat to honor, which is bred into bone and marrow, indifferent to the opinions of other men despite all other vanities, vices and weaknesses. I can read in the face before me the heritage and integrity of a house, the pride of a lineage and clan, the mark of a true warrior. John Quincy Adams is one of my kind. He is of my race. He will demand both justice and honor for me, I think. Even though he has done nothing to deserve it, I decide, this old man is the one white man worthy of the name Marda—Grandfather.

"But Marda, how many times am I to be tried?" I ask abruptly. "What have American men against me?"

"And what does Marda mean?"

"It means grandfather, sir. It is the Mende title of supreme honor, sir, the equivalent of Sire."

And I think I have nothing in common with this Marda, not a thought, not a feeling, not one act nor emotion. No word or action had ever coincided in our respective lives, nor will I ever be able to make clear to this man the simplest reason for any act of my existence, any desire of my heart, any fear of my spirit or principle of my honor. Yet my life depends upon him. . . .

The eyes of the old man and Covey lock in a test of wills. The flint-hard age-wily eyes of the old man win easily. Surely he has tangled with obstinate men who make Covey's stubbornness seem that of a three-year-old's.

"The judicial system of the United States," the Marda begins coldly, "provides for the right of appeal from a lower court to a higher court. . . ."

Even his voice, I think, sounds like the man Job in the Book. It is tuned for an eternal dirge.

"You are not being held in *slavery*, son, but for *trial* before . . . before . . . how do you translate it, Covey? The Supreme Court."

"The Council of Paramount Chiefs."

"You, too, Marda President, would be considered a Paramount Chief, for there is no division between those who rule and those who judge," I say.

In a few months, I think, both I and the Marda will have quit this earth. In quite different ways, I presume: one covered with age and honors, and the other, myself, young and at the end of a garrote. His fierce eyes blaze out of his creased face. When he speaks, almost pleading, his eyes coincide with what his lips are saying. Not like most white men, whose lips say one thing while their eyes say something else. I scrutinize the white-ruffled, black-draped, sour-smelling figure. I feel exasperated and helpless.

I think of Bayeh Bia. I have not lain beside her for more than thirty moons, have not curled around her soft fragrance, have not risen in the night to contemplate the face of my son. I have not swum the cataracts with my brother, nor smoked my clay pipe or dipped my hands into the icy spring that runs near my house, cupping my hands and drinking deeply, perfectly content. I have not hunted a leopard or read the stars for portents or felt the night dew or the exertions of love dampen my sleeping shirt. I have not done all this. Yet the river that runs through my village still flows, surely, its brown waters indifferently carrying friend or enemy, village people nursing love or hatred on its banks, watching it save a life here or give death there: a deliverance, a prison, a refuge or a grave.

"We lost three men in the fight aboard the *Amistad*. Since our capture the second time, Fa died in prison on the third of September last, Tua in prison on the eleventh of the same month and Welluwa on the fourteenth. Kapeli on October thirtieth, I believe, and Edge-of-the-Razor died on the last day of last year. And now we mourn Yammoni. In all I've already lost nine men."

"You mean six men have died since you've been here?" asks Marda Adams incredulously.

Covey answers. "Men are dying all the time," he says.

"Yes," answers the President. "Men die . . . all the time. . . ."

There is a long silence. It corresponds to the light flutter of white outside. Solitude closes in upon me. Familiar. Weeping and raging. I think of the broken stems and ripped flesh of saffron orchids after the rains.

Joseph Cinque's silence disturbed Quincy Adams. It seemed like a reproach. He understood that they were both attempting to read the heart of the other. Joseph Cinque's audacity was simply his unspoken question: if the life of a black man could

be safely confined to him. And he, John Quincy, didn't know
the answer.

John Quincy Adams had never broken bread with a black
man, had never had more than the most elementary conversation with his black servant. He had never received a black man
in his home, had never introduced a black man to his wife,
had never prayed with one. Despite all the anti-slavery petitions he had presented, despite the slave block just a few steps
from the White House, Joseph Cinque could just as well have
dropped from the planets.

Once, he had composed an analysis of Othello's tragedy.
Shakespeare had painted Desdemona as a lady of rather easy
virtue, whose sensual passions he had found so overardent as
to reconcile her to a passion for a black man.

Adams stared at the smooth dark face. What was he to make
of this "Othello," who was loved for the dangers he had passed,

> *. . . of moving accidents by flood and filled*
> *of hair-breath escapes*
> *of being taken by the insolent foe*
> *And sold into slavery . . . ?*

He, John Quincy Adams, considered himself, by virtue of
his public service, his age and his name, to be the embodi-
ment of the United States of America. He considered Joseph
Cinque the first and probably the only glimpse he would ever
have of a black man unpolluted by slavery. This then, he decided, was a conversation between America and Africa, not between the Republic and the slave.

He had nothing in common with this young man, thought
Adams, not a thought, not a feeling or one experience or emotion. *Not one word or action in their respective lives would
ever have coincided, nor would he ever be able to make clear
to Joseph Cinque the simplest reason for any act of his life,
any desire of his heart or any fear of his spirit, or principle of
his honor.* His face was an inexhaustible black, as if he, Adams,
had rambled into a starless night. And it was just as lonely.
The limpid round eyes surveying him were heavy-lidded and
luminous. The small head sat on the powerful column of his
neck like the point of an exclamation, aggressive, alert, ready

to spring like a panther, with the same prodigious energy. The face with its wide, high forehead, prominent cheekbones and fine features smouldered in the cold light like a banked fire. And John Quincy Adams was as attracted to the smooth, arrogant face of the man who might die quite soon as aged bones to a glowing fire.

In the past two years there had been anti-black riots in Philadelphia, Boston, New York and Chicago. The abolitionist Garrison had been mobbed, stripped naked and dragged by a rope through the streets of New York City until rescued by authorities, who put him in jail to save his life. A minister in New Hampshire had been jerked to his knees during an antislavery sermon and tried for inciting violence. Free colored people's churches, schoolhouses and dwellings had been mobbed, sacked and burned down in Providence, Cincinnati and Harrisburg. In St. Louis a slave had been burned to death over a slow fire in a public square, and Elijah Lovejoy, the only newspaper editor who had spoken out against it, had been smoked out of his publishing office and murdered, five bullet holes tearing open his chest. The message was clear, mused John Quincy. Negroes and white men who loved Negroes were not safe in this land, under this flag. He knew the motives of the other white men. For the Tappans and the Jocelyns, Cinque was an undreamed-of piece of providence. For the Gibbses he was a heathen to be Christianized just as Africa had only been invented to be saved. For the Maddens, Cinque was a quest, an unclosed case, an unfinished, overriding goal of a policeman fighting crime: a rare witness to be protected, examined, his captors pursued and prosecuted. For the Judsons, Cinque was an unwelcome nigger, to be disposed of in any way possible, as soon as possible. For the Van Burens and the Forsyths, Joseph Cinque was the reincarnation of Nat Turner, his rebellion, his clarion call to revolt to the whole South. He must be destroyed just as Turner and his men had been, not only as a living man, but as a ghost, an unnamable specter of insurrection and liberty. So dangerous was it for a white man to champion a black one in the national controversy between slavery and anti-slavery that John Quincy wondered if he was mad.

Had he any right to ask a man who had been ready to die for his liberty to happily rot in jail while the United States

split hairs about his exploits? He refused to prefix "poor" before Joseph Cinque's name as everyone did. Bad luck alone
had put him where he was, thought John Quincy. That, and
the color of his skin.

"You are a dangerous man," said John Quincy.

"For whom?"

"Mostly for me," laughed Adams.

"As far as I can see, only white men are dangerous, and I
have never been nor will I ever be a white man."

"It is not your color that worries me. It is your status as an
insurrectionist."

"They believe I have no soul."

"But you believe in God?"

"Of course."

"How is he called?"

"Gewo."

"One God?"

"Yes. Though he has deserted me."

"I have thought that many times, but have always been proven
wrong."

"That remains to be seen."

God. Gewo. He believed his God was God to all men. That
was enough. His irreducible innocence saved him from the
conversion he wore as lightly as Adams imagined he carried
his fighting weapons. And there was something else that shone
in his eyes, thought Adams: a belief in his own worth and in
his own goodness. Those hard, cynical, courageous eyes saw a
world not so different from his own.

"Under extreme provocation even white men will be just
whether they want to or not," said Joseph Cinque.

The words triggered a new idea in John Quincy's mind: the
unsettling discovery that the first men and women to struggle
for freedom, the first to think of themselves as free, were *freedmen*. Without slavery there could be no freedmen. There lay
the strange enigma; was he, he thought, to esteem slavery for
the definition it gave freedom? Should he cherish Joseph
Cinque's revolt for the same reason? Would it eventually de-
fine the republic he, Adams, had so perfectly embodied all his
life, or was the revolt of Joseph Cinque the very nemesis of
his life? He tried not to look surprised, but the younger man

saw his expression and changed his own from haughty resignation to the first smile ever bestowed on Adams by a man accused of murder.

Joseph Cinque's features blurred in the shifting light and Quincy Adams' erratic eyesight. The curly hair glistened with drops of silver. The wide sloping shoulders belied a lightly built frame, delicate and muscular at the same time. His hands are beautiful, thought Adams in astonishment. And they have never seen hard work. The night before, he had spent hours mulling over a map of Africa drawn by the explorer Mungo Park. The limits of the Mende nation had never been defined with much certainty. They were as vague as the limits of freedom or of self-defense. And they had never been visited by an unhostile white man. Where would *his* route take him? How was the heart of a man driven to the most extreme act of violence explored? Did one go straight to the center in a straight line, or did one circle around the perimeter, settling into a comfortable campsite and making quick excursions into the jungle? Or did one move from site to site around the edges, stumbling on remote pockets of inhabitants by chance, hoping that when all was completed, some pattern, some rationale would emerge?

The dark blue face, half hidden in the shadows of the lengthening afternoon, reflected neither light nor comprehension. Just like that dark continent. Not those puny strips of coastal land clinging to the Atlantic—the gold and ivory slave-stockade coasts, where greed and grief had been transplanted—but that other sorrow, that dark core which lay south of the Sahara and a thousand miles from the sea, crisscrossed with grand fleuves flourishing with uncharted rain forests and unnamed nations, where no white man had ever set foot. Joseph Cinque's eyes were like the source of the Congo River, thought Adams.

"And tell me, Mr. Cinque, how many days were you on the *Amistad*?"

"After I conquer the house that swims, fifty-nine suns. Time to return to Mendeland, Marda."

"And you thought you were going home?"

"Yes. No. I no know. I know only that canoe should head into the sun."

"And there was no one who could steer the ship except your enemy Montez, and your enemy Montez told you he was steering you towards home, towards the rising sun."

"There was no one. He told me. I realize there was no one, Marda."

"And you believed him?"

"I must believe, Marda."

"And you know now what he did?"

"Yes. He trick us through our own ignorance."

Cinque added nothing more in explication. He sank into a brooding silence.

Adams looked up in irritation at Covey, who had allowed Cinque to speak for himself during this exchange.

"Mr. Cinque hardly needs me, sir," said James Covey to Adams. "He understands everything you say to him and communicates with facility, if a little," he paused, "on the colorful side. I must add that there are certain expressions in Mende that do not exist in the English language, for example, the measure of time you call an hour or a day. You understand that sun is used for day and moon for the approximation of months. And there are certain expressions in English which do not exist in Mende, for example, democracy. But he understands a final appeal, for it is our custom too. And the Supreme Court corresponds to our great Council of the Paramount Chiefs. There is," Covey was quick to add as Adams looked at him sharply, "no concept, abstract or concrete, that cannot be expressed in one way or the other in Mende. What I mean to say, Mr. President, is that Joseph Cinque listens to what you say, retains this information, decides if this information is reliable and can be reasonably believed, and then he interprets it and he *reacts* to it; in other words, he answers back, and not always what a white man might care to hear."

"You have made yourself perfectly clear, Mr. Covey," Adams snapped back. "Just do your job. What I want is the truth. Not white truth or black truth, but the truth! And I don't need a lesson in cross-examination, Mr. Covey, I am here to provide as much extreme provocation as this old, old man can, I promise you."

"Then, sir, we run the same risks as the first trial in this new one before the Supreme Court?" asked Covey.

"Yes. But it is most serious, *most* serious. Translate most carefully, Covey. The warrant the President issued to put Joseph Cinque on board the *Grumpus* assumed a power that no American President has ever assumed before, one which is questionable if the most despotic government of Europe possessed it. Such a power puts the personal freedom of any citizen of the United States at the disposition of executive discretion, caprice or tyranny. It is the servile submission of an American President to the insolent dictation of a foreign minister; a lawless and tyrannical order, issued in cold-blooded cruelty, for the commanding officer of *Grumpus* has warned those who sent him on this errand that his vessel is too small to carry so large a cargo of human beings. You know what that means far better than I. And the Connecticut District Attorney has assured the Secretary of State that the decree of Judge Thompson will be as pliant to the vengeful thirst of the barracoon slave traders as that of Herod was in olden times to the demand of his dancing daughter for the head of John the Baptist!"

Joseph Cinque started at the tone of the old man's voice.

"The Spanish minister," continued John Quincy, "demands that the President of the United States first turn man-robber by removing you from the custody of the court of law; that he next turn jailer and keep you in his custody to prevent your escape; and last turn catch-poll and transport you to Havana to appease the public vengeance of the African slave traders!"

"But Mr. Adams," said Covey. "You, too, were the president of a slave-holding republic."

There was no reproach in the interpreter's voice, only a statement of fact, but the ex-President felt as if Covey had just clubbed him between the eyes. This accusation, of all those awful ones leveled against him, had never been made before, even in his most secret heart, even in the diaries in which he poured out his most intimate thoughts and desires, even by his worst enemy. Yet there it was. The god-awful truth. His presidency had been a fiasco, won by expediency and almost immediately riddled with dissension, and before two years were out, stymied by hostility to every idea of progress, reason and unity, the abolition of slavery included, he had ever possessed.

John Quincy scrutinized both young men. The two heads, Cinque's and Covey's, were like the front and back of the same Roman coin, so much did they resemble each other, the finely chiselled features of each slightly blunted as if by the passage of endless time. Covey, too suave, too cool, too handsomely fastidious, had a deep cleft in his chin that the coal-black prince Joseph Cinque did not have, but both had the same small, neat, round head, the fine mouth and chin without a trace of beard, the same thick column of neck traced out of wide sloping shoulders. Their expressions, the one and the other, were forbearing, distant and ferocious. Yet Adams felt for Joseph Cinque anything but the antipathy he felt for Covey. Could it be, thought Adams, flushing, that it was their respective situations that made the difference? Covey was a free black Englishman. The other was, until proven otherwise, a slave.

You, too, were the president of a slave-holding republic.

Covey's words hung in the air between them, like a drawn sword.

Adams rose wearily. He extended his hand to Covey and then to Joseph Cinque and made his way slowly, gingerly across the room as if he carried his own bones on a silver platter.

Roger Baldwin took Adams' arm as he stepped out of the jail onto the New Haven Green.

"Mr. President," said the lawyer. "Bad news . . . I have spoken to Francis Scott Key, District Attorney of the United States for the District of Columbia. . . ."

"Ah, that one," said John Quincy. He detested hymns—all of them.

"He says he is afraid there is no chance for the poor creatures; that the case of the *Antelope* will be used as a precedent against them. He himself had argued this case and the blacks lost."

Adams recalled the case where justice had been dispensed by lottery. It had been impossible to distinguish between the Ladino slaves and the African "slaves," and so the United States judge had simply divided the prisoners pell-mell by numbers, taking no account of their names or origins or histories, and sent the unhappy losers back to Cuba.

"Scott Key did suggest a solution," continued Baldwin. "Make up a purse, buy the captives back and send them home to Africa. This doesn't avoid the necessity, of course, of returning Cinque to Spain to be tried for murder."

"This was Mr. Francis Scott Key's solution?" asked Adams. "Make up a purse by private subscription, buy thirty-nine men and children in 'the land of the free and the home of the brave,' and then *deport* them?"

John Trumbull fixed his good eye on the dishevelled figure of John Quincy Adams as he greeted him. His top hat was askew, his greatcoat was shabby and gray with age and he was without either gloves or cane. The wind had blown the long woollen scarf he had wound around his neck into a tight, ridiculous ball like a pillow at the nape of his neck, which was the reason his top hat sat rakishly over one eye. Like father, like son, thought Trumbull, not without affection. John Adams had been no better a dresser and no richer a man, but what a tough little bastard he was, recalled Trumbull. He had laid in a good supply of Madeira for tonight, remembering John Quincy's prodigious knowledge and delighted consumption of good wine. It would be a bachelor dinner, since there had long since been no Mrs. Trumbull. He was happy to see his old friend. A lonely old man got fewer and fewer visits, as each year someone else took permanent leave to meet his Maker. Here they were, he mused, two last remnants of the Revolution. He and John Quincy were made of the same memories as they stepped into the painter's atelier. Artfully draped classical sculptures, models of famous buildings, plaster busts of John Quincy's father, of Jefferson and Benjamin Franklin were all around them. Like Trumbull's rank of colonel, there was something true and something exaggerated there. On the walls were small studies of Trumbull's mammoth historical paintings that dominated the Rotunda of the Capitol. And on a velvet-draped easel sat a replica of his painting of the *Signing of the Constitution*.

"So they have managed to talk you into defending him."

"Well, let's just say the abolitionists are urging me to indiscreet movements which would ruin me and weaken rather than strengthen their cause. They've been doing it for years," replied Adams.

"You're evading the question, John. You've already said yes."

"My son wants me to sever all connections with the abolitionists, and Louisa has become one. Between these two alter-
natives I am agitated almost to distraction. What I endured this
last session of Congress was greater than I had imagined possible."

"Come now, John. I've known you since you were twenty.
You're spoiling for a good fight. I can feel it. You've already
decided, come hell or high water."

"Joseph Cinque has engaged my emotions powerfully. . . .
I have just met him. This subject of slavery, to my great sorrow
and mortification, is absorbing all my faculties."

Trumbull was surprised to have lived as long as John Adams'
son. But from the looks of John Quincy, ten years his junior,
he might even succumb before his, John Trumbull's, bones
were put to rest. And what a poor grave it would be, he thought.
The painter carried many men's secrets behind that dreamy
one-eyed gaze, most by choice, having to do with love and
power. For he had spent his life amongst the rich, great and
famous, recording public moments with his brush. But it was
the private ones that haunted him, moments he had captured
in sketches and miniatures, which were his secret diary of power
and its price. This, he realized, was one of those moments.

"All I know, John, is that there is a great fermentation on
this subject of slavery in *all* parts of the Union," he said, his
glass eye gleaming in the fire light, his long body stretched
out, feet crossed. He poured another glass of wine for John
Quincy. He hadn't realized how lonely he was.

"Look at the abolitionist press. Look at the Amistad Committee formed in a twinkle. Anti-slavery *and* women's emancipation associations are forming everywhere in the country.
And they are working hand in glove with England." Trumbull's mouth turned down in distaste. "Funds are raised to cir-
culate inflammatory newspapers and pamphlets, and they send
multitudes to the slaves."

"Who can't read," said John Quincy dryly.

"Come now, John, this question has given you more than
one attack of apoplexy! We are in a state of profound peace,
John: an overpampered, prosperous nation, yet all the elements of exterminating war are in violent circulation, and no
one," said Trumbull, his voice slurred, his eyes staring blankly
into the fire that cast shadows as long and as black as the ques-

tion the two friends were discussing, "can scarcely foresee to what it will lead. . . ."

"I'll tell you where," said Adams. "The nation is being led by inches towards a war it is too weak to survive. I am playing for time."

John Quincy fell silent. He would continue to oppose the Gag Rule until he dropped dead. He would *talk* it away until he had no more strength. Instead of twenty anti-slavery petitions introduced and laid on the table, he would present a hundred.

John Quincy felt one of his terrible depressions coming on. They had plagued him all his life and he had fought them bitterly, reminding himself that they were visitations of Divine Providence, builders of character, marks of a chosen dynasty. He had fought them with obsessional work. It was what had always saved him. Work. Time. He had struggled the past five years without an interval of a day, while his mind and his body had been weakening under the daily, silent, unremitting erosion of Time. Failure had always been the heaviest load he had to carry. Failure to gain a second term as President, failure not to have himself turned the tide against slavery when he had been President, failure to have provided financial security and fortune for his family, failure not to have saved his youngest son, would all join hands with failure to free Joseph Cinque.

You, too, were the president of a slave-holding republic.

The abolitionists in their arrogance thought the name Adams, armed with the sword and shield of the Constitution, was enough to convince nine just men, all of them Southerners. But they were wrong, he thought.

"I," said John Quincy, "am not a . . . John Adams."

"But then I," said John Trumbull, "am not a John Sargent."

John Quincy said nothing. He could not protest that Trumbull was not a first-rate painter, though he admitted it in private. His picture of the signing of the Declaration of Independence was immeasurably below the dignity of the subject and his expectations. It might be said of Trumbull's talent like the Spaniards say of heros who were brave on a certain day: He has painted good pictures.

*   *   *

"He calls me Grandfather," said John Quincy. "According to
his interpreter that is the equivalent of Sire—the highest address of respect possible in Mende society. This man Covey is
more than a mere interpreter. He is Cinque's eyes and ears as
well as tongue. They seem more like twin brothers than anything else. Incredible that a few months ago they were strangers.
They seem to think the same—even to the naked eye of an
outsider. There is something quite Catholic in Cinque's thinking—more I would say medieval than savage. For Covey has
given us a literal translation of a noble and poetic language
that otherwise we would have no access to—and thus no true
access to Cinque or his men. For if Covey is a modern man,
Cinque has stepped out of some feudal romance. It may seem
strange to speak of a man who has no written language (Covey
says Mendes *do* have a written language but Cinque can't write)
in terms of books or paintings but there is a Socratian manner
not only of gesture but of speech and thought as well. Of course
he is very young, but others are older. Take Sessi, the Homer
and the 'historian' of the voyage. For him, only the past is important and the present, as in Socrates, is likened to a shadow
world to be passed through on the way to meet one's ancestors. I begin to believe that the idea of the present is much
less attractive to them than either the future, which is the suc-
ceeding generation, or the past, which is the ancestors. For the
present seems to imply free choice, which is the negation of
African belief in which predestination and determination play
a large role, as they did in classical times. . . . I'm afraid I'll
be calling myself Adams, il africano, from now on."

But he didn't stop there. "I know, I know I voted for the
Missouri Compromise because I believed it was all that could
be done under the Constitution and from fear, yes, fear of putting this Union in peril. But perhaps in hindsight twenty years
later, I would have been wiser to have persisted in the restric-
tion upon Missouri until it should have ended in a convention
of the states to revise and amend the Constitution. This would
have produced a new union of thirteen or fourteen states unpolluted with slavery and with the greatest and noblest of
causes, namely to rally the slave states to us one by one through
the universal emancipation of their slaves, to rejoin the United
States of America."

It was growing cold and dark in the atelier. Trumbull listened in consternation to Adams. He was speaking treason! The dissolution of the sacred Union! It was worse than Burr. But he wouldn't stop.

"You know, Trumbull, I've been thinking for a long time that perhaps I should move for a declaratory act that so long as an article of the Constitution of a slave state, say, North Carolina or Georgia, deprived a colored citizen of Massachusetts, for instance, of his rights as a citizen of the United States within a slave state, then the *white* citizen of the same Georgia or North Carolina should be held as an *alien* within the commonwealth of Massachusetts, not entitled to claim or enjoy there any right or privilege of a citizen of the United States."

"Mr. Adams!" exclaimed the painter, more and more anguished. It was the most extreme declaration Trumbull had ever heard Quincy make.

"And I would go further," he continued, "and declare that North Carolina (or Georgia) had disfranchised a portion of the citizens of Massachusetts (its Negro citizens) and had violated the Constitution and until those citizens should be reintegrated in the full enjoyment and possession of those rights . . ."

John Quincy had lost all sense of reality, thought Trumbull.

"I think you would do much better," he said softly, "to leave the Constitution alone, John. No slight occasion should tempt us to touch it. Better rather to habituate ourselves to think of it as . . . unalterable. Let it stand as it is. New hands have never touched it. The men who made it, your father, have done their work and have passed away. Who shall improve what they did?"

"There is nothing," said Adams stubbornly, "in the Constitution that condones slavery. Southerners insist on hiding behind states rights and the Constitution! It's wrong!"

"What about Queen Victoria's appeal to President Van Buren on behalf of the Amistaders?" said Trumbull, hoping to get the subject back to Cinque and his men.

"The Minister of Her Britannic Majesty, Victoria, Mr. Fox has told me, he has still received no answer to his note to the Secretary of State. He said he had heard with surprise that the decision of the Supreme Court would be to deliver up these unfortunate men. He left me two folio pamphlets of documents laid before Parliament relating to the slave trade. Then he explained to me in great detail what he, on orders of Palmerston, had looked into for me: the doctrine of continuity of voyages in cases of insurance which he thought applied to the case of the *Amistad* as a slave trader—the continuity of voyages," Adams repeated. "The voyage of the *Amistad* is only a continuation of the original voyage from Havana which itself is only the continuation of the pirate ship voyage of the *Tecora* . . ."

"Do you think it will work?"

"Well, it's one thing we will try. With the whole United States dressed against their freedom, we have to try anything."

"And everything."

"Oh, Gilpin, Van Buren and Forsyth are not fools. Nor are they particularly wicked men. They simply don't want slavery or this trial as an issue, now or ever, since they crave power. But it cannot be helped. The issue is here. The black man is here. A victory would be a revindication of everything America stands for and the future of the black man in this country."

"You think he *has* a future?"

"Of course, he does. As a citizen and as a freedman. I don't believe in colonization, Trumbull. Anything John J. Calhoun approves of has got to be wrong. After all we've done to them, shall we now set them down somewhere in the Gulf of Mexico?"

"It's a very seductive idea."

"Because it's a stupid one. One to rid the United States, not of slavery, but of free-born black citizens. Colonization is another word for deportation."

Adams drew together his fluted eyebrows. He was only a short time from that great equalizer, Death. There was much, he thought, in favor of risking one's life for justice.

Trumbull allowed the silence to envelop both of them. Adams turned his profile. John Quincy's mouth was dry. His eyes pricked. He felt sick to his stomach and took a sip of wine, hoping the gallish taste would disappear.

John Quincy had always saved his kindness for strangers and underdogs, thought Trumbull. He welcomed misfortune as a means of improving character and had driven one son to suicide with his demands for excellence and unattainable goals. He was a vengeful friend if crossed, an unforgiving father if disobeyed, a pitiless enemy if he believed himself wronged;

he had driven himself to paupery in the service of his country, and now this.

"If the Union must be dissolved," he said slowly, "it is precisely this question upon which it ought to break! If slavery be the destined sword to sever this Union, the same sword, believe me, will sunder the bonds of slavery itself. And perhaps Joseph Cinque is part of the plan of the destroying angel. . . ."

Slowly, almost shyly, John Quincy pulled out the same engraved portrait of himself that he had shown to Louisa. Trumbull stared at the signed bullet hole in the head. But to Trumbull, Adams showed the letter he had not shown to Louisa.

*Gracious heavens, my dear Sir, your mind is diseased on the subject of slavery. Pray, what had you to do with the captured ship? . . . You are great in everything else, but here, you show your weakness. Your name will descend to the latest posterity with this blot on it: Mr. Adams loves the Negroes too much—*UNCONSTITUTIONALLY.

—A Virginian

Quincy Adams closed his eyes in a moment of despair.

You, too, were the president of a slave-holding republic.

⟶ Joseph Cinque ⟵
November 1840

The sympathy of the Executive government, as it were of the nation, in favor of the slave-traders, and against these poor, unfortunate, helpless, tongueless, defenseless Africans, was the cause and foundation and motive of all those proceedings.
—*John Quincy Adams*

For a long time after he leaves I gaze after the short, shuffling figure. I wonder if I will ever see him again. It seems to me that this meeting is the key to an event that has more to do with the Marda President, as I begin to call him, than with me or my men. If he has decided, I think, he certainly doesn't show it. Yet the Marda President haunts me—his fierceness, his pride, his voice. His face resembles the great stone heads the village sculptors carve to commemorate the spirits of the chiefs. The features are powerful and calm and resemble actual men. We call them *mayen yate* and they have been strong medicine for two hundred years. In the end I managed to touch him. I grasped his hand American style, wordlessly, and he allowed it to remain in mine, small, dry, gnarled, and cold.

I decide to prepare myself for the new trial with or without the Marda. I close myself off from everything and everyone. I apply myself to learning from the white man's Book, hoping for a clue as to how they reason. I go over my arguments one by one, retracing every step of the war of the *Amistad*, reliving every gesture, every emotion, imagining my appearance before the judges, rehearsing my speech. But as the days wear on, I become more and more despondent. I begin to have nightmares again about the *Tecora*. Bayeh Bia visits me almost daily in my dreams. For the first time I refuse food. I begin to see the trial as a sinister, comical ritual with my men as the sacrifice. I try to remember the first trial, but it is a blur of faces and words in a sea of boredom and incomprehension. I have not understood any of it, nor anything that has happened since. I pretend to, but now, face to face with a new battle, I feel empty, used, despised.

Am I a good man? Or have I committed some unpardonable sin in this life or another which renders me unfit to live, unfit to lead, unfit to win? Have the acts of an ancestor brought down retribution upon me? Either I have brought the trial and slavery upon myself in some mysterious way, or the white man has imposed it upon me unjustly. It is up to me to decide if they have such power. In Mende, I could have consulted the Elders, the oracles, the Priests. I would have had the whole history of my clan recited to see where my *ndehun-bla* had failed. Then I would at least know for which ancient trespasses I am to pay. Then all of this would have some meaning.

"I have prepared my speech for the Big Court," I tell Covey proudly.

"But you," said Covey, "will not be allowed at the Big Court."

"What?"

"The men involved in such a case are never present. You see, it is the trial *itself* that is to be judged, not you. You as a person, as a man, are not the important thing. The importance is the validity of the first judge's opinions. You're only a symbol, a . . ." he searched for the word, "case, an argument, so many folders of paper."

"But how will they do this?"

"By proxy."

I am to be tried by proxy. A white man standing in my place. I am too ashamed to tell the men. I am angry. And I am afraid. I am deprived of my only consolation: the trial.

Up until the very end I believed all my efforts to understand their power would help me prevail. It is only at this final humiliation that I despair.

And so I live with the ghost of Ramon Ferrer, the spirit of the President Marda, and the specter of total failure. No one can comfort me, neither Covey nor Vivian, the Braithwaites nor the white men. I am at once frantic with the desire for action, yet held in thrall by a strange apathy, an apathy such as I imagine a man already condemned to death might have. It is both the relief to be freed of the anxiety of living and the intense desire to survive. It is such a strong and strange elation, it becomes almost a visitation. Only my eyes, as Crocodile tells me, betray me. They are bright with yearning, yet clouded with the anticipation of the trap, the spear, the knife, the club, the net: like a stalked animal. And around the net swirls a cyclone of words, documents, ambitions, politics, indignation, benevolence, misconception and what the white man calls "public opinion." As for me, I consider "public opinion" worthy of the same treatment I accorded the Spaniard's trouser leg. But I am wrong. I realize I have a power of my own. A power beyond the accusation of murder. It is a power that has until now been ignored not only by my defenders and my enemies, but even by myself. It is a power as ancient as history. It is the power of legend.

The memoirs of John Quincy Adams, Washington City, The twenty-sixth Congress, 1840

The second   My time slips away from under me week after week, while I am doing nothing. I was all this day absorbed in struggling to answer a letter from Messrs. Jocelyn, Leavitt, and Lewis Tappan, about the *Amistad* Africans, whose case involves deeply perplexing questions. I have not yet commenced. Upwards of two hours was consumed in reading the Parliamentary papers relating to the slave-trade, accumulating proofs of the duplicity of Spain and Portugal in their treaties with Great Britain and in their edicts against the slave-trade. With that same duplicity the Government of the United States stands charged; and with such defenses as Forsyth's dispatches and Trist's dissertations, compared with the last paragraph of Van Buren's last annual message to Congress, any American must hide his head for shame.

The third   I finished my letter to Simeon S. Jocelyn, Joshua Leavitt, and Lewis Tappan, declining a proposal made to me by them to commence a correspondence with Lord Palmerston respecting the case of the *Amistad* Africans. On full deliberation, I concluded that it would be improper.

If I begin to read anything else, daylight fades into twilight, and twilight into darkness, before I am aware that the day is gone and I have done nothing. I this day took up and made a minute of eight folio pamphlet documents, containing about thirteen hundred pages of papers communicated to the British Parliament in 1839, and forty relating to the slave-trade, divided into classes A, B, C, D, two sets of each. What can I do with them? It is impossible to separate the discussion upon the African slave-trade from the moral and political aspects of slavery; and that is with us a forbidden topic. It is the quicksand upon which Van Buren is stranded.

The seventh   I walked round the President's square at evening twilight, and waded along nearly through N. P. Trist's dissertation philippic addressed to the British Commissioners at the Havana—an elaborate, insolent, crafty, hypocritical treatise to sustain and justify the African slave-trade and negro slavery, under hollow professions of deep detestation of them both. This paper, and the whole of Trist's correspondence, and his conduct as United States Consul at Havana, are among the most remarkable phenomena of the death-struggle now in continual operation between the spirit of liberty and the spirit of bondage on this continent of North America. Trist has the ambition to act as a prime part in this great convulsion.

The fourteenth   I went, therefore, into the Supreme Court library room, and took out the volume of *Wheaton's Reports* containing the case of the *Antelope*. I read as much of it as I could, and longed to comment upon it as I could; but I have neither time nor head for it—nothing but the heart.

With increasing agitation of mind, now little short of agony, I rode in a hack to the Capitol, taking with me, in confused order, a number of books which I may have occasion to use. The very skeleton of my argument is not yet put together.

I went into the Congress library, and took out for use the thirty-seventh volume of *Niles's Register*, containing the speech of James Madison in the Virginia Convention on the double condition of slaves in that State, as persons and as property.

The seventeenth   I went to the Capitol about half an hour before the meeting of the House, and in the office of the Clerk of the Supreme Court I read the opinion of the District Judge, Davies, of Georgia, in February 1821, on the case of the *Antelope.* I want copies, but hesitate to charge the cost of them to the friends of the Africans.

The eighteenth   Mr. Fox came, and conversed with me concerning the *Amistad* case. He has not had any correspondence with this Government on the subject, and I advised him to address a note to the Secretary of State concerning it, immediately. He said he would prepare one and call on me again tomorrow evening and show it to me. He said he had recently heard, with great surprise, that the decision of the Supreme Court would be to deliver up these unfortunate men.

The twentieth   By an agreement this day between Mr. Baldwin and the Attorney General, Gilpin, the Supreme Court postponed the *Amistad* captives' case till the 16th of February; and Mr. Baldwin left the city this afternoon to return home. This gives me a long respite for further preparation; but my senseless distribution of time leaves me none for this all-important claim. I went into the Senate chamber and heard a closing debate.

The twenty-fifth   I finished the day in drudgery to assort and file my papers. . . . Household cares are more and more burdensome with the advance of years. Anxieties for the journey, for the return home, and for those I am to leave behind, an hourly reminder and daily-deepening consciousness of decay in body and mind, an unquenchable thirst for repose, yet a motive for clinging to public life till the last of my political friends shall cast me off—all this constitutes my present condition.

The twenty-sixth   Evening consumed in reviewing the case of the *Antelope,* which I did not half finish—a desperate, dangerous and, I fear, useless undertaking.

The twenty-eighth   I enquired of Mr. Fox if he had sent to the Department of State his note concerning the captives of the *Amistad*. He said he had, but had received no answer.

At the first meeting of the House, Pickens reproduced his call upon the President for information respecting the seizure of American vessels by British cruisers on the coast of Africa, and it was received without objection. I had prepared this morning, and now moved, an amendment calling for the correspondence with the British Government relating to the African slave-trade, and for all N. P. Trist's dispatches as Consul at the Havana to the Department of State, relating to the same subject.

We shall certainly not get Trist's dispatches—perhaps not the diplomatic correspondence, particularly Fox's last note about the *Amistad* captives; but a refusal, or an apology for withholding them, will be useful for the appeal to the people, to the world, and to posterity.

The thirtieth   An inflammation in my left eye threatens me with complete disability to perform my final duty before the Supreme Court in the case of the *Amistad* captives; while the daily and hourly increasing weight of the pressure of preparation aggravates the disability.

The fifth   Sleepless night. The step that I have taken absorbs all the faculties of my soul. I fear I have estimated too highly its importance. I fear my own incompetency to sustain it effectively and successfully. I know not what support I shall receive in or out of the House; I stand alone in this undertaking. Few, if any, of my colleagues appear to understand my purpose, and, from their deportment yesterday, I should conclude they thought it one of my eccentric, wild, extravagant freaks of passion. . . ."

I look up to see Covey standing over me as I squat against the wall, changing places to follow the winter sun. Since the day with Marda Adams, I call War Road only by his English name.

"Come," he says, "The *Amistad* is in New Haven harbor and they are towing her to New London for repairs. If you want to say good-bye to her, you must come now."

"Now?" I say, alarmed.

"She is going to be put in dry dock, cleaned and painted and regilded. Even her name is to be changed."

"My *Amistad*?"

"She is no longer yours, my friend," says another voice. Startled I realize Covey is not alone; Richard Purvis, the black abolitionist who commissioned my portrait from Reverend Jocelyn's brother, is standing in the doorway behind Covey. He looks regal and dangerous in his dark gray riding clothes and top hat.

"But the verdict has still to be decided," I protest to Covey.

"True," says Covey, "but just the same, the *Amistad* as we know her will no longer exist."

"By what power . . ."

"Evidently the Admiralty," says Purvis sadly. "They can't let such a ship rot. Take heart in the news that your war has lost President Van Buren the election. The returns from the West are in. The next President of the United States is William Henry Harrison."

So, I think, in the mad scramble of Paramount Chiefs the Americans call elections, our enemies have been defeated. But as far as I am concerned, presidents are interchangeable, Adams included. They are all white, and they all want to remain President. Paramount Chief Van Buren is gone, but then so is the *Amistad*. I feel like howling. Instead I say, "Take me to New Haven; I want to see it. . . ."

"Her," corrects Covey.

I put on every scrap of clothes I own, for the weather has turned cold, raw and windy. Covey lifts me onto his speckled mare named Buzzard and I ride double behind him while Purvis accompanies us on a black stallion called Abolition, the equal of which I have never seen. As we come into town, I try to ignore the curious stares of the villagers. Ever since Big Man and Python were attacked by gangs on the street and beaten, I have avoided New Haven. But I am the famous Joseph Cinque with my twin, Covey, and Robert Purvis is so intimidating, people make way for us. We go directly to the harbor. She is there, waiting. I take in her old, battered appearance in silence, comparing it with the newspaper image of her I carry even now, next to my heart.

"Her name will be changed, her color will disappear under new paint, her history will be cancelled," says Purvis, "but the spirit of the *Amistad* will always roam the sea and the blood of the captives who died on her decks will never be erased."

I am in awe of Purvis. I respect him as I would a noble of another tribe. But he is, for me, like Covey and Braithwaite, one of them.

"What happens now?" I ask.

"The trial," Purvis replies.

"That is Marda Adams' job," I say. I feel a certain protective affection for him. "He is my Speaker."

"And he speaks alone in this," says Purvis, "despite our many friends. I am beginning to agree with a young, new voice amongst us, a fugitive slave from London named Frederick Douglass who is beginning to make a name for himself as a debater of genius, that as concerns the man of color in this country, the American people are more often generous than just . . . all full of good intentions; but there is always more charity than justice."

"If it comes to that," laughs Covey, "I'll settle for generosity."

But Covey can't console me. It is like a funeral. If I had been in Mendeland, I would have shaved my head and torn my lappa and fasted for weeks. My eyes follow the tall, naked masts up to the sky and history comes rushing back so violently, I catch hold of one of the ropes mooring her to the quay to steady myself. The water reflects her forlorn hull, the paint has peeled like hanging skin, the ropes are all eaten away, the gold letters I can read now are almost invisible. Behind me, the din of the docks with their happy crowds of people, merchandise, sailors, cargos of printed cloth, hawkers of the ginger beer and candied apples I love, all remind me of village life and make me feel even more childlike, helpless and despairing. I turn away and spit in disgust, my heart shriveling. The shadow of the masts falls over the three of us as I finger the newspaper image inside my shirt. Except for ghosts, the *Amistad* is deserted. She has been sealed by the customs with large lead insignias and red wax in large X's. A cloth breaks loose from its cords and dances in the wind, making a hollow, thumping, ominous sound like a drum. Overhead the mast-head looms, a gigantic carved fetish, the torso of a voluptuous white woman with flowing yellow hair, naked breasts, empty blue eyes. One arm extends, holding a torch. I realize with a shock that I have never really seen her before. This uncanny sculpted and painted figure above the prow guided us for fifty-nine suns. What manner of diabolical sculptor fashioned this sky-eyed monstress?

"She represents Columbia," says either Covey or Purvis.

Forlornly, I look up at her in Covey's castoff pea jacket, my ragged clothes, filthy boots and rough woolen cap. I recall standing naked, clean, rubbed in palm oil on the *Amistad,* this sculptured woman beneath me, free. I reach out, but I am too far to touch her. The tow boats begin to pull her away from the quay. The vacant eyes leave mine with neither compassion nor recognition and the splendid bosom heaves with the sea.

"Father Siaffa," I shout into the freezing wind, "let it reach you; let it reach you that Columbia returns us!" I ignore the sour, despairing glance exchanged between Covey and Purvis as if all this was only a wild, extravagant freak of passion. . . .

Bayeh Bia saw billows of gray smoke and flying sparks light the sky over Dumbocorro and the river Gallinas. The white queen had declared war on the nation that had stolen Sengbe Pieh. And the English commander Denman's ship's cannon spit fire over the Lomboko barracoons. But was this queen powerful enough to return Sengbe Pieh to her? Bayeh Bia lay in Sengbe Pieh's carved bed, her blackened fingers caressing its ornate sculpting. Often, as now, in the quiet hours before day-break she would dream she heard Tau's little bell or Sengbe Pieh's light runner's step. She always rose, though she knew it was hopeless, expecting something uncanny and ravishing to happen, like her beloved Kabba Sei, crashing through the clusters of fuchsia lilies, laughing with news of Sengbe Pieh's return. But this strange, harsh, white man's news was real. Guns. Cannons. Fireballs. Dynamite. But King Siacca couldn't send all the bad white men home any more than he could bring Sengbe Pieh back. Bayeh Bia's long narrow feet stepped onto the earth floor. Without her sleeping shirt she stepped through the round door out into the pink ribbons of low mist. She began to pace to and fro, appearing then disappearing as she passed the opening, suddenly stopping short to listen for Gewo's breathing. Her thousand plaits swung loosely around her shoulders, the coral shells clicking like grasshoppers, leaping and glistening. She seemed encased in a deepening veil of wavering light that distorted her as in a flawed mirror. Her bare shoulders caught the first dawn light, but the rest of her nakedness was hidden by the pool of her own shadow, so that in its darkness she caressed her body and repeated her husband's name: a mindless incantation, not a real prayer of Return like those she performed twice a moon in the Sande Society's compound in the company of her mother-in-law and Sengbe Pieh's second wife. No, this was more like the unreasonable murmurings of lovemaking, here, here, here, as the moonlight left its thin silver line across her breast and the sun disputed the violet sky. Now. Now. Now. She leaned against the umbrella tree in the enclosure; the morning scent from opening lilies was so strong her nostrils quivered. The lilies bloomed just before the rains came and bowed their stems back, broke their fleshy petals and destroyed their beauty. Just like men who disappeared. Bayeh Bia wondered why they insisted on offering all their splendor to the rains, in suicide, by blossoming every season just at the wrong time, like women who yearn for men who leave them. How long would her family allow her to remain husbandless? Even if the ships of the white queen were a sign that Sengbe Pieh was not dead? She would stop wearing mourning. Tau had given birth to a girl, and Sengbe Pieh had fathered her second child his last night in Mende. Both children waited for his return to be named. In almost every village war had broken out. Men disappeared. Women disappeared. Whole villages fled into the tall-grassed savannas. Sengbe Pieh had been gone two years. It would be

another twelve moons before her uncle would insist on another marriage. At dawn she went to her mother-in-law's house
and knelt down wordlessly, and wordlessly the women of the
compound began to unweave her thousand braids, the doing
and undoing of which marked Bayeh Bia's waiting.

CORRESPONDENCE RELATIVE TO THE
DESTRUCTION OF THE SLAVE BARRACOONS
AT GALLINAS

Governor Doherty (Copy)
to Lord John
Russell.
7th Dec. 1840.

In consequence of the white slave dealers settled in the River
Gallinas having prevented the boats of Her Britannic Majesty's ships
from receiving the common rights of humanity when in distress
and seeking refuge in King Siacca's waters; in violation of his dignity, and of his rights, thus exposing him to differences with the
Queen of England, and also in consequence of a Sierra Leone boy
having been made a slave by these white men at the River Gallinas,
who was discovered and released by Commander Denman on the
19th instant.

1st. King Siacca engages totally to destroy the factories belonging to these white men without delay.

2dly. King Siacca engages to give up to Commander Denman
all the slaves who were in the barracoons of the white slave dealers
when he entered the river and have been carried off into the bush.

3dly. King Siacca engages to send these bad white men out of
his country by the first opportunity, and within four months from
this date.

4thly. King Siacca binds himself in the most solemn manner that
no white men shall ever for the future, settle in his country for
the purpose of slave dealing.

5thly. Captain Denman, upon the part of Her Britannic Majesty, promises never to molest any of the legitimate commerce of
the River Gallinas, but that, on the contrary, Her Majesty's ships
shall afford every assistance to King Siacca's subjects and take every
opportunity of promoting his commerce.

6thly. The Governor of Sierra Leone will use his influence to
get the Sierra Leone people to open the trade with King Siacca's
country.

7thly. No white man from Sierra Leone shall settle down in King Siacca's country without his full permission and consent.

8thly. All complaints that King Siacca may have to make hereafter against any of Her Majesty's ships he is requested to forward at once to Sierra Leone, and a full investigation, and such redress as the occasion may require, is solemnly promised to Commander Denman on the part of Her Britannic Majesty.

Done at Dumbocorro in the River Gallinas, this 21st day of November, 1840.

		his
(Signed)	PRINCE MANNA,	x
		mark.
	LUSINI ROGERS,	ditto
	JOHN SELEPHA ROGERS,	his
		x
		mark.

(Signed) JOSEPH DENMAN,
Commander and Senior Officer on the Sierra Leone Station.

Captain Denman, by the request of Prince Manna and the chiefs, hereby states, that he at first demanded that the trade goods of the white slave dealers should be destroyed with their factories, but King Siacca having declared that those persons have acted in defiance of his laws and that in consequence he considers their goods as forfeited to him, Captain Denman has withdrawn his demand upon this point and consented that King Siacca shall take possession of the said goods, on condition that they are immediately taken out of the factories and removed to Ghindemar, or some other place far from the coast.

(Signed) JOSEPH DENMAN,
Commander and Senior Officer.

Sent at 8 A.M. 25th.
TO KING LAMINA,
Dumbocorro,
25th November, 1840

I AGAIN demand the slaves that you have in your possession, which Prince Manna and the chiefs have engaged to give up to me.

Prince Manna will deliver this letter to you, and unless you give up every one of those slaves immediately, I will burn your town.

(Signed) JOSEPH DENMAN
Commander and Senior Officer
of Her Britannic Majesty's Vessels
Off the River Gallinas.

The captain, Honorable Joseph Denman, Esq., Commander of Her Britannic Majesty's African Patrol, stood on the forecastle of his brig of war the *Wonderer* and trained his telescope along the burning line of seacoast where flames had turned the already torrid air into wavering cyclones that tore down the white beaches from the Banana Islands to Lomboko. Clouds of heavy smoke rose upwards spilling black ink onto the pristine blue chart of the sky. The captain's loud-hailer hung loosely from a leather strap over his gold-braided shoulder, but he had no more use for it. The operation was over. Don Pedro's barracoons, like Don Pedro, no longer existed—at least for the moment. The tall, tough, obsessional English lord, steeled in prodigious hardship and privation, blessed with a constitution of iron and cursed with an irreparable lust for vengeance against slavers, turned his back on the singed coastline and, motioning his second lieutenant to his side, ordered two extra rations of rum for the crew.

"I think," said Robert Madden to the handsome, intense Captain, "that we can toast Her Royal Majesty. We have something great to celebrate."

Denman's anti-slave treaties with the King of Gallinas had now made him the most feared man on the Windward coast. Escorted by the brig *Rolls* and the schooner *Saracea*, Denman had blockaded the entire shore, daring Pedro Blanco and the House of Martinez to move one slave out of Lomboko. Unaware of Denman's new cruising tactics, Havana kept sending vessels full of goods to barter. The stocks had kept piling up and slaves died by the hundreds, as not one of the nine vessels blockaded by Denman dared embark them. Of the suffering of the captives in the barracoons, the captain's only remark had been, "Better as unlucky men in their own country at war than as animals in the Middle Passage." Day after day the *Wonderer* stalked to and fro outside the estuary, and finally, with the King of Gallinas' treaty in hand, Denman had left the coast and invaded the inlets, rivers and islands of Gallinas, nominally Portuguese territory, firing incendiary rockets, igniting the barracoons and liberating on the spot 841 slaves.

SUPREME COURT OF THE UNITED STATES

JANUARY TERM, 1841

THE UNITED STATES

v.

SINGUA

If the power existed, these proceedings are not against the Africans as persons, but as property merely. It is from the decision that they are not property that the United States have appealed.

The claim of property in the Africans is necessarily several, when each answers for himself and claims his own freedom, and there are no conflicting claims to them as property. The answer of each was sustained by the court below. The appellants have no controversy with them jointly; but with each separately on the question whether he is a person or a thing. To give jurisdiction to this court, therefore, it should appear that, as property, they are severally of the value of $2000. The four claimed by Montez are stated in his libel to be of the value of $1300. The forty-nine claimed by Ruiz are stated to be of the value of $22,000.

If the appeal should be sustained, the Africans, on the facts admitted and proved, are entitled to their freedom.

John Quincy Adams
February 1841

Is it possible that a President of the United States should be ignorant that the right of personal liberty is individual? That the right to it of every one, is his own—JUS SUUM; and that no greater violation of his official oath to protect and defend the Constitution of the United States could be committed than by an order to seize and deliver up at a foreign minister's demand, thirty-six persons, in a mass, under the general denomination of all, the negroes, late of the *Amistad*.

—*John Quincy Adams*

The cold shortened his breath and reddened his cheeks as John Quincy walked from the F Street house to the Capitol. It was a freezing February morning, the twenty-second, George Washington's birthday, and Adams struggled with one of the worst depressions of his life, his mind in such turmoil that even the simplest arguments, even sentences, seemed beyond his capacity. The thoughts, strategy, memoranda jotted down in the middle of the night, in the wee hours of the morning, at the draughty Court library after his meeting with Joseph Cinque, had all fled, leaving only fear: fear of failure, fear of ridicule, fear of punishment, fear that he would lose control of his violent, impetuous, explosive temper. It was one thing to attack an opponent in the House and quite another to argue soberly and masterfully before the Supreme Court. His mother had warned him to curb his excessive temper, but he had lost every battle he had ever had with it. Never rise to provocation, she had said. But he did. He did. It would cost him the trial, he knew it. And it would prove to Joseph Cinque that it was dangerous to trust any white man with one's life. . . .

People were crowded on the steps of the Senate when he arrived: applicants for office, suppliants for patronage, newly elected congressmen, those who had lost their seats in the elections, lobbyists, military men, all the apparatus of a new presidential dynasty buzzed around the honey dome of the Capitol. Joseph Cinque had cost Martin Van Buren the election. President William Henry Harrison would be sworn in in March. Newspaper boys darted in and out of the top-hatted, gray- and black-greatcoated, exclusively male mob, shouting the headlines. The trial of Joseph Cinque was front page news. John Quincy made his way through the wall of bodies, nodding here and there, distant enough to discourage conversation, and entered the packed Rotunda and a repetition of the crowds and noise outside, except that inside the atmosphere was more dense, more volatile and louder, since it was easier to speak in the warmth, and proximity to the source of power made the voices even more predatory.

"Good luck Mr. President," was all Nathan Langdon said, towering over him. Before Adams could acknowledge his greeting, the ex-census-taker had been swallowed up by the crowd. Adams entered the chamber of the Supreme Court, in the basement of the Senate. It was already full. He looked up. Chief Justice Taney's clock, set five minutes ahead to make the lawyers think they were late, ticked on. The brass glowed, the spittoons sat everywhere like fat bright frogs.

The mahogany chairs, all different in size and height to accommodate the various shapes and dimensions of their occupants, but all the same form, sat empty, facing him in a somber, intimidating line. The only fireplace in the chamber did not draw, causing a pall to descend over everything, with no way to dissipate the stinging fumes. The dim, smoke-filled windowless room with its thick arc of marble columns seemed more and more a dungeon to him rather than a court. Yesterday, in his pew at St. John's Church, he had offered a prayer for Quinquagesima, the last Sunday before Lent. The sermon had been from Hebrews, XII, 22, "and to an innumerable company of angels he spoke . . ." Company of angels, thought John Quincy. How cheering, mysterious and awful was that doctrine of angels. He felt the chamber fill with ministering spirits, messengers of weal and woe: numberless, they flew around his head in hierarchies, cherubim, seraphim, archangels, guardians of Kingdoms and, he supposed, Republics, and of individual lives, their nature inexplicable to man. Did he believe in them? he asked himself. Yesterday no. Today he was almost tempted to address them instead of the nine men who had started to file in. So little space was allotted to the Court that the judges had to dress after they had entered, in full view of the audience. Robed and wigged, they sat down as the Court crier droned the words John Quincy Adams had not heard in twenty years:

"Oyez, oyez, oyez
All persons having business before the Honorable, the Su-
preme Court of the United States, are admonished to draw in
and give their attention for the Court is now sitting. God save
the United States and this honorable Court."

Still thinking of cherubim, John Quincy whispered greetings to Sedgwick, Baldwin and Staples, and then sat down as the din of the chamber diminished into uneasy, expectant silence.

The tribunal now comprised nine judges instead of the original seven. Andrew Jackson, John Quincy recalled angrily, had added two more the day before he left office, another reason why he was glad he had left the White House by the back door in order to avoid shaking hands with the man who had deprived him of a second term. Only the two oldest members, Smith Thompson and Joseph Story, had sat on the court before Jackson. John Quincy studied the round-faced, bespectacled Justice Story of Massachusetts. He was a Harvard professor and the most erudite member of the Court. He sat next to Smith Thompson of New York, who had handed down the decision in the circuit court in favor of Cinque and his men. They had both served in Monroe's cabinet, thought John Quincy, and Thompson would have been Chief Justice if it had not been for Jackson's fear of him as "the most dangerous man in the Union." The present Chief Justice, Roger B. Taney, a Jackson man, opened the trial, his long black hair falling over his ears and collar, his melancholy face furrowed and compassionate. He owned slaves, and had emancipated them, but he remained convinced that slavery was a necessary evil so long as Negroes remained in the United States. The rest—John Catron, Philip Barbour, Henry Baldwin, John McKinley, John McLean and James M. Wayne—mused John Quincy, were all Jacksonians not only in mind and politics, but in commonness and mediocrity. He respected none of them and none would give him any quarter—not even, he thought bitterly, the time of day.

The Attorney General, Henry D. Gilpin, a Philadelphia lawyer and successor to Felix Grundy, who had died in the year between the trials, opened the argument for the government. "The United States cannot go behind the regularly documented papers of the *Amistad*," said Gilpin. "The United States must pursue the course required by the laws of nations; and if the Court is satisfied, on the first point, that there is due proof concerning this property, then this property ought to be delivered, so that it may be restored to the Spanish owners. If this be so, the Court below has erred, because it has not decreed any part of the property to be delivered entire, except the boy Antonio. From the vessel and cargo, it has deducted the salvage, diminishing them by that amount; and the Negroes it has entirely refused to direct to be delivered."

John Quincy listened stoically to the familiar arguments while he pondered a hierarchy of angels.

The men of the *Amistad* knew this was the day of their trial vaguely, as one recognizes certain forces over which one has no control, like the cycle of seasons. What they felt most was the unrelenting cold which made them morose and angry, while fear of another defeat made them belligerent. One by one they came to Covey with their complaints and anguish.

Covey's explanations that the *verdict* of the trial was to be judged and not the *men* of the trial, made no impression on them.

"How could a verdict be on trial without the flesh-and-blood men?" Crocodile wanted to know. "This is indeed the spirit world if an idea is more important than a man's life! Is the *verdict* to be tried by real men or by other *verdicts*?" Then Crocodile fashioned nine black-clad dolls to represent the nine judges, one to represent Quincy Adams and one, the biggest of all, to represent the Verdict. Then he found a long twig to represent the bridge that separated the two positions. He placed the nine judges at one end and the President and his verdict at the other.

"I would go to Washington in chains," said Big Sun, "but

even this honor is denied me. Perhaps they will let me attend my own hanging." He laughed.

"Hang the verdict, not us!" added Cricket, cheerfully.

But Bone was busy writing still another letter to "Dear Friend Mr. Adams," his small face under its red bonnet screwed up in effort.

The lawyers had considered moving Cinque from Farmington to the Washington jail, where he would attract both attention and compassion, but Joseph Cinque had insisted on remaining with his men. It was Antonio who was the most desperate of all.

"They will send me back to my owners no matter what they decide about you! It was in the first verdict! I am the Ladino bastard. They have to return me!"

Python tried to comfort Antonio, but his own depression made it hard for him to disbelieve Antonio's conviction. After saying good-bye to the men, finally Vivian, Covey and Braithwaite took the steamboat to Baltimore, crossed the Delaware by canal boat and rode the new horse-drawn railway cars overland to Washington. They were safer in steamboats and trains, where they could keep to their cabins and avoid as much contact as possible with the white population. Staring out at the cold, desolate landscape, with its black supplicating trees which seemed to be yearning for another country, it seemed to Joseph Cinque that only the children were oblivious to the gloom, the despair, the sense of betrayal he had felt ever since seeing the *Amistad* towed out of New Haven harbor. He unfolded his newspaper engraving of the *Amistad*. The talisman calmed him. Soon he would pass his name day here. He would be twenty-seven years old.

The Attorney General spoke for two hours. Then Roger Baldwin stood for the defendants.

"This case not only affects the destiny of these unfortunate Africans, but involves considerations affecting our national character in the eyes of the civilized world, as well as questions of power on the part of the government of the United States. It presents, for the very first time, the question whether the government, which was established for the promotion of JUSTICE, founded on the great principles of the Revolution, as proclaimed in the Declarations of Independence, can, consistently, become a party to proceedings of the enslavement of human beings cast upon our shores and found in the condition of freemen within the territorial limits of a FREE AND SOVEREIGN STATE.

"I shall appeal to no sectional prejudices, and assume no positions in which I shall not hope to be sustained by intelligent minds from the South as well as from the North.

"It is a remarkable circumstance," concluded Baldwin, "that though more than a year has elapsed since the decree of the district court denying the title of Ruiz and Montez, and pronouncing the Africans free, not a particle of evidence has since been produced in support of their claims. And yet, strange as it may seem, during all this time, not only the sympathies of the Spanish minister, but the powerful aid of our own government, have been enlisted in their behalf!"

There it was, thought John Quincy, the accusation of the Executive, of the President, the nail he would drive home into the very heart of this lame duck administration. He had caught the smell of controversy as an old war horse scents blood. He was suddenly a bright young colt frisking in a meadow of clover instead of a man who believed the world, the flesh and all the devils in hell were arrayed against him. The Court, he noted, had listened attentively to Baldwin's reasoned and constructed argument of the facts as they stood. Now he, Adams, who had been so deeply distressed, was ready. His spirit would not sink. "May it please Your Honors," John Quincy Adams began, "I derive consolation from the thought that this court is a Court of JUSTICE. The district court exercised its jurisdiction over the parties and found that the right was with the other party, not in accordance with the impulses of SYMPATHY. And consequently it now appears that everything which has flowed from this mistaken or misapplied SYMPATHY, was wrong from the beginning.

"For I inquire by what right all this SYMPATHY, from Lieutenant Gedney to the Secretary of State, and from the Secretary of State, as it were, to the nation, is to be extended to two Spaniards from Cuba and utterly denied to the fifty-two victims of their lawless violence? By what right is it denied to the men who restored themselves to freedom?

"There is no law, statute or constitution, no code, no treaty, applicable to the proceedings of the Executive or the Judiciary, except *that* law." John Quincy Adams pointed in the direction of a copy of the Declaration of Independence, hanging against one of the pillars of the chamber. "I know of no other law that reaches the case of my clients, but the law of Nature and of Nature's God on which our fathers placed our own national existence."

Adams paused here, not only for the shortness of his own breath, but for effect. The courtroom stirred and then settled back. They knew they were in good hands.

"The Africans were in possession, and had the presumptive right of ownership, of the *Amistad*. They were at peace with the United States, and truly, they were not pirates; they were on a voyage to their native home—their *dulces Argos*; they had acquired the right, and so far as their knowledge extended, they had the power, of prosecuting the voyage; the ship was in the territory of the state of New York and entitled to all the provisions of the law of nations, and the protection and comfort which the laws of that state secure to every human being within its limits. The whole of my argument will show that the proceedings on the part of the United States are all wrongful from the beginning.

"What combination of ideas led to the conclusion that the President of the United States had the power to decide such cases and to dispose of persons and of property, *mero motu*, at his own discretion? . . . That the President can issue a proclamation, declaring that no court in this country could hold cognizance of the case . . . ?

"May it please Your Honors—if the President of the United States has arbitrary power to do it in the case of Africans, and send them beyond seas for trial, he could do it by the same authority in the case of American citizens! Would this not disable forever the power of the Habeas Corpus? I say the Africans were here with their ship. The Africans, who had the prima facie title to the *Amistad,* did not bring the vessel into our waters themselves, but were brought here against their will, by deception. The original voyage from Lomboko, in Africa, was continued by the Spaniards in the *Amistad.* Pursuing that voyage was a violation of the laws of the United States, and the Spaniards are responsible for that offense; the deed begun in Africa was not consummated until the Negroes were landed at their port of final destination in Puerto Principe. The clandestine landing in Havana, the unlawful sale in the barracoons, the shipment on board the *Amistad,* were all parts of the original transaction. . . . If the good offices of the President are to be rendered to any proprietors of shipping in distress, they are *due to the Africans.* They were brought into our waters by their enemies, *who are still seeking to reduce them from freedom to slavery as a reward for having spared their lives!*

"The treaty under consideration cannot apply to slaves. It says ships and merchandise. Is that language applicable to human beings? Will this Court so affirm? It says they shall be restored entire. Is it a treaty between cannibal nations, that a stipulation is needed for the restoration of merchandise entire, to prevent parties from cutting off the legs and arms of human beings before they are delivered up?

"The sympathy of the Executive government, and as it were, of the nation, in favor of the slave traders, and against these unfortunate, helpless, tongueless, defenseless Africans, is the cause and foundation and motive of all these proceedings."

By this time Gilpin understood that John Quincy Adams was putting President Van Buren on trial. Furious, he leaped from his seat, interrupting Adams' speech.

"May it please the Court," Gilpin shouted. "Mr. Adams has pushed the argument a step beyond! The appearance of the Africans in the court below is now to be regarded as *destitute of right,* as well as their appearance here. They are not even mere *interlopers.* They are *dictators,* in the form of suppliants, and their suggestions to the Court, and their application for its judgment, upon solemn and important questions of fact, are distorted by an ingenious logic which it is difficult to follow. Applications, made without the slightest expression of a wish, except to obtain that judgment, and in a form which, it might be supposed, would secure admission into any court, are repudiated, under the harsh name of 'executive interference.' How can it be justly said that there has been any 'executive interference!' "

"*Gubernativamente,*" Adams continued imperturbably, "here is a word, used several times in correspondence, that no American translator has been able to translate into our language. It means, 'by the simple will of the Executive!' That is what the

Spaniard means by *gubernativamente*, when he asks the President of the United States, by his own feat, to seize these MEN, wrest them from the power and protection of the courts, and send them beyond seas! Is there any such law at Constantinople? Does the Celestial Empire allow a proceeding like this? Is the Khan of Tartary possessed of a power competent to meet demands like these? I know not where on the globe we should look for any such authority, unless it be with the Governor-General of Cuba with respect to Negroes.

"I put it to Your Honors to say what sort of regard is here exhibited for human life and for the liberties of these people. Did not the President *know*, when he signed that order for the delivery of MEN to the United States Navy to be carried beyond the seas, he was assuming a power that no President had ever assumed before?

"Here is no longer a demand for the delivery of slaves to their owners, nor for the surrender of the Africans as assassins, but an application to the PRESIDENT OF THE UNITED STATES, on his own authority, without evidence, without warrant of law, to transport forty INDIVIDUALS beyond the seas to be tried for their lives. Is there in the whole history of Europe an instance of such a demand made upon an independent government? I have never in the whole course of my life, in modern or ancient history, met with such a demand by one government on another. Or, if such a demand was ever made, it was when the nation on which it was made was not an independent power. . . .

"I ask the learned Attorney General what is the bearing of this on the liberties of the people? I ask him what authority there is for such an exercise of power by the Executive? I ask him if there is any authority for such a proceeding in the case of these unfortunate Africans, would it not be equally available, if any President thought proper to exercise it, to seize and send off forty citizens of the United States? THE PRESIDENT OF THE UNITED STATES was informed of the deep principles, involving the very foundation of the liberties of this country, that were concerned in the disposal of these men.

"All the proceedings of the government, Executive and Judicial, in this case has been founded on the assumption that the two Spanish slave dealers were the only parties aggrieved—that all the right was on their side, and all the wrong on the side of their surviving, self-emancipated victims. Is this JUSTICE?"

Hour after hour the Justices' eyes remained fixed on the old man. Justice Barbour marveled at the power and sarcasm and lucidity of Adams' arguments. Philip Barbour felt sorry for Adams. It was tragic that this great lawyer's last appearance before the Court was for a lost cause.

John Quincy had been speaking for almost five hours. His voice was almost gone. Behind him he could hear the discreet, excited buzz of the audience. They had been promised, and they were going to get a trial, of one President by another. Martin Van Buren was guilty as hell, and he intended to prove it beyond any reasonable doubt. Van Buren had wanted to separate the trial from the moral and political aspects of slavery, had wanted this forbidden subject out of sight. But as far as Adams was concerned, he had Martin Van Buren and his presidency by the throat.

Adams heard Roger Taney gavel the Court to adjournment for the day. He looked around in a daze. It was almost dark; he had been so lost in his argument he had lost track of time— any time. Now he would have to conclude tomorrow, if God give him the strength.

Baldwin suddenly appeared at his side, but all Adams could feel was the pain and itch of his inflamed eye, which was almost closed.

"Well done," said Baldwin, but John Quincy felt so tired he could have lain down on the bare defense table and slept forever. There was tomorrow. Somehow he had to find strength for tomorrow.

The judges rose in silence, pulled off their robes and left. There was scattered applause. People began to file out. Vivian, Covey and Braithwaite were staying with a white abolitionist family in Virginia, who accompanied them to and from the trial. As free coloreds they had no right to remain overnight in the District of Columbia, under penalty of jail, whipping or reenslavement. Baldwin had arranged their housing, and although both Braithwaite and Covey objected to Vivian's accompanying them on the dangerous journey below the Mason-Dixon line, they had not been able to persuade her to remain in safety. Braithwaite thought often of Increase's words and her nightmare—reenslavement by Negro kidnappers. The white man to whom they supposedly belonged, and from whom they carried a pass ascertaining this, sat behind them, an ever-watchful, mild-mannered, bespectacled freckled man who looked like Henry Braithwaite could have eaten him for breakfast.

Increase Braithwaite's carriage pulled up to the barn in Farmington. Everything had been arranged for Antonio's escape. Her deep, expressive eyes took in the men's unhappiness and disarray. They'll all die, she thought, if they're not freed. Joseph Cinque had even taken to carrying a Bible around, from which he would read at the slightest excuse. The lessons from the Yale Divinity School students still continued, but the men built their lives around the daily visits of the girls, Black Snake, Frog and Country. Country asked again and again where War Road was and why he had left. In the past year the girls had grown surprisingly, thought Increase, and were closer to being adolescents than children. But as children would, they had adapted more easily both to confinement and to the strangeness of their new world. Their narrow, somber faces shone out from beneath woollen bonnets and shawls, their legs in coarse stockings and heavy shoes made them seem frailer and more pathetic than ever. She had heard that the Pendletons worked them like slaves. But there was no way Increase could verify such a rumor, so she spent many hours worrying over their possible ill treatment. But they seemed to her healthy enough, and here they were the men's only comfort. Antonio was another problem. Whatever happened to the others, Antonio was the uncontested property of Ramon Ferrer and as such would be returned to him as merchandise. Little by little Increase had been gathering clothes, food and medicine to be put into the knapsack Antonio would take with him over the Canadian border. It was Robert Purvis' idea. When the verdict came, there would not be much time.

March first. The galleries were filled. More than once Adams' eyes turned to the young Braithwaite-Covey couple. They had come, as much as Cinque himself—especially in his absence—to symbolize for him the hope, life and liberty John Quincy had been arguing for two days now. His strength was failing, but his will was not. God, he thought, God speed me to the end.

When the ex-President rose this time, in the torpid, smol-
dering chamber, he rose with all the ravishment, vehemence
and passion of youth: that of Cinque, of Covey, of Vivian:

"I read to you the confidential answer of the Secretary of
State of the twelfth of January to the inquiries of the federal
marshal of New Haven, Connecticut. He says, 'I have to state
by direction of the President, that if the decision of the court
is such as is anticipated (that is, that the captives should be
delivered up as slaves), *the order of the President* is to be carried into execution, unless an appeal shall actually have been
interposed. You are not to take it for granted that it will be
interposed. And if on the contrary the decision of the court is
different, you are to take out an appeal, and allow things to
remain as they are until the appeal shall have been decided.'
The very phraseology of this instruction is characteristic of its
origin, and dispenses the Secretary of State from the necessity
of stating that it emanated from the *President* himself. The inquiry of the marshal was barefaced enough; whether, if the
Executive warrant and the judicial degree came into conflict,
he *should obey the President, or the judge*? No! says the Secretary of State. If the decree of the judge should be in our
favor, and you can steal a march upon the Negroes by foreclos-
ing their right of appeal, ship them off without mercy and
without delay: and if the decree should be in their favor, do
not fail to enter an instantaneous appeal to the Supreme Court
where the chances are more hostile to self-emancipated slaves.

"Was ever such a scene of Lilliputian trickery enacted by
the rulers of a great, magnanimous, and Christian nation? Contrast it with that act of self-emancipation by which the savage,
heathen barbarians, Cinque and Grabeau, liberated themselves and their suffering fellow countrymen.

"This review of all the proceedings of the Executive I make
with the utmost pain, because it is necessary to bring it fully
before Your Honors, to show that the course of that department
has been dictated, throughout, not by JUSTICE but by SYM-
PATHY—and a SYMPATHY most partial and unjust. And this
sympathy prevailed to such a degree, among all the persons
concerned in this business, as to have perverted their minds
to all the most sacred principles of law and right, on which the
liberties of the people of the United States are founded. This
Court should decide only on consideration of all the rights,

both natural and social, of EVERY ONE of these individuals. I have endeavored to show that they are entitled to their liberty from this Court. These Negroes had a right to assert their liberty. My argument in behalf of the captives of the *Amistad* is closed."

Adams looked up at the galleries where applause had broken out and found the two dark angels who were Covey and Vivian, smiling down at him. This, then, was the end, the very end of his long, anxious and turbulent service to the United States of America, Adams thought. He hoped for the approving sentence. He hoped for a well done, good and faithful servant: enter then into the joy of the Lord. If only from the men of the *Amistad* who had not been allowed as spectators at their own tumultuous trial. But at least the sitting President had been at his. He, Adams, had seen him lurking behind the pillars as he had finished his summation. John Quincy had now only to wait for the verdict.

Increase Braithwaite watched the Yale Divinity students cross the green, their greatcoats flapping in the wind, their caps pulled down over their ears. So, they were all back from Farmington. Lewis Tappan and Increase Braithwaite had decided that if they waited for the verdict, it might be too late to save Antonio. If he was freed, he could always come back. Increase smiled. Lewis Tappan, old, ugly, mild-mannered, pious—butter wouldn't melt—had the mind and cunning of a criminal. Tappan would spirit Antonio away from Farmington under a bundle of clothes and blankets, Cinque and the men would conceal his disappearance for a day, pleading that he was ill and in a bed that was in reality stuffed with rags. She would hide Antonio in the printing-press barn until the verdict arrived—either Antonio would be free or he would be on a boat to New York City and then Canada if the judges returned him to his master. Antonio was lowered into the small room under the floorboards of the Braithwaite printing depot, in the strong, ample arms of Increase, there to await the verdict.

That night Justice Philip Barbour died in his sleep. The trial was postponed so that the funeral could be held in the same courtroom where he had sat, a living, breathing man only two days before. Even Braithwaite, not a religious man, composed

an imaginary epithet in Baskerville Light: JUSTICE MEETS
DIVINE JUSTICE. When the public looked down from the
visitors' gallery again, it was the ninth day of March.

The Justices entered the courtroom, in procession and seemingly by height, headed by Chief Justice Taney. But it was
Justice Joseph Story who presented the majority opinion: "Before entering upon our verdict, in this interesting and important controversy, I want to say a few words of the case as it
now stands before us. It has been argued on behalf of the United
States that the Court is bound to deliver up the Negro defendants, according to the Treaty of 1819, ratified in 1821. To bring
the case within the article, it is essential to establish, first, that
these Negroes fall within the description of *merchandise* in
the sense of the treaty. Secondly, that there has been a rescue
of them on the high seas, out of the hands of the pirates and
robbers; which, in the present case, can only be, by showing
that they themselves are pirates and robbers; and, thirdly, that
Ruiz and Montez, the asserted proprietors, are the true proprietors, and have established their title by competent proof. Fraud
vitiates any, I repeat, even the most solemn transactions; and
an asserted title to property, founded upon fraud, is utterly void.

"If these Negroes were, at the time, lawfully held as slaves
under the laws of Spain, and recognized by those laws as property capable of being lawfully bought and sold, we see no reason why they may not justly be deemed within the intent. . . .

"As to the claim of Lieutenant Gedney for the salvage service, it is upheld under the very peculiar and embarrassing
circumstance of the case. We may lament the dreadful acts by
which Cinque and his men asserted their liberty and took possession of the *Amistad* and endeavored to regain their native
country; but they cannot be deemed pirates or robbers in the
sense of the law of nations.

"It is also a most important consideration in the present case,
which ought not to be lost sight of, that, supposing these African Negroes not to be slaves, but kidnapped, and free Negroes, the treaty with Spain cannot be obligatory upon them;
and the United States are bound to respect their rights. The
conflict of rights between the parties under such circumstances becomes inevitable, and must be decided upon the
eternal principles of justice and international law. Upon the

merits of the case, then, there does not seem to us to be any ground for doubt, that these Negroes ought to be deemed free."

And they shall not sigh for Africa in vain.

"The decree of the circuit and the district court is upheld, including the restitution of Antonio Ferrer to Cuba and his legal master Ramon Ferrer, and except so far as it directs the Negroes to be delivered to the President, to be transported to Africa. As to this, it is reversed. The said Negroes are declared to be free and go without delay."

Justice Story, speaking deliberately and slowly, had not finished saying the words "without delay" before stomping, hissing and cheers rose from the visitors' gallery. The entire courtroom was on its feet. Reporters ran to file their stories. Southerners screamed. Northerners applauded. James Covey raised a hand in the Poro gesture of victory.

"The captives are free," murmured John Quincy. "The captives are free but not unto us. Not unto us. Thanks to you. In the name of Justice . . ." he said to Joshua Leavitt.

"Then praise be to the God of Justice!" replied Leavitt.

Adams could not resist a passing thought on the vicissitudes of the presidency and of Martin Van Buren. But his contemplation was interrupted by Louisa's voice very near. He had not known that she was in the room.

"It is a great relief, Mr. Adams, that your cause is settled and well settled," she said.

John Quincy turned to his wife. He had agonized from the time he had pledged to defend Joseph Cinque until this very moment, because of Louisa's terror and Charles' opposition to the anticipated calamities he would bring upon all of them. For once John Quincy held his peace.

"I was pleading for more, much more than my own life, Mrs. Adams."

The voices of the Amistad Committee and dozens of abolitionists in the Court floated out into the excited courtroom. People around Adams spoke of deliverance, not of the captives, but of the United States.

"May the blessing of all those ready to perish fall upon you!" intoned Simeon Jocelyn.

"Glorious," cried Roger Baldwin. "Glorious not only as a triumph of humanity, but as a vindication of our national character from reproach and dishonor!"

The Constitution of the United States had been tested and had not been found wanting. Justice had triumped over prejudice and Sympathy, and slavery and the usurpation of the power of the Office of the President. Black men had appealed in the highest court of law in the land and been heard. John Quincy Adams was satisfied.

The former President walked directly from the Supreme Court to the floor of the House to face the sound and fury of praise and censure with a heart as light as an angel's.

Covey rode all day and all night, stopping only to change horses. When he arrived in Philadelphia Robert Purvis was waiting with passage on a steamboat to New Haven. When Covey stood before Joseph Cinque laughing, "The Paramount Chiefs have set you free!" the explosion of joy was thunderous. All the resentment the men had felt at not being allowed at their own trial dissolved in the general happiness. It was as if they had recovered a fortune they had lost through carelessness. They had been given a second chance. They laughed and they wept. They lifted their fists in the Poro gesture of victory. Everyone spoke at once, lapsing into a melee of Mende.

Although the marshal had sent word of the verdict, Cinque had waited for James Covey to arrive to assure his men. When he looked into the eyes of his interpreter, he knew it was true. Their two heads bent towards each other in a kiss on the lips— the Poro signal that war is ended.

"President Adams won a great victory in the Court—and then left without saying good-be," Covey told Cinque.

"We can say good-bye to him before we sail. And we can sail tomorrow." Cinque threw back his head and laughed. But Covey did not laugh.

"You don't have the *Amistad*, Sengbe Pieh. The award of the *Amistad* as salvage to Lieutenant Gedney, is upheld. We don't know how to get you and your men home."

"And the President? It was promised that we would be delivered to him to be transported across the waters."

"This, too, has been reversed. You are no longer in the cus-

tody of the President. You are immediately and forthwith a free
man. . . ."

Joseph Cinque fell silent for a moment. Then, despite his
disillusion, he said:

"I thank American men. I thank American men."

By the time Braithwaite and Vivian returned, the news had
spread throughout New Haven. Henry Braithwaite fired the
gleaming bronze cannon on his lawn in celebration of Cinque's
victory. It boomed out at twelve noon, scattering the black crows
in the leafless black trees, while Braithwaite's father-in-law rang
his church bell in response, and as church bell after church
bell echoed, all of New Haven's black citizens marched to Farmington bringing gifts for the men, and invitations to house
them away from their barn. On the way they sang, their voices
spiralling on the blue, cold air.

Snow lingered in patches on the brown grass, but the essence of a new spring was in the air. It hovered over the
marchers like an unrealized promise. It was the first time any
of them, on their way to Farmington, had ever heard of a story
of slavery with a happy ending. It was this more than anything
that drew them like a magnet to Farmington. The Return, as
they began to call it, began to converge in conversation after
conversation. Cries of deliverance and captivity took on a new
meaning. Black men had received justice in a white court. Joseph Cinque had been delivered. Joseph Cinque was going
back to Africa. His liberty was neither a gift nor a theft, but a
right recognized by the highest court in the land. And when
Joseph Cinque emerged from the darkness to greet them with
the words "Thank you, American men," they cried and cheered,
sang and shone.

Henry Braithwaite decided to spread the news the only way
he could really believe it: in black and white—the printed word.
He would print and distribute three thousand pamphlets an-
nouncing the triumph of Joseph Cinque. From the bottom of
his font drawer he took out his secret pride, a typeface he had
designed himself and had had cast in Boston more than fifteen
years ago. He had never utilized it and he had never named
it, certainly not after himself. It had seemed to him that no

occasion momentous enough had ever occurred in New Haven until now.

He gazed down at the black letters on the white proof page. He wondered if he should add an exclamation mark. The whole range of the ugly and the beautiful in both art and nature could be translated into mathematics. Not all things that had lines and curves could be reduced to geometry just as ideas like Justice and Independence could not be reduced to a single emotion, but still, Henry Braithwaite mused, everything in this world depended on proportion, the perfection of all the parts to the whole. This was true of the soul as well as the eye; for men as well as nations, thought the typographer.

☙ HAPPY ENDING ❧

he composed, letting the lead fall as delicately as precious gems from his fingers. He smiled when he realized he had just given Vivian and Covey, without his realizing it, his permission to marry. His children would also have a Happy Ending.

**THIS TEXT IS COMPOSED IN
CINQUE CONSTITUTION BOLDFACE
DESIGNED BY
HENRY BRAITHWAITE, ESQ.,
ON THE OCCASION OF THE VICTORY
OF
JOSEPH CINQUE
V.
THE UNITED STATES,
THE SUPREME COURT, MARCH NINTH,
THE YEAR OF OUR LORD A.D. 1841,
THE YEAR FIFTY-FOUR OF THE UNION
GOD BLESS AMERICA**

Covey placed the pale blue velvet box embossed with the name Charles Tiffany on Vivian's lap. When she opened it, she found a ring of gold chain set with a single ruby. Covey took her hands in his and slowly brought them to his lips. Then he took the ring from its throne and placed it on the fourth finger of Vivian's left hand. It was a perfect fit. He laughed.

"My eyesight is very good for measuring many kinds of distances," he said. He held her hand up against the winter sun's crimson brilliance. The gem caught the light and burned.

Vivian's hair was glossy against the veil of curtains in the Braithwaite's parlor. She was dressed in hunter-green serge, which had a wide ivory sash and a full walking-length skirt that showed her new boots and foamed in ruffles around her ankles. A cashmere shawl trimmed in Spanish fringe lay on her shoulders. "This victory is part of Cinque's victory," said Covey.

Vivian, loving Covey with a discerning anxiety, and not to break his heart by some misspoken word, said nothing. She watched him silently as he passed to and fro, as if he were pacing the deck of the *Buzzard*. Finally Covey turned, his tension and nervousness dissolving in a magnificent smile. "I could carry you off now. I could run with you in my arms and never stumble."

The low passionate voice had barely broken the silence when his hands were on her shoulders, pulling her to her feet. "Come with me," he said. "I need to breathe salt air, I need to move, I need to see the stars."

Covey wrapped Vivian possessively in her cloak and led her from the shelter of her father's house. Outside, the March thaw had bared the footpath leading to the cove.

"I have sailed six thousand miles four times over and never thought to find you," said Covey. "I am nothing you do not make me, and I live only for that making. A more loving, faithful and worshiping husband you will never find. You are my home. You are my one safe harbor."

He reached out and took Vivian's face in his, stroking its luminous curves with his long, strong hands as if they ignited the burning kisses he showered upon it.

Vivian neither swooned nor broke away frightened from Covey's passion, but endured its violence much like a young willow arches in upon itself to withstand a summer squall, supple, returning his now-lingering, insistent kisses with quiet power.

She was already his wife. He had a right to open and touch all the wellsprings of emotion deep inside her.

"War Road," she whispered, *"the road dangerous to travel for fear of being taken captive."*

For the first time Covey allowed his hands to roam blindly.

Vivian flashed and shimmered against him, pressing against that state she had so often brought him to while he lay helpless and ill, though it was now she who moaned with this new sickness, as they sank onto the hard rock and Covey pulled her hips closer. Then suddenly, as if awakening from a dream, he stopped.

"Are you afraid?"

"No."

"Nothing will happen, I swear, until we are man and wife."

"I know."

"It is so difficult," said Covey, "to remember suffering, miseries, crimes, when one holds one's heart's desire."

"Is it a crime to forget?" Vivian asked. "Are we not to be allowed happiness?"

If a marsh hawk, or a peregrine, or a mourning dove had flown over them, his eye would have seen them enlaced like seaweed, the long black figure of Covey like a dark rocky coast onto which Vivian flowed, her undone hair tributary rivers under his hands, her white petticoats the foam of ocean waves that rose and ebbed about them.

❧ Joseph Cinque ❧
April 1841

The vessel was engaged in the slave trade. The voyage in the
Amistad was a mere continuation of the original voyage in the
Tecora. The object of the Africans was to get to a port in Africa,
and their voyage was lawful.

—*John Quincy Adams*

The war is over, America.

We are free. Free to leave. Free to starve. Free to rot.

I don't remember when, or whose idea it was, to exhibit us.
But we learn from the Bible and read in public meetings. The
children spell and count. Remember, Waterfall, Twin, Big Sun
and Little Sun sing spirituals. People return to see us. Pendleton begins to charge admission again. Dressed in the costume
of a deacon, Bible under my arm, I am the famous Joseph
Cinque, self-liberator and murderer. Pass the beggar's bowl,
for how much was the *Amistad* worth and how much more to
buy a new ship? Ten thousand dollars? Twenty? How much
are we worth? According to Covey we were insured for twenty-
four thousand gold dollars.

I hear them arguing.

"Van Buren's order to return Cinque to the Spanish government should be engraved on his tombstone to rot with his
memory," one of them said to Arthur Tappan.

"We can always sue the government for unlawful, unreasonable and oppressive imprisonment, but I doubt if we can prove
it in a court of law."

"It is just as futile to prosecute Ruiz and Montez, who are
both back in Cuba!"

"What should be done with them now that they are free?"
they argued.

"They must return to Africa before they become a burden

345

on society," the lawyer Baldwin said to Joshua Leavitt.

"But should the costs be borne by them?"

"Certainly not. The Government of the United States is bound in honor and in justice to perform it!"

"In Mende," I say timidly, "damages are always awarded." They look at me as if I had declared that God was black.

"The Supreme Court of the United States," added Covey, "has pronounced them *free*, but the authorities of this country have seized their persons and their property, kept them in prison for eighteen months, taken their ship—without which they cannot accomplish their voyage home—and now turns them adrift in a strange land where they cannot subsist without help and where they cannot depart for their own country except with the aid of those same charitable hands!"

Charity, I think. We are reduced from slavery to beggary. We are a company of scavengers, a colony of bowls in hand. The white men continue to argue.

"I suppose with their freedom they may in this country earn their subsistence by their labor, but their desire to return to their own homes is reasonable and just."

"I think an address to the new President representing the facts and requesting that a vessel of the United States Navy be authorized to convey them to Sierra Leone, or somewhere on the coast of Africa where they may safely attain their native soil, is in order."

"It would be a suitable and proper atonement for the desecration of our navy, in the matter of the *Grumpus*."

The marshal comes for Antonio, but he is gone. He stayed in the Braithwaite cellar until Covey returned with the unhappy verdict for him. The bitterness we felt for Antonio is overshadowed by that sentence. The marshal threatens to arrest us all again, including the Tappans, Baldwin and Dr. Gibbs for obstruction of justice. His impotence makes us all laugh. For Antonio will soon be in New York City, his passage to Canada paid for by Robert Purvis.

We are all present: Vivian, Covey, all the Braithwaite boys and their parents, as the sun descends on Antonio Ferrer's new life as a fugitive slave.

"Forget you were ever a slave and you will never be one again," I say. "Look at any man in the eye and dare him to protest. If you are to impersonate a freedman, you must act and think like one. No white man has any claim either to your person, your labor, or your affections if he has not merited it by employing you, defending you, or loving you. I do not say this is impossible. For where would you be without the men who have saved you? But do not think this debt is eternal. It is only a part payment owed you by the generations before and the generations to come. Assume only the right to the respect you will have to earn from any man, black or white. Remember slavishness is finished. It never earned you anything but contempt."

There is fear, exhaustion and bitterness in Antonio's face as we put him on the boat. Soon there will be solitude.

"You will not be alone," I call out, hoping to comfort him.

"You cannot know the thousands who have passed this station to safety and freedom," says Henry Braithwaite. "Goodbye, Antonio."

"*Anuli-Sinamato*," I say, taking leave of Antonio Mende-style, my voice echoing. We stand there under a wide-branched oak tree whose roots drink from the canal, in a pall of color as dark as blood, our forms etched against the open fields, and watch the flatboat slowly glide away, soundlessly, broken only by the faint sobs of the fugitive. He grows smaller along with the silent pole man, a black man who will transport him to the next station. A rider passes, but he neither stops nor acknowledges our little group. I have the sense that it is someone I know, but I do not dare turn to look after him. We are all prepared for the unforeseen and accustomed to the unexpected. Antonio looks so young and pitiful standing on his raft that I have the impulse to dive into the canal and bring him back. The silence is potent with happiness and possibilities, yet I am utterly isolated from the world by unforgiving rage. Nothing can ever again be so bad as to surprise me. I am, by what life has already done to me, prepared for the worst. We had to return to our former lives, but Antonio was being born again. "*Anuli-Sinamato*," I call out for the last time.

Only Vivian senses the frustration of our having been set free only to live as specimens, or half humans, on the charity of our captors and missionary bodyguards.

Although there are many rich men surrounding us, none offers the simplest solution to our predicament: cash to pay our passage home. Each man has a reason: For Theodore Sedgwick it is the obligation of the President and the United States to pay our way home, and he will not do it for them; for Robert Purvis our being sent home is an illegality, involuntary deportation, and a way to rid the country of an embarrassment. One Tappan is insulted we do not wish to remain in this country blessed by Providence to savor the joys of salvation and civilization. The other Tappan feels we have not reached that pinnacle of Christian education that will prevent our ultimate backsliding, and that we should stay longer. Dr. Gibbs will pay only for teachers to accompany us, and nothing else. Amos Townsand thinks us stupid, ungrateful and lazy not to want, as a matter of principle, to stay long enough to earn our own passage home. He is, it seems, a self-made man whose bootstraps have lifted him to his present heights and wealth. This is the same man who had been willing to break the laws of his own nation to sail us to the Bahamas. Dr. Madden feels the British should sail us home, and has begged his Queen for a ship. She has promised one, but it is slow in coming and Captain Fitzgerald has orders not to interfere further with the internal affairs of the United States. The new President, Paramount Chief Tyler, has taken the place of Paramount Chief Harrison, dead after a reign of thirty days, and claims no responsibility for us and refuses to consider providing a ship. His Secretary of State, Daniel Webster, delights in irking the Spanish, but not enough to return the *Amistad* to us. Only Marda Adams is really so poor, according to Covey, that he can not even afford to pay for his seat in church. Besides, neither he nor the lawyer Baldwin have asked for payment for our defense as our Speakers. Moreover, it is impossible for black and white Christians, and black and white rich men, to work together. They remain distant and separate.

There are long and angry arguments over the coming tour. Vivian calls it a performing circus, a zoo, a disgrace to the United States government, but we have no choice. Charity. Robert Purvis donates Nathaniel Jocelyn's portrait of me to be exhibited in Philadelphia for money but it is refused as incitement to revolt for black people. The world has changed. From heroes we have become wards, from victims we have become dangerous aliens and mendicants. There is no choice now, but to resume the war. One day Vivian surprises the men singing.

"Cinque," she says, "what are they singing? I've never heard anything like it."

"It is a Poro warrior song," I say, "but it is almost . . . almost a love song. A lamentation. It is the story of a warrior who is far from home and who is yearning for his sweetheart. By magic she comes to him in the form of her name, which is Cheetah, in order to escape detection by the enemy camp. But the warrior, obsessed by the battle the next day, does not recognize her and kills her by mistake, thinking her to be what she appears to be. Too late, he realizes what he has done. The moral of the song is never mistake love for hate, a friend for an enemy, a stranger for a foe, a human soul in a different guise for a beast. . . ."

"Why does such a sad song sound so happy?" Vivian asks.

"Mende have a way of making sad songs sound happy," I reply.

Python carries his loneliness in him as if he had eaten clay. And Python believes that there exists white magic that will keep us here forever. Our bodies, not our spirits, have been rescued. And it is our spirit, our soul's memory, all the oracles that he guards, which torments him into the belief that we are doomed.

Python wonders in his heart of hearts if he does not half envy the white man's ignorance. He knows there is a fixed time between the moment a man bursts from his mother's womb and the moment he leaves the world to join his ancestors: that life is predestined by death. But the whites do not believe this. They divide time on earth, not into moons, or rains, or seasons, but minutes, seconds, hours, which they record with their beautiful instruments as truth and reality. But they do not even believe this. They fear death as Python has seen no men fear death. They run from it, they fight it, but most of all they disbelieve it.

The day Python takes off the white man's pantaloons and the white man's shirt and stands naked, poised on the edge of the pond at Farmington, my voice comes back to him as it did so often when we played and swum in this same place, and it says: "See who can dive under and stay the longest!" But Python already knows the willful pull of those depths. He dives into the water and comes up gasping, his limbs automatically thrashing. He strikes out slowly along the surface, west towards the sun, towards Mendeland, with lengthening, plodding strokes. From time to time he dives into the water's marrow until he no longer feels the need to resurface in fright, sucking in air. Has he not survived for fifty-nine suns without air? Has he not seen scores of chained men of the *Tecora* fling themselves by twos over the side of that house that swims?

Python had come to me not long ago, his cap in his hand, and had said, "If American men offer me enough gold to fill this cap, give me houses, land and wives so that I stay in this country, I say no! Is this the way of my father? Is this the way of my sister? Is this the way of my mother? Is this the way of my brother? No! I want to see my father, my mother, my brother, my sister."

Python and his wife had been captured at the same time. They had been marched in different coffles, side by side. A guard called out in Mende if any of the men recognized any of the women. And Python cried out, "I do, for this one is my wife!" Python thought since they had him, they would let her go. The Spaniards unshackled his wife and she ran to his side and knelt to acknowledge him. As Python bent down to kiss her, the butt of the Spanish man's rifle came down on the side of her head, smashing her skull open. She was dead even as she fell forwards, her eyes widened in surprise, her mouth open as she tried to speak while Python stood over her, still smiling.

Sumptuous liquid darkness closes over Python. His limbs spasm and his heart abdicates to the pain, yet he continues obstinately to flail. Sleep comes and goes more often, while the water pulls at his chest and arms. His heart beats in alarm but he does not listen to his heart, he listens to the voice of Mende. Come home. Come home, Python. Why wait to be carried home when it is so simple to return? Since Python can expect nothing from the mercy of God or from the mercy of white lords, he has left only the power to escape his amalgamation.

Python floats on his back and stares into the red sky, then

slowly, majestically, with great happiness and contentment, he sinks to the applause of the morning insects. All the blackness of which he is the inheritor and to which he has arrived embrace him. The sky disappears. He is blind. He has become one with his color. Python has at last fed at the Feast of the Return.

We lay Python in his grave with his feet facing westwards so that the thunderstorms that blow from the east may blow his spirit back home. I stand at the foot of the grave in the burying ground in Farmington and pray to Python's ghost, begging it to help him leave. The grave is a hole in the ground marked with a white marble stone. He would have preferred to have been buried in a running stream.

Python's real passage across the Waters occurs four days later, when we return to his grave to escort him to Deadland. We bring him food for his journey. We prepare rice and chicken and this is placed on the grave. We sit circling the stone marker and the newly turned earth, eating. The food will last Python's journey to join his ancestors. It is Waterfall, with his passion for orderliness, who reminds us that Python can not complete the Teindianali, the entering into the land of the dead, without his food and will return to haunt us. And so we all sit, willing Python home, amid the gravestones of the Farmington villagers, while I think of the *Amistad*.

Once Covey told me a true story of a whole ship of one hundred and sixty-two slaves who had all gone blind on the voyage across the waters. Then the thirty white men of the crew had all gone blind, until there was no one on the entire sailing vessel who could see except one white sailor who steered the ship as best he could alone for seventy-nine suns. And when he reached land with his blind slaves and his blind sailors, he, too, was struck blind. The ship was called the *Rodeur*. But for me her name would always be the *Amistad*.

The gentlest and wisest of all the captives has left a message we all understand: Do not spend another winter in this place.

It is Vivian, strangely enough, who, weeping bitterly, insists upon this. She takes the death of Python hardest. He had been one of her favorites, but it seems to me there is something too wild and inconsolable in her grief, as if she and Python have a vision of our destiny that we cannot see. Perhaps it is only fear for Covey, or doubts about his future in the New World, but she advances the date of her marriage from Christmas to Emancipation Day so that we can all attend the celebration and still be back in Mendeland before the first snowfall.

Lewis Tappan finds a ship to swim us home. It is called the *Gentleman*.

We recite by turns for a ladies' group that provides us with sixty-six shirts, thirty-three plastrons and sixty-six collars. A tailor makes us thirty-three coats and pantaloons costing fifty-eight dollars. Thus clothed, we send ten of the cleverest, our best Christians, on a new speaking tour. Now we need money not only for our passage home, but for a Christian mission in Mendeland.

In each hamlet and village we give the same program. We do not call them performances, for Dr. Gibbs finds some offense in this word, it being too close to circus and too far from prayer. So we call them "meetings," and three of the best readers take for a text a passage in the New Testament. Then Bone or Big Man recites the voyage of the *Amistad* in English. Then two or three Mende songs are sung, followed by hymns in which the audience joins in. When I am introduced, I speak in Mende. Ever since the trial in Hartford, the committee perceives the magic in my recitation. I hold audience after audience in thrall with my mysterious epic of the voyage of the *Amistad,* in a language which they cannot understand.

I persist as if I can by force of repetition teach those who listen another language. I use every trick I have ever heard from the Speakers in Mendeland, from the long, elaborate, never-ending trials and litigations before the Paramount Chiefs, to the interminable recitations of the epics that are the history of the Mende handed down from historian to historian in each village. I sweep my listeners away into the *Tecora,* the *Amistad,* the *Washington,* and now the new ship, *The Gentleman,* which will return us home. Large numbers of the audience rise and clasp my hand. Women weep. I marvel at the duplicity of the human heart. The same person who shakes my hand and weeps will refuse me a glass of water or a seat next to him in his own church. I learn the limits of charity and the good conscience of New Englanders. Big Man has become Lewis,

Bone has become George, Waterfall has become Henry. I have become Joseph. How long will I remember my own name?

Three moons pass. An appeal is printed in Tappan's newspaper and again we take to the road. This time I choose the men for their voices. These, I decide, are to be not meetings with songs, but songs with meetings. We are sixteen in all, and the first meeting is held in the colored church of Reverend Beman. When it is over, a black mechanic and his wife and child offer to return with us to Mendeland. A white man, Charles Finch Lowell, and a colored man, John Levi, offered to sail with us. We began to collect people as well as money. We became true evangelists. We had collected 1600 dollars before Python's death, and now the dollars multiply.

Day after day we continue to travel from town to town, from speech to speech, from revival to revival. Black Snake and Bone read and spell. The others sing and I speak. My voice has taken on a new sadness and a new urgency, even frenzy. We have to go home. Python commands it. At times I stretch my arms outwards in the sign of the cross and the sign of the masts of our ships: the *Tecora,* the *Buzzard,* the *Amistad.* The crowd goes wild with some particular ecstasy, stomping and singing and shouting amen. The women especially. If I feel I am losing my audience, I have only to make that one gesture to bring them all back to me. When I speak, I imagine every uplifted face that of my uncle, furious at my neglect and stupidity, judging my performance. And so I speak to my Mende clan. And every time, disguised in Mende, the Americans understand.

We travel by night to avoid dangerous confrontations with whites. And we sleep mostly in barns in the early morning before the meetings, for sometimes no inn nor boarding house will admit us and there are sometimes no black families' houses or stables to take their place. Sometimes we cannot be admitted as blacks and whites together. Then the blacks eat in the stables if there is no colored family, while the professors eat in abolitionist homes. At times, through force of circumstances (Tappan would always say God), we eat together.

Finally, in Lowell, Massachusetts, we expect to exceed the two thousand dollars we need. The church, St. Paul's, is crowded to overflowing with one hundred and fifty score people within and as many outside the church. A veritable army. This time we have our ship. We are taken through the streets of Lowell to the cotton mills. And if the workers stare at us, we stare at the lengths and lengths of multicolored cotton that seem to stretch forever, as if they could span the very ocean we have traversed. Yet there is only one man behind each machine. I ask if he is a hundred years old, for to have woven such a cloth he would have had to have been alive forever.

I am beginning to lose the need for Covey as an interpreter of words, but never of ideas. Still playing the part of our eyes, voice, ears, spirit, he stays with us, though I knew he longs to be back in New Haven with Vivian. "Not," he repeats, "until you are aboard the *Gentleman*! You are almost home. You are almost safe. This is the only thing that matters to Vivian and me. It is our farewell gift."

Covey has decided to remain in America with his new family. It is a wise thing to do, for it is too dangerous to risk the life of Vivian in our wild, war-torn country. So, after having had no *ndehun-bla* except the *Buzzard* and slavery, Covey now has his future wife's *ndehun-bla*. He has met them all, uncles and cousins, his future brothers-in-law, his grandfathers and aunts, a generous, numerous, loving family.

Vivian's people become the most important thing in life for him. He makes plans for his children. At night we speak of our future. For the first time he asks endless questions about my son Gewo, about Bayeh Bia, about Kabba Sei and my uncle, the Speaker, Kosokilisia.

The last meeting is held in the largest church in Boston, Marlboro Chapel, the last Saturday in July, a week before Emancipation Day and Covey's marriage. I make the best proclamation of my life. We collect the fattest purse. That night we travel northwards.

Our goal is reached.

❧ James Covey ❧
August 1841

In the Declaration of Independence the Laws of Nature are announced and appealed to as identical with the laws of nature's God, and as the foundation of all obligatory human laws.

—*John Quincy Adams*

Vivian followed Python to her grave so suddenly and so quickly that perhaps the cruelest of all was that Covey, who had lived only cruelty, known only cruelty, remembered only cruelty, should have been surprised that Nature's laws were so immutably indifferent to human pain and human destiny, but this was what happened, and the divinity students who had so earnestly and fervently taught that God worked in mysterious ways, now had Vivian's death to prove it.

❧ Joseph Cinque ❧
August 1841

The repetition of that single line, struck me as a moral principle, and made upon my mind an impression which I have carried with me through all the changes of my life, and which I shall carry with me to my grave.

—*John Quincy Adams*

Covey is orphaned and once more orphaned and thrice orphaned. Vivian is already dead of yellow fever, only days after we rush back.

We try to save her from the violent chills, the back pains, the bruises under her skin, the familiar and deadly fever followed by black vomiting and a sudden drop in body heat as vicious as its ascension. Through the open door I can see the bath draped with white sheets where Vivian's mother has submerged her again and again in ice water. The masses of towels, sheets, and coverlets are crumpled in agonized heaps like Mendeland's chain of mountains.

I look down at the haggard, yellowing cadaver that was once Vivian, brilliant and vibrant, her hand clutched in that of a wordless, sightless, suffering Covey.

Mysteriously, the stench of the slave ship rises from her hand as it cools.

Vivian's mother reaches over to disengage Covey's hand from that of Vivian, but he reacts so violently that she draws back into the summons of her own grief, leaving Covey a few more short seconds of belief that the love he has searched for for so long and that he has rushed back to New Haven in the fierce hope of seeing again, is still alive. Mother Increase retreats, taking the pale glow of the whale-oil lamp with her, but it does not matter. Covey sees Vivian clearly in the dark. He draws her into his arms, and they are as one, his left hand remaining in hers, his body flung over her as if to protect her even in Death, his right hand entwined in her hair.

The white lace curtains hang in coils with their delicate tracings of circles and flowers. The furniture draped in white sheeting is like a strange new landscape. The iron pots standing on the floor, the patchwork quilt that has slid onto the glowing pattern of the rugs, the bouquets of white flowers which stand in vases in various states of decay, like sentinels to the progression of Vivian's death, are as translucent as the still body. Every seam of Vivian's nightdress, every strand of her black hair, each feather of eyebrow, curve of eyelash, shadow between the closed eyes and the bridge of her nose, between nostril and hollow cheeks, the gleam of small teeth behind slightly parted lips, the deep blue outline of that precious mouth, become sharper and sharper until they dissolve in crepuscule. Covey bends low to kiss the dimple at the left side of Vivian's mouth and its twin, the soft contour of her chin. He counts the beauty rings of her neck and opens the V of her chemise. He fingers with his thumb the ruby ring on the graying flesh of her hand in his, never untwining his other hand from the tendrils of her hair flung out on the white pillows, like a river traced on a plain. From beyond the door comes a shred of light and audible movements: muffled sounds and sobs, but Covey remains immobile for a day and a night. Finally Increase enters the room and I hear the snip of scissors as she cuts the locks of Vivian's hair out of Covey's clutched fist and leads him away, his hand still trailing her hair.

I believe the death of Vivian is the price God has extracted for the freedom of the men of the *Amistad*. "It is my fault," I say, "Gewo took Vivian as his reward." The idea repulses Covey. "Gewo is a just God," he replies. "He would never do this." I do not argue with him.

Covey and I stand apart from both the Americans and the Mendians, on a small rise behind the white clapboard church, its spire as narrow and as tall as a mast. Only the ugly open grave disturbs the sumptuous green velvet of Vivian's grandfather's churchyard. The hot summer sun beats down and the women shade themselves with white parasols as they do in Africa, while the men wear straw panamas except when they uncover for prayer. The black of the costumes and of the faces floating beneath the canopies of white umbrellas give the congregation the aspect of a flock of crows perched amid the crosses, ready to take flight afterwards, back into the cloudless dome of the sky. I let the sun burn into my scalp, scalding the insoluble pain for brief seconds while my eyesight comes and goes as if I am going blind. The crowd appears, then disappears, wavering in the heat, as do the great oak and birch and chestnut trees, fluted and umbrageous like rigged green sails above me. I draw nearer as songs and chants of great beauty follow one upon the other and the women begin to moan, weeping as they hold each other, clustered around the half-swooning Mother Braithwaite.

I see Increase Braithwaite force herself to look at the inexpressible, almost repulsive grief in Covey's face. She draws away, not as if from the unbearable agony of having lost her eldest daughter, but from Covey's unbreachable rage. Across the open grave, the echo of Vivian's face reverberates in that of her sister Honor. Beside her, holding her hand, Henry Braithwaite seems to have shrunk within himself, his eyes as blank as an unwritten page. Covey stands apart from his other sons, a son-in-law without ever having been, and Increase Braithwaite stands even further away, in her own loneliness, as I watch her scrutinize all her sons' faces as if they, too, were somehow, yet she knew not how, doomed. Jeremiah. Cotton. Joseph. Jefferson. Jacob. Jasper.

At that moment Increase Braithwaite's most beautiful voice—famous, I have learned, for her prayers—begins to speak.

The full rich voice of the grieving mother lifts in cadences which I sense in the depths of my soul, so that I reply in Mende with the incantations for the dead. Like a low running brook, the Mende words mingle with her voice, which has retained remnants of its origin: the Windward Coast.

"There are mines for silver," Increase chants, "and places where men refine gold; where iron is won from the earth and copper smelted from the ore; the end of the seam lies in darkness, and it is followed to its furthest limit. Strangers cut the galleries; they are forgotten as they drive forward far from men. But where can wisdom be found? And where is the source of understanding? No man knows the way to it; it is not found in the land of living men. The depths of the ocean say 'It is not in us.' And the sea says 'It is not with me.' Red gold cannot buy it, nor can its price be weighed out in silver; it cannot be set in the scales against gold of Ophir, no creature on earth can see it, and it is hidden from the birds of the air. Destruction and death say, 'We know it only by report.' But God understands the way to it, he alone knows its source, for he can see to the ends of the earth and he surveys everything under heaven. When he made a counterpoise for the wind and measured out the waters in proportion, when he laid down a limit for the rain and a path for the thunderstorm, even then he saw wisdom and took stock of it, he considered it and fathomed its very depths. And he said to man: 'The fear of the Lord is wisdom, and to turn from evil is understanding.'

"I am a brother to dragons and a companion to owls, my skin is black upon me and my bones are burned with heat. My harp also is turned into mourning and my organ into the voice of them that weep."

"*Oga-wa-wa*, Oh great God

"*bi-a-bi-yan ding-go*. Thou art good

"*bi-a-bi ha-ni gbe le ba-te-ni*:

"Thou hast made all things happen . . . ," I answer.

❦ Joseph Cinque ❧
September 1841

However revolting to humanity may be the reflection, the laws of any country on the subject of the slave trade are nothing more in the eyes of any other nation than a class of the trade laws of the nation that enacts them.

—*John Quincy Adams*

All I now understand of the world is that the angry, grieving, half-crazed Covey will return to the sea. He will return to chasing, capturing and killing slave traders and burning slave ships. Of the rest, I understand nothing.

In New York whites strike according to the Book of Exodus. They spread the news that white families should keep their candles lit and stand before their windows so that they may be passed over; the white mob attacks houses with darkened windows or with dark faces. They sack the Negro district of New York City. They attack abolitionist merchants in Baltimore. They beat nuns in Massachusetts, they hang gamblers in Vicksburg, burn mail in Charleston, dynamite Negro houses in Philadelphia, fire a loaded cannon down the main street of the Negro ghetto in Cincinnati. The specter of what they call amalgamation rises as unknowingly and mysteriously from its grave as Vivian and Python have unknowingly and mysteriously descended into theirs.

Through the end of summer, fantastic rumors spread. One is that abolitionists ask their daughters to marry colored men; another is that a famous abolitionist has adopted black children. Still another is that Arthur Tappan has divorced his wife and married a Negress. That abolitionist ministers are conducting interracial marriages, that abolitionists encourage Negroes to assume "airs" and parade down Broadway on horseback in dandy dress, seeking white wives. From morning till night respectable white people speak earnestly about "sexual passion," even unmarried women. Citizens form vigilance committees to patrol Negro quarters, to question strangers, to search post offices, ships and stages for anti-slavery literature. Southern vigilance committees offer rewards for leading abolitionists. In East Feliciana, Louisiana, citizens post $50,000 for the delivery of Arthur Tappan, dead or alive; in Mount Meigs, Alabama, $50,000 for Arthur Tappan, dead or alive; in New Orleans, $100,000 for Arthur Tappan, dead. The grand jury of Tuscaloosa, Alabama, demands Lewis Tappan be sent South for trial. Hinds County, Mississippi, offers $100,000 for the Tappan brothers. "The American Anti-Slavery Society," says Lewis Tappan, "has thirteen agents and a $25,000 budget. If I could collect all of that money, I would even be willing to go to my Maker. . . ."

From Covey I learn that hatred of the black man prevailed in the North before the *Amistad* or before anyone had ever heard of the newspaper the *Liberator* or "immediate abolition without expatriation." Long before Vivian watched her school burn down, this new word, *amalgamation,* had come to mean miscegenation, the mulattolization of the white man's posterity, its mixture with black blood, the breakdown of distinctions between the races, the defilement by marriage of a nation of white men, the downfall of white America.

There is no longer a question of my men spending another winter in America.

Like possessed men in a magic ritual, we tour town after town, travelling by day, speaking each evening, never sure if we will find a place to sleep or eat in the small villages and towns that follow one upon another in a flow of halls, churches, barns, hotels; Northampton, Hartford, Springfield, Lowell, Philadelphia, until they all blur into one single image of an ocean of white, upturned faces, hostile, friendly, curious, shocked, avid, indifferent, guilty, outraged, fascinated, condescending, enthusiastic, dangerous.

I, too, have become a dangerous man. The war of the *Amistad* has become a rallying point for emancipators and the abolitionists and an example to the colored men of America. I am the symbol of insurrection, the amalgamation and lurking violence the slaveholder will not tolerate: that of self-emancipation. I am some marvelous phenomenon, a black man who has defied the courts of America, who has been recognized as having natural as well as legal rights in the highest court of the land. I am a hero. I am a revolutionary. I am a whole race of deported men, the mirror of a thousand minds. I am everything to anybody, and nothing at all. It is like catching the head of a spear in midair with one's bare hands. I stand in the pulpit or on the stage, feeling as if my body has been flogged by a million blows. As for Covey, the pain of Vivian's death gathers slowly until it breaks all the barriers he has built against unbearable despair. Is he the one who brought blood into the happy, safe, Braithwaite family? Did the suffering and death he has trailed behind him since a slave of nine bring the ghost of all those awful deaths into Vivian's chaste life? Was his dangerous, violent life her doom? No one can reconcile him to it. Not even I. I think of the magnificent grief of the King Kosokilisia for his Queen Miji, who abandoned his kingdom, his other wives, his children, and for seven years roamed the jungle, naked, his only weapon a spear, until the day he encountered his own grief in the form of a leopard and killed it and returned to his kingdom dressed in its skin, which he wore as his only dress until the day he died.

"Sengbe Pieh," Covey cries out one day, "take me home as well!"

It is the fourteenth of November. The Broadway Tabernacle in New York City is the final meeting. The *Gentleman*, rigged and provisioned, waits in the harbor. Another winter has started, but we will not see it. The church is packed. The admission is high, fifty cents. For the occasion we are to use our Christian names as a tribute to the Gospels. I have always been Joseph Cinque, but now Remember becomes Alexander Posey; Big Man, Lewis Johnson; Bone, George Lewis; Second Born, Henry Cowles. And so baptized a third time, in our black breeches and white sailor shirts, we present a Bible inscribed to John Quincy Adams. He has declined to appear on our behalf for, it seems, the sake of his only son's career, but he has sent a message that Covey reads.

"It was from the book you gave that I learned to espouse your cause when you were in trouble and to give thanks to God for your deliverance."

He has added a strange, uneasy message for Covey.

"When I heard of your tragedy, all I could think was,

> *Cold, Cold my girl!*
> *Even like thy chastity.*
> *O Cursed, cursed slave!—whip me devils*
> *From the possession of this heavenly sight!*
> *Blow me in steep—down gulfs of liquid fire!*
> *O Desdemon! Dead, Desdemon! Dead O."*

The lights dim and the gospels begin. The stage is lit by three rows of flickering oil lamps, their little flames pricking the skin and their glow bathing us all in a smokey, gold haze. At the back of the tabernacle, a fantastic instrument of hollow metal tubes and cylinders through which air is pumped by a man sitting at a white ivory and black ebony table, playing moving strips of wood, swells the first hymn. The heat of packed bodies rises to the rafters and hangs there like the notes of music amidst the gold and white ceiling, the palm-leaf decoration and the chandelier. Then it is time to rise and speak not as Joseph Cinque, but as the Speaker before the Paramount Chiefs, in defense of my blood relatives, my blood image, my *Nge gbembi.*

"And, out of Gallinas we come. Out of the womb of the world we come. All pleasure in feast and love forgotten. All rancor in feud and war forgotten. All joy in birth and circumcision forgotten. We come, the only merchandise that carries himself. A column of jet, quickening, gyrating in one celestial tribal dance, rolling and spreading like a giant dust devil, thickening, spinning itself into the white fireball of the New World, rending the cosmos in the season of *Konunqui.* We come out of Gallinas. Groaning across savannas and the pyramids of Vi, the landscape of mountains and sand and lagoons of the Windward Coast: rock and mine craters, charred clay and brimstone, from the underground pebbled with spirits and gold scum. To the land of white spirits we come. To eclipsed sun we come: to the negation of time we come. Our women a nation of banshees conned from every bankrupt and ravished nation. Mende and Lokko, Temne, Limba, Susu and Sherbro, Yalunka, Bullom, Krim. Wading waist-deep across rivers: Niger and Nile,

Gallinas and Gambia, Senegal and Quarra, and strung out in caravans we come, a stunned string of cowries like a centipede: one thousand, one thousand thousand, one thousand thousand thousand sprawling over the badlands carrying Death in every heart. Torn like belladonna lilies from our roots, we come, one savage wail swirling soundlessly, lashing the hot sand. The red flag of slavery, fluttering on the naked trees of the houses that swim, blots out hope and memory. Shark-licked skeletons like phalli mark watery graves strewn backwards. Fingers clutching at a chilled sun in cyclone while murder moves . . . Move murder move! Sacred vultures pick flesh bone clean but our lineage sits mute and horrified on its polished haunches, silent and powerless while we labor under an armor of glinting sweat through petrified mangrove forests, our mouths stuffed with pebbles. Bloodied lips beaten back at every step by clouds of locusts that flag our flesh like love-sick leeches. Our shackled necks bend and sway in malignancy, iron oiled with newborn's milk: the singing mother, her distant verse a children's chant muffled in the barren dust that shifts and bursts underfoot as light as charcoal, as deep as creation. Move murder move! Orphans sway like clinging monkeys suckled at wet nurses' breasts, mothers strangle in their own afterbirths. Dazed tribes of virgins trample hot beach to the music of the calabash, sha, sha, sha, believing this to be their only travail, sha, sha. Stupefied Mori-men and the Humui, slapped and weighted down with fetishes, stumble blindfolded, chained one to the other in perfidy. Empty mouths rail in useless supplications. Where is Gewo? But then we have no writing and no walls . . . Our ark is carried on slippery shoulders. Sand whips bright ebony breasts to the beat of the *Sangbei*. Our godheads roseate in the gathering dusk, Gewo is vanquished, no more will the tribes prostrate themselves before Ngafogoli, Yavei, Jobai, Dagbadaii. No longer will the Nation swallow the burning sperm of warlocks, for they have allowed the Race and the Gods to fall into this abomination. The multicolored powders of the Rites have blended into that which is the absence of all colors: Captivity. Boulders of grief block our way like the palm of Levi and the weight of it undoes us all, while in the brazen glare of Gallinas' shores one collective scream of agony rams the sullen sea, vibrating the python of the continent as tremors of our earthquake ripple back towards Mendeland, and in that last

moment with the sea and slavery to our backs, the Race, re-
splendent unto itself, dissolves and all our voyages, all our bio-
graphies, become one. In sanctified Black."

Covey is laughing.

"*Hooyo*," he shouts. It is the Poro war chant, which means
"bring them on, the enemies; we are ready to fight them," but
the audience thinks he has shouted Hallelujah and they follow
his lead. The whole tabernacle rises as one, clapping and
shouting, stamping and weeping. The great Hallelujah releases all the wonder and beauty of emancipation. And why
not? I think. Our freedom has been seized and endorsed in
blood and justice. And after all, what was *Hooyo* except Hallelujah?

❧ Joseph Cinque ❧ November 1841

Persons held illegally have the right to self-defense. This is the ultimate right of all human beings in extreme cases of oppression—to apply force against ruinous injustice.
—*The Supreme Court of the United States, January Term, 1841*

To the Hon. John Quincy Adams:
Most respected Sir—the Mende people give you thanks for all your kindness to them. They will never forget your defense of their rights before the great Court of Washington. They feel they owe to you in a large measure, their delivery from the Spaniards, and from slavery or death.

We are about to go home to Africa.

Our soul is escaped as a bird out of the snare of the fowler—the snare is broken and we are escaped. Our help is in the name of the Lord who made Heaven and Earth.

> For the Mende people,
> Cinque
> Kinna
> Kale.

The *Gentleman* is towed slowly out of New York harbor and onto the only home that remains to us: the Atlantic Ocean. Henry Braithwaite's thunderous voice rises above all the rest, drowning out his sons. Only Covey's lips remain silent, as do mine, our souls unable to lift our voices out of grief. In victory I am leading my men home.

At last, I can destroy the image of the *Amistad* I have carried all these years.

* * *

Our ship holds not only my own men but a small band of missionaries: The white man is inventing a new God for Africa. Our three little girls stayed in New Haven, Black Snake to be sent to Oberlin College in Ohio. Covey wears the ring he gave Vivian turned inwards, so that only the dull gold shows. But I am as much married to Vivian as he is, having brought her death.

Those departing as well as those remaining sing louder and louder in hope that their voices will carry across the expanding distance between our house and the shore. I can see Covey's tears as clearly as I can taste my own. But I am struck by the memory of the dark, jubilant gaze of Vivian, for it is she more than Covey who has given me a glimpse of the furthest reaches of our voyage.

"Cinque," she said to me, her eyes somber and gleaming, her incomparable voice stern and lovely, "for those you leave behind there is no Return. We must make our way with only half a voyage. We are orphans, standing on the blank page of America, waiting to be acknowledged. But you, more than any of us you leave behind, are truly free, for you have travelled not only the road to slavery but the Return. Never forget: you proved there is a round trip possible while six million of us, having made only the half, remain unfinished, the captives of America.

"The exodus of the thousand thousand thousand who made their voyage but in one direction still awaits the Return. Oh, not to Africa, but to *ourselves*. Then there are those who never arrived, whose voyage ended on the bottom of the Atlantic Ocean. Imagine a common grave for four million, a road stretching from the Windward coast to here; paved with iridescent skeletons. Imagine an Atlantic of African bones, people of all the clans: the greatest deportation in history.

"This time, at least, a slave's story has a happy ending. You found justice, white justice, flawed justice, compromised justice, but you found it. The voiceless and the powerless found it. But what you must understand is that the rich, the powerful, the well-born, found it as well. For what those who hold slaves do not realize is that the discovery of freedom is the very essence of the black man's destiny here—the very nature of slavery itself.

"And if the Negroes in this country belong to the whites,

why, the whites also belong to the Negroes. We are divided among them and mingled up with them, eating from the same storehouses, working the same land, dwelling in the same enclosures, populating the same countries, forming parts of the same families, a race distinct yet united. We are not more truly theirs than they are truly ours."

Vivian's voice rises and falls in streamers of silken sound amid the high grass of the Braithwaite farm. Her eyes, her face, her very body will me to understand. Her wide skirts wrap around her, the blue and white flashing between the green and gold. She holds her wide-brimmed hat in her hand and the red ribbon sweeps out in the breeze as her voice washes over me. The sun catches the long coil of her braid, which gleams in the afternoon light. The unshadowed face etches itself on my unworthy soul like the cleft of a powerful sword, or the sound of approaching drums. The brave stubbornness of her words inspire in me a baffled tenderness and incomprehension. Much of what she says I can only vaguely discern. I wish for Covey, but I am glad we are alone.

Her face is very close to mine; her fragrance mingles with the smell of August grass. Happy ending, I think. Yes, I suppose that day one could have called it a happy ending.

"Oh, Joseph Cinque, remember us, the orphans of the one-way voyage. Remember us."

Her name rushes to my lips, as if she were alive, as I begin to see that only those who have survived some form of slavery can ever know what it is to be really free.

My gaze never leaves the shore, as if I can will Vivian back beside her mother, on the quay.

I believe, as my ancestors did, in Fate. I believe in the onward rush of history beyond our birth and our death. I believe we are, black and white, Gewo's long biography in which all the faults and all the joys of the world are One.

Knowing our impatience, the captain crowds as much sail upon the masts as the *Gentleman* can carry. Bayeh Bia is now more real to me than the winter sea I travel upon. Her face is beside that of Vivian, and then little by little her face replaces Vivian's as the distance between America and the *Gentleman* increases. Bayeh Bia is, after all, alive, the flesh of the world I have conquered, my wife. I cherish her contours, her color, her odor, her sweet breath, the faint disturbance of the hem of her lappa as she passes close by, the feel of her delicate neck between my palms, her laughter, the way she holds her head when she speaks, which differs from when she laughs, or when she is in the company of others, the long eyes, dark labyrinths, yet candid beyond my strength to resist or to offer less than the truth. I imagine her on her walks with Gewo, for he must be walking now, lurching forwards on sturdy short legs, all polished black fat, fresh smooth skin, with wild heartbreaking limbs reaching out for the world, the world I know so much more about now. I will tell him the whole story, I decide, just as it had happened, sparing nothing, even to reliving it. I will hide the worst from Bayeh Bia. She will consider us gone to war and returned whole, with our victory and our scars and our souls intact.

For fifty-nine days I read the stars back to Mendeland.

❧ Joseph Cinque ❧
November 1842

In Gulliver's novels, he is represented as traveling among a
nation of beings who were very rational in many things,
although they were not exactly human, and they had a very
cool way of using language in reference to deeds that are not
laudable. When they wished to characterize a declaration as
absolutely contrary to truth, they say the man has "said the thing
that is not."

—John Quincy Adams
Argument in the case of the Amistad

The green and white shoreline I have never seen from the sea
now rises before me. It has been my destiny to have left and
to have come again, to have died and been reborn: to have
risen up and now to celebrate the Feast of the Return. The
three voyages, the three houses that swam, the three destinies
that I have endured, the three trials to which I have submitted,
have become the trinity of deliverance. I laugh as the ocean
sprays me. I will tell Bayeh Bia and Gewo of a whole nation
of beings, whites who fashioned a new world which exists because of our slavery. The *Gentleman* is quiet. Each man is
wrapped in his own dreams, or perhaps awakening from them.
I lean over the rail of the ship, expectant, searching the horizon for Gallinas. The language of the New World is already
forgotten. My thoughts are in Mende and that is all my lips
speak.

With landfall it is impossible to control the men. They kiss
the earth, they fling their clothes off, they cheer, they dance
nude; and, but for a handful, most head home. I, too, take off
my boots, sling them over my shoulders and begin the long
trek home. All alliance to the missionaries is postponed. Wa-

terfall, standing there stark naked, crazed with joy, remains with Covey, to join the *Buzzard*.

For suns I travel at a war trot, through the land that becomes more and more familiar to me, willing my body not to over-reach itself, hurtling over the grasslands, then dropping in my tracks for a few hours of sleep. Forgotten odors, shapes, land-scapes, plains, shadows, light, have been so long reinvented in my memory that they have become the memory of my mem-ory. For suns I run, but I am running through a tale I have told myself a thousand times, as if carried on the shoulders of all the white man's masteries. After all these years, as if I have grown taller, everything looks smaller, dustier, weaker, less glorious than what I had recited in my imagination through those years of dark prisons and barns, white presidents, police and trials.

On the twelfth day I sleep near the village so that I will not arrive tired. My heart lifts as I approach. Here, I think, is joy; why had I expected it before now? The walls of the town rise up. I run though my feet are blistered and bleeding. My feet have grown soft in captivity, and I have taken only the rough footpaths, never daring to travel by road.

Mbake sees me first, for he is outside the walls, in his rice fields. He rises, a shoot still in his hand, as it is planting time, and I am glad that I will begin work at once. He comes towards me, his lappa flying behind him, his arms outstretched.

"It is I, Mbake. Sengbe Pieh. What is an old man like you doing in the fields?"

Mbake's eyes become white globes. He takes my hand and leads me to the gates of my compound. At first I am not alarmed at the tears of a grown man and I repeat my name as if it were a question, although I do not mean it so, and then the name of my wife.

"Bayeh Bia?"

"Taken on the War Road."

"Madawea?"

"Taken on the War Road."

"Gewo!"

"Taken on the War Road."

"Kosokilisia?"

"Taken on the War Road."

"Father?"

"Gone on the War Road. All of them . . . I tell you, even to your mother. All, all, all," sobs Mbake, gesturing towards the empty compound. He clutches his shaven head, wrenching it from side to side on his thin neck as if he could thus decapitate himself. But I can only stare at him. In the three years I have been gone, all my family has been captured and sold into slavery.

I turn on my heel and start down the road from the emptied village towards the sea. I walk slowly because I am blind. I walk with great deliberation because I have to begin the journey back to the place from which I have just returned. Just beyond the walls of the village I stop suddenly. I may have stumbled, or perhaps I smell the arrival of the harmattan. When it blows, the earth is hot but the body is cold and the dryness of the air evaporates a man's sweat into frost. It is a terrible plague, this gale that irritates the soul and makes the limbs slack, turns a man's testicles inward and glazes his skin in ash. The lips become chapped and painful, the eyes, as if invaded by fine sand so that it is torture to keep them open. So I close mine and hear the harmattan that has blown in Mendeland for two hundred years, and this is the two hundredth.

I lift my arms outwards for enough breath to carry an otherworldly shout, terrible and maledictory, undulating back over the ocean I have just crossed.

For thirty-one years I forgot the *Amistad,* and now that I am dying at the mission at Komende in Sherbo, Black Snake, who has been Sarah Kinson all these seasons, tells me that on the day I speak of, the twenty-eighth of January, 1842, three thousand miles away, thunder, impossible in that month in New England, was heard over the New Haven jailhouse and across Montauk Bay. Like the echo of lions, it rumbled southwards along the Atlantic coast and the marshes of Delaware, across the Schuykill River Valley to a place they call Gettysburg.

✢ Epilogue ✢
1989

Eight years after the *Gentleman* anchored in the bay of Sierra Leone, James Covey, ill with a mysterious and apparently incurable disease and believing himself bewitched, returned from the sea to the Amistad mission where, barely thirty-three years old, he died and was buried. In January 1842, even as Joseph Cinque and his men debarked from the *Gentleman*, a motion was passed in Washington, D.C., to censure and expel John Quincy Adams from Congress. Quincy Adams had read before the House a petition from forty-six citizens of Haverhill, Massachusetts, praying to dissolve the Union of the United States. His enemies accused him of treason, and after waves of shouting and tumultuous protest, the motion was passed that Adams "had incurred the censure of the House." The representatives of the fifteen slave states rose one by one to attack him. This was their chance to rid themselves of John Quincy Adams forever. He was compared with Benedict Arnold and Aaron Burr. He stood alone. Only Joshua Leavitt and the husband of Angelina Grimké, Theodore Weld, founded a committee of two on his behalf. In answer to the motion, Adams rose and spoke in his own defense for six days, after which he informed the House that he needed another six days to complete the arguments for his defense. He then offered to sit down if anyone made the motion to table the question of censure forever, never to be taken up again. In despair the House, seconded by Virginian John Botts, passed this resolution by a vote of 106 to 93. John Quincy Adams had won. The very same day, Adams presented two hundred new petitions to the House, each of which was tabled one by one under the Gag Rule. Six years later Adams died at his desk in the House while presenting still another petition.

That same year, Louisa bought the title to a slave woman named Julia and freed her. She wrote in her *Adventures of a Nobody* that she was "as glad as if I was buying my own freedom."

Eight years later, in 1856, Chief Justice Roger B. Taney reversed himself in the Supreme Court decision of *Dred Scott v. United States*. He delivered the verdict of the majority that a Negro was not a citizen with standing in the courts or under the Constitution, that slaves represented property only, and that the Negro was an inferior class of humanity, "altogether unfit to associate with the white race," and "had no rights a white man was bound to respect."

Joseph Cinque lived to be an old man. He survived the American Civil War by fourteen years. After having disappeared for thirty-one years, he reappeared in 1873 at the Freetown Mission, died and was buried there next to James Covey.

The Amistad Committee's activity on behalf of Joseph Cinque's rebellion evolved into the basis for the reestablishment of practically the entire structure of Afro-American higher education, and was the founder of five great black universities: Fisk, Atlanta, Hampton, Talladega and Howard, the institution that educated Martin Luther King, Jr.

And between the first of May and the thirty-first of August, in any year, any of us, anywhere under the flag, can gaze up at the night sky and recognize the stars of the Summer Triangle, and listen for the distant echo of lions.

In the year of the 150th anniversary
of the rebellion of Joseph Cinque, A.D. 1989

✑ Acknowledgments ✑

A nonfiction novel requires exactly the same research as history or biography, although I feel that here, a bibliography would be long, and out of place. It suffices to say that I consulted all the current and classical works connected with the *Amistad* case although I tended toward nineteenth-century documents as close to "reality" in the sense of time and place that I could find. Among these are the actual manuscript transcripts of the two trials and the several investigations and accompanying testimonies in the federal archives at Waltham, Massachusetts, the papers, letters, diaries and memoirs of the main protagonists, John Quincy and Louisa Adams, R. R. Madden and the Tappans, Roger Baldwin's published argument before the Supreme Court as well as his recounting of the *Amistad* story. Here I must mention Samuel Flagg's superb *John Quincy Adams and the Union.* For the African experience I went much further abroad, depending again on eighteenth- and nineteenth-century "confessions" of slave traders, slave narratives, and Johnson U. J. Asiegbu's *Slavery and the Politics of Liberation, 1787–1861. A Study of British Anti-Slavery Policy.* For Mende culture, Kenneth Little's *The Mende of Sierra Leone* was invaluable, as well as a dictionary of Mende language, thought, and grammar published in 1909 by F.W.H. Migeod, as well as his *A View of Sierra Leone,* 1926.

For Henry Braithwaite, I relied a great deal on the letters, speeches, and writings of Frederick Douglass, and although Braithwaite's ideas may sound extremely modern to the reader's ear, they were expressed by that ex-fugitive slave turned writer, lecturer, and abolitionist as early as 1844 when he began speaking out of his own experience. I used the journals of Mungo Park, the manuscript log book and diaries of American Admiral Andrew Foote, who expressed as poetically and vividly as one could wish the experiences of the African Patrol and its *mission impossible*. A special thanks goes to Professor Howard A. Parnham of the New York City Planetarium for his superb navigational skills, by which Cinque and I sailed across the Atlantic and back again by the stars of the Summer Triangle. Finally, three seminal studies of slavery underpinned my conception of Joseph Cinque and his men: Orlando Patterson's *Slavery and Social Death* and David Brion David's *Slavery and Human Progress* and *The Problem of Slavery in the Age of Revolution*. I would like to thank my university's libraries, Yale's Sterling Memorial, and the Beinecke Rare Book Library, as well as the New Haven Colony and the Massachusetts Historical Societies, the New York Public Library, and the Library of Congress.

I would like to thank Assistant Librarian of Congress Ruth Ann Stewart not only for her invaluable help but for her long-time friendship, as well as my intrepid researcher, Clarencetta Jelks, formerly of the Library of Congress, who never let me down and who always got what she went after.

The name of my fictional Braithwaites is a family name on my mother's side, a name found among northeastern seventeenth- and eighteenth-century black families. But he could have been any of a number of "station masters" on the Connecticut Underground Railway, whose centers were Farmington and New Haven.

❧ Glossary ❧

MAJOR AFRICANS

Bartu = Sword
Bau = Broke
Burnah = Twin
Prince Fabanna = Remember
Faginna = Twin, the elder
Fooni = Python
Fuli = Sun
Fuliwa = Big Sun
Grabeau = Have-Mercy on Me
Kagne = Country
Kale = Bone
Kaba Kpekalay = Heart-of-the-Razor
Kaweli = War Road = James Covey
Kimbo = Cricket
Kinna = Big Man
Kosokilisia = War Sparrow
Margru = Black Snake
Prince Fabanna = Remember
Sessi = Crocodile
Shule = Waterfall
Shuma = Falling Water
Senghe Pieh = *Sangbei* = Drummer – Cinque = Joseph Cinque
Teme – Frog

THE BRAITHWAITE FAMILY

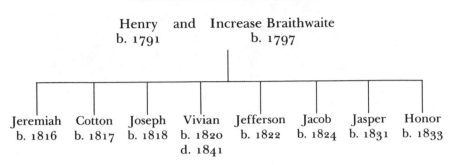

Henry   and   Increase Braithwaite
b. 1791   b. 1797

Jeremiah	Cotton	Joseph	Vivian	Jefferson	Jacob	Jasper	Honor
b. 1816	b. 1817	b. 1818	b. 1820	b. 1822	b. 1824	b. 1831	b. 1833
			d. 1841				

❧ A NOTE ON THE TYPEFACE ❧

The text of this book was set in Caledonia, a typeface designed by William Addison Dwiggins for the Mergenthaler Linotype Company in 1938. Caledonia is a "modern" type, although it resembles in elegance, the classic Bulmer, designed in 1890 by William Martin. With its lack of contrast between thick and thin, its proportionally ideal relation of height to width and its avoidance of eccentricities, Caledonia is a simple, readable typeface whose quality is in its feeling of fluidity, power and speed, combined with a pleasing, balanced medium lightness on the printed page.

W. A. Dwiggins (1880–1956) was associated with the Mergenthaler Linotype Company from 1929 until his death, and during that time, designed many popular typefaces, including Falcon, Metro, Electra, Eldorado and Caledonia.

This book was composed by the Maple-Vail Company 1988, and printed and bound by Haddon Craftsmen. Typography and binding design by Kathryn Parise.